STARRY-EYED

Also by Ted Michael

So You Wanna Be a Superstar?: The Ultimate Audition Guide

Other Running Press Teens anthologies include:

Cornered: 14 Stories of Bullying and Defiance
Edited by Rhoda Belleza

Willful Impropriety: 13 Tales of Society, Scandal, and Romance
Edited by Ekaterina Sedia

Brave New Love: 15 Dystopian Tales of Desire
Edited by Paula Guran

Truth & Dare: 20 Tales of Heartbreak and Happiness
Edited by Liz Miles

Corsets & Clockwork: 13 Steampunk Romances
Edited by Trisha Telep

Kiss Me Deadly: 13 Tales of Paranormal Love
Edited by Trisha Telep

The Eternal Kiss: 13 Vampire Tales of Blood and Desire
Edited by Trisha Telep

STARRY-EYED

16 STORIES that Steal the Spotlight

Edited by Ted Michael & Josh Pultz

Introduction by Clay Aiken

RP | TEENS
PHILADELPHIA • LONDON

Books published by Running Press are available at special discounts for bulk purchases in the United States by corporations, institutions, and other organizations. For more information, please contact the Special Markets Department at the Perseus Books Group, 2300 Chestnut Street, Suite 200, Philadelphia, PA 19103, or call (800) 810-4145, ext. 5000, or e-mail special.markets@perseusbooks.com.

ISBN 978-0-7624-4949-1

Library of Congress Control Number: 2013940578
E-book ISBN 978-0-7624-5078-7

9 8 7 6 5 4 3 2 1
Digit on the right indicates the number of this printing

Designed by Joshua McDonnell
Typography: Avenir, Bembo, and Mensch

Published by Running Press Teens
An Imprint of Running Press Book Publishers
A Member of the Perseus Books Group
2300 Chestnut Street
Philadelphia, PA 19103–4371

Visit us on the web!
www.runningpress.com/kids

Contents

FOR YOUNG
PERFORMERS
AND ARTISTS
EVERYWHERE

INTRODUCTION

If someone had asked me when I was a teenager if I ever dreamed of being where I am today, I would have told that person one thing: yes.

Imagine a ten- or eleven-year-old me. Though Mom might say otherwise, like most kids, I wasn't always the cutest or the best dressed or the most popular in school. What I did have, though, was drive, determination, and a passion for singing.

Whether it was a concert with the local boys' choir, a Sunday morning hymn at church, or a role in a community theater production, I always felt most alive when I was performing. The thrill of making music and the artistic friends that I made through my love for the arts made my teenage years enjoyable and planted the seed for my current career. But the glitz and glamour of Los Angeles and the bright lights of Broadway seemed miles away from my front porch in Raleigh, North Carolina, way back when.

Flash forward to May of 2003: To my left is *American Idol* contestant (and my competition) Ruben Studdard. To my right, host Ryan Seacrest holding a little piece of paper that would change my life forever.

American Idol may have introduced me to the world, but even now I still haven't forgotten where I've come from. I have been able to accomplish so many of my dreams as a performer, but the seed that was planted when I was a teenager, my love for music and singing, the joy that I feel onstage connecting with people, has grown into a career that is larger and brighter than anything I could have ever imagined.

Starry-Eyed is full of stories about passion for the arts, the challenges of stardom, the silly side of show business and the successes that come with just being you. Inside, you'll also find words of wisdom and encouragement from some names you'll definitely recognize. Maybe you've seen them on your favorite television show or in a blockbuster movie. Perhaps you've heard them on the radio or seen them perform in concert. Either way, they started out just like you and me: with a love for the arts and a dream. With a little luck, some hard work, and a lot of heart, they have some incredible stories to share with you. I hope you enjoy reading them as much as I have.

Clay Aiken

A NOTE FROM THE EDITORS

There's a reason that so many people love *Glee*—besides all of the musical numbers. And Jane Lynch.

Really, *Glee* is a show about the underdog, and no one knows what it feels like to be ignored, pushed aside, and made fun of like a teenager— especially one who loves the performing arts. Not only do *Glee* and other TV shows like *The Voice, The X Factor, American Idol, Smash, So You Think You Can Dance* (and many more) inspire us to believe in the power of music, they encourage us to follow our dreams. They teach us that with hard work and confidence, anything is possible. Because when it comes to the performing arts, it's not about fitting in—it's about standing out.

Which is why we wanted to craft a collection of stories that spoke to the very heart of what it means to be a teenager and to love performing. The stories in this anthology are written by some of today's most fantastic writers, and they are all inspired by the transformative power of music, dance, and drama. Whether you're a member of the audience, taking it all in, or up onstage, making it all happen, there's nothing quite like the magic of a fantastic performance.

In these pages, you will read about everything from the simple wonder of a first kiss to unlikely yet powerful friendships to the thrilling mystery of finding one's voice—literally. In addition to these stories, throughout this anthology, theater, television, and film actors have shared the moments that inspired their careers and exposed their personal failures and triumphs.

The seeds of *Starry-Eyed* were planted many years ago, when we were in school. For us, performing was the creative outlet we needed to make us feel special. From plays and musicals to chorus, band, and orchestra rehearsal, we were allowed to truly be ourselves. To pursue our dreams and reach for the stars. Our best friends were made during productions and musical summer camps. The arts provided us a home, a safe haven when we needed one, and for that we are forever grateful.

We hope that you enjoy *Starry-Eyed* as much as we have enjoyed putting it together.

Ted Michael & Josh Pultz

THE ACCOMPANIST

Eve Yohalem

When I was nine years old I smashed my pinky with a meat mallet so I wouldn't have to go onstage.

It was the night of Mrs. Komar's annual Christmas recital. She'd rented out Westview's Town Hall for her piano students, and it felt like half the town was there.

I stood in a corner of the green room (a file storage room by day) fingering the straps of my tote bag and listening to the older kids talk about how nervous they were, even though they really weren't. All that hugging and deep breathing and "oh-my-God-ing"? That was *excitement*. They couldn't wait to get out there and show the whole world how great they were. *Nervous* is when you beg your mother again and again not to make you do it, when you look up *phobia* in the dictionary before the scariest conversation you've ever had with your Eastern Bloc piano teacher, when your brother has a cold and you sneak dirty tissues out of his trash can and rub them on your face—and after all that fails, when you stuff a meat mallet into your tote bag, wedging it right between Chopin's waltzes and Beethoven's sonatas.

My black patent leather flats had rubbed blisters on my heels even though I was wearing tights like my mother told me to. She'd pulled my braids so tight I thought my eyeballs would pop out of my head. That way, she said, there was no chance my hair would fall in my eyes and distract me.

The problem with being able to play Mozart when you're nine years old? Everybody wants to see you do it. But all that wanting felt like taking, like everybody who listened to me play pinched off little Andie souvenirs, leaving me with Swiss cheese for a soul. And then there's the whole prodigy thing. People said *exceptional* and I heard *exception*. They said *outstanding* and I heard *oddity*.

"Andie, you okay?" Mrs. Komar's husband bent down to peer into my face. It was his job to keep order backstage. Histrionic teenagers were bad enough. The last thing he needed was an epic third grader meltdown.

"Yes," I whispered.

"You're gonna be great," he said.

"I have to go the bathroom."

Alone in the ladies' room with the door locked, I pulled the meat mallet out of my bag. It had a long wood handle and a big square metal block on one end for flattening chicken into cutlets. Two sides of the block were smooth, a third had spikes and the fourth had ridges. I picked a smooth side. I wanted pounding, not tenderizing.

I straightened my pinky on the Formica vanity. No hesitation. Just a good sharp *thwack*.

Freedom.

. . . .

Eight years and one healed pinky later, I still hate the spotlight. But tonight that's okay because I'm alone in the orchestra pit of my high school auditorium.

I look up . . .

. . . over the manuscript stand, beyond the stained top of my upright piano. I scan the rehearsal stage where there's a cardboard city plaza, circa 1930. Think old Europe at its quaintest: cobbled streets, ornate black streetlights, an array of charming shops around a fountain made out of a lawn swan and a plastered-over kiddie pool. The cast of Westview High School's *She Loves Me* are milling around, checking cell phones or trying out facial expressions. My eye goes to the wings, where the two leads Chloe Pavone and Ben Jazinsky are dancing. Waltzing, I think. They do this a lot.

Chloe Pavone of the high As and the grand jetés. She who can cry on demand, kill a punch line. She of heart-shaped face and round brown eyes and perfect boobs. And Jazinsky who went by the nickname BJ all through elementary school because he thought it sounded cool. In sixth grade he found out why it wasn't and told everyone to call him Ben.

Across from Chloe and Ben, Henry DeRuyter leans against the proscenium, already in character though the run-through hasn't started. What I mean by that is Henry DeRuyter played Danny Zuko in *Grease* last year and he was Henry DeRuyter. He played Gaston in *Beauty and the Beast* as a sophomore and he was Henry DeRuyter. Now he's Steven Kodaly, the arrogant, handsome ladies' man, but really he's Henry DeRuyter.

And, yes, I admit I used to lie in bed at night thinking about Henry with the soundtrack in my brain playing Debussy's *Prelude to the Afternoon of a Faun*. I would fan out my hair behind me on my pillow and let the music spill down my body like water, dreaming about exotic places I'd never been to, like Henry's bedroom on a Thursday afternoon while his parents were still at work.

By "used to" I mean last week.

From behind me floats the disembodied voice of our director, Mr. Sandburg:

"Okay everybody. We're going to start from the beginning and work straight through. Places for 'Good Morning, Good Day'! Andie, you ready?"

I drag my eyes off Henry and find Mr. Sandburg a few rows back in the audience. As the pianist for the school musical, I've been to every rehearsal. *She Loves Me* has a ridiculously difficult score, the kind of stuff that usually only classical musicians like me play. So even though we open in two nights, the music director is working with the rest of the band in the rehearsal studio, and tonight I'm on my own in the pit. Which is really just a clump of chairs and music stands off to one side and below the stage in the auditorium.

Being alone down here is fine—more than fine—by me.

"I'm ready," I say.

Mr. Sandburg isn't listening. He knows I'm ready. I'm always ready.

He gives me a nod and I launch into the overture. It's supposed to start with a virtuosic violin solo, so I improv that. Then I improv the rest of the orchestra.

Davis Lee, the only freshman in the show, wobbles onstage on a bicycle. He needs to nail his entrance or the rest of the cast will follow him off a cliff. "Good Morning, Good Day" has a tick-tock rhythm that right now mirrors the beating of my heart. *Tick-tock, tick-tock, come on Davis, and NOW!*

"Good morning!" he sings, right on cue. *Good man, Davis.*

Next I help Sophie, who plays Ilona the salesgirl, with timing. I accent the downbeats so she can find them.

The joke for the audience is that Ilona is complaining about being totally exhausted because she's been up all night romping with Kodaly. The joke for the cast is that Henry/Kodaly was actually up all night romping with Chloe/Amalia.

Henry makes his entrance without any extra help from me, and my pulse tick-tocks along with my heart and the song. He is, literally, tall, dark and handsome, like a poster boy for a Greek escort service, but his usual swagger does seem to be off a few degrees. I suppose thanks to last night with Chloe. Who has come down from the wings and is now sharing my piano bench.

"Andie," she whispers, turning a page for me. "Can I ask you something? I want you to be really, really honest. Totally honest. *Don't* be afraid of hurting my feelings."

I feed Ben his note so he'll be in the same key as everyone else.

"Do you think I'm getting . . . *boring*?"

How would I know? We've never shared a lunch table. You've never invited me to any of your parties. In fact, the only reason I know where you live is because everyone knows where you live. Because of all the parties you've never invited me to.

"No," I whisper. It's hard to count and massage Chloe's ego at the same time. Why hasn't Mr. Sandburg noticed her and sent her backstage to wait for her entrance?

"Are you sure? Don't say that just to be nice. I want the absolute truth."

I play louder and the cast follows. "Good Morning, Good Day" has turned into a round. Ben's timing is off but not enough to stop the song.

"You're not boring, Chloe. If you don't believe me, ask Henry."

"I can't ask Henry. We broke up."

Oh.

"Oh," I say out loud.

I look away from the music and risk a quick glance at Chloe. Her round brown eyes are even more luminous than usual.

"I mean *I* broke up with *him*."

Meaning that he broke up with her. And why is she telling *me* this?

"I'm sorry."

"Thanks." She squeezes my right arm so I have to cue with my left hand and half the cast misses it. "You're the best. You never get caught up in all the *drama*. God, I swear, I'm so sick of *all the drama*." Chloe actually has her hands threaded in her hair, like she's about to tear it out in frustration over the *drama*. The song ends and now I can give my full attention to Chloe and her monologue.

"I mean, we're all leaving for college in six months. Or at least you and I and Ben and Henry are. Can't we leave with our dignity intact? Can't we leave like *adults*?" Before I can inject an "um-hm" or a "yeah," Chloe continues and I realize she wasn't waiting for me to respond, she was just taking a beat. "It's all so *meaningless*! Like any of it really matters. Who dates who. Or who stars in what show. A year from now, who will remember any of it? Any of *us*?"

Is this another beat or am I supposed to answer?

"That's why Ben and I came up with a *thing*. A plan. For tonight. So we won't all fade away to nothing the minute we're out the door."

"Quiet in the pit!"

"Sorry, Mr. Sandberg." Only Chloe doesn't say the words—she sings them.

"Come backstage with me so I can tell you about *the plan*," Chloe says.

"I can't," I say. "It's almost time for 'Thank You, Madam.' And you have to go on in about three minutes."

"Fine, then let's hide down here."

She drags me under the piano. Except since it's an upright "under" just means crouching on the floor between the bench and the keyboard.

"We're going to make our mark on the school tonight. In a *prominent, permanent, personal* way."

"That sounds really great for you."

"Oh, um, no, I mean, you should totally do it with us if you want to." Chloe beams at me. "All you have to do is come up with something to do, something that will be here *forever* that shows the world who you really are."

"Thanks, b—"

Chloe lets out a little gasp. "I've got to go! Remember, don't breathe a *word* of this to anyone. Not anyone!" She kisses my cheek. "You're the *best*."

And so concludes the only conversation I've ever had with Chloe Pavone.

. . . .

I don't need to show the world who I really am. The idea of playing Beethoven for a thousand people just so they can applaud when I'm done makes me want to crawl inside a drycleaner bag and knot the bottom end. Which is a problem because my first college audition is in two weeks. In two weeks I have to go down to Philadelphia to the Curtis Institute of Music and play fifty minutes of classical music on a stage in a concert hall full of strangers so I can get accepted into their accompanist program.

Then I have to do it three more times at Yale, Juilliard, and Peabody.

Just thinking about it makes me want to smash all my fingers with a meat mallet.

Despite my "performance anxiety," I'd never give up piano. I love the music too much. After Mrs. Komar's recital, my mother and I negotiated a truce: I'd keep studying as long as I never had to perform alone in front of an audience. Which meant I became Westview's go-to accompanist. I do all the Music Society's musicales, the community theater shows, and the school shows. I draw the line at churches and temples, though. I find God in music, not the other way around.

Accompanying is different from solo performing. When I accompany, the audience thinks I'm just there for background. Sometimes the singer thinks so, too. They don't know that the notes I play to mark their entrance or find the right octave aren't written in the sheet music. Most of the time they don't realize they're following my lead, getting louder and softer with the piano or stretching a phrase to give it more impact. We're collaborating, even if I'm the only person who knows it.

. . . .

This morning I got up at 5:24, my internal clock being programmed to wake me exactly one minute before my alarm goes off. I shuffled down to the living room and sat down at the piano, a massive Steinway B that fills half the room. Black, curvaceous, alive. Not a *thing*, a *being*.

I don't square my shoulders or let out a deep breath or anything. I just start. With scales, octaves, arpeggios, fast as I can, super slow, putting the accent on different beats, never missing a note or breaking rhythm. I've done these warm-ups almost every day of my piano playing life, which is to say for the last ten years. I don't have to think about what I'm doing. I just do it.

Right now I'm working on four pieces for my auditions. Funny how the number four keeps popping up. Four pieces of music, four auditions, the Four Horsemen of the Apocalypse. The music isn't the problem. I love the music. My favorite is *Kreisleriana* by Robert Schumann. It's a monster of a piece, the hardest thing I've ever played. Schumann wrote it for his wife, Clara, in 1838. They had this incredible, tumultuous love affair. They fell in love when she was fifteen and he was twenty-five, but her father hated him and refused to let them marry for six years.

Schumann named *Kreisleriana* for this fictional character, Kreisler, who was a crazy manic-depressive musician. That's why it has so many highs and lows. But really, it's everything he felt for Clara. The fourth movement is the most beautiful. It's marked *sehr langsam*, which means "very slow." It's deep and peaceful. Like Robert and Clara talking to each other, just the two of them all alone.

I wonder what that feels like, being loved the way Robert loved Clara. For a while now, my romantic life has been mostly aspirational.

· · · · · · · · · ·

"Hold please!"

Mr. Sandberg calls a quick conference with Walter the Sound Guy. For some reason, all the body mics have stopped working. It's a problem because out of the entire cast, Chloe is the only person who can be heard past the tenth row without one.

"Take five, everyone," Mr. Sandberg says. "And I mean *five*."

I get up to go to the bathroom and run into Ben on the way there. He's in his Georg costume, a close-cut, gray three-piece suit. It looks good on him.

"Andie, com'ere." He drags me down the hall to the school lobby. "Chloe said you're going to leave your mark with us tonight. Here's mine."

I look at the glass display case he's pointing to, one filled with countless photographs of Westview, Connecticut, athletes and all their trophies.

"What am I missing?" I say. "I don't see anything."

"Look closer," Ben says, a big, satisfied smile on his face.

It's a picture of some kid who won the state championship in tennis in 1977. I've walked past it a thousand times on my way in and out of school. Only now he has Ben's head.

"Check out this one."

Ben leads me down the hall and shows me the 1985 football team with him as quarterback. And the swimmer who went to the 2000 Olympics after high school has Ben's head, too. Even some of the girls are now Ben-headed.

"Is Ben showing you his mark?"

Henry has come up behind me and is looking over my shoulder. He's half a head taller than me and I'm pretty tall. I catch Ben looking at Henry, and then Ben catches me catching him and we both half smile. Like me, Ben has spent a fair amount of high school dreaming about Henry's bedroom.

"Gotta love Photoshop," Henry says, bending over for a closer look. He's wearing the same gray suit as Ben, and it looks even better on him.

"Do you think anyone will notice?" I ask.

"Not for years and years. That's the whole point." Chloe has joined our little group. She's standing between me and Ben with her back to Henry so he's kind of excluded from the circle. "*Meine damen und herren, mesdames et messieurs . . .* La Sandburg is ready for us." Chloe links elbows with Ben and sweeps him down the hall.

"Ouch," I say to Henry.

He shrugs. "It's fine." We start back toward the auditorium and I realize I never made it to the bathroom. "So, have you decided what your mark on our future alma mater is going to be?"

"Nothing," I say. "I'm happy to leave as I entered, in total obscurity. How about you?"

"Chloe had a few ideas for me," Henry says, "but I think I'm gonna pass."

"You're happy just to live on in the memory of those you leave behind?"

Henry shakes his head. "God, I hope not."

I want to ask Henry what he means, why the star of every show, the object of envy or desire of most of the student body, wants to be forgotten, but we're inside the auditorium now and Mr. Sandberg is waving at me.

We're picking up at Chloe's big entrance scene. Walter the Sound Guy is still working on the body mics, but it doesn't matter to Chloe. You can hear every word, catch every gesture, every bat of an eyelash. She's dazzling. For the first time, I wonder what it's like to be Chloe Pavone. To come alive in front of a crowd, instead of withering. To *want* to be seen.

She's not dazzling to Henry, though. His character is supposed to lust after Chloe's, but instead he's squeezing the puffy ball of a perfume sprayer like it's one of those lung inflator bags you see on TV medical shows. As ever, Henry DeRuyter is playing Henry DeRuyter.

"Hold!" Mr. Sandburg shouts. "Where's the spotlight on Chloe? Why is she standing in the dark!"

Jenny Jackson in the lighting booth has been having an off night. She gets into a back-and-forth with Mr. Sandberg about how it's not her fault, the computer's not working, and a Bach partita churns in my head, soprano and tenor weaving over, under and around each other, *tick-tick-tick-tick . . .*

"Okay, let's take it from 'Thank You, Madam.'" Mr. Sandberg and Jenny have agreed to disagree, and I give the cast their opening chord.

· · · · ·

At nine o'clock we still haven't even finished the first act. So much for my first period history test tomorrow. Walter the Sound Guy left for coffee half an hour ago, Jenny Jackson is in tears, and Mr. Sandberg just called Ben an asshole for dropping a line and then threw everybody out of the auditorium for twenty minutes so he can scrape together a few shreds of sanity.

It's counterintuitive, I know, given the manual juice press around my temples, but I escape to the practice room. I take *Kreisleriana* out of my bag even though I know it by heart. Seeing the dove gray cover of the manuscript with its old-fashioned font grounds me.

I start with my favorite movement. The music is unhurried and gentle, a murmured conversation between two intimate lovers that I've imagined a thousand times. I hear the man's voice, deep and bold, full of stops and starts like he's holding back the full intensity of his feelings. The woman's answer is lyric and lovely, with no reservations whatsoever. The lovers' songs echo and sway, their music soothing and generous. A minute or so into it, the juice press around my head is gone and so am I. My eyes are open. I see the keyboard and the manuscript on the music stand, but I also see a drawing room in nineteenth-century Leipzig. I see women in empire waist dresses and men in gray waistcoats perched on settees and straight-back chairs. I see vases of white peonies, honeyed by candlelight.

I see Henry DeRuyter.

I yank my hands away from the piano.

"Holy cow, what was *that*?" he says.

"Um, *Kreisleriana*."

"Chrysler—what? No, I mean, I had no idea you could play the piano like that."

Henry is looking at me like you'd look at a centaur in your backyard. Or maybe a cyclops, I can't tell which.

"I usually only play classical for myself."

Henry leaves the doorway and stands in the crook of the piano. "Well, you shouldn't. You're incredible. That was the most incredible piece of music I've ever heard."

"Better than the Rolling Stones?" My face burns. Did I really say that out loud? Why did I say that? Maybe because the Rolling Stones are pretty much the only rock band I can name off the top of my head because my dad listens to them all the time and that's how big a loser I am.

But Henry laughs. "Way better. Nobody in the Rolling Stones could play—what's it called again?"

"Kreisleriana."

"Krice-leer-ee-ana," he says slowly, trying to get it right and succeeding. "Is it hard?"

"It's the hardest thing I've ever played."

"Really?" Henry walks around the piano to stand next to me. "Why?"

I'm overly conscious of Henry, standing inches from my arm, which makes it difficult to answer his question.

"Technically it's incredibly challenging. Can you read music?" I ask. Henry shakes his head. "It doesn't matter. Just look at it." I flip through the pages of the manuscript and show him an ocean of black notes surging over the paper. He leans down next to me and a soft curl of black hair brushes my cheek. I swallow hard. "The rhythms, the speed, the contrasts. It took me a really long time to get it down."

Henry is shaking his head again. "Why don't you ever play for anyone? You should be giving whole concerts by yourself, not just sitting under the stage spoon-feeding the unmusical our notes."

He noticed the spoon-feeding? Although, truth be told, Henry doesn't need much.

"I *like* accompanying. It's a collaboration."

"You *like* accompanying, but you love *Kreisleriana*. Don't deny it. Nobody plays music like that when they don't care about it."

I cross my arms in front of my chest. "I'm not denying anything. I freely admit I love classical music. I just don't like performing it."

"Bullshit. You're hiding your light under a bushel."

"What are you, my grandmother? And why do you care anyway?"

I scrutinize Henry's face. He looks really upset.

"Let's just say I've reached a point in my life where I've lost patience with people who pretend to be something they're not."

"Is this about Chloe?"

"Chloe?" he says, surprised. "Not at all. Chloe is a perfect example of someone who's *exactly* what she seems. Shallow, self-centered—"

"And hugely talented."

"And hugely talented," he agrees. "No, I was talking about myself."

"*You?*"

Henry DeRuyter who always plays Henry DeRuyter is telling me he's not Henry DeRuyter.

"Did you know I've got a brother?" I didn't. "James. He's nine years old and incredibly annoying. Anyway, a few weeks ago, James was bugging me about looking at his stamp collection, which is a lot less weird than the soda can pull-top collection that he's amassing to donate to the Shriners or his deep knowledge of monkdom across the centuries.

"Anyway, James wants me to look at his stamps, and I'm asking him why I have to deal with his hobbies, and suddenly it occurs to me that I've got no hobbies of my own. None. I haven't got one single personal interest. I read books I have to read for school; I see whatever movies happen to be out. Football is boring. I don't care about cars. You're going to say, what about theater? It's true, I like doing theater, but I don't like theater people, and this is probably going to be the last show I ever do. I keep asking myself how I made it to senior year of high school this way."

While he's been talking, Henry has been pacing back and forth, and while he was pacing, he loosened his tie and then unbuttoned the top button of his shirt. Now he's rubbing the back of his neck. He stops and points at me.

"But *you*," he says, "you've got this thing that you love, this thing you're amazing at, and you keep it a secret from the entire world."

I'm a tree falling in the forest.

"Play for me."

"Henry, I don't want to."

"You've got an unbelievable talent. I've just confessed to you that I've got nothing. I want to know what it feels like to be you."

"Trust me, you really don't."

"What's that supposed to mean?"

How can I explain my Swiss cheese soul to Henry? "It's just, when I play in front of people, I feel like I lose myself, piece by piece." I keep the part about feeling like a member of Barnum's Freak Show to myself.

Henry studies my face, and I hope I'm not still blushing.

"When was the last time you played for an audience?"

"When I was nine," I admit.

"So? It's been so long, how do you know you'll still feel the same way?" He puts his hand on my arm. "Try it. Just with me, like an experiment. Play *Kreisleriana*. From the beginning."

He doesn't know what he's asking. The first movement is wild, uncontrolled passion.

When I don't answer, he sits next to me on the bench. There's barely enough room and our hips touch, but both of us pretend not to notice.

"Please."

How many more ways can I say no? But the truth is, I kind of want to do it. Maybe Henry's right. Maybe it'll be different now.

There's a ball of ice in my stomach as I push the pages from left to right. Page one: *ausserst bewegt*. Extremely moving. *Agitatissimo*. Very agitated.

"Wait," Henry says, his expression a new and totally unfamiliar mixture of shyness and need. "I want to know what it feels like." He reaches his hands toward mine. "Can I? I mean, would you be able to play if I . . ."

I understand what he's trying to say. Can he hold my hands while I play *Kreisleriana*? The idea is terrifying and irresistible.

"It won't work like that," I say.

"Of course not. I understand. I'm sorry," he says, looking completely mortified, another unfamiliar expression.

"No, I mean I can't play if you're leaning across me," I say. "You'd need to sit behind me."

"Oh," he says. "Okay."

Henry gets up and I shift forward on the bench. Then he sits behind me, straddling me. "You mean like this?" he says. His mouth is just above my ear.

I have to tell myself to breathe. Henry's body is so warm. "Yes," I say. I put my hands on the keyboard, and Henry puts his hands on top of mine.

You know what it's like when you go to the beach in June on a hot day when the water is only about fifty-five degrees, and you're standing at the shoreline with the sun boiling your scalp and your toes numb in the frigid sand? That's how I feel right now.

I think about the rooms full of strangers at my auditions. I think about my mother's meat mallet. And then I push it all out of my head and think about Henry's thighs, which are currently sandwiching mine, and how the poor lonely tree falling in the forest with no one to hear it has always seemed so pathetic to me and I really don't want *that* to be the metaphor of my life.

One-two-three-go!

There's no introduction to the first movement of *Kreisleriana*, no way to get ready for the tidal wave of sound that overwhelms you from the first instant. My hands are like life rafts in a tumultuous sea of music. They fly to the extremes of the keyboard and Henry leans against me, following my body's movements to keep his hands from slipping off mine.

I can feel Henry's heart beating against my back, feel him breathing in fits and starts. I'm breathing hard, too, but it's okay. I'm okay. I'm playing *Kreisleriana* and Henry's here listening—*more* than listening—and I don't want to die.

The movement is building toward its final crescendo, the chords climbing higher and higher. It ends *sforzando*, as loud as I can make it, and while the blast of sound decays around us, Henry squeezes my hands and I feel the rise and fall of his chest on my back, his breath heavy in my ear. I turn my head, but before I can say anything we're kissing.

This is not the awkward too-wet fumblings of the boys at music camp. This is the kiss I've been waiting for. I twist around so I can put my hands on Henry's shoulders, and he grabs my legs and pulls me the rest of the way so now I'm the one straddling him.

Which is when the practice room door swings open.

Chloe.

Her hand flies to her mouth, and her eyes well up for an instant. Then just as quickly, she's pulled herself together.

Henry jumps off the bench, like if he can get away from me fast enough, maybe Chloe won't have noticed the way I was wrapped around him.

"I'm *so* sorry to interrupt," Chloe says, "but break ended five minutes ago. You remember—we're doing 'Dear Friend,' the song where Amalia *begs the love of her life not to humiliate her*? She's such a tool, Amalia."

This time, Chloe doesn't take a beat. She exits. Center stage.

. . . . .

I'm back at the piano in the auditorium watching Ben and Chloe go through their scene. Chloe seems distracted, and Ben keeps botching his staging.

"Hold!" Mr. Sandburg says for the umpteenth time. "Ben, you're supposed to take the book from Chloe. Why is this so hard?"

"I'm sorry, Mr. Sandburg," Ben says, looking straight at me. "Maybe if I sat next to her—or *maybe if I sat in her lap*—it would be easier."

"Just do the bit, Ben. Take it from when he tells her it's wrong for a man to keep a girl waiting."

I feel the tears well up like they always do when I'm mortified, but unlike Chloe I can't control them. They run down my face while I play "Dear Friend" for her. If Chloe notices, which I doubt, she doesn't care.

Henry, meanwhile, is backstage. Since he doesn't have to go on again until the second act, I can only assume he's hiding, asking himself why he ever thought it was a good idea to get within ten feet of freaky me and *Kreisleriana*. Or, like everyone else, he's entranced by Chloe's riveting performance. Or making out with Sophie. Or Ben.

This is what I get for sticking my neck out. Yes, Chloe's a diva and Ben, as it turns out, is a jerk, but if I'd never agreed to play for Henry, I wouldn't be sitting here now, melting away bit by bit.

After about a hundred years, my sleeve is encrusted with snot and Act I is over. Mr. Sandburg doesn't give us a break. Instead, we go straight into "Try Me," where Davis Lee begs his boss for a job. Davis is full of "Hey, world, I'm in ninth grade and I have a song!" exuberance. He doesn't care that it's ten thirty at night, and he doesn't know that his school is full of nasty egomaniacs, and a dirty mean part of me wants to grab him by the shirt and tell him.

But I don't. Instead I play "Days Gone By" and "Where's My Shoe?" and I give Ben all the notes he can never find on his own and I hold all the high notes just the way Chloe likes them—and stretch the ritards for her because she sounds even better that way. And Jenny Jackson keeps missing her cues and Walter the Sound Guy is AWOL and now it's past midnight and half the cast is asleep or in tears from pure fatigue. Did I mention that the audience is full of pissed off parents waiting to pick up kids who were supposed to be home hours ago?

Also, I haven't seen Henry since Kodaly got fired for sleeping with the boss's wife.

And then it's time for "Vanilla Ice Cream."

Not the dessert, the song. Chloe's last big song, where she flits around her bedroom in a nightgown charming the pants off everyone. I'm about to cue her when she leans over the stage and beckons me until her face is about two inches from mine. "Watch me make my mark," she says.

I know instantly what she's going to do. "Vanilla Ice Cream" is the best song in the show, mainly because Chloe is the one who sings it. It's the one everyone's going to walk out humming. It's hard because it's so high, which you'd never know because Chloe makes it look easy. But there's one note even Chloe hasn't gone for yet. An optional high B at the very end when the singer is bound to be tired. And you can't just touch it, you have to hold it.

I don't know what Chloe had planned to do before to make her mark, but she's changed her mind. She's going for the high B.

. . . . .

Chloe, fragile and angelic in her cream-colored negligee, is at her desk, writing to her lover. Jenny dims the lights and shines a spot on her. As soon as the first lines are out of Chloe's mouth, the buzz in the auditorium dissolves. Cranky parents lean forward in their seats to catch every word. Mr. Sandburg stops talking to the music director.

Chloe looks up from her letter, distracted by a shiny new thought: *Ice cream!*

Smiles spread across all the tired, furious faces. She's that good. And suddenly I see Chloe's performance for what it is: a gift. Even though she didn't intend it to be. Even though she's doing her thing just to show the world how great she is, the fact remains that watching someone great do what they do shines a light on the rest of us.

I'm infuriated by my own sappiness, but I still can't take my eyes off Chloe. Neither can Henry, who's now watching from the wings with the rest of the cast.

She's nearing the end. I can see her getting ready for the high B, planting her feet, rolling back her shoulders—when every single light in the auditorium goes out.

We're all sitting in pitch black.

Dead silence and then Chloe screams, "*JEENNNNYY!!*"

From the dark comes Ben's voice, "Chlo, com'ere. It's okay," at the same time that Henry says, "Oh, for fuck's sake."

From Jenny in the lighting booth, "It wasn't me! I swear! I didn't touch anything!"

From Mr. Sandburg, "What the hell is going on! *Walter!*"

From Walter the Sound Guy, ". . ."

You can hear parents jumping up from their seats and their cries of "Enough!", "Sandburg!", and "One o'clock in the frigging morning!" Onstage kids are wailing and someone is screaming, "Stop it! Just stop it! Stop it!"

Which is exactly how I feel. I can't breathe. The noise is a vortex that sucks every molecule of air from the room.

"*Help!*" says a voice.

I could help.

I could replace the screaming and crying with something else. Something beautiful. I could replace it with the fourth movement of *Kreisleriana*.

It wouldn't be about Andie the Oddity. It wouldn't be about *me* at all. It would be a gift. For all of us.

I think about Robert and Clara Schumann. I think about the look on Henry's face when he said, "Holy cow, what was *that*?" And then I think about the kiss I'd been waiting for and I start to play.

It helps—a lot—that the lights are still off. The movement begins like a whisper, lyric and ethereal, and I'm not sure anyone can hear me. But, gradually, musical tendrils gentle the whirlwind and fill the auditorium, the sound building in power until every crevice is smooth.

The houselights come back on and although my eyes are glued to my hands, I'm aware that the hall has gone silent and people are coming up the aisles and down from the stage. I feel their eyes on me, but instead of melting away I'm growing warm, coming alive like a daffodil after winter.

I finish playing and the silence that follows is a respite, a moment of grace. It hovers over the room and its inhabitants like a slow breath after a long cry.

I look up.

The whole cast is crowded around the piano, their parents behind them. I scan their faces—Chloe, Ben, Davis Lee, Jenny Jackson, Mr. Sandburg—looking for envy or greed or weirded out, but I don't find anything remotely like that. Instead, Henry catches my eye and tilts his head to the side, conveying an unspoken message that I can feel as clearly as if he had whispered the words directly into my ear.

I scan my soul and it's whole.

....

ANECDOTE: JESSE TYLER FERGUSON

....

I have been charmed with a few things in life. My hair is the hue of crimson that can never be achieved from a bottle; I have a fairly healthy if somewhat slowing metabolism; and I have always known what I wanted to "be" when I grew up.

I have gone back in my mind to try and pin down the exact moment I knew I wanted to be an actor. I always seem to end up back at the uterus. I am using the word *uterus* literally here. It isn't the name of a downtown improv group I started at. Also, if I ever start a downtown improv group it WILL be called the Uterus so . . . consider it trademarked.

I know I nagged my parents about letting me join the local Albuquerque's Children Theater after seeing one of the plays they produced, but I can't even remember what play it was. I have told interviewers and talk show hosts that it was *Alice in Wonderland*. I have no idea if that is true but it is on my Wikipedia page now so it is basically written in stone. I guess I really WAS one of those kids who came into the world with jazz hands and great extension. (I curse myself for not stretching daily to maintain my flexible newborn muscles.)

Now, there is a HUGE difference between knowing you want to *be* a professional actor and knowing that you *like* acting.

Someone who knows they *like* acting might be comfortable spending their entire stage career in Middletown, USA, building a résumé of roles ranging from Harold Hill to the first Caucasian Coalhouse Walker Jr.

The crossover to wanting to *be* a professional actor comes with the reality that you WILL be a small fish in a big pond. People use this metaphor a lot. They always fail to add that the small fish species is a guppy and the big pond is actually a piranha river. Wanting to be a professional actor is accepting that you will be unemployed more often than not. It means you are ready to leave the comfort of suburbia to barely afford rent in a studio smaller than the size of your childhood bedroom.

I had to really sit down and think: What in the world could possibly have had the magnetism to allure me into this insane world of acting?

It can only be one thing. The Tony Awards.

It really was my only consistent outlet when I was growing up in Albuquerque, New Mexico. Sure, every once in a while a non-union production of *Cats* or *Something's Afoot* would roll through town but it was the Tony Awards that really captured my attention.

As much as I still enjoy this Awards Show, I will always have a soft spot in my heart for the Tony Awards of the eighties and early nineties. Every category came with an amazing montage of clips from the musicals and plays nominated that year. This was before the age of YouTube and DVR so I would sit close to the TV . . . trying to absorb every moment.

Side note: A few years ago, at the age of thirty-four I found myself back in Albuquerque on the night of the Tony Awards. We already had plans to have dinner at my aunt and uncle's house, but they assured me dinner would be over before the telecast started. A game was also on that night so I was demoted to the tiny TV that sat on the kitchen counter. You would have thought it was still 1989. Here I was crouched in front of a twelve-inch screen begging my family to "keep it down, I'm trying to watch the Tony Awards!"

But I digress. The show that really captured my attention when I was a kid was a bizarre little musical called *Falsettos*. It was written by some guy named William Finn and directed by James Lapine. Research told me this was the same guy that directed and wrote my CURRENT favorite show, *Sunday in the Park with George*. I don't know what it was about *Falsettos* that entranced me. The actors were rolling around on bleachers and singing about baseball, lesbians, and Jews. It was bizarre . . . and I loved it! I remember thinking at that moment: if I ever get to work with someone like William Finn and James Lapine my life will be complete.

I made my first trip to NYC with my local community theater when I was sixteen. It was one of those whirlwind tour groups that packed six shows and a tour of Radio City Music Hall into a long weekend. I separated from the group on my first night, went to TKTS, and bought a ticket to see *Falsettos*, making it the first Broadway show I ever saw. It was late into its run. The house was half-full, and many of the cast members I remembered from the Tony Awards were different. I do remember Barbara Walsh was still in the show, and I looked upon her with the same awe that a modern-day Jesse would look upon Lady Gaga, Cher, or Jennifer Aniston. It was a truly an amazing night, one that I have NEVER forgotten.

Those who are as obsessed with theater history as I am may know where this story is ending up.

At the ripe age of twenty-nine, I was asked to workshop the role of a twelve-year-old kid in a bizarre new musical about a spelling bee. It was written by some guy named William Finn and directed by that guy James Lapine, who directed *Sunday in the Park with George*. To say I was having a full-circle moment would be an understatement. We even had rolling bleachers in the production!

The show was called *The 25th Annual Putnam County Spelling Bee*. Since it was nominated for Best Musical that year we were invited to perform on the Tony Awards. As we were onstage that night (killing it, I might add), I couldn't help but think: somewhere there is a kid watching this on a twelve-inch screen TV, screaming at his or her parents to "keep it down, I'm watching the Tony Awards." I imagine that kid thinking: "I want to do that someday. I want to be an actor."

The jaded part of me wanted to say: "No, it's too hard! They don't tell you the part about the piranhas! Turn back! Save yourself!!!!!" But the part of me that knew there is nothing you can do to dim that spark said: "I understand. Buckle up. Have a good time. Oh . . . and remove 'Caucasian Coalhouse Walker Jr.' from your resume."

JESSE TYLER FERGUSON currently stars as Mitchell Pritchett on ABC's *Modern Family*, for which he has received three Emmy Award nominations for Outstanding Supporting Actor in a Comedy Series. No stranger to television, Ferguson received rave reviews and was honored by the *Hollywood Reporter* in 2006 as one of "Ten to Watch" for his role on the sitcom *The Class*. His additional television credits include *Do Not Disturb* and *Ugly Betty*. His film credits include *Untraceable* and *Wonderful World*.

Ferguson attended the American Musical and Dramatic Academy and made his Broadway debut at twenty-one as Chip in *On the Town*. He later originated the role of Leaf Coneybear in *The 25th Annual Putnam County Spelling Bee* (Drama League "Distinguished Performance" nominee) and has worked extensively with the New York Public Theater in *The Merchant of Venice*, *A Winter's Tale*, and *A Midsummer Night's Dream* (Drama League "Distinguished Performance" nominee). Other theater credits include world premieres of Christopher Shinn's *Where Do We Live* and Michael John LaChiusa's *Little Fish* and Leo Bloom in *The Producers* at the Hollywood Bowl.

Ferguson is an advocate and supporter of the Human Rights Campaign and, in 2011, was honored with the HRC's Media Award for establishing a positive, increased awareness of LGBT issues in the media. Most recently, he co-founded Tie the Knot (www.tietheknot.org), a non-profit organization featuring bow ties designed by Ferguson, with sales going toward organizations fighting for marriage equality.

MC 'WAX

Josh Berk

INT.—A VERY UNCOOL SUBARU, 11:22 P.M.

TRESTA: You know, Javon used to rap for me.

My blood suddenly turns very, very cold. There most definitely should be a law about girls mentioning their ex-boyfriends. It would be a simple law: DON'T DO IT. Especially in situations such as these. *Parked car* sorts of situations. Especially if their ex-boyfriend is Javon freaking Harris.

I don't hate Javon Harris. That's not the problem. I *love* Javon Harris. Everybody does. *That's* the problem.

I'm in a lot of plays, so I sometimes imagine life as a script. Let's take it from the top. The full conversation goes like this:

ME: Come on, Tresta, just a little kiss. . . .

TRESTA: I don't know. I'm kind of not in the mood.

ME: Well maybe there's something I can do to *get* you in the mood.

(Awkward pause. Tresta puts her finger to her lips as if deep in thought.)

TRESTA: You know, Javon used to rap for me.

Well, shit. A whole host of thoughts run through my head, but that is the first and most eloquent. *Well, shit.*

First of all, know this about me: I am white. Very white. I will get a raging sunburn just from standing near an old person's birthday cake. I have red hair and red eyebrows and a love of musical theater. I live in a suburban home with a big green yard and two Subarus in the driveway. (My parents are both teachers. They *have* to own Subarus. I suspect it's in their contract.)

When me and Tresta are hanging out, I sometimes forget that I'm white and she is not. But when she mentions say, rap, or say her ex-boyfriend Javon freaking Harris, I become quite aware. You know Javon Harris. He is in a big horror film that comes out next month. Everyone knows he is on his way to becoming a real movie star. Probably a rap star too. Tresta dated him before he graduated and moved to California last summer.

I try to make a joke out of it. "I could sing you something from *Phantom*," I say. I gesture widely and start to warm up my throat. *La-la-la-laaaaa*.

"Uh, no," she says, cutting me off.

"*Into the Woods?*" I ask.

"Believe it or not," she says. "Sondheim does not get me hot."

"Liar!" I say. "Blasphemer!"

She laughs. She *does* like Sondheim. I know that she does. And I know that she likes that I like Sondheim. We have that theater thing going on. It's probably the only reason I've gotten this far with her.

Maybe it's not captain of the football team, but I did win a Joey award last year. Best Male Performance in a High School Musical. It's not a Tony, but it's a pretty big deal. Every school across four counties here in my corner of Pennsylvania competes. Something like twenty high schools are eligible, counting the Catholic schools, which never win. The award show is shown live on local TV. There's a red carpet and everything. So when you win, people notice.

Girls notice.

Tresta was nominated too. She was a great Motormouth Maybelle in her school's *Hairspray*. She goes to Robeson High downtown in the gritty city. I, on the other hand go to Woodland out in the wasteland of suburbia. The school district covers a huge county, so there are tons of high schools, as different as night and day from one another. Tresta was nominated, but she did not win a Joey because there is a county-wide law (possibly state or federal law) that Ann Nekin from Westlawn has to win everything. Cosette? Please. *Les Miz* is so overdone. So even though Tresta did not get to take home the trophy, she did meet me at the after-party. And we've been hanging out ever since. So in a way, she *did* win.

I decide to start fake-rapping in the dorkiest white-guy way possible, moving my arms in choppy robotic dance moves. "My name is Wax. Making out with me is as inevitable as income tax." (My name really is Wax. Well, okay, it's actually "Max." But when I was a little kid I wrote my *M*'s upside down all the time. People thought I was dyslexic. They also thought my name was Wax. It stuck. Haha.)

Tresta snorts. "Javon's rhymes did not typically use the word 'inevitable,'" she says. "And they weren't typically about paying one's taxes."

Hopes of getting a little backseat action are disappearing. The night went pretty well. I took her out to Hard Wok Cafe for sushi, which she loves. (I'm lukewarm on sushi, but a *huge* fan of bad puns.) Then we went for coffee and then a walk in the park. Now we're here. Parked near the park on a very quiet and very lovely and *very* private road north of where I live, where the suburbs give way to full-on forest. I still have to drive Tresta all the way downtown. And even on a Friday I have be to home by midnight or this Subaru turns into a pumpkin.

"So uh, what *were* Javon's oh so awesome rhymes about?" I ask.

"Oh you know." She touches her finger to her lips again. "Mostly about stuff he wanted to do with me."

Hmm, I think to myself. What rhymes with "caress those torpedoes"? . . . "We messed our tuxedoes"? I, um, may not be a great rapper. Time to change the subject.

"Hello, Tresta Evans," I say, sticking out my hand as if for a formal handshake. "I am not sure if we have met. My name is Wax O'Donnell." I repeat my last name in a loud stage whisper. "O'Donnell."

"What does that mean?" she asks.

"It means if you're hanging out with a guy named Wax O'Donnell, you shouldn't be surprised that he's not a tremendous rapper." I slap the steering wheel with both hands.

"Too bad for you," she says. "It really gets me in the mood. Maybe I'll ask Javon—I hear he's back in town. . . ."

I have no idea what to do next. So I turn on the engine and drive. The radio comes on loud. The whole time to Hard Wok we had been singing along. Now we just listen in silence.

After a very unenjoyable drive, I pull up to her house. There is nowhere to park so she's like, "Just double-park for a minute. It's fine."

Then she gives me a dry kiss on the cheek. She doesn't even take off her seat belt first! What a letdown. It was like a kick-ass show with a rotten third act. Instead of a fabulous finale you had the flattest, most off-key piece of crap ever.

Tresta takes off the seat belt, gets out of the car, and starts to walk up the cracked pavement to her house.

"Uh, see you later, I guess?" I call out of the car.

"Aw, it's sweet that you think that," she says over her shoulder.

"What the hell?" I say.

"Relax, Wax," she says, stopping and turning back to me. A stray strand of her hair gets stuck in her mouth as she whips her head around. She crinkles her nose and spits it out. For some reason I could never explain, this is the cutest thing I've ever seen. "Just kidding," she says. "I'll text you later, okay?"

"Okay" I say, still feeling like a sad, rain-soaked kitten. "Text me later."

. . . . .

I take the long way home. I'm feeling awful. It's so ridiculous because before I started doing theater, before I started winning awards and finding my true Wax-ness onstage, I would have never even *dreamed* of getting close to a girl like Tresta. To any girl. And now I actually get to go out on dates with such girls!? I've come so far. Why does it feel like it's not far enough?

The dashboard clock blinks from 11:58 to 11:59 right as I pull into the driveway—just before my midnight curfew. I sprint up the walk, fly in the door, bound up the steps, and dive into bed.

I fall asleep, having myriad confusing dreams of torpedoes and hip-hop stars, of sushi rolls and questionable neighborhoods.

One thing my dream doesn't have any of, is music.

· · · · ·

I wake up to a sound I can't quite place. It is faint, like the rustling of leaves. Then it gets louder, more urgent. Then it says "ahem."

"What do you want, Dad?" I mumble, shielding my eyes from the bright light.

"Oh, did I wake you?" he asks, snapping the newspaper again. They still love their newspaper, the O'Donnells' do. Newspapers, coffee with Splenda, crossword puzzles, NPR. They start their day white and only get whiter as the day goes on.

"You know you woke me," I grumble, trying to hide in my bed.

"Listen," he says, standing there in the doorway. He folds the paper and scratches his stubbly chin. His is not a face prone to smiling and the current expression is no exception. "We have to talk about something."

"I was home by 11:59!" I say reflexively, pulling the pillow off my face.

"Oh, believe me, I know that. This isn't about that. This is . . . well it's kind of bad." He folds the newspaper tightly into itself and throws it at me like a Frisbee. I do not catch it. I try, but it deflects off my hands, and takes flight in a birdlike arc, then thuds on the floor.

Dad smirks. How bad I am at sports is alternatingly hilarious and maddening to him. You wouldn't know it from looking at him now, with his mountainous slope of a belly, but he was apparently quite a jock back in the day. He's a sports-guy. He'd rather I do the high jump than sing the high C.

I look over at the newspaper lying on the floor. There is a headline screaming about football and a huge photo of a guy from Tresta's school celebrating a touchdown. I assume Dad's comment wasn't about that. Dad's face is looking very serious.

I flip the paper over to get a look at the nonfootball headline. It *is* bad.

COUNTY SCHOOL BUDGET PASSED 4–3. MAJOR CUTS.

"Holy crap," I say. "Are you guys losing your jobs?"

"No. You're losing your theater."

My eyes race through the article. There is a lot of boring stuff about credit swaps and budgetary whatnots. Some shady dealings by East Atlantic Bank I don't quite understand . . . and then there is this, in simple black and white.

> *Major cuts are coming to the many of the district's*
> *noncore classes. Extracurricular programs,*
> *including theater, music, and other clubs will be*
> *on permanent hiatus.*

"Um, hiatus doesn't sound so bad, right?" I say hopefully.

"It's the *permanent* part you have to worry about," Dad says. "They say *hiatus* to try to deflect the heat. But this budget is brutal. It's not coming back anytime soon."

"What the hell? What happened to softening the blow?"

"That's the administrators' job. My job is to tell it like it is. And I'm telling you. Theater is done."

Do I detect a bit of happiness in his voice? He never understood. How could I expect him to know what it would feel like to lose it? The backstage shenanigans. The onstage glory. The feel of the lights, the sound of the applause. The one place I ever felt truly alive and truly great and truly me . . . gone.

"Where's Mom?" I ask.

"I'm here." She sticks her head in from the hallway. She is rushing, like always. Mom is the busiest woman in the world.

"Mom. You see this budget story?"

"I know, dear," she says, already gone. "It's really such a shame. We'll talk about it later."

"This sucks so bad. I notice they aren't cutting football."

"You don't want to make it a fight between sports and arts in this town," Dad says. "Not in any town."

"No, not a fight," I say. "That's not fair. Unless it's a dance-fight. Or maybe a sing-off?" I'm being sarcastic because the alternative is to get really angry. I feel my face turning hot.

"Sports mean a lot to people," Dad says.

"So does theater!" I yell. "So does music! So does art!"

He clears his throat. "Well, sure, but for some kids—sports are the only reason they keep their grades up and stay in school."

"For some kids, theater is the only reason they stay alive!" I snap.

"Now you're being melodramatic."

"I'm not! It's true!" Without a creative outlet, without a place to fit in, without a spotlight in which to bask . . . well, what would the point of life be? How do I explain to him what it feels like to get lost in a song? How in that first moment when I stepped on a stage, something clicked. Maybe it didn't make everything perfect, but it was a hell of a lot better. That *is* life. My life anyway.

Dad keeps talking, but I stop listening to him. I stop listening and begin singing loudly in my head, the words to a musical I've been working on. It's called *Shut Up!* That is also the reprise.

WAX: (singing) Shut up! Shut up! SHUT UP!!!

Dad does not shut up. Eventually I tell him I have to go to the bathroom. I text Tresta from the john. I sit there a long time but she does not respond. I feel incredibly mopey.

Then I text Alex, a theater-friend. A good friend. I text and he calls me right back. Not texts: *calls*. Clue #1 that this is serious.

"Oh my God," he says. "You have got to be kidding me with this. I'm like beyond outraged."

"So you saw it then?"

"No," he says. "I'm just outraged for no apparent reason."

To be honest, it wouldn't be the first time. Outrage is Alex's primary mode of being. I am glad he is already in the loop and I don't have to break the bad news.

"Without theater I'll die, Wax," he says. "You might think I'm kidding, but I'm being perfectly serious."

"Oh, I know," I say. "This is as serious as a heart attack."

"I'd rather have like a million heart attacks all at once than have them cut the theater program!"

"I'm with you, brother. I'm with you."

"So what are we going to do about it?"

This is one of the many things I love about Alex. I am resignation. He's all action.

"Get off the toilet," he says. "I'm coming over."

. . . . .

Alex bounds into the kitchen without bothering to knock, blowing in like a strong breeze through an open window. I am sitting at the kitchen table, drinking coffee and sort of checking my phone every two seconds.

Tresta has not yet texted me back. Should I text her again?

"Want to get some coffee?" Alex says without seeming like he needed any. He is full of energy, almost vibrating in his shoes. He runs his hand through his hair, which appears to be messily tousled but I know to be painstakingly arranged. He looks like a headshot magically sprung to life. I'm not ashamed to admit it: he's a good-looking dude. They call *me* gay all the time, probably because I'm in theater, probably because I hang out with Alex all the time. I usually tell them to ask their moms if I'm gay.

I hold up my mug to indicate that I already have a full cup. "Can't ever have too much coffee," he says.

"No. I think you can."

"*You* can. I'm coffee-proof. My addiction is strong."

"Your addiction to that guy who works at Bertrand's is strong," I say.

"Maybe. May-be."

So we hop in Alex's car—an immaculate silver Audi—and drive to Bertrand's, the hipster coffee shop on the west end of town. You have to pass like twelve perfectly good Dunkin' Donuts to get there, but I know better than to say anything. As we drive, we talk about our plight and before we even get in the door at Bertrand's, have the beginnings of a plan.

INT—BERTRAND'S COFFEE

(As Wax and Alex enter, Alex speaks loudly.)

ALEX: So then I say to the curator: I don't care if he is a little person, no one should drink that much Chardonnay. . . .

Alex has the habit of saying something loud and fascinating in case someone is listening. No one is. It is just girls working the counter so he quiets down. "I like the idea of going to the school board meeting but we can't just go wait in line and give some speech," he says. "They've just been waiting to kill theater. It's their political *agenda*. And this was their chance. Their minds are set."

"I don't think it's really about politics," I say as we wait for our overpriced and bitter drinks. "I read that whole article. Okay, most of it. It was bank bullshit. The school district got ripped off by East Atlantic Bank. Shady investments, that kind of thing."

"Ew, East Atlantic Bank sucks. I hate their commercials too."

"They're the worst and now the school district is broke."

"Well, we have to do something big. It has to be epic. Not just a speech at the school board meeting," Alex says, his voice getting loud again. "Yes! A performance! You're thinking just what I'm thinking, Wax: We razzle-dazzle this bitch up?"

"Well, not in so many words, but okay . . ."

We proceed to formulate our plan. We talk about the specifics, me offering as much as I can about the political and economic side. I had just read only the one article and half listened to my dad talk about it, so it isn't all that much. The school board got screwed by the bank and can't raise taxes because of some law. So they have no choice but to start cutting every "noncore" thing they can think of. Forgetting of course that theater *is* the core of many of us.

We settle on who we were pissed at: everyone.

The school, East Atlantic Bank, the jocks, our parents, the newspaper. And if they think they can silence us they are wrong. They can take away our stage, but they can't silence our voices. We ARE going to razzle-dazzle this bitch. We are going to plan a guerilla theater performance, LIVE at the next school board meeting.

I remember from the article that they meet the second and fourth Tuesday of each month. That gives us two weeks. Not a lot of time, but we are up to the task.

. . . . .

The first step is to recruit some musicians. Okay, the *first* step is to obsess about how to get Tresta on board and maybe write a part for her to sing since she still hasn't texted me back. But the second step (maybe the hundred-and-first step, since the first step is repeated one hundred times) is to recruit some musicians.

Alex and I settle on the plan via text over the next two days.

> ME: marching band? that would make an entrance.

ALEX: can't sing over marching band.

> ME: jazz band?

ALEX: ew, i hate jazz.

> ME: guitar club?

ALEX: bingo. let's go recruit on monday.

INT.—MR. ORTIZ'S ROOM, MONDAY, AFTER SCHOOL.

We walk into Mr. Ortiz's room, the science classroom where Guitar Club is held after school. It is a crazy cacophony of high buzz-sawing guitars and low bass note rumbles. Electric and acoustic and someone banging on a table for percussion (I guess). Mr. Ortiz is nowhere to be found.

"Who should we ask first?" I ask Alex.

He shrugs and turns his palms upward. I'm not sure if that means he doesn't know who to ask or if he can't hear what I am asking him.

It is extremely loud. So I jump on a table and start to tap dance. Just a quick few steps. Shuffle, ball change. Shuffle, ball change.

It gets everyone's attention.

The torrent of noise dribbles to a stop like a leaky faucet. *Squeak. Plunk. Crunch.*

"Hello, Guitar Club," I say in my best stage barker voice. "I, as you no doubt know, am Wax O'Donnell."

I do this thing where whenever I say my name: I wait for applause. I don't mean to do it, I just do. You never know. Sometimes there might be applause. This time there is not. I continue.

"I am here today to talk to you about some terrible news." I wish I had the newspaper with me. Every good speech needs a prop. "The proposed school district budget includes massive cuts to the arts."

"For real?" says a kid named Bo Hertzman. He is a white kid with hipster glasses and dreadlocks pulled back into a black bandana.

"For super-real," I say in a solemn tone.

"Is Mr. Ortiz going to get fired?" asks a kid named Martin, who apparently does not read the news.

"No," I offer. "Yes. Maybe. Wait: Do you want him to get fired?"

"Why would we want Mr. Ortiz to get fired? He rules," Martin says.

"Okay, yeah, I mean, if you help us, it probably would help him not get fired." Alex chimes in.

"The point here is that we have to stick together!" I announce loudly.

"We're all in this together. Artists. Musicians. Actors. Guitar Club *will* get canceled like everything else. Theater will be canceled. Orchestra. Jazz Club. All of it. Canceled."

Bo stands up. He starts talking loudly and pointing right at me. "You never gave a shit about us for like a minute of your life, Wax. Remember when I played that song I wrote for the talent show? And I introduced it by saying that I was at a point in my life where I was either going to start writing music or kill myself? And then after I was done you said I made the wrong choice?"

"Well, you kind of did set me up for that," I mumble.

"You don't give a shit about us until you need something from us. I see how it is."

I am losing the crowd. Some of them start strumming their instruments again. "Do you see how it is?" I ask, my voice rising into its upper register. "This isn't about me. This is about something much bigger. None of you will give up a few precious hours of your oh-so-busy lives to help me write a song and save the freaking arts?! What kind of world do you want to live in? That literally is the question here."

The only response is silence.

"Maybe we *should* go ask the Jazz Club," I whisper to Alex.

"Ew, I told you I hate jazz," Alex says. "Listening to jazz is like watching old people do it."

Then a girl named Hannah Senko stands up. "I'll do it. Music *should* be used to say something. Like Dylan, you know?"

I am not sure what Dylan Moscowitz from the stage crew has to do with anything, but I nod in agreement. Alex is not so sure.

"We're not looking for like, peace, love, and hand-holding," he says. "We're looking to stir things up. We need some energy!"

"You think I don't have any energy?" Hannah mumbles. I try hard not to laugh, because she's like . . . well, picture a stoned and very sleepy bulldog yawning and being like, "You think I don't have any energy?"

Then she jumps up and throws her acoustic guitar into its case. She grabs an electric instead and cranks the volume up and starts *wailing!*

She starts shaking her hair, and it turns her head into a ball of fire. The music is amazing! I get chills and I don't get chills easily.

"Ladies and gentlemen: We have our guitarist," Alex says. "The rest of you can pluck yourselves."

· · · · ·

So I spend my after-school hours every day now in Hannah Senko's wood-paneled basement. The song is coming together okay. She has these little battery-powered amps that you can wear on your belt which blast at surprisingly loud volume. Alex and I plug our microphones into ours, and she plugs in her guitar. The song is a little weird but sort of *awesome*.

It turns out that Hannah wasn't talking about Dylan Moscowitz from stage crew, but rather Bob Dylan, the songwriter. She played us some of his old songs—I like "Positively 4th Street" best because it is so freaking bitter. Fits my mood. I like how it accuses some unnamed "you" of all sorts of shit.

We keep the same structure but pen some lyrics all our own.

ALEX: You say the money's gone.

ME: You say your hands are tied.

BOTH: We say it's all a con—a big fat lieeee.

ALEX: I'm talking to you, Walter Peters.

ME: Save our theaters, Mr. Peters!

BOTH: Save our theaters!

It's a happy coincidence that the school board president is named Walt Peters so we pretty much ride that rhyme as far as we can. I'm not saying we're Dylan (either one), but it is catchy. And at least I can carry a tune.

We practice it over and over again. Theater kids can work harder than anyone. Putting on a show is no small feat. It takes hours. Days. Months. Blood and sweat and jazz hands. We've learned discipline. Devotion. We've learned to work hard. No: We *have* to work hard. It's what we do.

Hannah works hard too. She never seems to tire of playing the song day after day as the big show approaches. I mean: school board meeting. It is hard not to think of it as a *show*. My stomach gets the same amped up feeling it does leading up to opening night. It never seems like it's going to come together, but somehow it always does.

Which is why just a few days before the big show, I am shocked when Alex says, "No offense you guys. Obviously we're great. But the song is, I don't know . . . lacking something?"

"Lacking what?" Hannah looks genuinely shocked, her big eyes growing wider.

"I don't know," Alex says. "I can't put my finger on it. It's just like, something that isn't there, you know?"

We sit quietly for a minute. The truth hurts the most when it's most true. The song *is* lacking something.

"I know what it needs," I say. And I do. Suddenly it's clear, a blazing spotlight in my brain. "And no offense, Alex. But what it needs is star power. Hollywood star power."

"You have an idea as to how to land a Hollywood star to help us perform at the school board meeting?" Hannah says.

"Yup," I say. "Yup, I do."

And I swear to you that this has *nothing* with a desire to talk to Tresta even though it has been DAYS since our date and she still hasn't texted me back. It only has to do with my altruistic desire to save our theater.

"The person we need," I say, "is Javon Harris."

"You know him?" Hannah asks.

"I, uh, I know someone who knows him, uh, pretty well . . . "

"Well, call him up—"

"Who is it that you know that is BFF with Javon freaking Harris and why have you never told me about this?" Alex interrupts, looking shocked.

"Dude. It's Tresta."

"Who is Tresta?" Hannah asks.

"I thought you said you guys were done," Alex says.

"She hasn't texted me back in a while. But desperate times call for desperate measures. Let's go."

. . . . .

The three of us pile into Alex's Audi and drive purposefully downtown. I am not quite sure why Hannah is with us, other than we are like a *band* now and thus have to do everything together.

She sits in the back and jabbers enthusiastically about how awesome it would be to have Javon Harris show up at our school board meeting. Alex agrees. It would make a dramatic third act to this melodrama, the surprise happy ending every good show needs.

I am getting psyched too, listening to her talk. Though of course it is the longest of shots. For all I know, Tresta was kidding when she said he was back in town. He could be in Los Angeles, sunning himself on the beach or napping on a pile of money. For all I know, Tresta isn't even talking to me anymore and we won't even get to ask him.

"You guys stay in the car," I say as Alex circles the block trying to find a parking spot. "This probably won't be long anyway."

I walk up to the door, take a deep breath, and knock. No response. I hear some shuffling behind the door. Is she ignoring me?

Then the door opens!

"What on earth are you doing, Wax O'Donnell?" Tresta says. She is wearing hot pink yoga pants, a boy band T-shirt, and a bandana tied tight around her head. I think it's safe to say she wasn't expecting guests. She's smiling though, a huge, toothy smile.

"Tresta!" I sing.

"Make it quick," she says. "I'm grounded. My mom is at the store. If she comes back and seems your skinny ass on the step, I won't see the sun for a year."

"You're grounded? Why?"

"*Somebody* got me home past curfew."

"We were in before twelve!"

"Yeah, well, my curfew is eleven. My mom is strict as hell."

"You never told me to bring you home by eleven," I say. She smiles. Oh, the smile. I am confused for a minute. Then I do the math. "Aw, you knew you'd be home after curfew, but you didn't want to stop hanging out with me. You broke curfew for me!"

She smiles again. "Yeah, and a lot of good it did me too. Mom took my phone. That's why I haven't texted you or anybody. It's been hell. She grounded my ass. And you heard they're cutting art and music and theater?"

"Yeah, I heard. That's actually why I'm here. And I mean, also just to see those beautiful eyes."

She smiles again. I smile. We're just standing there smiling.

Then I hear a quick double-honk. Alex gives me a hand gesture telling me to hurry up. They are just a few feet away, close enough to hear and, unfortunately, talk to us.

"Who is in the car?" Tresta says.

"Alex. I told you about him before."

"And who else?"

"Oh, that's Hannah. She plays guitar," I say. Hannah waves.

"I don't text you back and all of a sudden you're hanging out with some other girl? Don't tell me she's with Alex. I know he's your gay friend."

"I'm so much more than the gay friend," Alex says with a wave. "Seriously."

"I just play guitar," Hannah says, leaning out the window.

"Yeah, well that better be all you do."

Hannah rolls her eyes. I like this!

"So why all you all here again?" Tresta says.

"Here's the thing," I say. "We're going to protest at the school board meeting on Tuesday. Guerilla theater! Hannah is going to play guitar, and we were going to ask you to sing. . . ." (I am hoping here that Alex and Hannah would just roll with it.) "But since you're grounded, we're wondering if maybe you could see if maybe Javon was in town. He's a graduate of this theater program too. Maybe he could . . ."

"Shit!" Tresta says. "I think I just saw my mom's car up the street. She must be looking for parking. I gotta get inside! Text Javon, tell him I gave you the number!"

She shouts out Javon's number and slams the door. Gone again.

I keep repeating the number out loud, over and over, so I won't forget it. A little voice in my head is like "Hey, why does she still have his number memorized?" I try to drown that voice out. I don't want to forget the number.

· · · · ·

I scramble into the car and duck down so Tresta's mom can't see me. I hunch low in the passenger seat like a felon fleeing the police. All the while I'm saying the number over and over again, staring up at the ceiling. I feel the car pull away from the curb. I am trying to make a plan—what do we say when we text Javon? Then I hear Alex start to talk.

"Hi, Javon Harris," Alex is saying into his phone in a singsong voice.

"Dude!" I say. Alex shushes me.

"You don't know me but I'm a friend of Tresta's. Friend-of-a-friend really. Anyway, she gave me your number. Don't worry, I won't share it with TMZ or anything. . . . I'm just calling to see if you happen to still be back in your old hometown this Tuesday. We're doing a protest to save the theater department and would just love you to come. Call or text me back. Okay, thanks. Love you. Bye."

"What the hell?" I say.

Alex has a huge smile on his face. "Well, not like *literal* love. It's just a Hollywood thing to say. Everyone knows that."

"I can't believe you just called him," Hannah says from the back.

"Ain't nothing to it but to do it," Alex says. "Now we just wait." He drums on the steering wheel with his thumbs. His phone chirps loudly. He ignores both the law and common sense wisdom against reading a text while driving and checks his phone. "Dude!" I jump up and grab the phone.

I read the text. It does indeed appear to be from Javon! It takes a bit of time to decipher the rapper lingo, but it appears to read upon being translated to regular English: "Tresta is a great girl. I happily accept your invitation. Please instruct me via text message as to what time and location to arrive and you have my word that I shall attend."

Alex pulls the car over. The three of us sit in stunned silence until Hannah speaks.

"I can't believe that worked."

"Me neither," Alex and I say in unison.

He grabs the phone back and starts texting furiously.

In just a few seconds Javon texts back.

"He's in," Alex says. "He's in."

· · · · ·

The day of the big school board meeting is finally here. It's a Tuesday, hardly a good time for a show. These people know nothing about theatrics. They are about to learn.

Alex picks me up, and swings by Hannah's house. She's pacing on the street out front, her guitar and amps sitting on the curb. As soon as she sees the car, she sprints toward us so fast that her ball of red hair shoots out behind her, waving like a flag in the wind. She leaps in, throwing her guitar and a crate with our microphones and amps in beside her.

"Slow your roll, Senko," I say. "We don't go on for like an hour."

"I know. I'm just excited! *Weeeee!*" She literally says *weeeee*. I try not to judge. Preshow jitters do different things to different people.

"You have everything we need?" Alex asks.

She points to the guitar and the crate o' gear. "Now we just hope Javon shows up."

After that, no one says anything. We don't talk about the plan anymore. We don't practice the song anymore. We just sit quietly, almost meditatively.

When we finally reach the nondescript school district administrative building on the east side of town, Alex parks the car and says two words.

"It's showtime."

. . . . .

We have to be a little sneaky about our presence. These meetings are open to the public, so we have every right to be here. There is a part at the beginning where anyone who wants to can sign up to speak. So we signed up. Only, of course, no one is expecting microphones and rock guitars.

The plan is for Alex, who really looks the part of the clean-cut-all-American boy when he wants to, to wait in line for his turn to speak. A minute before it's his turn, he'll text me. This will alert me, Javon, and Hannah—waiting backstage—to burst out, guitars-a-blazing.

The only problem is that Javon Harris is nowhere to be seen. We are hanging out in the parking lot, watching people arrive, trying to be relaxed. It's easy for Alex—he is one of those guys who gets just super cool and icy before a show. He turns his big eyes to me and says, "It's fine. He said he'll be here so we have every reason to believe that he'll be here."

I wish I could share his confidence. We wait. I pace. Hannah paces. Alex stays cool.

"Well, could you at least just text him to see if he's coming?" I say.

"Don't you think I thought of that?" he hisses. His eyes bug out huge for half a second; his face flashes panic. Maybe he's not as confident as I thought. "I've texted him like a million times. No response."

"Dude," I start to say, then I hear a guy yell to some other guy hustling across the parking lot. "Gavel comes down in two minutes. Get in here, Walt!" He laughs. *Walt Peters.* He opens the door and closes it behind him. It thuds like the end of a sentence.

Alex follows Walt, and we follow Alex. Alex takes his place in the auditorium while we wait down the hall. I peek into the auditorium. Rows of dark chairs face the stage. On the stage are seven seats—one for each member of the school board. Behind them are more American flags than could possibly be necessary. I watch as the school board members assemble, like an Avengers of evil. I see Walt Peters, that bastard. My heart is pounding in the region of my shoes. Where is Javon? I text Alex: **still no javon.**

I can see him, smiling and happily waiting his place in line. Somehow he texts back without even looking at his phone. I don't think he even takes it out of his pocket.

"What did he say?" Hannah asks, looking over my shoulder.

"He said," I say with a gulp, "the show must go on."

The meeting starts with the public comments, but there are a handful of people in front of Alex in line so we have to wait. I crane my neck every five seconds to try to see the parking lot like I'm waiting for the Great Pumpkin to arrive. The Great Pumpkin is never going to arrive!

My phone beeps. It's our turn to go on. No Javon. What the heck are we going to do? There will be a big awkward instrumental part in the middle that is supposed to have a rap part. The whole thing is going to suck!

Hannah and I walk into the room. She turns on her guitar and lets out a massively loud minor chord. Alex starts to sing. Then my phone beeps again. Another text. This one is Tresta. **Break a leg,** it says.

I look up. She is in the audience! She must have snuck out! She broke curfew *and* she snuck out of being grounded! For me! Or did she only come for Javon. . . .

I see a few other kids from theater: Claudia, Tanner, even Ann Nekin. Me and Alex sort of let it slip that something was going down tonight. We couldn't tell them *exactly* what because then they'd be jostling for stage time and stepping on our lines. . . .

Hannah smacks me with her guitar. I'm supposed to be following her. The song is starting!

The school board guys just look confused. Hannah is strumming her guitar loudly and Alex is singing his Bob Dylan-ish best, "You say the money's gone . . ."

I scramble to sing my part. "You say your hands are tied . . ." And then it clicks. The performance instinct kicks in, and I'm lost in the moment. Our harmonies are tight. Our melodies are strong. The crowd isn't in an uproar. If I had to describe their reaction, I would pretty much say "polite bemusement." We hit the breakdown. The time for the rap to start. No Javon. But it's clear. I know what I have to do.

Wax O'Donnell has to freestyle rap.

I take a deep breath and step to the center of the stage. Hannah plays this jerky little rhythm thing she's been practicing that is perfect for rapping over. Okay. Deep breath, Wax . . .

INT.—SCHOOL BOARD MEETING, 6:30P.M.

Wax struggles to come up with words. He is not a good rapper.

WAX: (haltingly) Aw, yeah, the budget is cut? That . . . judge . . . is a slut.

Okay, not the best first line. What judge? Doesn't matter. It rhymes with budget. Sort of. What rhymes with slut?

WAX: (cont.) Put a horn in your . . . butt.

What am I saying right now? Time to bring it back to at least something somewhat relevant.

WAX: (cont.) East Atlantic Bank killed theater, and I hate their silly faces!

Hannah stops playing. Mouths drop open. Do I hear crickets? I know I hear laughter. Just a little at first. Then a lot more. Rapping is hard! Shut up!

I run offstage, never to be seen from again.

. . . . .

I run right out of the school board building and head back to my house. It's a long walk and it takes forever, but I don't want to face anyone. I can't stop replaying the scene in my mind. *I hate their silly faces?* Oh, for all that is holy and just, please just kill me now. I run into the house, slam the door to my room, throw myself on the bed, and decide to hide for a few thousand years.

Not only have I failed to save theater, but I have made an ass out of myself. In front of my friends, in front of Tresta, in front of Walt Peters and a dozen American flags. And—oh no—my heart sinks further if that's even possible. There is no doubt that someone recorded it. You can't bust out a hard rock school board guerilla theater anthem and not have someone whip out a cell phone. I try to remember the audience—did I see anyone with a phone? I can picture Walt Peters's face, which was pretty epic. And Tresta's, which was . . . not.

Why did I have to try to rap? Why did I try to be Javon Harris? Why did Tresta have to mention Javon's rapping in the first place? Why didn't Javon show up? Why couldn't I be eloquent?

I had my one chance to say what I know to be true. That this theater department means everything to me, to all of us. You can't put a price on that.

. . . . .

When I wake up the next morning, it's not to Dad rustling his newspaper. It's to my phone, going crazy. It's beeping a million times, like an extended beep solo. I debate throwing it out the window, but I really like this phone.

I look at the screen. It's worse than I expected: 47 million missed calls and 863 billion text messages. *Slight* exaggeration. I don't even want to read any of them. Then the phone rings again. It is Alex.

INT.—WAX'S BEDROOM, WEDNESDAY MORNING.

Wax O'Donnell has bed head but looks adorable.
ME: Hello?
ALEX: Hello? That's all you got is hello?
ME: Was it as bad as I think it was?
ALEX: How bad do you think it was?
ME: Like the stinkiest stink to ever stink up earth?
ALEX: Worse.

ME: Thanks.

ALEX: But dude, something amazing happened.

ME: Don't tell me: Someone filmed it. The video exploded. Nine million views overnight.

ALEX: Yup.

ME: You're joking.

ALEX: Nope.

(Wax contemplates suicide.)

ME: I—I was joking.

ALEX: It gets better.

ME: Could it get worse?

ALEX: It gets much better! I've been reading the comments. Most everyone just laughs at you. But one of them is from a bank.

ME: What?

ALEX: Western Hills. I swear it's legit. They're a competitor to East Atlantic. They've been trying to contact you. They want to use your rap in a commercial. "East Atlantic Bank killed theater, and I hate their silly faces!" is the most famous phrase on the Internet right now. Also they're going to make a donation to save the theater program! And all of the other arts programs that were going to get cut!

(Wax's head explodes.)

ALEX (cont.): Dude! We did it! *You* did it.

ME: Hold on—I have another call. It's Tresta!

(Wax switches to the other call.)

ME: (cont.) Hello?

TRESTA: Dude, you're a terrible rapper.

ME: I know.

(There is the longest of pauses.)

TRESTA: But a pretty great guy.

. . . . .

A few short (long) months after the day I saved the arts/became the world's laughingstock, Tresta and I are again in an idling Subaru at the park. It's dark and quiet. The dashboard clock blinks 10:45.

"I should go," she says. "I don't want to get grounded."

"Again," I say.

"Again. I have got to be the only girl who ever got grounded for sneaking out to go to a school board meeting."

"Was it worth it?" I ask. She kisses me. Again. We have been kissing a lot.

"Maybe."

There is a brief pause. The crickets sing to us from outside. And this time *I* break the cardinal rule. *I* bring up a girl's ex-boyfriend in a parked car. "Um, so hey—did we ever figure out why Javon didn't show up at the school board meeting?"

"Yeah," she mumbles. "I thought I told you." But the way her voice gets quiet and her eyes stare out the window tells me that she's lying.

"I'm pretty sure you didn't," I say.

"Oh, well, I don't really know." She looks down.

"You know, for a great actress, you're a really bad liar." The icicles-on-my-skin feeling returns. *What is she hiding?*

"Shut up." She punches me. "I really *am* a great actress. Say that part again and kiss me."

"You're trying to change the subject."

"It's working," she says, kissing me again.

"It really isn't," I say.

"Don't get all weird. Can we just go back to kissing?"

"No. No, we cannot."

"Ah, you got weird." She throws up her hands.

"I did not!" I say, though I totally felt myself getting weird.

"Fine. Read for yourself." She taps her phone a few times and hands it to me. I will paraphrase the texts so as to save your brain melting from grammar sickness.

TRESTA: Dude, what the hell—where
were you the other night?

JAVON: Where was I supposed
to be, baby?

TRESTA: You don't remember?
You promised to come to the
school board meeting and help us
save theater.

JAVON: Oh hell, sorry, I forgot. I got
invited to a party up in NYC—couldn't
miss it. I'll make it up to you. You know
I still love you, baby.

I feel my ears turning red. "Keep reading," she says.

TRESTA: The feeling is not mutual.

JAVON: Give me one more
chance. ONE MORE CHANCE.

TRESTA: I told you, I fell in love
with somebody else.

To this, Javon apparently did not respond.

I stare at the phone, out the window, and finally at Tresta. The girl in my car. The girl who apparently loves me.

"You broke up with *him*?" I say. "Who did you fall in love with? Do I know the fella?"

She looks at me with those big, beautiful eyes and smiles.

"What can I say?" she says. "You're a star. And besides, I told you Sondheim makes me hot." We kiss again. A long, slow, soft, and beautiful kiss. "Just don't ever rap again."

....

ANECDOTE: IAN HARDING

....

I remember the exact moment I decided acting was my life's passion. This epiphany, if one could call it such, came out of someone else's mistake.

I was a senior in high school, and had already auditioned for several colleges and acting conservatories, but I was still a little uncertain. I had been performing throughout high school, loved doing the work, and was reasonably talented, but could I actually do it for the rest of my life? Did I have what it takes?

The show was *How to Succeed in Business Without Really Trying*, and I was cast as Mr. Biggley, a crotchety older man who runs the World Wide Wicket Company. I forget the exact point in the story, but in one performance the actress playing Rosemary, the young love interest, completely missed her entrance, leaving myself and the other actress onstage with nothing to do. In that moment, having never taken an improv class and without even being conscious of my actions, I started making up lines.

Something going wrong in a show is never fun. And trying to cover for someone else's mistake can be heart-wrenchingly nervous. Would people think I was the one who messed up? Would they be weirded out? Would the director be upset with me? But "the show must go on." At that moment, keeping the audience entertained was all I could focus on—not whether I was scared or anxious about what might happen next. I remember referencing the other actor onstage. Then, seeing she was terrified and completely lost as to what was going on, I made some crack about her and being deaf for some reason. The audience lost it.

Finally, Rosemary walked out, also completely bewildered as to where I was in the script, and I covered that as well. We broke into song and dance as one is wont to do in a musical, and then Rosemary exited. In doing so, the door she left from came off its hinge, swaying awkwardly, revealing all of the other actors getting ready to come onstage for their entrances.

Again it happened.

I made some comment about budget cuts, told the people standing in view of the audience to get back to work (I was playing their boss after all . . .), and slammed the door into place. The audience laughed and applauded, which startled me since I was used to applause at the fall of the curtain. The scene ended, and I left feeling something I couldn't articulate. To this day I don't know what I said, or even if what happened was any good. In that moment though, I got the certainty I needed: I was an actor.

It's not the applause, the laughter, nor the praise, (in fact, I've mostly received the opposite of praise). It was the alive-ness. I know that's not a word, but that's what it is. Danger, excitement, connectivity, the moment, and what comes out when those things are combined. Just throwing myself out there. That's why I do it. It doesn't matter if I'm brilliant, terrible, ugly, beautiful, happy, or sad. It's getting out there anyway and knowing it will turn out as it should.

IAN HARDING is an American actor whose work can be seen in several films and television shows, most notably on ABC Family's *Pretty Little Liars* as Ezra Fitz. He attended the Carnegie Mellon School of Drama, and would like to thank his friends Ted Malawer and Nic Cory for their totally unfounded faith in his talent. Along with his above anecdote, Ian would like to add that he is still learning the ins and outs of show biz, and would encourage the reader to remain forever a curious student.

TESSITURA

Maryrose Wood

"Sing a little something for us, Fiona. Come on, love, give us a song."

A table full of bleary eyes and eager smiles swivels my way, like a bank of searchlights converging on an escaped prisoner. I flinch, can't help it. Then I laugh, to make like it's all right. They're Niall's friends, after all. I have to be nice. I'll sing whatever they like.

"Sure, Fiona, let's have a song. Sing 'Molly Malone.'"

"Sing 'Johnny, I Hardly Knew Ye.' Gets me every time."

"Bit military for a birthday, don't you think?"

"'Tis, you're right. Sing 'Danny Boy' then."

"'Danny Boy,' that's it!"

Look, they're crying already. Just say the words "Danny Boy" to this crowd and their eyes turn to faucets. The Japanese may have invented karaoke, but we Irish have our own version. We call it *life*. We can't gather for five minutes without someone calling for a song. At least, that's the way it goes in Niall's circle of friends. They're all creative types to begin with, of course. Fiddlers, drummers, dancers, poets. New arrivals and nostalgic expats, their Irishness seems to double the minute they arrive in Woodlawn. And I don't mean the cemetery, though that's here too.

Woodlawn is the Bronx's own Little Ireland. Take a walk down Katonah Avenue; you'll see what I mean. You'll hear it too. The brogues are thicker than the head on a pint of Guinness, and contagious as a yawn. Listen to me, for fek's sake. I talk like an American at school—I was born here after all, though my parents weren't—but when I'm around this lot....

"'Danny Boy'! 'Danny Boy'!"

Like an under-rehearsed choir of drunken ghouls, they start moaning the tune in four different keys at once. Niall rolls his eyes and checks his iPhone. He's a busy fellow, even in a pub with friends. Even on his birthday. The Kilcommons Irish Culture Institute never sleeps. Might you be interested in a step-dancing class? How about some Gaelic lessons? Is it your lifelong dream to learn to play the uilleann pipes? If so, Niall's your man. He's all incorporated and everything. If I ask him for a few bucks and he won't give it, here's his reply: "Sorry, love, but I'm a nonprofit organization." You can't imagine how often I've heard that one.

The moaning's over; now they're all lighting their cigarettes. There's no smoking allowed in New York City unless you're hunkered in your own bath with the windows nailed shut, but we're in the private party room at Kelly Ryan's pub, and it's Niall Kilcommons's birthday, after all. Rules do not apply. Frankly it's a relief to see people enjoying a smoke for a change, instead of standing huddled on the sidewalks in front of buildings, shoulders hunched in shame, eyes flitting about like murder suspects. I hear you can't smoke in a pub in Ireland anymore, either. That's a sure sign of the apocalypse, if ever there was one.

"Somebody get Fiona the microphone, now. Come on, love. Sing a song for your da."

Yeah, Niall's my da, but I call him Niall. If I said my da, most people wouldn't understand who I meant. Fathering is not what he's known for. But he is known, make no mistake. He's famous in certain circles, among the barkeeps and bagpipers, the cops and the Catholic priests. He knows every fire chief in the five boroughs by his middle name. It's not much of a feat of memory, mind you, as about ninety percent have got Patrick for a middle name. That's another of Niall's jokes. Every one a groaner. I only repeat them so you know what I've been up against my whole life.

Niall's vast reputation makes Evelyn and me famous too, on the rare occasions we're all three together. Niall Kilcommons's two gifted daughters are we. I'm the teenaged singer, the sassy one with the big chest, and Evelyn's the dancer and the looker. And a dental hygienist too, but Niall doesn't mention that part. Twenty-six years of life as Niall's daughter has blessed Evelyn with a sense of the practical, if only in self-defense. She was a brilliant dancer in her day, though. She used to win all the step-dancing contests, before she traded in her dancing slippers and beautiful costumes for her current wardrobe of powder-blue polyester jackets, boxy and unflattering, even on a tall, slim girl like Evelyn.

If there'd been a third Kilcommons daughter, she'd have played the fiddle no doubt, or maybe the flute, but after I was born, my mum declined to bear any more talent for Niall's unpaid employ. Instead she took up with a biker fellow with fearsome tattoos wrapped about both arms. His name is George and he's swarthy. Of Greek extraction, and therefore statuesque (that's a joke of my own making, but George is certainly well muscled in the classical style, not that I've noticed). He works construction and is a quiet type. By quiet I don't mean shy, or mumbling, or weak. George is anything but weak. But he's not a talker. He just gets up and does the thing. No preamble. No excuses. Can you imagine? The silence of George must have been a blessed relief for Mum, after all those years of listening to Niall talk about Niall.

Needless to say, there's not one drop of Irish blood in George's brawny, swarthy, nonloquacious physique. He has thick, blunt fingers, strong and reliable. Too thick to dance along the neck of a fiddle like pale fluttering birds, the way Niall's do. But his arms are strong enough to lift a tired woman's life into an easier place. So I can't blame her one bit, really.

. . . . .

The room is thick with smoke by now, and somebody's rigging up a microphone to the amp. I catch a glimpse of myself in an open spot on the hazy mirror on the back wall, my reflection slivered in between a poster for the Irish Rugby Football Union and a list of the day's specials. My father's daughter? Sure, I guess there's a resemblance. He's got curly dark hair shot with wires of gray, uncombable. A broad pale face, like mine, and milky blue eyes capped by high, dark eyebrows that give him a look of perpetual happy surprise. Maybe that's why everyone likes him at first glance. He always looks glad to see you. Don't be fooled. It's just the eyebrows.

People are always crazy about Niall when they meet him. Then they get to know him a bit, and they like him well enough. After a few years they grit their teeth. Full-on abandonment comes soon after, sure as a hangover follows a binge, but it doesn't matter. He's always collecting new followers. Niall looks soft, like a pushover, a sentimental sap even, the way he caresses his fiddle and cries like a baby at an old song, but he's steely at the core. All right, he's a proper bastard sometimes.

He calls it being demanding. He's "demanding" of me and Evelyn, and of his students, and his women, and himself too, I suppose. Says high expectations are the only true compliment. Says it's the only way to achieve greatness. I used to think he was a hero, a grand whatever-it-is. Visionary. But you can't fool me, not anymore. Mean is mean, there's no need to tie a bow on it and call it something respectable.

· · · · ·

"'Danny Boy'! 'Danny Boy'!" They're like vultures on a carcass, this crowd. Evelyn comes behind me and puts her hands on my shoulders. She smells minty, like she always does. It's an occupational hazard.

"Leave Fiona be," Evelyn scolds the table. "She has school tomorrow. She needs to go home and to bed."

A roar of protest.

"Just one song, love, before you go. It's Niall's birthday! Comes but once a year!"

"She'll wreck her voice singing in all this din, trying to be heard over your craic." Evelyn smiles her disturbingly white smile, but she's dead serious. (The smile's another occupational hazard; her boss gives her free bleachings so he won't have to pay her fair wages.) Always bossing me around, that Evie, ever since our mum moved to Tampa with George. His Mediterranean blood craved the heat, he'd said. Poor, fair, freckled Mum. She must keep the sunscreen companies in business down there. "Leave her be, I say."

"Sing one for Niall. Do, Fiona!"

I look at the man, my father dear, who seems completely indifferent about whether I sing, go home, or do a striptease on the bar.

Evelyn gives it her last, best shot. "Don't be selfish, now. She's to sing for a famous teacher tomorrow. She shouldn't even be here, out so late. She's supposed to be home resting her voice."

Supposed to be? *Supposed* to be? Well, sorry, Evie, but that's all I need to hear. I get up and head for the makeshift stage, and the cheers start all over again.

I take the microphone in my hand. And Niall grins so everyone can see his paternal pride, and he laughs too loud and drapes his arm around a girl not much older than Evelyn, Terry, I think her name is, and she looks at him adoringly and they kiss with beery lips while I sing. Can't refuse a fellow on his birthday, right? Poor Terry. Her song of love is just beginning, and it'll be over before the second verse.

. . . . .

I sing until the wee hours, you might say, meaning I sing until I have to wee. Only my bladder gets me offstage. I'm underage, of course, but no one tosses Niall Kilcommons's daughter out of the private party room at Kelly Ryan's pub on the man's own birthday. Or looks askance when she pours herself a drink from the beer pitcher, either.

I sing everything everyone asks for, and more. "Danny Boy," oh boy, did they hear "Danny Boy." Four or five times, at least. Me and songs is like my uncle Frank and a pint. Should've stopped at two, but I didn't.

Niall keeps up the jolly act for the first song, and the second. On the third his face locks up into a mask. The smile is frozen in place, but his mind has gone elsewhere. And why isn't it him with the microphone, anyway? Him in the spotlight, instead of me? That's his natural position in life. Just ask him, he'll tell you.

· · · · ·

By the time Evie drags me home, my hair stinks of pub and my voice is a rasp. I sleep in my makeup, too lazy to wash up. In the morning, I scrub my raccoon face in the shower and emerge in a girlish cloud of Herbal Essences. I didn't dare try to make a sound, even in the soothing steam of the shower. I knew I'd done myself in.

I get to school a bit late, just in time to hear the bells of doom tolling. My best friend, Lily, looks at me with big wild eyes as I slip into my seat. She's the type who'd show up to vocal technique class twenty minutes early on the day the great Sabrina Krause was coming. She's the type who'd have risen at 6 a.m. to warm up at home, in case she got picked by the great, famous Sabrina Krause to do a demonstration. She's the type to be punctual, prepared, and in good voice, on the day the great, famous, world-renowned soprano Sabrina Krause was coming to our snooty, private, hard-to-get-into performing arts high school to give the voice majors a master class, which is all we'd heard about, over and over and over again, for three Sabrina Krause–obsessed weeks.

Me, I am not the same type that Lily is. Obviously. And I don't just mean that her family pays and I'm on scholarship, although knowing this fact makes the epic scale of my stupidity all the more clear.

"Dammit, Fee!" Her whisper's so sharp, it's like a poke in the ribs. "How could you forget?"

I give her my best "hey, I'm a jerk" shrug. Still daren't speak. Anyway, Mr. Scharf, head of the vocal studies department, is about to introduce the woman of the hour. Doubtless his knees are trembling in his trousers (well, something in his trousers is trembling, I bet) to stand so close to the twinkling aura of greatness.

"... made her debut at La Scala ... starred at the Metropolitan Opera ... recordings ... concerts ... Grammy Awards ..." Blah blah blah, she's famous and we're not, we get it. And then: "It is an astounding privilege for us here at the Professional Academy for the Performing Arts to welcome the one and only, the *legendary* Sabrina Krause."

"Legendary? I thought she was mythical," I wisecrack to Lily, or try to, but my voice is a small dry pea stuck to the back of my throat. I'm left making jokes in my own head. The *manticore*, Sabrina Krause. The *griffin*, Sabrina Krause! Mythical creatures, see? I think it's hilarious. Poor Lily doesn't know what she's missing.

Everybody claps, and the unicorn Sabrina Krause herself takes the stage. Tall, straight as a ladder-back chair, with about as much meat on her bones. Carries a cane but doesn't seem to lean on it much. Probably uses it for delivering beatings, I say to myself, wittily. It's truly a shame Lily can't hear what's in my brain. She'd be in stitches.

The minotaur Sabrina Krause nods in slow motion and sits her skinny arse on the piano bench. No words of intro from her, she's all business. We stand up, and she runs us through vocal warm-ups. We *bzzz*, we *brrr*, we *nyah nyah nyah*.

Well, everyone else *bzzz*s and *brrr*s. I just make the faces. My throat's too raw to produce any sound. I feel like one of those fire-eaters at the circus—an incompetent one, the kind who sets her own throat on fire and has be doused with a hose in front of all the terrified children. Sorry about that, kids!

Scharf takes the mic again. "As you know, Miss Krause has opted to teach demonstration lessons, rather than give a lecture. In the interests of being fair, I am simply going to pull names out of a hat." He smiles as he holds up a big straw boater left over from last year's production of *The Music Man*. "Don't worry, you're all in here," he says, and reaches in.

I stare at the hat with all my might, trying to make it ignite with the pure force of my eyeballs. A name is drawn, a paper unfurls.

"Fiona Kilcommons, to the stage, please."

All those "Danny Boys," yet the luck of the Irish was nowhere near. I'm halfway to the stage before I think of appendicitis. Appendicitis! Brilliant. First I'll double over, then groan, then collapse, then vomit, then they'll call an ambulance. . . .

Too late. I'm already on the stage, grinning like a dolt and trying not to catch Lily's horrified eye. Krause plays a simple arpeggio, one measly octave, right in the sirloin of my range. "On the syllable *nay*, please," she says. "*Nay-nay-nay-nay-nay-nay-nay.* Ready?"

I nod. She begins to play. I open my mouth. Out comes a hoarse croak, full of phlegm. Then a few tight, pitchy *nays* and a top note that's mostly air, until it cracks completely.

Her hands fly up as if the piano keys have suddenly turned into snakes. "Horrible, horrible! What have you done to your voice? Are you sick?"

"Not—ahem—not exactly." I sound like a man. Crap.

She tips her head and peers at me over her glasses. Cute frames, I think. Expensive-looking. Little sparkly bits in the corners.

"You were yelling at a rock concert, hmm?" She sneers. "Or a football game?"

"No, ma'am. I sang at a party last night. It was my father's birthday," I add, like that'll help.

She waves a hand, signaling that I'm no longer worthy of her disdain. "Sit down. You cannot sing today." She swivels sideways on the piano bench and looks at Mr. Scharf. "May I have another student, please? This time, one that isn't broken?"

Scharf's face turns red at that little zinger. The man's having a hot flash of shame thanks to me. "Of course, Miss Krause." Hastily he pulls another name from the hat. "Anthony Rutigliano," he calls out.

Our resident Italian tenor jumps to his feet, both hands in the air. Did he really just double fist pump getting picked to sing? The lameness has no limit.

As he bounds up the stairs to the stage, the succubus Krause gives me a hard look. Then she bows her head to the keyboard and plays a rapid two-octave scale that drips with sarcasm. My exit music, I guess.

· · · · ·

For the rest of the day, no one dares look me in the eye, since we all know humiliation is contagious. Now it's half past two. I'm almost out the door of the school. Almost. So close to being out—

"Fiona!" Mr. Scharf bellows. He's right there by the exit. No escape.

I slink over, and he hands me a folded note. Thick ivory paper, big "Krause" at the top in flowing script.

I read. "'Send the broken singer to my studio. Saturday morning, nine o'clock.'" The address is written below. Central Park West. Fancy.

"You're going," he says.

"Nine o'clock on Saturday is kind of early." No way am I facing the dragon in her lair. She hates me. She probably wants to kill me with that cane, and use the polished shards of my bones to add more sparkles to her eyeglass frames.

"Consider it a mandatory make-up class for the one you blew off today by being unprepared." Then, with a different kind of heat in his voice, "What an opportunity, Fiona! Sabrina Krause *asked* for you. You have to go. If you don't . . ." He doesn't need to say it. We both know he'll flunk me in a heartbeat, scholarship or no scholarship. The threat hangs in the air like a rancid fart.

I mumble yes, I'll go, and shove the note with the address in the pocket of my jeans. The "broken singer"? That's just mean. Mean mean mean.

And then, *crap*, I think. *If Niall finds out about this* . . . Auditioning for the private performing arts school had been my idea. Niall was firmly opposed. He didn't think I'd fit in, he said. Didn't want me mixing with the privileged. It'd just piss me off, or fill my head with longing for things I'd likely never have. "An artist's life is not about luxury," he'd said to me, weirdly earnest. "We've already lost Evelyn to the money-making world. But music is your calling, Fee! Real music, from the heart, for good working people who crave a bit of beauty in their lives."

That Evelyn becoming a dental hygienist was somehow selling out to the temptations of luxury was news to me. Then again, Niall's idea of luxury was paying the rent on time. And from my point of view, him begging me not to do it was reason enough to try. When I shocked us both by getting the scholarship, something went cold between us, and it hasn't warmed up since.

Would he act triumphant if I flunked out? I'd never forgive him if he did. And he'd never forgive me if I succeeded. Clearly, Niall and I were not going to get along again, ever.

But there was good news in all this, too: with my ample bust, I'd never be able to pull off one of those boxy, blue polyester jackets with the pockets full of dental floss. Losing a second daughter to the ritzy, champagne-swilling world of "rinse and spit" is one thing Niall will never have to worry about.

He'll just lose me to something else.

. . . . .

Saturday it rains like a punishment. As it turns out, on a day of good Irish weather like this, Central Park West is as gloomy and gray as even the low-rent parts of New York, with the added charm of wet horse poop piled in the streets from the carriage horses across the way. The thought occurs: *Perhaps I might step in some of that fine, fresh manure and track it into the Legendary Mythological apartment, and make like, oops.* But I'm rather fond of the boots I've got on, so nevermind.

The elevator is a cage with a man in it, and when he heaves open the black gate at Sabrina Krause's floor, we're already in the living room. The woman herself stands there, leaning on her cane, waiting. I have the urge to duck.

"Thank you, Dominic," she says, not looking at me.

"My pleasure, Miss K." He tips his hat. "No need to ring the bell. I'll be back in an hour."

She shakes her head. "Thirty minutes today. Perhaps an hour next week. We shall see."

Next week! Kill me now. Mr. Scharf said nothing about next week.

Dominic gives me a pitying look, and pulls the door shut with a mighty *creak*. The cage goes shivering back down the way it came. I'm trapped.

"Good morning," I say, just to break the ice.

"Umbrella in the bucket, please. And take off your boots." She arranges herself on the piano bench and hangs the cane on the edge of the piano. I do as she says. My big toe with the chipped black polish pokes proudly out the hole in the front of my sock. Classy.

"So. You came."

I smile sweetly.

"How is the voice? Still broken? Any more birthday parties?"

"I'm feeling much better, thanks."

She tilts her head to one side. "So I hear. Let us begin." She runs her fingers over the piano keyboard like she's stroking a long black and white cat, from head to tip of tail. I ready myself to sing, feet planted, back straight, chin down, belly loose. I'm here, after all. Might as well knock her socks off.

She pauses, takes her hands off the keys, and folds them in her lap.

"So, broken voice girl. Why do you sing?"

"Why?"

She nods.

"Well, people say I've a good voice."

Her face doesn't change, but somehow she looks like she might vomit.

"I like to sing. It's fun," I venture.

Her eyes bore twin holes in my forehead, and my brains spill out. "I love music," I say, desperate. "I just love music, that's all. Even when I was a baby, I sang all day, that's what my mum says. Made up songs about the potty and so on."

At that Sabrina Krause laughs once, short and sharp. Even her laugh is resonant, like a trumpet blast. "I would like to hear these potty songs someday. So. You sing because you love music. I believe you. But why *should* you sing? Why should I? Why should anyone? Will it cure the sick? Will it feed the hungry? Will it end all wars?"

"No."

She sizes me up. "Will it make you more beautiful than you are?"

I snort. "No!"

"You are wrong. Of course it will. All great singers are mesmerizing. The world falls at their feet. Singing makes us beautiful. What else does it do?"

"It makes me happy." I remember Niall's friends at the pub, and their cheers. "It makes other people happy too."

"And these 'other people' you speak of—will it make them love you?"

I'm about to say no, because the question's so stupid. But what comes out is something else. "Maybe." I think of Niall and that look of fake pride on his face. It used to be real, once. "Yes. It might."

"Now you are telling the truth. Good." She plays a few chords, melancholy ones. "You cannot take a real breath, a singer's breath"—she demonstrates, and her skinny body balloons like a blowfish on the dock—"and lie. A true singer's breath will only reveal the truth."

Um, what?

"If you lie, you cannot sing. The note will die in the throat." She makes a choking sound. Her hands float back to the keys. "Ready?"

I don't know if we're talking or singing or what anymore. I'm lost. "What do you want me to do?" I ask.

"Breathe," she says. "And tell the truth."

. . . . .

We sing. Only scales, some sustained notes. Soft and loud, on different vowels. She's taking me for a test drive, kicking the tires. It's irritating, like being under a microscope. After a while, she asks, "How good a singer do you wish to be?"

"Better than I am now," I say.

"You have a voice." She says it more to herself than to me. "You could be a singer, if you work."

"I'd like to be as famous as you are," I blurt. The legendary, mythological Fiona Kilcommons, why not? I can aim for the moon as well as the next person.

"Famous!" She spits out the word. "Why?"

"It must make you feel special, doesn't it?"

A cloud suddenly covers the sun, except we're inside. "That is what you want singing to give you? This specialness?" She taps herself on the chest, and it makes a hollow sound. "This loneliness?"

"Yes." Can't be any lonelier than a mum in Tampa and a father who's given up on me. And at least I'd be famous.

One penciled eyebrow lifts high on the face of Sabrina Krause. Her lips press closed into a thin red line.

"Come back next week, then."

. . . . .

The next week, we start with warm-ups. Lip trills, up and down the scale. Placement exercises, to get the voice buzzing. Position of the tongue. Breath support. It's all the usual stuff, but Krause has her own way of listening to me, and correcting me. Like she can tell what I'm doing wrong before I do it. Soon I feel sound coming from spaces inside my head and body I didn't even know were there. I'm vibrating like a tuning fork, and it's making me light-headed. I wish I could sit down for a bit. But Krause is all business, intense, like we're going to run out of time. Which is dumb, because she doesn't have a student after me. I know this because last week I waited in the lobby for a full hour to see who else might show up. There was no one.

"Now, a song," she says. "What do you have? Show me."

I put my binder of music on the piano. She flips pages, flips, flips. Nothing pleases her.

"Sing this," she says at last. She taps a long yellow fingernail against the page, once, twice. *"'O mio babbino caro.'"*

Scharf is always trying to get me to sing this one too. He makes all the girls learn it. "It's a bit high for me," I protest.

"It is not high at all. An A-flat." She plays a run of notes. "You just vocalized to a C-sharp, and could have gone higher. A-flat is the cream of your voice, not even the top."

"Still, it's not—"

"Tessitura." She cuts me off. "You know what that is?"

"It's, like, your range. Where you're most comfortable singing."

"You do not decide what your voice is. Your voice decides, and you obey. You cannot wish yourself other than what you are, Fiona. Remember that." Her hands hover over the keys. "Now. *'O mio babbino caro.'* Tell me what the words mean."

I try to think. "Oh," I begin. Got the first word all right. "Oh, my beloved father." I stop.

"Go on."

I can't for some reason. "Sorry," I say. "I just think it's too high."

She looks at me. A staring contest ensues, like two alley cats across an open can of tuna fish. It goes on for at least a year.

I lose. My eyes drop to the carpet.

"*You* do not decide where your tessitura is," she says, very stern. "Your voice decides. Whoever *gave* your voice decided, long ago. You can only sing in the voice you have."

"Sorry," I mumble. My face is hot. I don't know why I feel so—I don't know. Ashamed, I guess. That I can't even sing a stupid aria in front of this skinny old woman. What's the point?

"I will sing it for you, then," she says.

And she does.

> *"O mio babbino caro,*
> *mi piace, è bello bello . . ."*

I'm pretty much a puddle by the end. Her body is frail, but her voice comes out of someplace else. Like she opens her mouth and a river of music, of beauty, gushes of its own free will. Like she's not the one singing at all.

The notes soar and float, and the sound expands until the room can hardly contain it. I've never stood so close to singing like this. Who has? I can feel it in my body, too. It's almost too much to bear. *Dear God*, I wonder. *What would it feel like, to be able to make a noise like that?*

When she's done, the room lets the music go, reluctantly, I imagine. Now it's just the sound of her breathing, me breathing, the ticking of the clock.

"That was"—I almost said awesome—"that was beautiful," I manage.

"Oh, my beloved father," she says, her voice dreamy. "Lauretta begs her father to allow her to marry the man she loves. She wants him to give her his blessing. If he doesn't . . ."

"She'll throw herself off the Ponte Vecchio." That part I remember. Bit of a drama queen, this girl Lauretta, but I've acted the fool over a boy a time or two myself, as poor Lily could tell you.

"Yes. She would rather die than be without love. Now you try."

Me? Is she kidding? "But—but Miss Krause, I could never sing it as well as you."

She shakes her head. "Forget me, forget everyone. You must sing it as *you*. In *your* voice. Now ask your father for his blessing. Ask him as if your life depends on it."

I picture myself standing on that old bridge in Florence, tottering on the edge, ready to hurl myself into the rushing waters of the Arno. For some reason it works. The music swells and I make a sound like I've never made before. Big, open, sailing out of me like someone's pulling it out by a string. The feeling lasts, all the way to the end.

> "Babbo, pietà, pietà!
> Babbo, pietà, pietà!"

My voice is much bigger than I am, I realize.

"Not bad," she says, and jots something in her calendar. "Not bad. Come back next week."

. . . . .

Niall hears me singing in the shower this morning, I know he does, because he pounds on the door while I'm in the middle of the aria. I sound like an angel in there, to be honest.

"Fee!" he roars. "Will ya get out? It's the only bathroom we have, you know!"

I realize he's probably got to do something that can't wait. We've all been there, when it comes to needing the bathroom.

But would it have killed him to say something about the song?

. . . . .

It's my third trip to Central Park West in as many weeks, and I feel like a regular, but Miss Krause is not up to speed. She looks like crap, frankly. A skeleton in a Chanel suit. (Sure, I know what a Chanel suit is, doesn't everyone? Watch an Audrey Hepburn film, for Pete's sake.)

It's not much of a lesson today. She's tired or something. We stop after a bit, and she closes the piano and hobbles to her armchair. I figure we're done, and pick up my coat. I'm disappointed, really. I've been singing that aria all week. Mr. Scharf even gave me a thumbs-up at school when he heard me in the practice room.

"Don't go yet," she says, leaning back in the chair. "Sing me a song you knew as a child. Not something you learned for school."

"Not the potty songs?" I ask, alarmed.

She smiles. "No, not the potty songs. Sing . . . sing what you sang for your father. On his birthday."

Really? At school they never want to hear my pub repertoire. That's all a bit low rent for Scharf's taste.

"All right," I say. "But I've no music."

"A cappella," she says, and closes her eyes.

Not knowing what else to do, I sing. I do it quietly, though, in case she falls asleep.

> *"Oh, Danny boy,*
> *The pipes, the pipes are calling . . ."*

It's a lovely tune, really. One forgets that. I think I did all right with it. Ended soft as a whisper.

Well, the old girl doesn't say a word. I wait.

"Miss Krause, are you all right?"

Her eyes float open. "Why do you ask?"

I look at her face. Her skin seems papery to me. Thin, like a light could shine right through it.

"You look pale, is all. A bit yellow. You might take some vitamins, you know. My sister, Evelyn, swears by them."

She looks at me. "Is your sister a doctor?"

"A dental hygienist," I say.

At that, the world famous Sabrina Krause does something I'd never thought I'd live to see. She grins, and she opens that resonant cavern of a mouth, and she laughs, deep from the belly. And believe me, there is no laugh like the laugh of the greatest diva of the modern age. It is an opera, that laugh. A symphony of symphonies. The music of the spheres is in it.

"Danny boy," she murmurs, after a bit. "That was lovely, Fiona." One thin hand flutters upward, fragile and bent as an origami crane, and presses against her chest. "It came from your heart. I could tell." She gives me a sly look. "I could never have sung it so well as you."

That gets me too emotional to even say thank you, so I just stand there fumbling with my coat buttons. "Shall I come again Saturday?" I say at the door. She usually mentions it herself and jots it in her datebook, right there at the piano, but today her book is nowhere to be seen.

"Of course, Fiona." Her eyes close once more. "Come Saturday. I would like that."

· · · · ·

Monday it's in all the papers.

They'd found her Sunday morning, in bed, music playing on the radio, dead as stone. I figure it must have been that elevator guy Dominic who found her. He was probably delivering the newspaper or her morning caviar or something.

Amazing, how much there is to say about a person when she's dead. The obituary goes on for pages. I read every word.

Her real name was Stanislava Kuskowski. Born a Polish Catholic, her parents were killed in the war for trying to hide their local priest from the Nazis (the obituary explains how the Nazis rounded up most of the Catholic priests in Poland and sent them to the concentration camps, which was a bit of history I didn't know). Somehow she made her way alone to England as a teenager, when she was about my age I guess. She got a job as a dresser at the Royal Opera House in London. She changed her name and told people she was a runaway Slavic princess, or the dis-owned daughter of unimaginably wealthy parents, or whatever tale suited her on the day. She married one powerful man after another, each one lifting her to the next rung of her career. She didn't become a legend; she made herself one. And she never, ever talked about that orphan girl from Poland, the dead parents, the terrible things she must have done just to sur-vive. Hardly a soul on earth knew about her real past, just as no one knew about the cancer that had eaten her up for the last year.

"After a lifetime of accolades for her work on the operatic stage," the newspaper says, "in the end, her greatest role was the one she played in life: the role of Sabrina Krause, illustrious diva."

. . . . .

I go through them page by page, but there's nothing in any of the newspapers about the services. I'm not a huge fan of churches, mind you, but I was raised never to miss a good funeral. It's an Irish thing. I figure Dominic will know. That man knows everything, you can just tell. I take the bus uptown after school and lurk around the lobby of Miss Krause's building until I find him.

The funeral mass is Saturday morning, he tells me, at St. Aloysius in midtown. He won't be there, though; he has to work. And anyway, he'd already said his good-byes.

So Saturday morning I'm putting on a black dress, and not the kind you'd wear to a club. Niall and I pass each other in the hall. He notices.

"Where you goin', love?"

"Funeral," I mumble.

"Ah." He wipes the shaving cream out of the crease of his mouth with a finger. Shaving on a Saturday? Man must have a date. "Ah. Whose?"

"My singing teacher," I say, and I'm done. Crying like a kid, tears, snot, everything.

He stands there for a bit, taking it all in. Then he tries to hug, but I pull away. It's just awkward.

"Right," he says, looking at me. "Well. I'm coming with you, then."

"No, you don't have to." But I can't stop crying.

Ten minutes later he's in his black suit, rolling the lint brush on his lapels with one hand, on the phone with Terry with the other. Canceling his date, I guess.

Well, he put on his suit, and I'm in no shape to go by myself, so what can I say? At least he can pay for the cab.

. . . . .

Somehow the secret must have leaked, because there's a crowd in front of the church. No one is being let in, though.

"Maybe it's already full inside," I say, ready to give up. Niall ignores me and weaves his way through, determined, until he gets to the velvet ropes.

"We've come to pay our respects," he says to the young man in the suit who's barricading the doors.

"You and everyone else. We were told immediate family only. As per the wishes of the deceased." The young man folds his arms. Niall grins.

"What part of Dublin are you from, lad?" The fellow startles, but Niall's got him; he can tell a Dublin accent down to the block you grew up on. A little banter is exchanged, about possible mutual acquaintances in Ireland and here, too—sure, Niall knows his brother-in-law's cousin in Woodlawn! She had the face of her Cavalier King Charles Spaniel tattooed on her own calf because she loved the dog so. More faithful than any man she'd ever known, she said! Soon they're laughing and clapping each other on the back like brothers.

"And tell Father O'Rourke that Niall Kilcommons sends his regards, will you, John?" Niall says to his new best friend, as the fellow slips us past the ropes.

"Niall Kilcommons! Why didn't you say so?"

. . . . .

Without pausing for thanks, Niall leads me into the dark chill of the church. I don't want to barge in on her family's private grief. I just want to have a peek from the back. And she did tell me to come on Saturday, didn't she? I'm pretty sure she must have known what that meant, even if I didn't at the time.

But the place is empty, save for the priest puttering in his priestly way up front, and a gleaming dark coffin laid out before the altar.

We slip into a pew in the rear of the nave. "Why isn't anyone here?" I whisper.

Niall frowns. "I don't know. Maybe she has no family living."

"Then why say family only?"

Niall shakes his head. "People are mysterious, love. You can't solve 'em like a riddle. You just take 'em and love 'em as they are, warts and all."

I want to ask him what this means, but the priest is talking now. He mumbles his canned bits of funeral mass to an empty house. He talks too fast, like he has to get to his next gig. The organ brays out a few hymns, and that's it as far as music is concerned.

"Well, this is a poor excuse for a funeral," Niall says, a bit too loud. He stands up and gives the edge of his jacket a tug downward. Tugs once, sharp, at the end of each sleeve. I know this move.

"God, Niall. What are you doing?"

"Paying my respects, love, that's all."

"But you didn't know her."

He takes my chin in one hand and tips my face up, toward the light. "What I see in your eyes right now says something good about her. That's all I need to know."

A moment later the man is kneeling by the casket, lips moving. I find myself wondering what prayers Niall remembers, though I suppose you never forget those kinds of words, even if you haven't been to church in a dog's age.

All at once there's music.

> *"Oh, Danny boy,*
> *The pipes, the pipes are calling . . ."*

It's the sweetest Irish tenor you'll hear this side of County Sligo. That's right. Niall Kilcommons is serenading the corpse of Stanislava Kuskowski.

It's a lovely voice, he has. Years of use and abuse have spared it, somehow. Niall's voice is like that man in the famous story, where the fellow stays young forever while the portrait in his attic ages like all hell. The story's by Oscar Wilde, which I only remember because he was Irish.

I expect that somewhere in our apartment, crammed in the back of some closet, there's a painting of my da's voice that'd freeze your blood. He sounds like a boy when he sings, wild gray hairs and all.

Miss Krause would have liked his voice, I think.

I sob a little, to hear him singing. Who wouldn't? Niall looks back over his shoulder at me. Those eyebrows lift an invitation, and a hand slips out of that long black sleeve. A pale, long-fingered hand, graceful as a bird. Just open to me, waiting.

Well, what am I to do but join in?

. . . . .

Me and my da, we give her a proper send-off. Maybe we should've stopped at two, but we don't. When I sing "*O mio babbino caro*," he sheds a few tears himself. I nail the A-flat, too. Miss Krause would've given me a fist pump, if she'd heard it.

"Is that what they're teaching you at school?" Niall says, a bit awestruck.

I shrug. "Miss Krause liked 'Danny Boy' the best. It's . . ." I was going to say, it was the last thing I sang for her, but I can't get the words out, I'm too choked up. Doesn't matter. I let Niall hug me this time. After I dry up a bit, we go back to singing.

The organist is gone by now. He didn't seem to mind us taking things over. Probably he went outside for a smoke.

"There's nothing like making music in a church," Da whispers to me at one point. "Your voice echoes all the way up to heaven."

"Sure beats singing in the shower," I agree, and slip my hand inside his. I'd forgotten how good we sound together.

....

ANECDOTE: SIERRA BOGGESS

....

I knew I liked performing from an early age. But there was one person in particular who helped me plant the seeds to become an artist. That woman was my high school drama teacher: Nancy Priest. As I recall my time with her, I want you to keep in mind some things: this was not a performing arts high school. This was not a private high school. This was not even a rich school. This all happened at an inner-city public high school in Denver, Colorado.

High school consists of some of the toughest years of growth a person can face. You are going through so many changes, discovering who you are, who your friends are, you are trying to figure out which college to go to, and what classes you have to take. Through all of this, it is so helpful to have someone guide you, and I swear if it weren't for my four years of drama class with Mrs. Priest, I wouldn't have even made it through! Her classes, her teaching, her being, gave me a reason for wanting to stay in school and solidified my passion for the theater.

Nancy Priest taught for thirty years at George Washington High School, and her drama class was no "easy A." It wasn't the kind of drama class where you just hung out with friends and did weird acting exercises. In fact, more was expected of me in drama then I was used to. We did Shakespeare; we did Neil Simon; we studied the origin of musicals. We did scene work nearly every week and worked on memorization and creativity. We learned how to give feedback to one another and formulate helpful opinions about our work.

I remember the day that she asked each of us to raise our hand and "tell the class something you like about yourself." As an insecure teenager, I immediately started going through my mental list of things that I hated about myself: my body, my skin, my legs, my clothes . . . the list seemed to be endless. But the point of the lesson was to learn not just to criticize yourself or other people, but to see the good in each of us. This set the tone for how we were to critique each other when we did scene assignments. Someone gets up to perform, we applaud. Priest asks us for critiques, and we were to *always* start with the positive! You can always find the good in what you see. I try to live that way every day and am so grateful for that lesson.

There was also more to learn than just being good at scene work. There was the design element. I remember we watched *South Pacific* so that we could create our own costume renderings for the show. Well, I figured since I *knew* I don't want to be a designer, I would be funny and draw basic clothes on stick models and draw pineapples for their heads. I thought I was hilarious. Mrs. Priest was not impressed. She reprimanded me for not taking it seriously and failed my drawings. You better believe I did them over and handed them in again! I *wanted* to succeed in her class. I *wanted* to impress her. I *wanted* to learn how to appreciate all the aspects of this industry that I loved so much. She knew how much I wanted to do this for a living, and she pushed me to care about every side of it! It was important that I paid attention to each part.

She also taught us how to make set models. We designed our sets for *Noises Off* and *Rent*. We listened to the cassette tapes of *Rent* so we would know the show in order to make amazing models. I was *terrible* at this, but I had to do it anyway. I mostly just liked going to Hobby Lobby and picking out cute things to glue on my set. But we actually had to measure things and use our math skills. Well, suddenly in order to get an A in drama, I needed to listen up in math more. To get an A in drama I needed to attend my other classes. What a concept!

Outside of class were the school shows. We put on four shows a year, which in itself was an incredible feat for a poor inner-city high school in Denver and because there wasn't much money, we all helped out. Mrs. Priest taught us how to paint sets, sew costumes, and build scenery. No matter how long you had been a part of her class, everyone auditioned for every show. I always wanted to be the star of each show and she saw my potential early on, but she *never* let me rest on my talent alone. She never made it easy for me; I had my fair share of disappointments.

My senior year I wanted to be the lead in *Moon Over Buffalo* so badly. I did my *best* audition, and I was sure I got it. But when I got to school the next day, I ran to look at the cast list to see I was not in the show at all. She made me the stage manager. Stage manager?! Mrs. Priest knew I didn't want to be behind the scenes, I wanted to be onstage!

But she had a point: she knew I needed to learn all aspects of the the-ater, not just about being onstage. In my four years of drama class, I starred in shows, I stage managed others; I did makeup, costumes, and sound; I choreographed, and I assistant directed. There were times I was even an usher, but I was always involved. Priest taught us the importance of being supportive no matter what part you have.

She also taught us the importance of coming together as a team. Before every show, we did something called "circle." Everyone in the cast, orchestra, and crew stood in a circle in the lunchroom (our backstage, of course), and if anyone had any thanks they wanted to give, we said it one at a time. Then Priest would say the final words of thanks and inspiration. We would then join hands and jump up and down chanting: "aaaaahhhhh ONE, TWO, YOU KNOW WHAT TO DO! UNITED WE STAND! DIVIDED WE FALL! LET'S MAKE THIS SHOW THE BEST OF ALL! GIVE 'EM HELL!"

My senior year, Priest announced that she was retiring. Oh, the tears. Even though I was graduating, it still felt like such a loss for the school. This woman would be a tough act to follow. We got the auditorium to be named after her in her honor. It was the least we could do for someone who ignited such passion in each of us. It didn't matter that we had been a school without a lot of money. It didn't matter that most of us didn't come from privileged backgrounds. It just mattered that we were there for each other. And I realized, *that* is why I want to be in this business. I want to be part of a community like the one Mrs. Priest created. A community of artists who always can find the positive in one another, who care about the importance of jobs onstage and offstage and most of all who live by the code "united we stand, divided we fall."

So what made me want to do this for a career? I had the world's greatest drama teacher. Her name is Nancy Priest.

SIERRA BOGGESS has starred on Broadway as the title character in Disney's *The Little Mermaid* (for which she received Drama League and Drama Desk nominations), opposite Tyne Daly in *Master Class*, and as Christine Daaé in *The Phantom of the Opera*. She received an Olivier Award nomination for her work in *Love Never Dies*, starred as Fantine in *Les Misérables,* and returned to the London stage for the 25th Anniversary Gala of *The Phantom of the Opera*. Concerts include BBC Proms (Royal Albert Hall), American Songbook Series: The Lyrics of David Zippel and New York Pops (Lincoln Center), and Broadway by the Year (Town Hall). Her TV appearances include *Today*, *Good Morning America*, *The View*, *Entertainment Tonight*, the Macy's Thanksgiving Day Parade, and the 62nd Annual Tony Awards. Sierra has been heard on the recording of *The Phantom of the Opera* 25th Anniversary Gala (also DVD), *Love Never Dies* (symphonic recording), *The Little Mermaid* (original cast), and Andrew Lippa's *A Little Princess*. She holds a BFA from Millikin University.

HOW DO YOU SOLVE A PROBLEM LIKE MARIA?

Marc Acito

"*What* are you doing?"

Gale stops typing, startled back to reality, a place she avoids whenever possible. She looks around the camp office, the room thick with soupy summer air, the only sound the chirrup of cicadas—*whirring like a thousand tiny helicopters*, she thinks, narrating her life. With a British accent.

She sees no one except a small boy with an unblinking gaze and unexpected hair. In the summer of 1969 even small boys at Camp Algonquin have long hair—not long-long like the counselors, with their hippie dos that make the Squares say they look like girls—but long enough to make them look like sheepdogs.

This kid, however, has sculpted his hair into a sturdy pompadour, a granite cliff perched on his head. With an aristocratic tilt of his chin, and a stick-up-his-butt posture, he reminds Gale of Captain von Trapp—shrunk in the wash. Maybe that's because she has *The Sound of Music* on her brain. Where it frequently does battle with *Funny Girl*.

She hez a chronic condition, she thinks, this time sounding like a German psychiatrist. *Tsis overly imaginative fifteen-year-old camper suffers frum a "Maria Fanny Fixation."*

The boy repeats himself, a tiny wind preceding the *wh* as he says,

"*What* are you doing," his tongue crossing the *t*. His voice is high and musical, the diction precise and almost British—like Julie Andrews.

"I'm typing up a script," Gale says. "Larry the camp director is too cheap to get the rights to *The Sound of Music*, so I'm writing it myself. From memory."

Her voice sounds defensive, and she's instantly embarrassed, reports the Newscaster in Her Brain. But she does feel embarrassed. Not just that she's explaining herself to a little kid, but actually ashamed that in both junior high *and* summer camp she's had to endure performing such babyish drivel as *The Haunting of Spook House* and *The Mystery of the Missing Sandwich*.

However . . .

This summer is gonna be different. This summer astronauts will walk on the moon. The moon! This summer Gale Rosalyn Rubenstein will direct, star in, and otherwise rouse the conformist complacency of Camp Algonquin with her own wondrous version of *The Sound of Music*. This summer she'll return to Long Island and start high school, where she'll finally audition for a REAL play. And when she does, she'll be able to say, "Experience? Well, I just played Maria this summer. Maria von Trapp . . ."

Back in reality, the boy's blue eyes suddenly shine like sapphires.

"I LOVE *The Sound of Music*," he says. "I've seen it FIFTY Times."

This seems highly unlikely to Gale. After all, she's fifteen and only seen *The Sound of Music* ten times. "How old are you?" she asks.

"I am nine years old," the boy replies, pronouncing each word as if it were Holy Writ. "I am small for my age."

And then he launches:

"The movie of *The Sound of Music* had its world premiere at the Rivoli Theatre in New York City in March of 1965—exactly twenty-two blocks from my house—and it stayed there for ninety-three weeks until November of 1966. My father has visitation every other weekend and I told him I had no interest in the Bronx Zoo, the Central Park Zoo, or anything other than *The Sound of Music*. When I went the fiftieth time, the ushers gave me free candy and popcorn."

There's no denying it—this kid is strange, in a way that makes Gale slightly uncomfortable. Not creepy uncomfortable, more unsettled, like the room is suddenly askew. But she can't help but be impressed with his knowledge and finds herself addressing the child conspiratorially, as if they were the same age.

"I wanted to do *Funny Girl*," she says, "but Larry said it was inappropriate."

The boy gasps asthmatically. "I LOVE *Funny Girl*! You know the scene where Fanny is in the Ziegfeld Follies and she feels embarrassed having to sing about being the beautiful reflection of her love's affection, so she puts a pillow under her costume to be a pregnant bride?"

Of course Gale knows the scene. She knows just about everything there is to know about Barbra Streisand. If Jews could have patron saints, then loudmouth girls with unconventional looks like Gale would worship Barbra. The Holy Nose.

"The pregnant bride is the fourth best scene," Gale says. "After 'Don't Rain on My Parade,' 'I'm the Greatest Star,' and 'People.'"

"I KNOW," the kid says. "Barbra's going to do *Hello, Dolly!* next. I can't WAIT. I saw *Hello, Dolly!* on Broadway. Not with Carol Channing, but I have the original cast album. I saw Ginger Rogers. She danced with Fred Astaire. Not in *Hello, Dolly!*, but in the olden days. I've seen TEN Broadway shows: *1776*, *Fiddler on the Roof*, *Judy Garland at the Palace*. . . ."

This is Gale's sixth summer at Camp Algonquin, an experience she inherited from her parents, who met here in the 1950s when it was practically a Talmudic Law that all Jews migrate every summer to the Catskills. Over the years, Gale's shot arrows, thrown pots, paddled canoes, roasted many a marshmallow, and told many a ghost story. Neither popular nor unpopular, she has one True Friend here, Amanda Horowitz, a tall, mannish girl who rides horses and whose enthusiasm for movie westerns rivals Gale's obsession with musicals.

But . . .

Never before has she met anyone who shares her passion, a slightly guilty pleasure because it is so decidedly uncool. Cool kids listen to the Stones and the Who, while she'd rather hear the original cast albums of *My Fair Lady* and *South Pacific*. But she certainly never imagined she would share that passion with an overly articulate nine-year-old boy. Who immediately takes it upon himself to criticize her work.

"No, no, no," the boy says as he looks over the pages she's already typed. "Friedrich doesn't introduce himself by saying he's incorrigible. He says he's IMPOSSIBLE. The younger brother Kurt is the one who says he's INCORRIGIBLE."

He's interrupted by the arrival of Larry, a big bearded man who looks like a grouchy Santa Claus. One glance at the kid and Larry groans. "What is it now, Sterling?" His voice is edged with irritation. "Other boys giving you trouble again?"

Sterling. Of course the kid has a name like Sterling. Sterling's jaw tightens and flexes, his upright posture turning rigid. In an instant Gale pictures him as the hero of *Oliver Twist*, which she read because she loves the musical:

The ruffians of Boys Bunk Two bullied the poor lad, mocking him with mincing gestures, the cruelest of taunts spewing from their tongues like rotting food they had spit upon the ground. Crueler still, Sterling found no comfort in the camp director, a hulking furnace of a man who thrummered and thorshed, yet did not emit the slightest trace of warmth.

The roles are clear: if Sterling is the hero and Larry is the villain, then Gale is the savior, just like Nancy in *Oliver!*, who wears saucy costumes and has lots of great songs and dies nobly to protect a child.

"He's helping me," Gale says to Larry. "With my script."

By her side, she feels Sterling exhale, turning to her like a flower facing the sun.

. . . . .

Gale scans the assembled cast, a patchwork of other campers who she cajoled, coerced, herded, and even bribed into doing the show. She savors the moment, preserving it for her future biographer:

The aspiring thespian, authoritative beyond her tender years, scanned the roomful of uncertain faces in the aptly named Drama Shack, a three-sided wooden fire hazard with an outdoor stage used primarily for movie nights, sing-alongs, alleged talent shows, and the occasional play. With a tin roof that clacked in the rain and screenless windows that allowed in bugs, birds, and bats, the Drama Shack called to mind a hastily remodeled carport because, indeed, that's what it was.

Sterling hands out the scripts to each cast member, smiling and nodding in a manner that reminds Gale of airline stewardesses. The title page reads, "*The Sound of Music* by Rodgers and Hammerstein, adapted by Gale Rosalyn Rubenstein and Sterling Clark Jr."

Like R & H, theirs is a true collaboration, Sterling having dictated the entire movie while Gale ruthlessly edited that which couldn't be recreated in the Drama Shack, like singing "Do-Re-Mi" through a dozen locations in Salzburg, performing "The Lonely Goatherd" with the Bil Baird Marionettes and having any party guests to address "So Long, Farewell" to. Based on limited space—and even less interest—the cast consists solely of the von Trapp children, the All-Jewish Nuns Chorus, some stray prepubescent Nazis . . . and Aaron Messner.

Aaron peruses the pages with his dark, unfathomable eyes. With his black curls and hawky profile, he resembles what Gale has always imagined King David looked like. As usual, he's barefoot, his cut-off shorts revealing sturdy, tan legs, corded with muscle like the trunks of two young trees. Instead of a shirt, he wears a groovy deerskin vest with fringe and Gale imagines for the thousandth time what it would feel like to have his lean, sinewy arms around her. He glances up, catching Gale staring at him and the movie in her mind goes into freeze frame for an internal musical thought:

Aaron Messner, Aaron Messner, what a beautiful, beautiful name . . .

Aaron Messner, who can identify every plant and tree. Aaron Messner, who can start a campfire faster than anyone. Aaron Messner, who Gale can't resist mocking anytime they speak, calling him "Nature Boy," even though she wants to French kiss him to death.

Despite never having set foot upon a stage, Aaron agreed to play the Captain because his best friend, Conrad, wanted to play Rolf, the Nazi messenger boy. Conrad wanted to play Rolf to be near Barbie Bittman, who's playing Liesl. Gale wanted Barbie to play Liesl so Conrad would convince Aaron to play the Captain.

See "French kiss," above. This month, astronauts will walk on the moon for the first time. Anything is possible.

"All right, settle down," Gale says, trying to sound settled even though she feels like her veins are pumping Fresca. "Let's read through the script."

Joni, the counselor nominally in charge, doesn't look up from her copy of *Rolling Stone* as the cast members fidget and squirm like amoeba under a microscope, buzzing as loud as the cicadas outside. How Joni can read through purple-tinted shades is anyone's guess. Then again, she's a major pothead, so who knows what she's thinking?

Amanda, being a True Friend, rises to her Full Height, asserting herself like a western sheriff ready to rid Prairie Junction of Black Bart and his Gang. "C'mon, people," she barks, "listen up."

The cast obeys, which is one of the reasons Gale cast Amanda as the authoritative Reverend Mother, despite Amanda being a female baritone who'll have to sing "Climb Ev'ry Mountain" an octave lower than it is normally performed. They pick up their scripts, freshly inked in purple from the ditto machine. Several kids raise the limp pages to their noses to inhale the clean, sinus-tickling aroma, the Scent of Possibility.

But not Barbie Bittman, who's sliding a comb through her smooth sheath of hair, making Gale feel vaguely homicidal. Not once in Gale's life has a comb ever slid through her hair. Combs are Instruments of Torture designed to Inflict Pain. Combs snag, tangle, and once even broke off on the left side of Gale's head, requiring an Emergency Hair-ectomy.

Like America, God has graced Barbie's fortunate head with amber waves of grain. Born with the name "Barbara," she renamed herself after a plastic doll whose feet are permanently pointed for high heels. By way of comparison, Barbra Streisand dropped an *a*, making her truly original, which is why Gale dropped the *y* from her name, so she could be a true original just like Barbra.

Gale casts a grateful glance to Amanda, telepathically thought-ballooning a "thank you," then readdresses the cast. "For now, we'll skip the songs, so let's start with Scene Two at the Abbey."

Over Amanda's shoulder, Gale can see her co-author Sterling, his eyes like high beams, completely unaware that his lips are mouthing the words of the teenage nuns. At his insistence, Sterling will play Kurt ("I've ALWAYS wanted to be INCORRIGIBLE"), though he's better suited to play Marta, the von Trapp who wants a pink parasol for her birthday. Which explains why he has no friends in Boys Bunk Two.

The first scene plays just like the movie until they reach the song. When Amanda sees the stage direction reading, "The Nuns sing 'Maria,'" she tosses the script aside and croons:

> "Ma-riiii-a . . .
> I just kissed a nun named Maria . . ."

Not everyone gets the joke—including Aaron—but those who do think it's hilarious, no one more so than Sterling, who laughs so hard he gets a nosebleed.

It only takes a couple of days to learn the music because they're singing in unison out of the Hal Leonard Vocal Selections. Their accompaniment is provided by Joni, who reluctantly parts from reading a collection of beat poetry to strum a guitar. Sterling complains that playing the whole show on guitar "doesn't sound ANYTHING like the movie," but Aaron likes that it's "less Rodgers and Hammerstein and more Simon and Garfunkel." Gale secretly agrees with Sterling, but enjoys any opportunity to watch Aaron's very kissable mouth say anything.

The two-week rehearsal period was a frenzy of activity, Gale practices for her memoirs, *exciting, scary, Fresca-vein inducing.* Whatever she does to prepare the show, there is Sterling next to her to help, eagerly skipping all other camp activities to aid in painting an Alpine landscape on the few existing flats or pick through the optimistically named Costume Shop. Together, they assemble nuns' wimples and Nazi armbands, giddily making up fake lyrics:

> *So long, farewell, our feet are saying good-bye . . .*

> *Climb ev'ry mountain, fall in every stream . . .*

> *I am sixteen, going on seventeen, I know that I'm not Eve . . .*

There's not enough time or fabric to create dirndls and lederhosen out of curtains, so the von Trapp children remain in white Oxfords with blue sailors' neckerchiefs. This lack of authenticity bothers Sterling, who quickly gets on everyone's nerves by continually starting sentences with the phrase, "In the MOVIE . . ." He insists on wearing a nightshirt in the thunderstorm scene, which he accomplishes by auditioning several girls' nightgowns, choosing the most masculine (not very), and drawing stripes on it with a magic marker.

Since he knows every frame of the film, he becomes the unofficial choreographer, putting the campers in the unusual position of taking orders from a nine-year-old. But he speaks with such authority—not to mention multisyllabic words—that he earns their bewildered respect. Indeed, his exuberant demonstration of flit-float-fleetly-fleeing-fly will be remembered for years to come by all who witnessed it.

"Far out," Aaron says, not unkindly.

Despite being the director, Gale often finds herself standing aside and watching Sterling, shaking her head in astonishment. His passion is irrepressible, spurting out of him like a soda can that's been shaken. Secretly, she envies his flamboyance—never before has she met anyone who acts how she feels, who actually says what she thinks. Even here, in the shady sanctuary of the Drama Shack, she represses herself—standing sideways when she's next to Barbie so she looks thinner; trying to control the pinball machine that's her mind so she doesn't keep insulting Aaron.

Gale's mouth: Hey, Nature Boy, you've got more hair on the tops of your feet than a Hobbit.

Gale's mind: Throw me down and kiss me, you mad beast.

But Sterling laughs every time, the Best Audience Ever. ("A HOBBIT! That's HILARIOUS! Amanda could be Gandalf—her voice is deep enough!")

As the pressure builds toward the performance, however, Sterling grows increasingly agitated. "No, no, no!" he cries as Gale starts to sing "Something Good" to Aaron. "You're supposed to kiss BEFORE the song."

Gale tries to communicate telepathically with Sterling, widening her eyes to send a thought balloon reading, "Leave this alone." Yes, she wants Aaron to kiss her. But it should happen naturally, easily, and then . . .

Gale quivered with excitement, her bosom palpitating against his hairy chest as she left the loveless ranks of the unkissed behind her forever, her very essence entwining inexorably with that of her lover. . . .

Sterling sighs ostentatiously, putting the kibosh on the romance novel in Gale's mind. "In the MOVIE," he says, "the Captain takes Maria's face in both hands and kisses her before she sings—on the MOUTH."

This kid is not going to live to see ten, Gale thinks.

Sterling continues. "Then at the end they stand in silhouette with Maria's neck stuck out like one of those swivel desk lamps." Sterling snaps his fingers at Joni. "Music! Let's go back to before the song."

Joni shrugs, taking the command in stride. Being a pothead, nothing bothers her.

"You have to stand close enough to touch," Sterling says, "like Conrad does with Barbie." This elicits laughter from the prepubescent Nazis, which only seems to annoy Sterling. "It's TRUE," he cries. "They're like Siamese twins!"

It's moments like these that remind Gale that Sterling is only nine and doesn't understand that We Don't Talk About These Things.

Aaron takes a couple of steps toward Gale, so at home in his taut, tawny skin. He smells of leather and sweat and romance.

"We don't have to do this now," Gale says, addressing her sandals.

"It's okay," Aaron says. His tender lips—well, she assumes they're tender—curl upward in a shy smile, turning Gale's legs to Jell-O. *It's going to happen. It's really going to happen.* Over Aaron's shoulder, Gale spies the Jewish Nuns Chorus peeking around an Alp to watch.

Aaron's face is so close that Gale can see his pores, which somehow makes him seem even more irresistible.

"I'm not going to marry the Baroness," he says.

"You're not?" Gale replies, her voice scarcely a whisper.

"How can I," he continues, "when I'm in love with someone else?"

It feels So Real. Gale's heart beats everywhere in her body—behind her ears, between her shoulder blades, and in the arches of her feet. Aaron tilts his head toward hers. Gale closes her eyes and . . .

"No, no, no!" Sterling shouts. "Grab her face. Grab. Her. Face."

Aaron reaches up with his whole hand, palming Gale's face like she was a basketball. The spell broken, they both laugh.

"Yeesh," Sterling says. "You two are so immature."

. . . . .

The remaining days fleetly flee and fly. Gale and Aaron never get around to practicing the kiss, making another joke of it during their one and only dress rehearsal. It will happen for the first time onstage—which is somehow less terrifying than the thought of kissing Aaron alone, yet also more terrifying because all of Camp Algonquin will be watching. *Them's lose-lose odds*, says a bookie in her brain.

The night of the show, Gale tries to make herself as pretty and kissable as possible, with the usual dispiriting results. With orange juice can curlers, a horse brush, and Immense Rigor, she can just manage to tame her willful hair into obedience. Makeup helps, but then again, the whole cast is wearing makeup, so the bar for prettiness is raised. Even the boys look lovelier.

There is much hugging backstage. It feels like the show simply can't start until every cast member has squeezed each and every person like they're getting juice out of fruit. With at least two-dozen people buzzing about behind the scenes, Gale calculates that's over five hundred hugs, though math isn't her best subject. Still, it's Affection Concentrate.

Sterling zips around like a firefly, his face beaming bright in the twilight. He looks like how Gale feels, her internal pinball machine *clanging* and *dinging* inside her ribcage. Amanda pretends to smoke and drink shots because everything is funnier in a nun's costume. One of the prepubescent Nazis does a card trick for the von Trapp children. On the other side of the flats on which she personally painted an Alpine vista, Gale can hear the flustery rustle of the gathering audience, the unmistakable sound of Expectation. She steps out the back of the Drama Shack for one last deep breath, perhaps a prayer to the Holy Nose.

And then she sees them. Standing close. His hands cupping her face. French kissing. Barbie. Aaron.

Even worse, they see her.

The pair part, wiping their mouths.

Stupid, stupid, stupid, Gale thinks, not narratively, just smacking herself with her thoughts. How could she ever think that Aaron would want to kiss her that way? They don't even look guilty, so it's obvious Aaron had no idea how Gale felt.

"Break a leg," Gale says, and does a little time-step the way Fanny does when she says good-bye to Nicky Arnstein for the first time in *Funny Girl.* Then she wheels around and heads straight for the Alps.

· · · · ·

Onstage, alone, singing the opening number to Joni's folky accompaniment, Gale feels safe again. She understands better than ever why Maria goes to the hills when her heart is lonely. The stage lights are warm on her face and she can feel the audience listening. It's molecular. She doesn't understand the physics, but she knows that something chemical is happening. Her voice floats into the air and onto the ears of the audience and into their bodies, filling them up until they release it back to her with applause. A scientist could fill a chalkboard breaking down the process.

The show goes on.

No one's sure why the audience finds everything Amanda says funny. Maybe it's because she delivers the Reverend Mother's lines like she's heading to the last round-up. But it's okay. Both actors and audience are having a good time. Gale has confidence in sunshine, rain, and the campers of Camp Algonquin.

Then the von Trapp children march in. They all look appropriately stern, with the notable exception of Sterling, who's practically vibrating with excitement, the corners of his mouth twitching upward like there's a bumblebee trying to get out. It's obvious to Gale in an instant that he's deliriously happy to be there. And repressing his enthusiasm is not his strong suit.

Gale moves down the line, interviewing each child: Liesl, Friedrich, Louisa, and . . .

"I'm Kurt. I'm INCORRIGIBLE!"

To Gale's surprise, the line gets a laugh, perhaps because Sterling screams it like he's yelling "Fire!" in a crowded movie theater.

But there's an audible scoff from a red-headed, freckle-faced kid down front, plainly visible in the stage light. In a microsecond, Sterling's jaw tightens and Gale feels her gut clench.

Gale continues down the line to talk about pink parasols with Marta, but out of the corner of her eye she sees that the boy in the front row hasn't let up and is mouthing the words "I'm incorrigible" for his sniggering bunkmates, batting his eyelashes and flapping his hands limp-wristedly.

Gale moves on to the youngest, Gretl, determines that she's five, then delivers Maria's line about how Gretl is such a big girl.

From the audience, the freckle-faced boy says, "So's Kurt."

Gale's whole body tenses, an animal in the wild sensing a predator. But before she's had a moment to respond, it starts.

Laughter. Excruciating, sweat-inducing laughter. The cast stands there, prisoners lined up for a firing squad, von Trapped. Down front, the freckle-faced demon smiles, pleased with himself as his two companions punch him in the arm approvingly, rolling backward with laughter. A cicada-like buzz moves through the crowd. Those who didn't hear it are asking those that did, and the laughter burbles up again. Sensing that no one is putting out the spreading wildfire, Gale speeds through her lines, trying to end the scene as fast as possible.

By the time the von Trapp children have exited, Jerry has lumbered down to the front of the crowd, asserting his authority by placing his hands on his hips and rocking on his heels like a prison warden.

The show goes on.

Barbie and Conrad perform "Sixteen Going on Seventeen." Conrad turns out to be surprisingly good—he even sings with vibrato. But Barbie can't carry a tune in a bucket. Her grasp of the melody is so tenuous she seems to be inventing her own microchromatic scale, singing notes that lie right between pitches. But what she lacks in musical ability she makes up for by looking winsome while tossing her hair.

Gale searches for Sterling backstage, but the only light in the Drama Shack comes from the rising moon. She doesn't see him until he runs onstage for "My Favorite Things."

The entrance of Kurt and Friedrich is supposed to be a laugh, the cue being, "Boys aren't afraid of thunder and lightning." But the fact that Sterling runs on wearing—to the untutored eye—a nightgown only arouses another round of sniggers and mutters from the audience. The sparkle in Sterling's eyes has gone out, replaced with grim determination.

As Gale sings about dogs biting and bees stinging, she flicks her glance toward the heckler in the front row, desperately trying to thought-balloon to Sterling that Oscar Hammerstein has a solution to his troubles: he just needs to think of his Favorite Things. But Sterling has fallen deep inside himself, his dream come true now a waking nightmare. Gale says a silent prayer of thanks to the Holy Nose that they didn't have fabric to make playclothes out of floral pattern drapery or else they'd lose all control of the show. Still, the prey is wounded and is suffering a painful, lingering death.

Sterling moves through "Do-Re-Mi" joylessly, robotically, his wings clipped. And he doesn't sing his Kurt's show-offy high note in "So Long, Farewell," but gives a clipped "Good-bye" and runs off like he's afraid someone will throw something at him.

During intermission, the cast is united in their condemnation of the heckler. Amanda even rolls up her nun's sleeves, promising to "beat the snot out of that kid." But the talk quickly turns autobiographical: *Did you see how I slipped during that number?/How did I sound?/Couldja tell I sang "Lonely Goat Turd"?*

Gale risks witnessing Aaron licking Barbie's tonsils again by looking for Sterling on the back steps of the Drama Shack. Just above the blackened trees, the rising half-moon shimmers, the stars seeming to multiply by the second.

"Can you believe the astronauts are almost all the way to the moon?" she says. "It's like science fiction."

Sterling doesn't look up. Gale sits down next to him. "That kid is a jerkoff. Don't pay attention to him."

Sterling turns to her, his eyes like mirrors. "EVERYONE paid attention to him. You know they did. I wish I'd never come here. I wish I wasn't born."

Without thinking, Gale thrusts her arm on him, the way her mother does when she makes a sudden stop in the car. Since her mother's a lousy driver, that happens a lot.

"Don't say that," Gale says. "Don't *ever* say that. If you weren't born, how could I do *The Sound of Music* without you?"

"I wish you had."

He rises and leaves, taking a piece of Gale's heart with him.

The show goes on.

Gale's love scene with Aaron feels nothing like she thought it would be. When he takes her face in his hands to kiss her, all she can think about is Barbie Bittman—not just Barbie herself but all the Barbies in the world, girls who have lives waiting for them on their doorsteps, instead of the Barbras, who have to beat the doors down.

The audience goes "*oooooh*" when they kiss, and Gale just wants to scream. They're so immature, they deserve *The Haunting of the Sandwich*. Particularly after how they treated poor Sterling.

She thinks about Sterling as she sings "Something Good" and the lyrics about the wicked, miserable past suddenly come into high relief, as if she were carving them into her brain. He has no idea the good he's done. Not just making the show better, but for Gale herself. For getting the cosmic joke. For getting her. For the first time in her life, she feels like someone understands her, instantly, intuitively. For the past two weeks, she's come down to breakfast and been greeted by a boy who can cross his eyes and imitate Barbra Streisand saying, "Hello, gorgeous." It's sort of like love, but better. It's being seen.

And now half the camp just took a crap on him.

While the Jewish Nuns Chorus makes a stately procession onstage to kill time, Barbie Bittman helps Gale into her wedding dress. Gale wishes she didn't, because it just makes her more self-conscious of how poorly she compares to the aptly named Barbie. Like the universe, Gale's hips and thighs are continually expanding while her boobs don't seem to get the message from below. But when Barbie steps back after she adjusts the veil on Gale's head and whispers, "You look beautiful," Gale knows exactly what to do.

Stuffing a pillow under her dress, she makes Maria von Trapp a pregnant bride.

Just as it does for Barbra Streisand in *Funny Girl*, the audience goes ape with laughter, particularly since the nuns are singing the reprise of "How Do You Solve a Problem Like Maria?" It's a true roar, a palpable quake that shakes the molecules in the air, a sonic boom. It rolls in waves onto the stage as Gale continues to work the bit, walking a few steps, then stopping and clutching her side as if she's had a labor pain. She bends over, hyperventilating and crossing her eyes for maximum comic effect. Another thunder clap of laughter.

Gale's internal pinball machine *dings* and *bings*, flashing feelings ricocheting throughout her body. The laughter feels like approval, even love, but how can she enjoy it when it comes from those cruel mouths?

She crosses to Aaron, who's staring at the ground, trying to remain composed, but all she can see is Sterling quivering behind him. The child almost appears to be in pain as he clutches his sides, tears streaming down his cheeks as he barely suppresses an epileptic fit of laughter. An hour ago, they were dying onstage, now she's killing them, slaughtering them.

Then, like a volcano erupting, a geyser of blood red snot explodes out of Sterling's nose. The audience lets out a horror-movie scream and for a split second it's like the Zapruder footage of President Kennedy getting shot.

That stops the show—literally. Jerry steps up onstage and says, "Okay, that's enough. Show's over."

The audience groans in disappointment.

"C'mon, everybody back to their bunks."

The more obedient rise, but a contingent of appreciative teens in the back start the applause, forcing Jerry to step aside and allow the cast to take a ramshackle curtain call.

By now the camp nurse has rushed to Sterling's side and is holding his head back, yelling for ice. Gale moves toward him, but is stopped by Jerry.

"In my office," he says.

"But—"

"Now."

He takes her by the elbow, as if he were arresting her. *Just like Ziegfeld does in* Funny Girl, Gale thinks. But her sacrifice is worth it. *Just like Nancy in* Oliver!

For the next two days, all anyone can talk about is Gale's stunt—whether she will be sent home or not (she's not)—and the carnage that exploded out of Sterling's face. The boys of Bunk Two, who have a deep appreciation for disgusting bodily functions, spend the rest of the summer trying to make him laugh in hopes he'll spring another leak. He doesn't.

The subject changes. Astronauts walk on the moon, Barbie dumps Aaron for Conrad and rallies a group of counselors to quit early to take off for "an Aquarian exposition of Peace and Music" in a field in Woodstock, New York. The comments of one rude red-headed heckler are forgotten, never mentioned again.

Neither Gale nor Sterling return to Camp Algonquin, but in the years to come they meet in the city to see a show. They LOVE *Pippin, A Chorus Line, Nine, Sunday in the Park with George, Miss Saigon, Rent, Ragtime, Wicked, The Scottsboro Boys. . . .*

But they're still waiting for a revival of *Funny Girl.*

....

ANECDOTE: ALI STROKER

....

Picture this:

The Jersey shore. Summer of 1994. I was a shy seven-year-old girl with bleached blond hair halfway down my back. I was riding at the time in a gold and green splashed wheelchair.

My family had just moved into a house on the corner of Minnevoy and Oceana. The house was on the corner right across the street from the beach. Our next-door neighbors were introduced to us at the beginning of the summer. They had three kids as well. Their oldest daughter, who was twelve, had just come home from theater camp in the Berkshires. She was captivating, and I remember I was immediately drawn to her.

She was an "older girl," and I was always drawn to the more mature girls. Rachel announced to the neighborhood kids that she would be directing a production, which was following last summer's production of *The Little Mermaid*. The show would be presented at the end of the summer on our back deck. Rachel asked me to audition by singing a song. I told her I didn't know any songs at all. She asked if I knew the song, "Twinkle, Twinkle, Little Star." I couldn't lie about knowing "Twinkle, Twinkle" so I nodded my head slightly and took a deep breath. I sang the song, and at the end she smiled. I knew I had made the cut. The next thing I knew, she told me I had landed the lead role of *Annie*.

We rehearsed day in and day out. I remember watching the movie musical *Annie*, over and over again. Learning and mimicking and studying. The show went up at the end of the summer. We had a full backdrop painted by one of the cast member's moms and we sang to the movie soundtrack on a small tape player. The whole neighborhood lined up for tickets, and the local newspaper even showed up. To me it felt like hundreds.

I remember feeling like I was going to explode. I was ready! I knew my lyrics and lines, but I had never felt this nervous in my life.

The show went spectacularly! When I took my final bow, I felt like the world became silent. Like in one of those movies where it goes into slow motion and you watch the audience cheer and applaud. After the show everyone congratulated me on my performance. Rachel gave out special awards to the entire cast that were handmade with markers and paper plates. I felt like I had won a Tony!

This was the summer I remember my life actually beginning. I don't have clear memories of my life before *Annie*. I became whole when I found musical theater because I no longer had to fear being "the girl in the wheelchair" for the rest of my life. I became a new girl. Ali: the singer and actress. I was given the gift of performance. I had fallen in love with theater! Thank you, *Annie*, and Rachel, for changing my life.

ALI STROKER is best known for being a top finalist on the second season of *The Glee Project*. She graduated from New York University's Tisch School of the Arts, but she has actually been a New York City actress and singer for more than three quarters of her life. Paralyzed from the chest down, and a wheelchair user since the age of two, she strives to inspire all those with disabilities who want to pursue a career in performance to fearlessly follow their dreams. Ali's favorite role is Olive in *The 25th Annual Putnum County Spelling Bee*. It was a dream come true when she booked the role at Paper Mill Playhouse in Millburn, New Jersey. Ali is a spokesperson for the Christopher and Dana Reeve Foundation, Be More Heroic, and Colours Wheelchairs. www.alistroker.com.

ECHO

Kiersten White

The reflection staring back at me is wrong.

I'm terrified. I *know* I'm terrified. I can barely breathe, hyperaware of my heartbeat, aware that I should not be so aware of it. It can't be healthy, this racing thing my heart is doing. I can feel sweat breaking out along my hairline, feel my eyelids open too wide, feel the sheer horrified panic paralyzing me and keeping me from walking out of the bathroom in time to make my audition slot.

But my reflection doesn't show me the Loti I know. The me in the mirror looks . . . angry?

"I can't do it," I whisper. "I can't." I want to—wanted to—but faced with the reality of singing in front of other students at my high school, I know I was wrong to believe I could. I felt so brave, so reckless when I signed my name on the spring talent show audition sheet. But writing my name silently and using the voice that no one in this school would even recognize are very different things.

"I can't I can't I can't," I whisper, but my reflection spits the words back at me.

Someone bangs into the door and I startle—no one ever uses this bathroom because the stall door latches don't work. My heel catches on a slick spot under the sink and I overcorrect, slipping forward until my head connects with the mirror in a cracking bright burst of pain.

. . . . .

"Are you okay?"

I peel my eyes open, my head ringing. Why am I looking up at a girl I don't know?

I nod and sit, gingerly probing the tender spot at the back of my head where I must have slammed it into the floor. The dirty tile floor of the worst girls' bathroom at Bear Lake High School, where I have apparently been lying for who knows how long.

"Do you want me to call the nurse? You're bleeding." She shuffles her feet, shoulders hunched around her backpack straps. She keeps glancing at the tampon vending machine, embarrassed. That explains why she'd come to this bathroom; it's probably the only dispenser that stays stocked.

I pull my fingers in front of my face, frowning at them. I'm not bleeding. She nods toward the mirror, and I use the sink to stand, still shaking and disoriented. The mirror I was looking in earlier is cracked, spiderwebbing out in lines from an impact near the bottom right corner. The glass there is smeared with a teaspoon of dark red.

My shattered reflection shows me the small cut on my forehead, with a single trickle of blood disappearing into my hairline, staining the blonde hair above my ear.

"Oh," I say softly. "I'm okay. Slipped." I grab some paper towels, getting them wet with cold water to wash my forehead and assess the damage. The girl hasn't left. She's watching me, eyes darting to the dispenser. It's so embarrassing for both of us I don't know what to do. I'm glad I don't know her, that we don't have any classes together.

The blood comes away and reveals a tiny cut, not even stitch-worthy. I don't look at the girl again, and she seems to accept the evidence that I am fine. She digs in her pocket for a quarter, and I slide out of the restroom as fast as I can.

A head wound is what I get for thinking I could dare to open my mouth. It figures.

. . . . .

That evening I braid Oma's hair, humming to myself. She nods sleepily, the long, silken curls of pure white twisting around my hands.

"How was school today?" she asks in German. She's the only one I'll speak with in German. My parents get mad at me, but I refuse to answer them in anything other than English. I haven't spoken a word of German to them since I was eight years old.

"It was fine," I answer.

She lets out an annoyed huff I'm familiar with. "You are a terrible liar, my Loti. You wear the truth on your face, and lies twist your mouth into a sad, ugly shape."

I laugh and lean forward to kiss the top of her head. "You are so sweet, Oma."

She waves dismissively. "Were those kids mean to you again?"

Those kids she refers to are now teens, not cruel third graders snickering Heil Hitlers behind my back, but I blush anyway. "No one is mean to me." In order to be mean to me they'd have to know I exist. I've done my best to be invisible in the eight years since we moved from Germany to Idaho, and now, even when I don't want to be, I can't help but make myself disappear.

When I close my eyes, I can see my name on the audition list. Stupid. I desperately want music to be a part of my life, more than just singing at home and filling my small room with the sound of my voice. But like that? In front of my whole school? Of course I bailed. It's one thing to pour your soul out singing along with opera stars in the safety of your own room. For all I know, I suck.

Oma jabs a finger at my chest. "You should be proud of where you come from."

I sigh. "I am, Oma. Promise."

The truth is, ever since those kids made fun of me in elementary school, I've done my best to expunge any and all traces of where I came from. But sometimes a vowel comes out the wrong way, or a consonant isn't formed just so, and I realize I cannot escape my otherness. I'd rather be invisible than a target. My past has an iron grip on my tongue, and iron makes very good prison cell bars.

. . . . .

I slip into school the next morning, early enough to get to my classes without racing, but late enough that the halls are full and I don't stand out.

I drop my backpack at my feet in front of my locker. Grabbing my books for first period English and second period U.S. history, I don't realize the person behind me saying, "Hey!" is talking to me until I'm tapped on the shoulder.

I turn. My mouth drops open. Brianna Johnson is standing there, smiling at me.

"You're Loti, right?"

Correction: Brianna Johnson is standing there, smiling at me, *and she knows my name.* Brianna Johnson. Lead in the show choir. Lead in the last four musicals. Student Body Vice President.

Several seconds too late, I nod.

"Congrats on making callbacks! I didn't know you were a singer. Will you be singing the same thing? I can't decide on my piece. I'm so nervous! Anyway. Just wanted to say congrats and I hope we're in the talent show together!"

She squeezes my shoulder, the brunette embodiment of cheerfulness, and weaves away into the crowd. Her hair is shorter than it was when we were in sixth grade and she invited me to sit by her at lunch. I said no, knowing I'd have to talk if I sat by her, and I've regretted it ever since. The invitation never came again, not from her or anyone else.

I'm so shocked that she remembers my name and talked to me that it takes me a few heartbeats to realize what she said.

I made callbacks.

For the audition I missed while hiding and unconscious in the bathroom.

I dart through the stream of bodies until I hit the double doors leading to the auditorium. Most days I walk by without even looking at them, because they make my heart do this squeezing thing that feels like equal parts hope and hurt.

I have this recurring dream. The stage is there, alone, an island of light in a sea of darkness. And then I'm there, and there's a microphone, calling to me with its silent siren song. Not the fancy headsets the school used a grant to get, but one of those beautiful old ones—sleek silver stand, face-sized capsule at the top, like the screen sirens of another age used. I'm dressed the part, with my hair in gentle waves and a satin dress draping all the way to the floor.

And then I open my mouth, and all the music, all the notes, and all the sound I've bottled inside through the years floods out of me, a torrent of noise, heartbreakingly beautiful and precious because it's *me*, unfiltered, utterly naked in a way that no other music can be. There is no instrument between me and the world, no barrier. Just my voice. Just me.

It is the single most exhilarating feeling I've ever experienced, elation and fulfillment transforming me into something bigger than myself, carrying me outside of myself, freeing me.

After I've sung a song I can never remember afterward, I look out and realize there's an entire audience, silent, watching. I'm filled with equal parts terror and elation, waiting to see their reaction, and then—

I wake up. Always.

Now, that feeling I have at the end of the dream twists in my stomach, making everything around me feel fuzzy and unreal. I am standing outside of the auditorium where there's a sheet taped to the cinderblock wall next to the doorframe. I have to blink several times before the letters make sense. And when they *do* make sense, they still don't.

Brianna was right. My name is on the list, with a five-minute slot today during lunch for my callback performance, to be sung in front of all the other students who made callbacks.

For a minute my soul sings with joy, until it crashes to the scuffed linoleum beneath me. It's a mistake. I didn't audition, and no one here has ever heard me sing, so there's no way I'd be called back. Now I have to tell Ms. Jolley, the choir director, that my name shouldn't be on the list.

The bell rings and I swear softly in German, which is the only time it slips from me. I run to class, feeling as far away from my dream as I ever have.

. . . . .

I'd meant to find a time to let Ms. Jolley know about the mistake, but it's lunch before I have a chance. And then I know where she'll be—in the auditorium, with the people who actually made callbacks. The idea of walking in there in front of all of them, especially Brianna after she was so nice this morning, makes me so upset I duck into the bathroom, afraid I'm going to puke.

I pace in front of the sinks, noting the still-broken mirror with a twinge of guilt. The spot of blood is gone, at least.

I still have time to make it to the auditorium, but it doesn't matter. I won't show, Ms. Jolley will realize I was never supposed to be on the list in the first place, and everything will go back to the way it was before.

Quiet.

So very, very quiet and invisible.

That's the thing about living in a small town and going to a small high school with the same kids you've known since elementary school. You are assigned your slot, and unless you do something crazy to change it, you stay put. My slot is the quiet German girl. I have become part of the background, unseen the same way you cease even noticing the poster tacked to the back of the door you see every single day.

I splash some cold water on my face, put my hand on the back of my neck, and try to get over the panic. It's fine. It doesn't matter. I look up to the splintered mirror to make sure my mascara didn't run, but—

I'm sick. This isn't nerves. I'm actually sick, I have to be, because the me in the mirror doesn't have her hand on the back of her neck. She has it pressed up against the center of the spiderwebbing cracks in the mirror.

My head spinning, I raise my trembling hand to match my reflection. I have to match my reflection. If I match it, then I'm not going crazy.

When my fingers touch the sharp glass, the me in the mirror smiles triumphantly, and with a spinning twist of mirrors and sinks and pale pink stalls, everything once again goes black.

· · · · ·

I wake up with my cheek smashed against the cold tile floor, my backpack digging into my spine. I really should not be making a habit of this. I sit and hold my aching head, still overcome with dizzy vertigo. Maybe I should go home. I must be ill, not getting enough sleep, something.

I use the wall to leverage myself up, leaning heavily against it. A couple of girls come in, chattering to each other, and I pull my backpack around to pretend to be looking for something. It's another trick for being invisible. Always have something to do, some barrier between you and eye contact.

"What happened to the mirror?" one of them asks, and I don't look up, can't without admitting it was my fault.

"Is that blood?" the other asks, leaning in close.

My eyes snap to the shattered section and—yes, there, in the middle, where I touched. There's blood again. I know there wasn't before. From where it's safely hidden in my backpack, I twist my hand around and see a smear of blood from a knick on my finger.

I must have cut it on the mirror. The mirror that . . . *schiess, schiess,* the mirror that wasn't doing what it was supposed to. My eyes wide with fear, I look at myself, but everything matches. Both me's are doing the same thing. Though I swear—and this is paranoia talking, it has to be, I'm losing my mind—I swear that my reflection's eyes are narrowed in a way mine aren't.

The bell rings. I've missed lunch entirely. Was I really passed out for that long? I stumble into the hall, thinking to go see the nurse, but the world rights itself and I feel better, so I go to precalc like I'm supposed to.

When classes are finally over for the day, I trudge toward the parking lot where my fifteen-year-old Volkswagen Rabbit waits for me. My backpack is too heavy, digging into my shoulders, and the whole day—the whole *year*—feels like it's weighing me down. Classes. Home. Homework. Classes. Home. Homework.

My life has no real music in it. No joy. I listen to music, sure, but it's not the same as making it. I don't know if I can take two more years of high school. And what after?

I pass the auditorium. There's a new sheet posted, and bitter, resigned curiosity pushes me forward to look. I'm sure Brianna made it. I've gone to all of the school's choir performances, all of the musicals. The way the singers draw energy from each other, each performing better than they ever could alone, never stops amazing me. Brianna is one of the best. I wonder if it helps, having a talent that everyone knows, this wonderful thing about you they can use to identify you. She always seems happy.

I wait until a couple of seniors move away and lean forward, glancing at the list. A couple of dramatic monologues, a drum solo, a magic act, and of course, Brianna with a solo and as part of a quartet. Good for her. The rest of the list are the usual suspects: Jake Temple, an amazing baritone in the senior class; Carly Hansen, a beautiful soprano who played Maria in *West Side Story* last year; and the other members of the show choir.

Except one.

My name is on the list, again, for a solo.

For one split second, seeing my name on there with everyone else fills me with elation, belonging. Which is immediately washed away as angry, embarrassed tears burn in my eyes. One mess-up I can understand, but there is *not* another Loti König at this school. I'm sure Ms. Jolley didn't do it on purpose, but it feels like I'm being mocked for my cowardice. There's no way I was automatically put on after skipping my audition in the first place.

My anger propels me to the music wing of the school, into the choir room with its built-in risers. I've never actually been in here before, though I walk as slowly as possible past the large windows looking in on it every day. Actually coming in, seeing a pile of music scattered on the piano bench, hurts.

It hurts.

There's a glass-walled office and I shuffle my feet, staring at it, all my anger evaporated into humiliation.

Ms. Jolley, her short gray hair curled around cat-eye glasses, walks out of the office, a stack of papers in her arms.

She looks up and almost drops them. "Oh! Loti! I didn't hear you come in."

I frown, surprised she knows my name, since I've never spoken with her.

"Did you decide to stop depriving me of that gorgeous alto and transfer into choir?" Her face lights up. "I'll sign the slip right now."

I shake my head, my voice coming out a mumble. "Umm, no, it's about the talent show? The list?"

"I posted it! Didn't you see? Just promise me you'll sing what you sang today at callbacks. We'll need the name of the number for the program, if you can find it. You can't tell this to anyone, but that's the first time a student's voice has brought me to tears. Where have you been hiding?" She beams at me, then someone calls her name and she looks out the door. "I'll be right there!" As she's leaving, she turns around and says in a playful tone, "And don't think I'm dropping my campaign to get you in my choir. See you at rehearsal next week!"

I watch her go with my mouth hanging open. It's official: either I've gone mad, or the rest of the world has.

· · · · ·

My parents don't know I don't talk at school. It's amazing how easy it is to slide right under the radar—of parents, of teachers, of fellow students. I pull good grades; I keep my head down; I never raise my hand. Whenever I have to talk, I do so as quietly and succinctly as possible. I slip through.

But Oma knows something is wrong the moment I walk in the door.

"What happened?" she demands, arms open for a hug. I let her fold me in and rest my cheek against the polyester sleeve on her shoulder. She smells like dried flowers. I know this isn't what Düsseldorf smelled like, but in my head the two are intertwined. I wonder who I would have been if we had stayed there, if I had grown up where opening my mouth didn't get me made fun of.

She pats me on the back. "Let me feed you, and you tell me what has you looking like a ghost of yourself."

I follow her into the kitchen and slump at the counter. She has one of her old albums on, Mozart's *The Magic Flute*. My favorite opera, usually, because Mozart wrote it to so many different talent levels. Some of the parts are simple, heavily supported by the orchestra, but the Queen of the Night's solos are insanely hard, showcasing her voice alone.

Today it sounds lifeless.

"You'll think I'm crazy, Oma."

She clucks reproachfully, scooping a steaming spoonful of apple pudding cake onto a plate and sprinkling cinnamon on top. Then she climbs heavily onto the stool next to me. "Go on. Tell me."

I push the cake around my plate with my fork. What have I got to lose? Besides my mind, which maybe has already happened. Keeping my eyes on my food, I tell her almost everything: signing up to audition, chickening out, hitting my head, waking up to find my name on the callbacks, passing out in the bathroom again, waking up to find my name on the final list.

"But it's not a mistake, because Ms. Jolley knew who I was—she told me herself my singing had made her cry! But I never sang, Oma, and I don't know how this is happening or what's going on."

When I finally look up at her, it's not confusion or pity on her face. It's terror.

"Tell me about the mirror," she says, her normally strong voice trembling.

"The mirror? It's broken. I broke it."

"Did you see anything in it before you broke it? Did it look wrong?"

My eyes widen. I hadn't wanted to admit it to myself, had left it out of the story entirely. Finally, I nod. "I didn't match my reflection."

"Did you give it something of yours? Hair? Jewelry?"

I shake my head. "No, nothing, I—" I stop, rub my thumb over the raised spot on my finger where I cut it. Then I bring my hand to the small cut along my hairline. "Blood. My blood got on the mirror both times."

Her hand catches mine, squeezing it in a trembling grip. "Double walker," she whispers, and it takes me a few moments to realize I'd heard the German term before: *doppelgänger*.

She feels my forehead, looks in my eyes, and tugs my chin until I open my mouth to let her look at my tongue. Oma questions me ruthlessly about details from our life together, things only she and I would know. I get more and more scared until finally I scream, "Stop it! Tell me what's going on!"

Her shoulders are stooped, and she looks much older than she did when I got home. "It's bad, *Liebchen*. Double walkers steal your soul. They steal your life. Whatever you do, stay away from that mirror. Cross yourself when you pass by that bathroom."

She straightens, walks out of the room as though possessed with a new purpose. I want to run after her, ask what she was talking about, but I can't. A doppelgänger? A double of me, trying to steal my life?

Who on earth would want my life?

When I finally walk out of the kitchen, I stop short. Oma has covered the large mirror hanging over the mantel. I drift through the hall to the bathroom we share. The mirror there, too, is completely blocked by towels. I make it to my room in time to see her dragging out the long mirror that hung on the back of my closet door.

"No one is stealing you," she says, steel back in place in her German consonants.

I lean against the doorframe, looking at the empty space where the mirror was. I don't say anything, but I can't help but wonder: If this spirit is evil, why did it get me a spot in the talent show?

. . . . .

Oma has watched me like a hawk all week. But she's not at school, and I haven't been able to stop thinking about this, to stop wondering.

The first rehearsal is this afternoon. I can't go. I can't. But Brianna Johnson has smiled and waved at me every day this week. And a few other kids—Carly, Jake, a few juniors not in show choir yet—have all started saying hi to me, too.

It's amazing how normal, how accepted, something as simple as a smile and a wave can make me feel. I'm on the edge of being part of a group, and it makes the last few years feel even emptier than they did before.

I researched doppelgängers. They're supposed to make your life worse. This doesn't feel worse to me.

That is, other than the massive, sick pit in my stomach in the afternoon as I hover, hiding in a recessed doorway one hall over from the auditorium. They all know me now. They're expecting me. They're counting on me. I have a slot in the talent show, which means someone who wanted one doesn't. I've thought of everything: faking sick, telling them I've lost my voice. At one feverish point last night, I even considered running away.

I have to be at the rehearsal in two minutes. It's the only one before the show next week, so everyone can see the order and fix blocking for the group numbers. But I cannot—cannot—sing in front of people.

I've never done it before, and I have no idea if I'm good. What if what comes out of my mouth is so horrible no one says anything? Worse: What if they laugh? I can't handle being laughed at, or pitied. I just can't.

I can't risk it.

As long as my voice is mine and mine alone, I don't have to know whether or not I'm good. I can keep treasuring music as my own secret, special thing. If I put it out there for the rest of the world, I have to be judged.

I can't go to the rehearsal.

But . . . maybe *I* don't have to.

Before I talk myself out of it I slam through the door and burst into the bathroom. The mirror still isn't fixed, and before I'm even all the way in front of it, my reflection is smirking at me.

"I know what you are," I say, avoiding looking into my own pale blue eyes when they aren't really mine. I don't know if I expected her to answer, but finally I look her full in the face. She has one blonde eyebrow raised in derision, my full lips pushed into a smirk. "Why are you doing this?"

She rolls her—my—eyes, and points to her throat.

"Oh. You can't talk?"

She claps slowly, all of her actions dipped in sarcasm.

"Listen. I—I don't want you to take over my life or anything, but I've been thinking about it, and I always come back to myself after, right? So maybe you just borrow my life for a few minutes, and what's the harm in that?" My voice is getting faster and higher, I'm so nervous I can barely breathe. "The rehearsal is right now. I can't go. But . . . you can?"

A tiny smile pulls at one corner of her mouth and she nods.

"Okay." I take a deep breath. "Go ahead."

She holds out her hand expectantly.

"Oh. Right. Blood." I bite my lip, nervous, and before I can think better of it, I push my finger against the center of the cracks in the mirror.

This time before things go totally black, I hear laughter.

It's not coming out of my mouth.

· · · · ·

I wake up to the now familiar sensation of cold, grimy tile against my cheek. Every muscle is sore. And the bathroom is way too dim. Are my eyes damaged?

I probe for tender spots as I stand, my knees shaking. My head feels intact. But why—

It's *actually* dim. Not just my eyes. The narrow windows along the wall next to the ceiling don't let in the brilliant afternoon light they should. It's evening out there. Only a single emergency light is on in the bathroom.

I can't see my reflection, and I'm glad. I stumble out of the bathroom and through the halls, passing a janitor who has his back turned to me, floor waxer loud enough to cover my flight. My phone informs me it's 8:00 p.m. That means I've been unconscious for seven—SEVEN—hours. My phone also informs me I missed a call from my parents.

I'm in so much trouble.

Fortunately the doors leading to the parking lot don't lock on the inside, and I push through into the spring-chilled evening. My car is where I left it, along with a note from the campus security guard that cars parked overnight will be towed.

Trembling so hard I can barely steer, I drive the familiar streets back home. I can barely look in the rearview mirror. I don't know what I'll see. Or what I want to see. What happened this afternoon? Did I—I mean, my double—make it to practice? Did she do a good job? Why was I out for so long?

The first time it was just a few minutes. But now that I think about it, the second was all of lunch period. If it's getting progressively longer each time . . .

I can't think about it right now. I stop at my spot on the curb in front of my house and take a deep breath. If I tell my parents I was unconscious for seven hours, they'll make me go to the doctor. Probably the hospital.

Maybe I should.

But I don't want to. I know what happened. Sort of, anyway. And it's not an explanation that will show up in an MRI or through blood tests. Locking the car, I go up the walkway and open the door as quietly as I can, like if I'm silent they won't have noticed how late I am.

I nearly scream when I see my parents, snuggled up on the couch with a bowl of popcorn between them.

"Hey, Loti-bug," Dad says. "I thought you were spending the night?"

"I was? I mean. I was. I told you that, right? I, uh, decided to come home."

"You sounded like you were having fun when you called from your friend's phone. You ate, right?"

I nod, trying to force a smile. "Yeah. I got tired, is all. Wanted to go to bed early."

My mom holds out her arms and I lean forward, letting her kiss me on the forehead. "I'm so glad you've made good friends, Loti. I worry about you. And we can't wait for the talent show next week."

I grimace a smile and, sneaking my dad's phone off of the side table, lock myself in the bathroom. I scroll through the incoming call history to find out who called to tell him I was out with friends.

It was Brianna Johnson. Or her phone, at least. And my dad knows my voice—he wouldn't believe anyone else calling and imitating me. Which means not only did my double walker go to rehearsal . . . it means she had so much fun the other kids invited her to hang out with them afterward. I wonder what happened, if she could feel me waking up and made an excuse, or if she just disappeared?

All I know is she was having a blast while I was passed out on the floor in the bathroom.

Turns out my double is better at my own life than I am.

. . . . .

I have the dream every night in the week leading up to the talent show.

The microphone, the dress, the dark auditorium, waking up just before I get the audience's reaction—it's all the same, except one detail has changed. Now I can remember the song.

It's a lullaby, an old German tune Oma used to sing me. The tune is simple, haunting, the sounds and syllables of my childhood. And it feels *true* as I sing it, it feels like I am singing my soul, and I know it could be German or English, it doesn't matter. What matters is my voice with the song.

It's the song Oma is humming softly next to me as we ride in the back of the car to the school for the concert.

I could kill my double for that phone call where she mentioned the talent show to my dad. I tried to get out of it—telling my parents it was no big deal, telling them I'd changed my mind and didn't want to do it. But they were so excited, so happy and *relieved*. It was the relief that killed me.

I thought I was fooling them all these years, but I can see in their happiness just how worried they've been. I can't let them down. Even if it's not me who is finally becoming what they've hoped I could be.

My parents are both dressed up like they're going to the symphony. Oma gave me her strand of pearls, the only jewelry she has left from Opa, and my mother took me out for a new dress.

It's not quite the satin screen siren of my dreams, but it's a creamy off-white, the cut making me look older, braver, and prettier. In this dress I look like someone who can stand in front of an audience and sing.

Or at least that's what the me in the mirror looks like. Oma still has all the mirrors at home covered, much to my parents' consternation, but there was one in the dressing room at the store. I know the dress was on my body, but I swear my reflection wore it better.

When we get to the school, I wave my parents ahead, claiming I need to be backstage. I have no idea where I need to be—I wasn't at rehearsal. Oma watches me, her eyes wary. Before she goes into the auditorium, she pulls me into a hug.

"I love you, Loti," she says, her lips almost against my ear. "Don't ever hold yourself back from what you can be. No one else can be it for you."

Guilt joins the terror in my stomach. She knows. She knows what I did, what I'm planning to do. But I can't go up there. I can't. And I can't back down, not now that my parents are here waiting, not now that Brianna has asked me to eat lunch with her and the other choir kids every day. Not now that I'm accepted. Part of a group.

I can't lose this new life, even if it's not mine.

Oma pats my back and leaves me. My feet feel like lead as I escape the buzzing area around the auditorium and head for the bathroom.

My bathroom.

She's waiting for me when I go in, and I was right—the dress *does* look better on her. I wear it, but she owns it, shoulders thrown back confidently.

I analyze her through the cracked glass. "How long will it last this time?" I ask. I don't want to be lying here for hours before I wake up or someone finds me. And I wonder, too, if maybe, eventually . . . maybe she'll be me and I'll be the reflection.

She shrugs, smiling. I think I look kinder than that when I smile.

"Are you me?" I ask.

She raises a hand and twists it at the wrist, in a so-so sort of gesture. Then, my red lipstick forming the words, she mouths: *I'm better.*

I slump against the wall. It's true. She's better at being me. She's braver and stronger and a better singer, and . . .

The door opens and I jump. Brianna grins, breathless, her dress a short, flirty green number. "Loti! I'm so excited! I get so nervous before performances. That's probably why you came here, to be alone. Great hiding place—this bathroom is the worst. But now I'm totally ruining your solitude. I just wanted to say how happy I am that we've finally gotten to know each other!" She pulls me into a hug and squeezes me tight, her perfume tickling my sinuses. "And I'm going to say it right now so it's not awkward: If you beat me out for lead on the next musical there are no hard feelings, okay? About time this school had another alto who could carry her weight!"

"Thank—thank you," I whisper. "Good luck tonight."

She laughs, skipping to the door and pulling it open wide. "We don't need luck! Just our fabulous vocal cords. See you in there!"

I watch the door swing shut behind her, the room feeling smaller and colder in her wake. She doesn't need luck. I don't, either. I need to be someone else, is all. I turn back to my reflection. She's tapping her finger against the glass impatiently, mouthing something silently.

Wait.

"You have my voice," I mumble, remembering the call that my dad couldn't tell wasn't me.

She shrugs impatiently, nodding as she jabs her finger at the sharp center of cracks in the mirror.

I stand up straighter, still watching her in the mirror. I move my shoulders back, trying out the same posture she has. Lifting my chin. Looking boldly forward. "You don't have any voice until you take mine," I say, and this time I do not mumble or whisper. I speak clearly and I speak loudly. "It's my voice. My voice in the audition, my voice that made Mrs. Jolley cry, my voice that Brianna thinks is as good as hers."

She looks puzzled, and then her eyes flash slyly. She raises an eyebrow at me. She pantomimes singing into a microphone, and mouths the words: *so many people.* She opens her mouth like she's singing and grabs her throat, eyes widening in terror. Dropping her hands, she smiles at me again. *You can't,* she mouths, shaking her head.

My shoulders drop. She's right. I can't. I can't face the fear, the worry that if I open my mouth and let my soul out, I'll be laughed at. I've hidden for so long, I don't know how to handle the idea of being seen for who I really am.

I close my eyes. I will never know how the dream ends. I will never know how the audience reacts. I lift my hand, ready to cut my finger, ready to check out and let my double take my place. I cling to the dream, to the only space I'll ever be able to sing.

And just before my finger touches the glass, I stop. Because I have evidence now, from Brianna and Mrs. Jolley, that I *can* sing well enough to avoid embarrassing myself. But even more, I've realized something about the dream I never saw before.

I always thought I was waiting for the audience's reaction, but the truth is it doesn't matter. They don't matter. The way I feel when I'm singing, the truth of my soul coming out in the notes—that's what the dream is about. That's where the magic is. That's where my heart is.

The audience doesn't react because *I don't need them.*

My voice is mine.

"Mine," I say, opening my eyes. I pull my hand back and my double looks up at me, her eyes as sharp as the razor edges of the mirror.

I step back, smoothing the front of my dress. "It's not about them," I say. "All these years I thought so, but I was wrong. It's about me. I'm the one who chose to hide. I didn't need to. And I can stop now."

Her face contorts in rage, and she silently screams at me. She brings her fist up and slams it against the glass, again and again. And I step back again, suddenly scared that maybe she'll break her way out.

She smashes her palm into the glass a final time, and with a loud crack the mirror splits in two, coming loose from the pegs that hold it to the wall. I duck, covering my face. When the noise of shards raining onto the tile ends, I turn, dreading what I'll find.

But when I look down, all I see back are a hundred versions of my own face. I look scared, the same as I feel. I also look . . . hopeful.

And I hope I look brave.

I walk into the hall and toward the auditorium. Ms. Jolley is standing outside the stage entrance doors.

"There you are! You're next!" She beams at me as I walk past her and into the dim, cord-strewn backstage. I can see a free-standing microphone in an island of light on the dark stage.

I can see the audience, too. But they don't matter. This song, and every song after it forever, is mine. I smile, and walk out onto the stage.

I've finally found my voice.

ANECDOTE: GRETA GERWIG

Clues that I have always wanted to be an actor/writer/director/annoying:

I.

When I was five, my parents enrolled me in a kiddie tap class. We had a recital, tapping to "Johnny Be Good" and wearing bee costumes. There was one girl who didn't know it so well. I became increasingly aggravated by her and finally, halfway through the song, I pushed her into the wings. Then I tapped back onstage to finish the routine, much relieved that she could no longer muddy up the stage picture.

II.

In kindergarten I became obsessed with *Starlight Express*. I used to ask the other children on the playground if they wanted to be in the school-yard version I was directing. I'd play most of the parts and they (the two who agreed) would "skate" around me. I was always disappointed by their lack of commitment to the material.

III.

At seven, I participated in a children's summer theater production of *Peter Pan*. I was annoyed that I'd been relegated to the background, one of the dozens of "lost children." To amend this situation, I memorized the entire script. If one of the lucky children who had a big part did not say their line IMMEDIATELY, I would jump in to say it for them.

IV.

In high school I ran for student council every year. Not because I had a burning desire to be part of student government, but because I *loved* doing the speech. Each September, I would create an original rap that I would perform in front of the entire school. And I wasn't one of those well-loved students that everyone thought "Oh, Greta, she's such a personality!" I'm not even sure that a single person besides me enjoyed it. I never won, but I had an audience for my material, and that was all I really wanted to begin with.

V.

But the REAL moment for me, the biggest of the big and utterly sincere, happened my senior year in high school.

During high school—I grew up in Sacramento, California—I had done all the shows and musicals I possibly could, but I had never gotten a lead. The best I could hope for was a sidekick kind of role, which was fun and funny but not THE part. So senior year, the school held auditions for the spring musical: *The Wizard of Oz*.

It was already a tense time in my house—we were talking about colleges. It must not be easy for your kid to say "I want to be an actor" when you are looking at taking out tens of thousands of dollars in loans. I kept saying "I want to be an actor," but I wasn't sure I really believed it. I still lacked that inner trust and confidence. So when my mom said to me "Do you *really* think you're as good as Meryl Streep?" and I responded "I just have to be as good as ME," there was still a great deal of unacknowledged doubt.

In any case, we were in one of those classic parent struggles, and my mom asked why I would want to audition for *The Wizard of Oz*—what would I hope to get? I said, "I'd play a Munchkin just to be onstage!" (Side note: I was, and am, five foot nine. I should also mention that I had a shaved head due to an infatuation with Ani DiFranco. And wore a lot of cargo pants. I did not look very Lullaby-League.)

The audition: We sang, we read scenes, and then there were cuts—I stayed. Again singing, again scenes, again I stayed. And then, to my amazement, the director asked me to sing "Over the Rainbow." And then I was asked to read for Dorothy with two other girls. It seemed like a mistake.

The other girls had hair and could sing really well and looked like girls. I looked and sounded like . . . me. I did the best I could and went home, telling my mom I was sure I'd at least be a Flying Monkey.

When I looked at the casting list the next day, there it was: *I* was Dorothy. ME.

Mom asked if they were doing something "weird." It turns out they really were. The director (who is still one of the best directors I've ever worked with) had us show up to the first day of rehearsal with the script and a red pen. Over the course of the rehearsal process, the student cast completely rewrote *The Wizard of Oz*. We put in jokes and asides. We decided that the tornado should be represented by two guys holding leaf blowers. Dorothy became kind of a punk rocker (ruby-red Converse). We made it our own.

The months that followed were what put the finishing touches (or nail in the coffin, depending on your perspective) on my lifelong love of being on the stage and behind the scenes. Rehearsal for *The Wizard of Oz* is what made me know that storytelling was what I wanted to do with my life, and that I *could* do it. I had never been encouraged in that way before, to create original content and then perform it.

When the play finally went up, and I was onstage, getting laughs for jokes I had written myself—well, basically nothing has ever felt better and I have essentially spent the rest of my life trying to re-create that feeling. I finally felt like there was a way for me to make sense of all of the things inside of me that had never quite fit clearly into one path or goal.

Deep down, I've always known this is what I wanted to do, but I never would have done it if I hadn't had the good fortune of knowing the people who showed me the way. People like the high school theater director who saw that this strange, tall buzzcut girl could be Dorothy.

It is so easy to doubt and fall and not be true to your heart. But I had been right—I did only have to be as good as me.

P.S. My mom is now very proud of me and happy for me.

GRETA GERWIG is an actress, writer, and director. She stars in the film *Frances Ha*, a comedy she cowrote with Noah Baumbach. Gerwig also starred in Woody Allen's *To Rome with Love* and Whit Stillman's *Damsels in Distress*. Other credits include *Greenberg* with Ben Stiller, *Arthur* with Russell Brand and Helen Mirren, and *No Strings Attached* with Natalie Portman and Ashton Kutcher. She cowrote *Hannah Takes the Stairs*, and co-wrote and co-directed *Nights and Weekends*. Gerwig graduated magna cum laude from Barnard College, and currently resides in New York City.

TALENT

Claudia Gray

"Don't be upset."

It was sweet of Claire to comfort him, Landon thought—especially since she had to be elated.

"Mercutio is a great role," Claire continued, "and everybody knows the only reason you didn't get Romeo is because Mrs. K is saving you for Harold Hill."

This was comforting largely because it was true. Landon had decided before auditions for *Romeo and Juliet* began that he'd rather have the lead in *The Music Man*, and Mrs. Kowalski never chose the same students to star in both the fall play and the spring musical. Mercutio was precisely the part he'd wanted. Claire, meanwhile, had succeeded on pure talent—which Landon admired even more than he envied.

"That, plus you're the *only* possible choice for Juliet," Landon said, "and fate decreed the best actress in our school should be three full inches taller than the best actor."

Claire held her hand to her forehead, a showy silent-movie gesture. It was a game they played: mocking the stereotype of over-the-top drama students, which Landon knew they mostly did so they'd never have to find out how close to the stereotype they really came. "I can't help it that I'm built like a model," she said.

"And I can't help it that I'm . . . portable." It was becoming clear to Landon that five foot seven was about as tall as he was going to get. "I figure if it didn't stop Tom Cruise, it doesn't have to prevent my own ascent to superstardom." He tossed his floppy brown hair, doing his best impersonation of Tom Cruise's plastic grin.

Claire pretended to bow before him. "Only a matter of time, darling. You know nobody can resist you."

It was only a joke, one she couldn't have known would make him cringe. So he tried to hide his reaction, picking up the pace as they walked toward Claire's car. She caught up within a few steps, her bracelets jangling on her wrists. "Hey, don't let it get to you. Sean—he's talented, but he doesn't begin to compare to you as an actor. You know that, right?"

"I'm not jealous of Sean Pryor." The sooner he could stop talking about himself, Landon figured, the better. "You know, I didn't even pay attention to the other roles once you started screaming. Any surprises?"

"Exactly what we predicted, except for one bona fide shocker." Claire clutched at his jacket sleeve in a way Landon knew meant major revelations were in store. "Tybalt? Is *Jesse Pearce*."

Jesse Pearce wasn't involved in the theater program. It was pretty much the only program, team, or activity at Scotsville High Jesse hadn't yet conquered. He was the school's star swimmer, enrolled in the honors courses, voted Most Handsome twice already and expected to three-peat this year. There were all kinds of rumors about Jesse—who he was dating, what schools were throwing scholarships at his feet, whether he was a wonderful human being or actually a stuck-up jerk who thought nobody at Scotsville was good enough for him. Landon hadn't actually seen Jesse's audition since he'd read early on, skipped watching the other auditions to cram for a chemistry test, and only caught a glimpse of Jesse standing around staring at his script. At the time, he'd wondered whether the attention had gone to Jesse's head and made him believe he could do anything. But apparently, he *could* do anything.

"He can act, too? It's not fair." Landon was more intrigued than jealous. "Wait. Tybalt's the one who kills Mercutio. Jesse's going to run me through with a sword. How . . . symbolic."

Claire elbowed him. "Remember how Jesse practically mated in public with Hannah Silverberg all last spring? Your team is the only one Jesse's not on."

Landon sighed. "I'll get to look at him up close, anyway."

"Who knows? Maybe you can change his mind."

She was only teasing. Landon knew that. But a chill swept through him, and he wanted to get out of there. So he lied, "I forgot—I have to do some stuff for my parents at the house. We'll hit Starbucks next time, okay?"

"Yeah, okay, sure." Usually Claire was like a divining rod, drawn straight to any shift in his mood, but apparently today she was too happy to notice he was upset. She jogged toward her car, silky brown hair bouncing with every step. "Congrats, Mercutio!"

"Congratulations, Juliet."

Then Landon went home to deal once again with the fact that he was a total fraud.

· · · · ·

The thing was, Landon Avery wasn't an actor. He paid attention in acting class, watched Oscar-winning performances and noticed what people like Jack Nicholson and Meryl Streep did to capture the inner lives of their characters, and intended to major in theater in college. Usually he did his best, which was probably terrible. Deep down, he was sure he'd never done a day's acting in his life.

His real talent was far stranger than that.

He couldn't say whether he was born with it, or if it came to him later, or why he had it. All Landon knew for sure was that he'd become aware of his talent—and capable of consciously using it—just over a year ago, the summer between his sophomore and junior year. That was when his mother came home from choir practice and walked into his room at the exact moment he'd pulled up a full-screen naked picture of Michael Fassbender.

"What are you doing?" The hard edge of panic in her voice cut him to the quick. "Why are you looking at—*that*?"

It just came up on Google. Somebody sent it to me as a joke. But the excuses wouldn't come out of his mouth. He could only gape at his mother, rolling over so at least she wouldn't see his pajama bottoms were tented out.

Didn't matter. She *knew*.

"Oh, my God. I don't believe this," she said, and he didn't think she was talking about how good Michael Fassbender looked. It was the single most terrifying moment of his life. Landon had stared up at her, unable to speak, seeing only her pale face, the way she opened and closed her mouth, how her hands clasped together so hard the knuckles were white—

—*don't*, he thought. *Don't hate me. Please, Mom. Just don't hate me*—

—and he felt it. A soft *thump* against his chest, though he wasn't the one struck; he was the one striking out.

What it came down to was this: He wanted his mother to accept him. He *willed* her to do it. And she did.

"Oh, sweetheart, it's okay," she said. A hollow smile came over her face, and her hands relaxed as color returned to her cheeks. All her shock seemed to have been emptied out. "You like boys, don't you? I understand."

"You do?" Landon knew he'd done this, made her accept him, but he still didn't understand *how*. His heart was pounding so hard it felt as though it would break his ribs, cave him in. "Are you sure?"

"Of course I'm sure." Mom patted his shoulder, like he'd just told her something . . . minor. "Maybe I should leave you alone for a bit."

That night, Mom took it upon herself to tell Dad over dinner. By instinct, Landon had done it again, *thump*, and Dad's frown had vanished. "You're my boy, same as ever. Okay, Landon?"

"Okay," Landon had said faintly. But his fork remained poised over his plate, touching nothing.

The next day, Landon had headed to the movie theater—the first place he'd thought of where he might find a lot of people together that he didn't know. There he'd tried a few tests. He figured out that when he used this mysterious talent of his on someone, he could influence that person's emotions. No, not just influence: *control*. But his power went no further than that.

He couldn't make someone start dancing wildly in the lobby. He couldn't make the bored girl behind the concession stand start giving out free Raisinets. But he *could* make people think they were hungry, and then snack sales rose.

The Adam Sandler movie was just about the stupidest film Landon had ever seen, and the audience sat there in silent boredom—until he wished for them to find the jokes funnier, and funnier, feeling the *thump* in his chest each time he did it, until by the end they were applauding and wiping away tears of laughter. Other tests in other places over the next several weeks confirmed his conclusion: He couldn't control actions, but he could control emotions. People felt whatever Landon wanted them to feel. What they did about their feelings remained up to them.

Landon had ultimately decided that was a relief. Controlling people like puppets would be completely creepy. Even controlling their emotions was weird—he was a freak and now he knew it—but it wasn't, well, *evil*. Not if all he did was make sure his parents didn't hate him for being gay, or let people believe a bad movie was hilarious.

When he'd asked himself how he could use his talent in a way that wouldn't hurt anyone, immediately he'd realized the answer: acting.

His whole life, Landon had dreamed of being an actor. Most people who said they wanted to go into acting really just wanted to be famous. But Landon hoped to seriously pursue drama, to create characters from the inside out. When other little kids were watching cartoons, he'd been watching reruns of *Inside the Actors Studio*. But he'd never had the self-confidence to believe he could actually get up on a stage and convince other people he was this completely different person . . . until his strange new talent showed him a way in.

He threw himself into the drama department. Every time he auditioned, Mrs. K was blown away, and even the other students trying out for the same part said he should get the role. When he performed onstage, the audience came alive. If he wasn't *really* acting, he was at least using his natural talents, right? Just making people happy. That had to be okay.

There were other uses, as well. When Mitchell McLanc and his thick-necked friends started coughing "fag" under their breath at him, Landon made them feel ashamed of themselves. After that, he noticed most of those guys became not only nicer to him, but also to the other kids in school believed to be gay. Emboldened, Landon came out. While some people still hated him for it, he made sure none of them felt like saying anything about it to his face. He used his talent for others, too: whenever Claire started looking worried about exams or auditions or anything else, he made sure she felt like everything would work out.

And now his parents were members of PFLAG. They proudly supported him no matter what. Only Landon wondered how deep their acceptance went, whether anything like love was behind their constant smiles. All he knew was that every time the subject came up, he instinctively used his talent again, felt the *thump*, and ensured that they'd think they still loved him . . . even if maybe, deep down, they didn't.

That was why Landon had never dated anyone, or even kissed another guy. What if he accidentally willed someone into liking him back? It was bad enough to not know if his parents really liked him anymore. Landon thought being alone forever couldn't be half as horrible as always having to wonder if the person you loved would love you back. Or if they had any choice.

. . . . .

Scotsville High was a pretty big school, and Landon didn't make a habit of attending swim meets, so he'd never actually seen Jesse Pearce except at a distance. The guy turned out to be even better looking close up, which ought to have been impossible.

Jesse was tall—six feet or so. He had coal-black hair and eyes so dark they seemed to match. Swimming had given him broad shoulders, muscular arms, and a tapered waist. But he wasn't vain or loudmouthed like most of the jocks. He was, as Claire had whispered once, "the strong, silent type."

Landon had never known that was his type. He knew now.

After the first read-through, Landon understood why Jesse had been cast. Mrs. K always liked to throw a small role to one of the nondrama students—*see, everyone can get involved!*—but Jesse had a quality of barely controlled power that just *worked* for Tybalt. Instead of playing his character as the stereotypical hothead, Jesse infused Tybalt with a kind of quiet menace.

As if he's angry, Landon thought as he lay in the wings, his head pillowed on his balled-up jacket. Jesse stood onstage as Mrs. K blocked out his first scene. *Like there's this fury waiting to boil over, right beneath the surface—*

"Someone's got a *cruuuu-uuush,*" Claire singsonged in his ear, softly enough that no one else would hear.

"I know it's hopeless. But I can look, can't I?"

"As long as I can look too." She stretched on her belly beside him, miniskirt only kept decent by the black tights she wore. "But stop being so cold to Jesse, okay? You've spent the past three weeks trying so hard not to show how crushed out you are that you're *broadcasting* it. Like, the volume is up to eleven, Landon. Turn it down."

"I'm not being unfriendly," he protested, but she was right. While he hadn't been outright rude, he'd never joked around with Jesse, struck up conversations, or anything like that. "Not so he's noticed, anyway."

"He's noticed. Sometimes I see him looking at you. Like he's wondering what's what."

There had been other moments, ones Claire apparently hadn't seen. Jesse had asked Landon to interpret a couple Shakespearian phrases into modern-human-speak; they'd leaned together over the script, working out what a "runagate" was, or why it was insulting to be called "goodman boy." Jesse always asked nicely, always said thank you. The only reason anybody thought Jesse was stuck up was because he was so quiet, but that was just his way. He could be drawn out, probably, if you had the chance and the time. But whenever they spoke, Landon felt like he had to escape before he did something stupid.

Landon sighed. Jesse would never know that Landon was dodging him for his own protection. And he didn't see how he could spend much more time around Jesse and not wish for Jesse to want him back.

At the end of rehearsal, though, despite Landon's best efforts to steer clear, Jesse walked right up to him.

"Hi." Jesse had a deeper voice than most guys. "Listen, I'd like to go over the fight scene sometime. You and me. Sean and I worked on it, but the early part, where you draw and we get started, it's tricky."

"Yeah. It . . . definitely is." *Oh, God, did he hear me talking to Claire? He didn't. Okay. But now he's talking to me, and I feel like I should run away. Or kiss him. Or kiss him and then run away.* How was he supposed to get out of this one?

But as Landon looked up at Jesse, the two of them together in a half-dark hallway behind the stage, everyone else in the world seemingly far in the distance, his resolve weakened.

Jesse's straight. *Totally straight. It's not like I could make a straight guy fall for me, even if I tried, which I wouldn't,* Landon rationalized. He could affect emotions, not actions. Worst-case scenario, he might make Jesse . . . question himself, but not even his strange talent could make Jesse do something they'd both regret. *Besides, I need to stop broadcasting. Act natural.*

"Yeah. Let's do it." Their eyes met, and Landon had to swallow hard before asking, "When?"

. . . . .

When turned out to be Thursday night, and *where* turned out to be Jesse's house, which was only about a mile away from Landon's. Landon rode his bike over after class rather than ask for a ride from his mom. It was no big deal, just an extra rehearsal; Landon was proud of himself for not even changing clothes before heading over.

But that morning he'd been sure to put on the black T-shirt Claire always said made him look hot.

He had always assumed Jesse was one of the rich kids; most of the really popular people at Scotsville had money. But the Pearce house wasn't that different from Landon's own home, except for all of Jesse's trophies in the living room. Jesse's parents were out for the night—an unexpected bonus.

"Hey." Jesse smiled, and only then did Landon realize how rare that smile was. "Glad you came. I wasn't sure you would."

That had to be a reference to Landon's standoffishness. Landon decided it was best glossed over. "You're right. We should nail this scene. It's the most important one in the play."

"More important than the balcony scene?"

"First rule of acting: *your* big scene is always the most important one, no matter who you're playing." That made Jesse smile again, which made Landon feel witty, intelligent, and sort of like he might be melting inside. "Besides that," Landon continued, "the fight between Mercutio and Tybalt is key. Before the fight, *Romeo and Juliet* is mostly a comedy, you know? You have to kill me before it turns into a tragedy."

"Good point."

It had occurred to Landon that if they really wanted to perfect this scene, they ought to have asked over the other actors who appeared in it. But neither of them had brought it up.

Jesse's room was almost scarily neat, with a lot of empty floor space they could use. His fat Siamese cat slept in the desk chair, which they sometimes rolled into place so that the cat could be Benvolio or Romeo as the moment demanded. They wound up using old Nerf bats as their swords, but Landon didn't care. Not as long as he and Jesse were having fun.

"Okay, so, Mercutio is the one who starts it," Landon said. "He's full of himself, and it's like he doesn't even get that swords can actually hurt people."

"Right." Jesse wasn't off-book yet; he held his copy in his Nerf-swordless hand. "And Mercutio doesn't really care much about the whole family feud thing. It's Tybalt himself he doesn't like. Mostly because he's a good swordfighter, though that doesn't make sense. Why would Mercutio care?"

"He's jealous," Landon suggested. "Let's say Mercutio's mostly jealous of Tybalt. You know, Tybalt's good at swordfighting—he's good at *everything*, and Mercutio knows he's only ever going to be second-best."

"But Mercutio's funny. Everybody likes him."

"He'll never be important the way Tybalt already is. Come on. Let's try it that way."

Jesse went into a fighting stance. Just seeing Jesse's muscles flex beneath his T-shirt was enough to make Landon almost forget his lines. Luckily, Jesse spoke first: "Well, peace be with you, sir. Here comes my man."

As Jesse tried lowering his sword, Landon pushed forward, using his own Nerf blade to knock Jesse's back into dueling position. "'But I'll be hang'd, sir, if he wear your livery—'"

"Wait," Jesse cut in. "Is it, like—we decided Mercutio's jealous of Tybalt, but he's protecting Romeo."

"A lot of productions portray Mercutio being in love with Romeo." Landon couldn't quite meet Jesse's eyes. Yeah, he was out and everybody in school knew it; that didn't make it much easier to talk about it. "Romeo doesn't love him back. Obviously. The play's not *Romeo and Mercutio*. But that's one reason Mercutio might be so—over the top here. Not that he's not over the top everywhere."

That made Jesse smile again. "So does he think Tybalt's a rival?"

Maybe it was just an acting suggestion. But the idea that Mercutio could be gay—layered on the well-known fact that Landon was gay—and this didn't seem to turn Jesse off, and in fact Jesse seemed to want to play with the concept . . . well, it was all *extremely interesting*.

Heart thumping, Landon tried to speak casually. "What if maybe Mercutio's only pretending to be into Romeo? What if he's trying to make Tybalt jealous for a change?"

"What do you mean?"

"Like, Mercutio wants to see how Tybalt would react. To find out if maybe—maybe Tybalt would wish Mercutio was into him instead of Romeo." Had he actually spoken those words out loud? Too late to take them back now. Landon plowed ahead. "Which of course is a long shot and maybe even kind of crazy, but that's how Mercutio acts a lot of the time."

Jesse just went back into a fighting stance. "Let's try it."

They tried it, and the scene went from merely okay to bottled lightning. Or so it seemed to Landon. He was acting now, *really* acting, or at least it felt like it. But the thrill came from more than just feeling like he could play a scene without having to cheat. Every time his eyes met Jesse's, he was free to show all the longing he felt—the hopeless, helpless desire. And every time, the mysterious dark fire in Jesse's gaze answered him.

After three or four run-throughs, Landon felt like they had it.

They ran through it twelve times.

Then they made pizza bites. Then they played *Resident Evil* for an hour. Then they hung out up in Jesse's room, lying on the floor, listening to the Kills, and Landon stopped looking at the time. Even if he broke curfew for once, he could make sure his parents didn't care.

Which depressed him, as usual. So Landon decided to stop thinking about himself for a while. "What are you putting into Tybalt?"

"What do you mean?" Jesse lay next to him. Their feet were touching, but that was probably accidental. Probably.

Landon kept staring at their feet, instead of Jesse's face; that seemed easier. "He's so angry, but it's all beneath the surface. How did you come up with that?"

Jesse was quiet for a while. The only sound was the music. By now Jesse could have pulled his foot back, but he hadn't. "Well. I thought maybe Tybalt's the golden boy, you know? Capulet doesn't have a son, so he puts it all on him. Tybalt has to be the next in line. The best at everything. And he's good at a lot of stuff, but it's never enough. He just wishes he could stop doing what everyone else wants him to do and find out what *he* wants to do. But he can't. So he lashes out. He thinks attacking the Montagues will make him feel stronger, but it's not them he hates. It's everybody who keeps putting pressure on him."

For a few minutes more, they lay there together. The floor seemed to vibrate with the bass beat. Finally Landon said, "Why did you try out for the play?"

"My parents thought my college applications needed to be 'well-rounded.'"

"That's crazy. You're already good at everything. How many trophies are there in your living room? What, like, three dozen?"

Jesse shrugged.

It occurred to Landon that none of the trophies were in Jesse's room. No team photos, either. His parents were the ones who wanted to look at them. He remembered the bitter edge in Jesse's voice as he'd said *the golden boy*. "So you never even wanted to try theater?"

"I don't know. I thought about it, but I never—well, it always seemed like I had too much to do, before." He turned his head sideways just as Landon did. Their eyes met, and suddenly Landon felt like he could hardly breathe. "Turns out I like being in the play, though."

"Yeah?"

"Some parts of it." Jesse's gaze had drifted from Landon's eyes to his mouth.

I'm not doing this, Landon thought desperately. *I'm not. No* thump. *I'm not doing this, so it can't be happening, but I'm pretty sure it's happening, but it* can't be—

"Like what?" Landon said. The words came out unsteady.

But Jesse didn't seem to notice. He didn't answer, either. He just rolled onto his side, bringing his face closer to Landon's—not close enough to kiss, but too close for it to be nothing. Way too close for that. They hesitated there for a moment. Landon wasn't going to make the first move. He couldn't, knowing what he knew about himself. But he realized he'd parted his lips, and he wasn't going to pull away.

Jesse kissed him.

In that first instant, Landon felt nothing but shock. *Ohmigod Jesse's kissing me and I'm kissing him back and it's nothing like I thought it would be.*

But then their lips met again, and Landon got pulled out of his overactive brain and into his skin. Into the way that they touched, the way they started to breathe in and out in a rhythm, in the way Jesse moved and tasted. There weren't any words left in his brain, except maybe Jesse's name.

They tangled together on the floor, kissing faster and slower, shallow and deep. Jesse's fingers wound through Landon's hair; Landon's fingers found the belt loops of Jesse's jeans. Landon's body seemed to be taking over for his mind more every moment, but nothing his body felt was more powerful than this unfamiliar, incredible joy.

Jesse rolled Landon onto his back, and Landon helped tug Jesse on top of him—but that was the moment the song ended, the moment they heard a woman's voice call, "Jesse?"

"Mom." Eyes wide, Jesse scrambled off Landon about as fast as Landon scrambled out from under him. As footsteps came closer to the door, they both jumped to their feet. Jesse's long T-shirt gave him some coverage, but Landon realized he needed camouflage right away. He flung himself into Jesse's desk chair, scooping up the drowsy cat and depositing her in his lap so Mrs. Pearce wouldn't see just how much fun they'd been having.

When she opened the bedroom door, she suspected nothing. ("Well, I'm glad you kids want to do your best! But isn't it getting late? Jesse, you know you've got swim practice tomorrow morning.") Then they had to say their good-byes quickly, with Mrs. Pearce standing right there, which meant the most incredible first kiss imaginable ended with an awkward wave and a promise to see each other in class tomorrow. Within five minutes, Landon was back outside, walking his bike to the curb, almost shaky from the jolt of panic and arousal together.

He tried burning off the energy by pedaling home fast; the whole way, he composed text messages to Jesse. No two were the same, because he had no idea what to say.

I had fun tonight. No. *Want to "rehearse" again this weekend? ;)* Absolutely no. That was awful. *Sorry if that got weird.* Even worse. Maybe he should try the absolute truth. *All I can think about is what it was like to kiss you.*

Oh, no. Definitely not that. He might as well text, *Hi, my name's Landon, and I'll be your creepy gay stalker this evening.*

As soon as he pulled into his own yard, though, his phone chimed. Landon lifted it to see a text from Jesse: **Quick thinking up there. But my cat might need therapy.**

It would be so easy to laugh. To send back a joke, something else, anything. Instead, he could only stand there staring at the phone.

Another text from Jesse: **See you tomorrow?**

Landon typed, **Yeah, see you then.**

Which was a whole lot less than he wanted to say. So much less than he felt.

But all Landon could think was, *Did I make that happen?*

· · · · ·

Jesse's one study hall had turned out to be the same period as drama class, so ever since he'd been cast, he'd sat in with the rest of them, taking notes as Mrs. K talked about acting as a way of telling the truth, about how finding common feeling between you and your character was a way of being honest in any scene. Landon took these notes too, though lately he'd mostly been writing as though on autopilot while staring at Jesse the whole time.

The morning after their private rehearsal, Jesse came in late—right at the bell. Landon's heart turned over at the sight of him, especially when Jesse smiled at Landon before grabbing a seat in the back. Knowing he didn't deserve that smile made him want to be sick.

Of course, Mrs. K decided this was the perfect day for Landon to give the "Queen Mab" speech as an example of finding emotion in a monologue. Landon had worked hard on the "Queen Mab" speech, but today he hardly felt like he could face his classmates. When he got up to perform, he simply recited the speech, putting no feeling into it whatsoever. But he projected toward the class—even to Jesse, as unforgivable as it was to screw with his mind yet again—the sense that this was pure brilliance.

"'And in this state she gallops night by night.'" *Thump.* "'Through lovers' brains, and then they dream of love.'"

Faking it with his mysterious talent always made him feel like crap. Today, feeling like crap was exactly what he deserved.

When everyone clapped at the end, Landon could only stare at the floor. He couldn't bear to look at any of their faces, Jesse's least of all.

Landon didn't see Jesse again until lunch. Claire was at the orthodontist, so he sat alone at a bench at the far end of the outdoor eating area. He could have texted her (he had thought about it approximately eight zillion times since last night), but he still hadn't figured out what to say. The weather had turned cold enough that most people didn't eat outside any longer. Landon huddled in his jacket and started on his sandwich, hoping to be alone—until Jesse sat down across from him.

"Hey," Jesse said, unpacking one sandwich, and another, and another, plus an apple and an entire quart of milk. "You okay?"

"Uh, yeah." Landon didn't quite know what to say. "Wow. That's a lot of lunch."

"Swimming makes me hungry." Jesse took out a Kit Kat bar. "But I'll split this with you."

Okay, when you went all gooey inside just from somebody offering to break their Kit Kat in half, you had it bad. Landon summoned his courage. "Can I ask you something?"

"Sure."

Landon made certain everybody else eating outside suddenly got really interested in the far side of the quad before he looked Jesse in the eye. "Are you gay?"

Jesse didn't immediately answer. Landon's hopes rose. But Jesse said only, "I don't know."

"What do you mean, you don't know?"

"I'm not trying to make excuses, all right? Or push you away. It's just—I didn't expect this." Jesse sighed and stared at the gray sky for a few moments. "Last year, you know, I was hanging out with this girl—"

"Hannah Silverberg."

"I guess we were kind of obvious about it. Anyway. The thing is, I liked being with Hannah. But last night, with you—I liked that too." Jesse's shy expression felt like it might rip Landon open.

"Yeah. I mean, so did I." But Landon couldn't smile back, knowing this wasn't real.

Jesse continued, "So I'm just not sure. It's kind of scary, because maybe I'm not the person I thought I was. But when we were hanging out, I got less scared. So maybe we could, you know, see if we . . . fit."

Landon couldn't speak. Couldn't meet Jesse's eyes any longer.

More quietly, Jesse said, "I mean, if you want."

It should have been the most amazing moment of Landon's whole life. This incredible guy said he wanted to be with him, the kind of guy Landon had only ever been able to dream about, somebody he'd never have thought would actually like him back. But knowing the real reason for Jesse's feelings—it ruined everything.

By now Jesse knew something was up. He just sat there, looking more and more awkward, until it became unbearable. Nothing was worse than Jesse thinking maybe Landon didn't want him. It was so wrong, so crazy, that it made Landon do something he'd intended never to do in his entire life.

It made him tell the truth.

"You don't really like me," he blurted out. "Not really."

"Yeah, I do."

"No, you don't. I made you like me. I didn't mean to—I swear to God, I never meant to, I wouldn't—but this isn't something you feel. This is something I did."

"You're not making sense."

How could he prove it? Landon looked around at the dozen or so people who were also braving the chill outside. "Okay, watch. All these people are about to decide it's way too cold out here. Maybe they'll go in, maybe they won't, but they're all going to think it's freezing. You'll see."

"What are you—"

"Just watch." Landon went very still as he concentrated completely on his talent. *Thump.* Suddenly people sat up straighter, pulled the necks of their sweaters over their chins, yanked their sleeves down over their fingers. Most of them grabbed what was left of their lunches and headed for the cafeteria; a few simply started eating faster.

Jesse's eyes widened. "What just happened?"

"I made them do that." Landon felt almost dizzy with horror. He was revealing his strangest, most shameful secret, but what other choice did he have? It was one thing to let kids in class think he was a brilliant actor. Making somebody think they wanted to be with a person they didn't want at all—that was evil, like slipping roofies into a girl's drink or something. He wasn't going there, not ever, particularly not with someone as good as Jesse. "I can make people feel what I need them to feel," Landon said. "I always thought it was something I had to do on purpose, but apparently I can do it accidentally. Like I did with you."

"That can't be real. It was just a breeze, or something."

Landon pointed at Coach Pang, who was walking along the sidewalk at the perimeter of the quad. "He's going to decide he's late. I don't even know for what. But he's going to think he needs to get where he's going right away." Almost immediately, Coach Pang jerked his head upright and started jogging toward the gym. Then Landon nodded toward a girl who was eating by herself, a lost expression on her face. "She's going to be in a better mood. She's going to stop letting it bother her, whatever 'it' is." Slowly the girl began to grin as she tore open her bag of chips. "Do you see now?"

"Oh, my God." Jesse said. "Whoa. What did you—you did that. *You did that.*"

"I only try to do good things with it, or at least things that don't matter. Like, I made Mitch leave me alone, you know? Me and some of the other kids they used to push around. I didn't let my parents hate me for being gay. Sometimes I try to cheer people up, stuff like that. And acting class. I can't act. I just do my thing."

Jesse stared at him then. "We were acting last night. I don't mean . . . not when we . . . but during the scene."

Landon breathed out in frustration. "Sometimes I try, yeah. Because I wish I could act for real. And with you, it seemed easy." His throat was starting to tighten. "But I cheat. I make people think I'm awesome when I'm not. Like today? The 'Queen Mab' speech?"

"*That's* why everyone clapped?" Jesse looked confused. "I thought they were being polite."

"What?"

"You weren't acting at all! You just spoke the words. Totally flat. I thought maybe you were distracted. Because of, you know, everything." Jesse's expression was changing to one of total astonishment. The truth was beginning to sink in. "But you did the—made the—you put the mind whammy on everybody. Holy crap."

"Wait. You didn't think it was great?"

"You were *awful*. But nobody else saw it, did they?"

Landon didn't understand. Apparently he had influenced everyone's minds . . . except Jesse's.

If he hadn't bent Jesse's mind today, then maybe he hadn't done it last night, either.

Jesse began repacking his enormous lunch in a hurry. "Okay. Wow. All right. I have to think about this."

"Please don't tell anyone," Landon whispered.

For a moment Jesse went still, his dark eyes meeting Landon's. "I'd never do that to you. Not ever."

That was the moment Landon knew he hadn't messed with Jesse's head at all. Whatever Jesse felt for him was real.

Except that now Jesse was walking away.

Now Jesse knew he was a freak.

. . . . .

So then everything sucked.

Landon basically hid in his room all weekend. Occasionally his phone would chime with a text and his heart would turn over, but it was usually Claire asking him how he was feeling. (He'd pretended to be sick, the only way to tactfully ditch their Saturday plans, a twisted Netflix double feature of *Little Shop of Horrors* and *Sweeney Todd*.) Once it was this girl from his psychology class asking for last week's notes.

It was never Jesse.

At least half a dozen times, Landon nearly broke down and called Claire. It would have felt so good to talk to someone about this—but what could he have said? He'd never told Claire about his talent. He'd been too scared to, and seeing Jesse's reaction to the news wasn't encouraging. No way he could stand losing Jesse and Claire both.

He could just have said that he liked someone but it wasn't working out. But Claire had already noticed his crush, so she would know he meant Jesse. If she realized something had happened between them, then Landon would basically have outed Jesse without his permission. That was incredibly not okay.

So Landon had to lie there alone and try to figure it out for himself.

Was Jesse actually immune to Landon's talent? It was almost a relief to think that his power wasn't, well, all-powerful. If only he could have figured out Jesse wasn't affected in some other way besides revealing his secret: *Hi, I'm a total weirdo out of a science fiction movie, so maybe you should run really fast in the other direction* right now.

Sunday morning was the worst. Landon had never used his talent in church; it felt sacrilegious, the kind of thing that would get you struck by lightning. This meant a lot of people there felt about him the way his parents would've felt if he hadn't given them what Jesse had called the "mind whammy." Every single Sunday, he could feel the rest of the congregation staring at him, their eyes boring through his back. Not everybody there knew he was gay—but enough of them did, and most of the ones who knew weren't okay with it, not by a long shot. Landon was able to keep persuading his parents, but he couldn't keep going around town convincing everyone all the time that his sexuality was just awesome. It was a bleak reminder of the limits of his talent.

But seeing what he *couldn't* do wasn't the worst part. The worst part was when his mother smiled at him, or his dad put his arm around Landon's shoulders. It was when he saw exactly what he *could* do.

That was when he had to remember they only loved him because he'd made them do it.

. . . . .

Monday's rehearsal included his death scene. Which meant he'd be staring Jesse in the face all day. *Great.*

By coming in late and spending plenty of time talking to Mrs. K, Landon managed to avoid Jesse until the rehearsal itself. He'd never felt more exposed than he did standing in the auditorium in front of hundreds of empty seats, on a bare stage, waiting for Tybalt's entrance.

And he'd thought he felt as bad as he could feel until the moment Jesse walked out, so handsome and yet so remote, and Landon couldn't even believe he'd been able to touch him, or that he'd never get the chance again.

But Jesse looked right into Landon's eyes as he spoke: "'A word with one of you.'"

Is he playing it the way we practiced it? Like he knows I want him and doesn't know what to do? He is.

So Landon put all his longing and shattered hopes into his next line: "'And but one word with one of us? Couple it with something; make it a word and a blow.'"

When the fight began, their wooden swords smashed against each other with real force. Landon stumbled back, genuinely startled, and Jesse seemed to be equally surprised . . . even as Sean Pryor moved between them as Romeo, and Jesse stabbed his sword beneath Sean's arm, against Landon's side.

The force wasn't any harder than it should have been; their stage-fighting workshops had paid off. But Landon crumpled immediately, like there were no bones left in his legs. It was as if he let his despair drag him down.

Then it was his death scene, his biggest moment in the play, and for once, Landon knew he didn't have to project anything for anyone else to feel. He didn't even have to act.

"'A plague on both your houses!'" he said, his voice weak with strain. Though the stage directions called for Tybalt to go offstage, Mrs. K had blocked it out so that instead Jesse stood at the far corner of the fray, as if being held back by his friends. Landon forced himself to focus on Sean-as-Romeo instead. "'They have made worms' meat of me. I have it, and soundly too. Your houses!'"

With that, Landon let his head drop back onto the floor. For the rest of the scene, he'd just lie here and try to look dead. Should be easy. He felt dead.

Tybalt challenged Romeo. Romeo, maddened with grief for his friend, struck back. Within moments, Jesse fell to the ground by Landon's side. He was so close—but Landon didn't dare open his eyes to see.

"'O! I am Fortune's fool!'" Sean shouted.

"And scene!" Mrs. K started the applause, but then the whole class went nuts from the wings. Landon sat up, Jesse beside him, neither of them looking at one another. "Guys, that was fantastic! Landon, with you, I expect the best. But Jesse—who knew?"

"Landon's helped me," Jesse said quietly. "We've been practicing."

"It shows." Mrs. K patted Landon's shoulder. "That fight isn't just two guys acting out. It's personal. It's powerful. And frankly, it raises the bar for all the rest of you. Tybalt's reaction when Mercutio dies—you feel real pain there, real horror at the consequences of his actions."

Landon couldn't help imagining what Jesse's face must have looked like, or wondering what emotions had been behind it.

Mrs. K finished, "Romeo, Juliet, if you don't want to get outshone, you'd better get cracking."

Sean glared, but Claire grinned at Landon; she mouthed the word *Yay!* His heart ached to see her so guilelessly happy to see him praised in front of the class, so completely unaware of his secret misery about Jesse. She was his one true friend, the one person he never had to doubt. Landon had come out to her before anyone else, and months before he'd discovered his talent. He'd kept his talent a secret from her, but he'd always believed it was absolutely the only thing he couldn't tell Claire. Apparently he'd been wrong, because now he couldn't tell her about Jesse either—it wasn't his secret alone to share.

Jesse still sat next to him, breathing hard from the fight, not looking in Landon's direction.

But as the bell rang, Jesse said, "Want to cut?"

"Sure."

They hung around backstage as everyone else filtered out, Mrs. K included. Finally they were alone, sitting behind the old red velvet drapes—so old the color was starting to change, worn pink in some places, stained dark in others. Landon kept rubbing a fold of the curtains with his finger, still unwilling to meet Jesse's eyes.

Landon managed to ask, "You get sad when Mercutio dies?"

"Yeah. Right then, I realize that I hurt you. That I really hurt you. None of it was real before that." They finally looked at each other then, and Landon knew even if he'd lost Jesse as a potential—whatever he might have been—Jesse at least didn't hate him. "You were great, by the way. You really went for it. None of the—you know."

"I didn't do it that time."

"I was thinking about that all weekend. The thing you do. Your—"

"Talent." That was the least scary word for it Landon had ever been able to come up with.

"Okay. Your talent. I kept thinking about how you used it to be an actor."

"You mean, how I cheated."

But Jesse shook his head. "That's not what I meant. You have this talent, and you could mess with people's heads all the time. Most people's anyway, apparently not mine."

"No. Not that I ever tried to mess with your head," Landon hastily added. "Except with acting. Not ever besides that, I swear."

"I know. Because, Landon—do you realize how the average person would behave if they figured out they had that talent? They'd manipulate everyone. They'd screw with everybody's head to get whatever they wanted. But not you." Slowly, Jesse started to smile. "You only got people off your back, when they shouldn't have been giving you a hard time to start with. And you made things easier for other people who were getting picked on too. You wanted to act, to make people enjoy themselves. You were so scared you might have made me like you that you told me the biggest secret you had. The biggest secret anyone ever had, probably. Just to protect me."

Landon had never looked at it this way. Like he shouldn't feel ashamed—like instead he had something to be proud of. "I never wanted to hurt anybody. Least of all you."

Jesse didn't acknowledge that, but he stretched out his legs so that once again their feet brushed against each other. For a little while they were quiet together, and something painfully tight around Landon's chest began to loosen so he could again breathe free.

Finally Landon said, "Do you have any idea why it doesn't affect you? My talent, I mean."

"No clue. It's not like it would have come up before."

"So you're not, like, the seventh son of a seventh son, or part of a secret necromancers' guild?" When Jesse laughed, Landon could too. "This isn't the part where you tell me only I can open the Magic Portal of the Something?"

"That comes later." Jesse's foot thumped against Landon's. "I always knew you didn't force me to like you."

"Even though I'm the first guy you ever—wait. I am the first guy, right?"

"Yeah. You are." By now Jesse looked almost bashful. "But I might have noticed you before we started going over lines together."

"Oh, really?"

"Maybe during tryouts," he confessed. "You were so . . . alive up there. Having fun."

"I love being onstage. I just wish I could act for real."

"But you can. Come on, Landon! Today, during your death scene, you were in the moment, like Mrs. K says. That wasn't fake. That was genuine."

It was like a tiny candle inside Landon flickering into flame. "I guess."

"You told me you study other actors' performances. And you try to do the things they do. That's acting, right?"

"Yeah. But I always thought, because I used my talent too, that it . . . didn't count."

"I don't see why you shouldn't use it as, like, extra," Jesse said. Landon must have looked astonished, because Jesse shrugged. "Talent is talent, right? But you should learn how to act without always leaning on your more, uh, unconventional ability."

"Because it's more honest."

"Yeah. You know, every time I can tell I'm doing it right onstage, it's not because I'm pretending to be Tybalt. It's because I'm not pretending at all." Jesse paused, obviously trying to find the words to say something difficult. "I know what it's like to have people expect everything of you, and not to know whether there's anything you could ever do that would get them off your back. So when I say Tybalt's lines, I'm telling the truth for the first time. That's what I never got about acting before I tried it. That it's a way to be completely honest instead of being fake."

Maybe that was why Landon had always felt so awful about using his talent onstage. Because he'd been using it to get away with a lie he was telling himself.

Landon let his hand rest on Jesse's calf, and when Jesse didn't pull away—when, instead, he smiled—Landon hadn't known he could be that happy and have it last. "Does this mean we can figure things out together?"

Jesse's voice was warm now, sleepy but not sleepy. "What kind of things?"

"Whether you're gay, or bi, or Landonsexual, whatever." That made Jesse laugh, so Landon kept going. "If we fit."

"We fit." Jesse leaned closer.

Their lips met again, and this kiss was better than all the others put together, because Landon knew this one was real.

. . . . .

As he walked into his house after school, Landon started imagining how it would go. Claire was coming by later, so he'd make her swear every promise in the book, and then he'd tell her about him and Jesse, and—oh, she'd be bouncing off the walls. No, no, first he had to make her drink a Coke Zero. Or they should get coffee. No, espresso! It would be like shaking a bottle of pop before opening it.

Then it hit him: Should he tell Claire about his talent too? If Jesse could accept it, maybe she could as well.

I'll think about it, Landon decided. *But for today, learning about Jesse and me is a big enough surprise. I don't want Claire to actually* explode.

"Landon?" His mother had a late shift at the pharmacy today. When that happened, she was usually going out as he came in. "There's lasagna in the fridge for dinner. You just need to put it in the oven."

"Bake at three seventy-five for thirty minutes. I know. Thanks, Mom."

"You look like you're in a good mood. Anything exciting happen at school today?" She stood there at the door, all hopeful in her uniform smock. This was the part where he normally said nothing had happened— but today something had. And he wanted to tell her about it.

He wanted to find out how she'd really react.

Landon took a deep breath. "There's a guy I've been spending time with. We're—hanging out, I guess."

"A new friend, you mean?"

"Like, a boyfriend."

It took every bit of his courage, but he didn't smooth it over. Didn't use his power. It was past time for him to face what his parents really felt.

But Mom smiled. It was awkward, and a little unsure, but a smile all the same. "Yeah?"

"Yeah."

"Do you really like him?" He nodded. She said, "Does he like you back?"

"Yeah. He does." Landon kept waiting for the sky to fall. Maybe she was just in shock.

Instead she patted his shoulder. "Then, well, good. That's good."

He had to swallow hard. "All right."

It wasn't the plastic, ever-ready happiness he'd made them feel every time before. But it wasn't hate, either. If he hadn't used his talent, maybe Mom and Dad wouldn't have taken it as easily when he first came out, but it would have been okay.

Jesse had been right about his talent. It wasn't the only way he could get through the world. It was just . . . extra.

Landon had never thought about enjoying his talent before. About trusting it, or himself.

But if he thought of it as trusting Jesse, and what Jesse saw in him, then maybe he could give it a try.

....

ANECDOTE: GAVIN LEE

....

It all started on a chilly February afternoon in 1983. It was a Sunday, and I was eleven years old.

I had been involved in community theater in my little hometown of Woodbridge, England, for a couple of years and was taking tap and disco dancing classes. Hey, it was the '80s!

I heard a commercial on the radio for an audition, in London, for a brand-new show opening on the West End based on the film *Bugsy Malone*—which had made a child star of Jodie Foster. This was one of my favorite films: a 1920s gangster musical with the entire cast being played by kids. Sounds cool, right? I begged my mum and dad to take me, but there was a wrinkle in that plan.

The audition was on the same Sunday as my community theater's dress rehearsal for *Dick Whittington*. I was playing the park of Idle Jack, and it was my first speaking role. How could I miss this rehearsal? Well, my dad secretly arranged with the director that we could leave early—at 4:00—so that I could make the audition. I couldn't believe my luck!

Now the audition was in Earls Court, West London, and we lived about two hours from there. I remember my dad usually being a safe, sensible driver but that day he sped down the highway and straight through central London like a maniac. It was as if we were on *The Amazing Race* and had to win!

We parked and ran, sweating, to the audition building and literally bashed into the front door—it was locked. It was 6:05 p.m. We watched as the doorman took down the BUGSY AUDITIONS, 10–6, THIS WAY sign. My dad and I told him our situation, we did a bit of groveling, and eventually he let us in.

I was the last kid to audition for the day. My name was put on a card and pinned to my chest, and I was shoved into a room with the last group of forty kids, where we were all taught a pretty easy dance combination. The director and choreographer came in, and we did the routine another three times—then we all got a green, yellow, or red sticker placed on our card. We stood in a large circle and all sang "Happy Birthday" in unison as two guys listened closely to us sing—again, another sticker was put on each of our cards.

I later learned the "traffic light" scoring system. Red = *Stop* (and go home. Fine job but this isn't the show for you). Yellow = *Okay* (let's try this again). Green = *Go* (onto the next audition). Thankfully I had two green stickers, woo-hoo!

Ten thousand kids auditioned that day, and every single one of us left with a badge that said I AUDITIONED FOR "BUGSY MALONE" and a Snickers bar. But more important than a badge and a candy bar, some of us left with callbacks too.

Over the next three weeks, I had two more trips to London. The auditions got harder, especially the tap combinations. The final callback was at the Globe Theatre on Shaftesbury Avenue in the West End. There were about 150 of us left. I was so nervous that I wouldn't do the tap combination well that I plucked up the courage to go up to Gillian Gregory, the choreographer, after my name was called. I told her that she had made a mistake and that I wasn't "a tapper." I didn't want to be embarrassed by dancing badly in front of the other kids.

She looked, confused, at her notes and said, Okay, wait for the "non-tapper" routine. Then I sat in the auditorium watching the other boys learn and perform *the easiest tap routine ever!*

I very nearly cried. I could do *this* routine—should I just run up onto the stage and join in? What to do? What to do?!

In the end, I sat it out and just knew I had to do a good job for the rest of the day.

After a full hyper-nervous day of auditioning and being switched into different groups, all of us were tired. We were finally told to sit in the auditorium and wait.

After what seemed like a lifetime of nail biting, the creative team finally came back to the stage from their decision-making meeting. The energy and tension in the theater could have powered the city of London.

They told us how amazing we all had done. We thought, "yeah, yeah, but who got the job?" Then they said, "We are casting four separate companies of kids to appear in the show throughout the first year, and each of you will be appearing in one of those casts!"

Wait? You mean, we all got the job?

I think the roof of the theater actually lifted off! We screamed and cheered as all of our nerves were released. It was the loudest, most joyous sound I'd ever heard.

Then the producer said, "We are now going to announce the forty-eight of you that we would like to be the very first opening cast." Suddenly the silence, tension, and nerves were back in the auditorium. Of course we *all* wanted this icing on the cake.

I was a lucky, lucky lad that day. Just four weeks later, my mum and dad were dropping me off at the Holiday Inn at Marble Arch, where I met my fellow, opening castmates for the first time. This was where we would stay during rehearsals. I shared a room with three other kids, and it became our home away from home.

The next four months were full of brilliant new experiences from fittings for tailor-made costumes, fancy new haircuts, tech runs on dangerous giant, moving sets, opening night parties, television specials, and standing ovations.

For most of us this was our first and only experience as professional performers. Every single moment from that first nervous dance call to the bows after our final show (picture a stage full of kids blubbering hysterically) made me realize *this is it*. This was what I had to do when I grew up! And I'm so, so lucky to have been able to make a living following my ambitious dream.

GAVIN LEE originated the role of Bert in the London production of *Mary Poppins*, for which he was Olivier Award–nominated. He went on to play the role on Broadway, for which he received Drama Desk and Theatre World Awards as well as a Tony Award nomination. While in New York City, Gavin has appeared at Carnegie Hall in *Show Boat* and, on TV, guest starred in *Law & Order: SVU* and *The Good Wife*. His other London credits include *Crazy for You*, *Peggy Sue Got Married*, *Me and My Girl*, *Over My Shoulder*, *Oklahoma!*, *Contact*, and *Top Hat*. His regional theater credits include *Singin' in the Rain*, *Snoopy*, Noël Coward's *Masterpieces*, *Of Thee I Sing*, *Saturday Night*, Alan Ayckbourn's *Whenever,* and *Chicago*.

OTHER LIFE

Garret Freymann-Weyr

When Megan Walker was trying to survive being young, she spent almost three years as a moderately successful model and actress.

Megan had landed her first job at twelve, when a woman named Erika Bauer, who was from her mother's other life, visited New York. She lived in Berlin (almost everyone from the other life lived in Europe) and had come to the States to shoot an ad campaign for a couture label, which had been taken over by a luxury conglomerate. Erika had been hired to reintroduce the label by using one of the models from its old advertisements and Megan's mother was the one chosen. Back when her name was Lena Legarde instead of Lena Walker, her mother had been a very successful model referred to in the trades as *High Fashion's Movie Star*. Megan often thought of Lena's other life as an old and valuable fur coat, wrapped in tissue paper and put away.

It was always exciting and confusing when anyone from the other life appeared, making Lena's daughters and husband remember this precious, unworn garment. This time, however, the talk turned to actually using it. There were new technologies, Erika Bauer told them when she came to the apartment for drinks. She could manipulate old photos and blend them in a way that had once been a dark room trick, but was now quite simple.

Megan's father was uncharacteristically quiet, just listening to Erika talk. Lena sipped at her wine, her usual half smile in place; it was always impossible to tell what she was thinking. Megan's sister sat without moving, a sign that Liv was bored.

Trying not to stare at Erika, Megan instead studied her family and made herself useful by passing the cheese plate. Erika was the first woman Megan had ever seen whose face suggested that beauty could look more like strength than adornment. Erika's body was long and spare, and her big hands moved in rhythm with her talking so that it looked as if two large birds were fluttering all around her.

"I take it that this is not exactly a social call," Jesse Walker finally said, surprising his daughters by the hardness in his voice and eyes.

Normally Jesse loved having guests, lavishing them with welcome.

"No, not entirely," Erika said.

"Lena said that would be the case," their father said, as if their mother weren't sitting right next to him and perfectly capable of speaking for herself.

"Did she?" Erika asked.

"Either way, I am delighted for the chance to see you," Lena said finally. "Of course."

"As am I," Erika said, the back of her hand briefly brushing against Megan's as she accepted another piece of Port Salut. "Of course."

If she hadn't been holding the tray, Megan would have snatched her hand away. Touching Erika was as surprising as winter's static electricity, which flew off of door handles and people's cold fingers. Except that Erika's skin was warm and made Megan super aware of her own. It wasn't unpleasant but it was still a shock.

"Tell me, how is Stéphanie?" Lena asked.

Stéphanie, it turned out, was Erika's friend (or roommate, it wasn't clear) and a former model who was now a fabric designer. Megan always loved to hear about women who had once worked with her mother. She wondered if this Stéphanie also had a box like the big leather hat box which Lena kept under the bed. In it were eleven magazine covers, sixty-seven print ads, and endless pictures of her modeling all manner of clothes, walking down runways.

Megan and Liv understood that their mother, though no longer famous for it, was still seriously beautiful. They could see it in the way people—not only men—were almost stunned into a silent appreciation. The odd part, for Megan at least, was how Lena didn't even notice. Whenever mention of her fame arose, Lena would always say, "Briefly famous. And for such a silly thing."

While Erika and Lena spoke about what had convinced Stéphanie to move from Paris to Berlin ("Lord knows, it wasn't me," Erika said, citing a job offer with more creative control), Megan remembered the time she'd asked her mother what it felt like to be beautiful.

"It's like having a Siamese twin," Lena had said. "You don't love walking through life joined to this other being, but . . . it's part of how you live."

"I have the old negatives of you from that campaign," Erika was saying. "The agency wants to use the ones from Rome."

"The spring collection," Lena said. "Yes, that makes sense."

Liv arched her neck while flexing and pointing her feet, indicating that she was well past bored and was now irritated. Liv, who spent most of her waking hours at ballet class, knew a lot about how to plié, but wasn't interested in much else. Megan had seen her sister dance professionally many times, in awe of how the years of hard work turned to magic on the stage, but being bored as much as Liv was seemed too high a price to pay for art.

Or magic.

"I have an idea that the company loves," Erika said, slowly dragging out her words. "I would like to shoot you with your daughters."

Megan thought that Erika was studying Liv. Everyone always looked at Liv, whose body practically shrieked, *Soon, I will be a prima ballerina.* Megan felt that she had, over the years, learned a lot by watching people look at both her mother and her sister.

"Would you," Lena said. It was not a question.

"Absolutely not," Jesse said, in his I-am-the-Dean-of-Faculty-and-I-know-best voice.

"Darling, it's up to the girls," Lena said, looking at her daughters as if seeing them for the first time.

It often seemed to Megan that her mother was surprised by who she and Liv were. It was as if Lena were forever meeting them for the first time. Sometimes she was clearly pleased to know them—but not always.

"I'm a dancer, not a model," Liv said, her voice dripping with disdain.

Liv was fifteen and viewed everything about her mother as being beneath contempt. Megan could never understand how her graceful and talented sister didn't see how she too was walking through life with almost the same Siamese twin as their mother's.

Most of the time, Megan was content not to have a similar burden. It was true that people often remarked that Megan was beautiful, but she thought they were probably being polite. Her face and body each had nice bits, but there was nothing about either that would make her famous.

"Thank God you have some sense," Jesse said to Liv.

"You always say I have no sense," Liv reminded her father.

Jesse did not think much of his eldest daughter, who tested through the roof, wanting to become a dancer. Even though the director of Liv's school said fame was waiting in the wings for her and it was clear that she loved it, their father stayed focused on how a dancer's fame was fleeting.

"Today you do," Jesse said, and then to Lena, "This is a bad idea."

Lena, her half smile firmly in place, shrugged lightly. It was the great and infuriating thing about Lena; she rarely got upset or overly involved in family decisions (from what to eat to where they spent vacations). Megan could never tell if her mother didn't care what any of them did or if she simply found their deliberations pointless.

"It might be, but it's not my idea or my decision," Lena told Jesse. "Neither is it yours."

Watching Erika listen to her parents, Megan wondered what it would be like to watch people who were looking, for once, at her. She thought she might see herself in a new way. She had not yet had her growth spurt and was, as far as she could tell, hopelessly ordinary while also being unlike anybody else at her small, private school.

"I think we should say no," her father said calmly, as if perhaps Lena had mistaken his displeasure with the idea for agreement.

In a month, Megan would enter seventh grade, and was more interested in horses than boys. Her uncle owned a farm in North Carolina, and Megan loved taking care of his horses, mucking out the stalls, and cleaning their hooves with the sort of enthusiasm with which smart kids played chess and superpopular ones listened to music. She had friends (she belonged to a mildly popular group that held bake sales, got involved in Yearbook, and handed in homework on time), but Megan knew she had no real desire to spend time with any of them.

"Yes, you have been clear on that," Lena said. "Nevertheless, it's up to the girls."

Of course, none of the facts she could point to (loving horses or being neither an overly smart kid or a superpopular one) explained how deeply odd she knew herself to be.

"I'll do it," Megan said, unable to stay in her thoughts any longer.

Surely a camera held by the unusually beautiful Erika Bauer would produce a photo that would show how she belonged, not just to her family, but in the world.

"No," her father said, as if her wishes didn't matter. "You will not."

"But I want to," she told him, scrambling for a reason that wouldn't reveal anything too embarrassing. "I've always liked hearing about Mum's other life and this way I could see it for myself."

This, at least, was true. She was curious about what a photo shoot was like.

"Models are stupid," Liv said, rather pointedly looking at their mother.

"Beauty is a form of genius," Megan shot back, not sure where she had heard that, but fairly certain someone important had said it.

"I doubt Oscar Wilde had clothes and silly pictures in mind when he wrote that," Jesse Walker said.

Erika Bauer laughed, a rich sound that traveled right into Megan's bones. She looked at Megan as if she were seeing through her. As if Jesse had not spoken and as if neither Lena nor Liv were of any importance to her.

"If your father will let me," Erika said, "I will turn you into a genius."

. . . . .

Megan did not turn into a genius, but a photo of her and Lena made to look as if they were sitting at a café table in Rome sharing a coffee with the Lena of twenty years ago ran as a two-page spread in a lot of magazines. The campaign was written up in one of the city's daily papers, and that was how Megan got a manager.

Her uncle told her that the horses would wait for her until *all this silly business blew over*. Jesse, still dead set against it all, insisted that Megan promise to quit the minute her grades fell.

"And you need to take typing," he said. "Every actress has a second job."

"Okay, I'll take typing," she said, trying not to laugh.

A second job? She barely had a first.

"And we're going to the theater more often," he said. "There's no point in having you grow up thinking actors only work in front of a camera."

Megan nodded. Sure. She had always loved everything about going to the theater. The seats that looked comfortable but weren't, the silent darkness that held stories, costumes, people, sets, and light that pooled on the stage and bounced off the actors, making them pale but also very alive.

"And don't think that just because Erika gave you that absurd camera that you know a thing about photography."

Megan nodded again. She and her father had been over this many times, starting when Erika, before flying home to Berlin, had a well-padded package delivered to the apartment with a note: *Dear Megan, I enjoyed your curiosity. May this be of use to a fellow traveler through all that is strange and beautiful, EB.* Inside, surrounded by bubble wrap, had been a camera. A Minolta XD-11, Megan learned, studying the almost incomprehensible instruction booklet that read as if it had been translated one too many times.

Jesse had wanted Megan to give it back, saying a twelve-year-old girl couldn't possibly use such an expensive camera.

"What could Erika be thinking to spend so much money on a child?" he asked Lena.

"I'm sure the camera company gave it to her," she told him. "For what she does, she's very famous, and she is always being sent equipment to try."

"Her camera is one that there were only nine thousand made," Megan told her father, having found during the shoot that the best way to spend time with Erika, instead of the hair and makeup people who flocked to Lena, was to ask a lot of questions. "She said that the best way to become a photographer is to pay attention to what you see."

"Of course she did," Jesse said. "You are not to take that thing all around the city or to and from school. You'll get mugged or you'll lose it."

Megan said yes, okay, she would use it on weekends and pay attention on other days. She would have agreed to anything if it meant she had a chance to be one of Erika's *fellow travelers*. Whatever that meant.

. . . . .

The manager, whose voice sounded like it was two octaves too low for her, sent Megan all over the city to meet with people. After school, when her classmates had tutoring, music lessons, or some sort of athletic practice, Megan had auditions, go-sees, and every now and then, callbacks. The auditions were for the acting part of her career. She would read from a script and make smalltalk with a casting agent or director. The go-sees were the same as auditions, but for modeling jobs. She didn't have to read a script, but had to make awkward smalltalk while being stared at by casting agents, magazine editors, art directors, or catalog houses.

Casting agents were a nuisance, as it was their job to figure out why you weren't good enough to be hired, but they were, her manager said, important people to impress. Megan had heard a rumor that casting agents knew of *every single* actor and model in the city. Sometimes Jesse would take a train home in time to meet Megan in the lobby of whatever building her audition was in, but most of the time she went by herself.

Eventually, it all became routine. At auditions, she signed in, handed over her headshot, and waited. Go-sees were boring and the most anyone asked her to do was walk up and down or turn this way and that. She preferred being asked to *do* something, even if it was only reading from a script. Jesse not only took her to a lot of theater (they even went to Brooklyn to see the Royal Shakespeare Company perform *Richard II*), but she signed up for an acting class that met on Saturday mornings at the Neighborhood Playhouse on East 54th Street. There she learned how to break down a script, identify motive, and establish character.

The other students were either other actress-models or older teenagers hoping to get into Juilliard. Megan felt somewhat fraudulent in a room full of such seriously ambitious kids, but she loved the class. It gave her hope that if she simply worked harder, she'd do better at her auditions. And if she didn't get a job after an audition, at least the decision was partly based on something other than her looks.

She could still go to the theater with her father and to acting class no matter what happened at auditions. Not getting a job after a go-see felt awful since it was entirely based on what she was—her height, shape, face, hair. When she told her manager she only wanted to be sent out for acting jobs, the woman said,

"Honey, you've got height now, you're flat, and your face has good bones, are you sure?"

Megan was sure. She knew she was tall, she was indifferent to her bra size, and her face's bones, no matter how good, would never rival the perfection of her mother's. She shed the modeling part of her career and turned toward acting and theater with more care. Even though she was unsure about wanting to perform, she continued chasing the possibility that she would find a way to see herself through the process of other people seeing her.

For a year or two, she got enough work, and the money went into her college fund, making it all seem worthwhile. She kept mementos of auditions, slipping them into her schoolbag on the way out. She'd save a page of the script, some girl's discarded headshot, or simply a note she had written to herself describing one of the other girls waiting to audition. She told herself that it was a way to pay attention to what she saw, good training for when she did use the camera (very carefully and only of her family or certain favorite parts of Central Park).

Her father said a real photographer developed her own photos, but that the ones she was taking had *real coherence of image* and were *not at all terrible*. Megan knew he meant it as a compliment, but she wished she could take the camera to auditions and record what she saw at them, instead of collecting bits and writing herself notes.

Long fingers, does she play piano? A note might ask. Or one would say, *Wavy hair, green eyes, hoop earrings.* Megan stashed the notes, the saved headshots, and script sheets in a file that she kept in her locked desk drawer. The key was in an old pair of socks.

She knew there was something more than private in the way she hid the file, something furtive, only she wasn't sure why her collection made her feel so guilty and anxious. Maybe, she reasoned, it was because it held evidence of how little she was like the other girls auditioning for the same part.

In the waiting rooms, Megan gave the men a cursory look, but intensely examined the women and the other girls, perhaps hoping to discover what she herself must clearly lack. Not just as an actress, but as a girl.

At school, Megan had a much better sense of why she didn't fit in with the girls who giggled, tossed their hair, and used the words *so gay* and *lame* as if they were weapons. Those were the girls whom the cool boys in eleventh and twelfth grade wanted to spend time with and date. Megan had friends who were boys in both of those grades, but they were not the boys you dated. Even if you had wanted to, they were busy doing things (like studying chess or prepping for debate club), not hanging out being cool.

At Megan's school, no one had to be cool to be popular, which was, Liv liked to say, lucky.

For the most part, Megan understood life at school and where she belonged in it. Auditions were much harder to gauge, and during the last six months of her career, there were no jobs and almost no callbacks. Casting agents were forever talking about her appearance, as if she were at a go-see. If it hadn't been for the times she met with directors, Megan probably would have told her manager she was quitting.

Directors asked questions that she answered with a great deal of care, as if they were guests at her parents' dinner parties instead of men asking her to read from a script, saying, *Go ahead, I'll read with you. Gabe here is just going to tape it.* Casting agents, on the other hand, looked from her to the headshot and sighed, saying, *You grew.* She was, they said, too tall for how very young she looked. The directors never commented on her appearance, content just to chat.

They listened to her talk about school, laughed at her various trials and tribulations with homework. Sometimes directors had seen the print ad Megan was in with her mother and therefore put together who her mother was, but if so, they always asked about Lena Legarde very nicely. As if the connection made Megan an old friend instead of the puzzling offspring of a woman famous for her beauty.

"God, I haven't read a book in years," the director of a movie about eight orphans in Kansas said, after Megan told him her English teacher's obsession with *Great Expectations.* "All I ever look at are scripts."

"Well, that's part of your job," she said politely, feeling somewhat triumphant that she was always reading a book and not only as part of her homework.

"You realize, don't you," the director said, "that girls like you grow up to be women who don't know what a novel is."

Megan was reading for the part of the sixteen-year-old orphan whose first boyfriend is the son of a bank officer intent on repossessing the home where the orphans lived. She'd gone to the first audition to read for the twelve-year-old tomboy orphan, but had been found wanting.

"Too tall," the casting agents had said when she read for the tomboy. "But she should come back and read for the older girl. Hal might love her look for that part."

So for this callback, in an attempt to look as old as she was tall, Megan had blown-dry her hair and used mascara. She did not ask Hal (the directors always went by their first names) what he thought of her look, but she read for the part, relieved not to be in a room with casting people. It wasn't until she was on the M10 bus home that she thought to wonder what sort of a woman didn't know what a novel was.

· · · · ·

One night late in October, Megan's manager called. The casting people whom she'd seen the day before (and who had not mentioned her height) thought she might be a good fit for the daughter of the lead actress in a sequel to a movie about a football-playing detective. The callback was for tomorrow at four. Megan wrote down the name and address—it was a building on Broadway in the 40s that she had already been to many times.

As descriptions went, *daughter of the lead actress* didn't offer a lot of clues about what they were looking for. To auditions that might matter, Megan tended to opt for a pair of jeans that had cost an obscene amount of money, but which Lena had said made her legs look long and shapely instead of just long. But they were in the laundry so she pulled out a favorite black skirt that was sprigged with green flowers and had flounces and lace. She had a scoop-neck sweater that matched the green of the flowers, and with a pair of flat shoes and black tights, all that was left to worry about was her hair.

Megan could never tell if she looked older with her hair up or down, so she usually compromised by pulling the top part back into a barrette so that all of it hung down her back. She aimed for neat, but curly hair had a way of doing what it wanted and she had long since made peace with the fact that it would never look like her mother's.

Even before reading the scene, Megan knew she wouldn't get the part. The waiting room was full of girls auditioning for the daughter, and they each looked like perfect, delicately formed versions of a type. Half of them were short and curvy (and dressed in short skirts and plunging necklines) and the other half were tall and willowy (and dressed as if their jeans and sporty tops had been ironed onto them). Nevertheless, she signed in, handed over her headshot, and got the pages she would be reading from.

As she had guessed, the daughter was described in ways that might as well have said NOT MEGAN WALKER. After familiarizing herself with her lines, Megan began her usual study of the other girls. She let her eyes wander from the bare knees of the girls looking to play the daughter as a vixen to the covered shoulders of the ones looking to play her as a tomboy.

One girl stood out from the others, keeping a hold on Megan's attention. Her hair was as neat, straight, and gleaming as the rest, but it was cut short in such a severe way that it made the girl incredibly pretty. Her thinness was not like Liv's (delicate, graceful, commanding). Instead, her body (lean, strong, elegant) made Megan think of Erika Bauer's hands. It was ridiculous that they were auditioning for the same part.

She wished she had the nerve to switch seats and see what color eyes the other girl had. Instead, she wrote, *Sharp, clean, thin*, on a folded piece of notebook paper that she stuffed into her bag.

Eventually, well after the girl had gone in for her audition and left, Megan's name was called. She picked up her schoolbag, jacket, and script and went into the usual sort of room. In it was a table with two men sitting behind it, a couple of empty chairs, and, in the corner, a big, black camera balanced on a sturdy tripod.

Megan smiled at them and started to answer their questions (school, had she enjoyed shooting the pilot, what did she do for fun) when she thought about the girl in the waiting room. That girl had stood exactly here and done the same thing Megan was doing. In fact, all afternoon, girls would smile and chat and read and for what? The chance to play a character with no name, but described as, *Coltish, sullen, blooming.*

"This is silly. I'm not what you're looking for," she said, not wanting to point it out, but unable not to speak. "I'll read and you'll tape me, but it's pointless. I'm not it."

The man who had been asking the questions (he'd said his name was Steve. Or was it Mark?) started to laugh, saying, *That's a new one.* He also turned to the other man and said, *She's telling us that she's not it.*

Megan realized what she must have known for months or years since the first time she'd seen what was inside Lena's hat box. That what everyone was always looking for was an *it.*

"So let me ask you, um," Steve/Mark looked down at the papers on the table. "Megan, let me ask you, how did you get into this business?"

She had a simple answer to this question and it had the advantage of being true, but mentioning her mother and Erika in front of a director was not something she had ever willingly done. She thought of telling him why she liked her acting class and going to the theater (her father had taken her to see O'Neill's *Ah, Wilderness* the previous weekend). She thought of saying, *I love to watch acting. I love how a character made of words is turned into a living, breathing person with gesture, posture, and clothes. I love being part of the magic, even if it's only by watching.*

But Megan realized that her love of plays and of the intense, focused energy in her class was not something to be used as a lie. It was its own truth, and so she told them about Erika Bauer, her mother, and the ad campaign.

"That was you? I saw that ad fifty times," Steve/Mark said. "I must have only been looking at Lena. I couldn't believe how great she still looked."

"Yes," Megan said. "My mother is very beautiful."

"As are you," Steve/Mark said somewhat perfunctorily. "And you're smart. You're right, you're not it, but that's just because I'm looking for a type."

"Okay," Megan said, relieved to hear him confirm what she thought. "Thank you."

She was not a type. Whatever else was wrong with her, it was not that.

"Don't run out of here yet," Steve/Mark said, writing on the back of one the script sheets. "A friend of mine is in town. He's at the Chelsea, seeing girls. I've read his script. He's looking for a face. A real face, but a beautiful one."

"Jesus, Mark, you can't just send her all over town," the other man said. "If it's not an open audition, she breaks a ton of union rules going without an appointment."

"As soon as she leaves here, I'm going to put a call in to her manager and to Tomas."

Mark handed Megan the paper he'd written on.

"Tomas Grudnik is the real deal," he said, pronouncing it as *Tomash Groodnick*. "He only comes to the States for funding and casting."

"Thank you," Megan said, fairly certain that going to a hotel between 7th and 8th Avenues to meet a man that her manager hadn't talked to was a bad idea.

One she couldn't wait to do, and she left the room without responding to Mark's *Good luck*.

. . . . .

Tomas Grudnik answered the door himself, even though there were two other people in the room, women he introduced as his assistants. They were packing up a video camera and a folding table. Tomas was tired-looking with lines etched into his face and wearing glasses. He was delicate looking, but still weirdly handsome.

She handed him her headshot, smiled at the assistants as they said good-bye, and sat on the edge of the couch in the hotel suite's front room. This was it. She was alone with a strange man in a hotel room. Jesse would not be coming to pick her up, and if he knew where she was right now, he would have a fit.

Tomas asked her if she wanted anything to drink and she shook her head no, asking, "Is there a script? Do you want me to wait outside and knock when I've read it?"

"No, no," he said. "It's not how I work. This time, we just talk."

Megan relaxed a bit as she organized her little joke about pigs who were communists (her English class was now halfway through *Animal Farm*).

"I make notes," he said, picking up a pad and pulling a pen from his shirt pocket. "About our talk. Is okay?"

For the first time, she noticed that he had an accent and she smiled, thinking of Erika Bauer and her whole crew of assistants. On the day of the shoot, everyone's English had sounded like music.

"I have seen your picture in magazine," Tomas told her. "With your mother."

"Yes," Megan said and then, to spare him having to say it, "my mother is very beautiful."

"She is," he said. "She was. When I am young, she is very famous. Is brave choice to pose with you."

"I wanted to do it," Megan said, trying to figure out what he meant by brave. "Lots of people thought she looked even better than her younger self."

"Yes, she did. She does," Tomas said, "but the photo with you tell us why she is beautiful."

Megan was silent. She hardly thought it worth pointing out that no one needed a photo to see that Lena was beautiful. When people spoke of Lena's beauty, it was as if they were speaking about beauty itself. Not about Lena.

"When your mother look at the camera, she invite us to look at her, but when you look, all you do is look at it."

"You're supposed to look at the camera," Megan said, trying to recall everything that Erika had said to her that day. "Or through it or something."

"Lena, how do you say . . . she responds to camera," Tomas said. "You study it."

"Am I too tall?" Megan asked him.

She did not want to sit here and talk about Lena and her own short-comings, especially if it was going to turn out that she was not what he was looking for.

He shook his head, smiled. "No, not at all. I'm going to have drink; it's been long day."

Tomas walked over to the suite's small kitchen and opened an already open bottle of wine, pouring it into the sort of glass that hotels leave in bathrooms, next to the sink. Megan went from being relaxed to incredibly nervous. Which made no sense, as there was no reason that Tomas having a glass of wine should make her brain scatter into pieces.

"So they tell you too tall," Tomas said, sitting down on the other end of the couch across from her with his wine and a small dish of nuts he had taken out of a cupboard. "What else do they say?"

"It depends." She told him about the man who said she would grow up to be a woman who didn't know what a novel was.

"Probably not chance for that," Tomas told her, "but I tell you the problem you have."

"I know what it is," Megan said, not wanting to hear it from him, "I'm too tall for how young I look."

"Is true, but not problem," he said. "I would use as part of package. No. Problem is you are not open."

"You mean private?" Megan thought of her locked away file, the key hidden in a sock.

"Tell me, what is you like about being actress? You not like what people say about you, and Mark say you are very stern with him. So, who is making you do these things?"

"No one," Megan said, thinking of how her auditions produced disappointment in her father's eyes, curiosity in her mother's, and disgust in Liv's. "I thought it would be more interesting."

Or rather, she'd thought *she* would be more interesting. Or more understandable.

"But is not?" he asked, getting up and bringing the bottle of wine from the kitchen to the low table by the couch where he and Megan were sitting, and refilling his glass.

"Parts of it are," she said, and just then, all the pieces of her brain unscattered and fell into place in a new and clear way. "Parts are very interesting, but maybe not important."

Or important without being interesting, she thought, while realizing that she had been saving up many more notes and images than had made it to the file. And, as if a dam had burst, they all tumbled out into Tomas Grudnik's hotel suite.

"Like, when I come out of an audition and it's already dark, or almost dark, and the whole city is rushing home, and I step into it," she said. "I'm small and big all at once. And the waiting is so boring, in the rooms before they call your name, but it's always women who take your headshot, and have you noticed that they're almost always blonde and wear too much makeup? The men who are waiting to audition, well, they like to talk and act as if they're not nervous. I've never seen anyone auditioning to play a father or something like that read their script, but the women are so tight and . . . strained. Even the really pretty ones who are thin and pretty enough to be famous for it look nervous."

Megan stopped for a breath and looked at Tomas looking at her.

"I wonder if that's the problem," she said. "I never get that nervous until after, when I'm hoping I might get the job, but know I won't."

"I don't think nerves are problem, not even lack of them," he said. "When you wait, what else you see?"

What else did she see? Well, there were all of those girls she couldn't help but see.

"All the girls, it's like there are so many of us," Megan said. "There's this endless supply of girls and obviously we're different, but we're also exactly the same. This collection of arms and legs and . . ." She hesitated, not wanting to talk about girls' bodies or her own body. "Well, faces. It's like the people in charge are looking for something, only they don't know what, but if you look, each and every girl, even the ones who are totally a type have a way of being . . . amazing."

Appealing, lovely, funny, knees, wrist, hands—especially hands, Megan loved girls' hands—necks, hair that was short, hair that escaped its pins and barrettes, hair that curled around ears . . .

These words poured through her mind until they stopped with a thud and she suddenly saw what the file was. It wasn't a collection of keepsakes or even notes on what she had seen, but evidence of desire. Not of wanting to look like other girls, but of a wanting nonetheless. She looked up at Tomas, half of her finally aware of what she had always known and half of her hoping she still had a secret.

"Yes, right there is problem," he said and she thought, *He knows. If he knows, it's true.*

"Lena invites us into her beauty, but you keep us out by looking at beauty," he said.

Her heart was beating so fast she thought the noise might come out of her ears and fill the room. She had no idea what he was saying.

"I can't use you and this is not business for you," he said, putting down his empty wine glass. "You are in business of understanding, not of being."

So he didn't know. Or he hadn't listened or couldn't hear what was running around her brain and body like an escaped, crazed monkey happy to be free while desperately looking for a place to hide. Tomas thought Lena invited people into her beauty while she, Megan, kept people out by looking at beauty?

That wasn't it at all. She looked because she had no idea how to have. How could she be in the business of understanding when she was just now seeing all she did not understand? Although maybe, just maybe, paying attention to what confused her was a way of understanding.

"Who shot campaign?" he asked. "Was Erika Bauer, no?"

"Yes, it was."

"She made interesting choice." He yawned, standing up. "You must forgive me, I have long flight yesterday and is already very late my time."

Megan stood as well, holding out her hand to shake good-bye. "So I'm not it."

"You're not," he told her. "But I thank Mark for, how you say, referencing you?"

"Referring," she said, wondering if she should thank Mark as well.

Would it have been better not to know this? Would she have to tell anyone now? What did she know about girls who liked girls? She thought suddenly of Stéphanie, who was not Erika's friend or roommate, but both.

Or neither.

Megan let go of Tomas's hand.

"I do love plays," she said. "Seeing them. Studying them."

"I am glad to know this," he said. "Theater is haven for all."

. . . . .

She made her way down the stairs and onto the street. She turned, heading toward 8th Avenue, where her bus home would be stopping. If her three years as a model and actress had ended in Tomas's hotel room, her life as a fellow traveler through the strange and the beautiful was well on its way. Had Erika guessed that Megan loved girls? Or had she, like Tomas, understood that a mildly beautiful girl (the daughter of a great beauty) could see what others failed to notice?

Megan supposed it didn't matter as long as she used the camera to record not just other girls, but each of the images she stored up and, until now, had kept secret. She might not take another acting class (her father was right, a real photographer learned to develop her own photos), but she knew she would always have a home in one of those uncomfortable seats that offered a glimpse of the silent darkness and its pooling light.

All around her, throughout the city, people moved, intent on catching a bus or the subway, on running one last errand. If Megan paid attention, she would find a way to turn each person into a picture. She stood still

for a minute, trying to absorb that everyone she saw offered up the mak-
ings of a photograph. She shook her head and moved forward with the
crowd that was blissfully unaware Megan Walker now had her own
Siamese twin traveling with her. It would not lead to the sort of fame
Lena once had or that was waiting for Liv, but if Megan were lucky, there
would be beauty in it.

....

ANECDOTE: ANDREA McARDLE

....

My love of performing, and dreams of being a singer and dancer, began when I was very, very young. People are surprised by that, even though I was doing eight shows a week on Broadway in *Annie* when I was a "little girl." Most people don't know that I was pretty much raring to go not long after I popped out of my mother's womb!

When I was a baby, I'd swoon when my parents played Sinatra or Rosemary Clooney records. I'd force my little brother Michael to be part of my homegrown theatrics, and I lived for Saturday mornings at Miss Rita Rue's Dance Class.

But if I can pin it down to one moment, one exact moment when the idea of actually being a part of the creative community appealed to me most, it was when I sang at *Tony Grant's Stars of Tomorrow* on Atlantic City's Steel Pier.

While sadly Steel Pier is no longer a destination for live entertainment, at one time it showcased the likes of Guy Lombardo, Benny Goodman, Jimmy Dorsey, Mae West, Charlie Chaplin, the Three Stooges, Bob Hope, Amos 'n' Andy, Al Jolson, Paul Anka, the Rolling Stones, Ricky Nelson, and even my favorite, Frank Sinatra! The location also presented the famous Diving Horse and was where the Miss America Pageant first was held. It was a fantasy land for a little starry-eyed girl like me!

Growing up in Northeast Philadelphia allowed us to take trips down to the Jersey shore with relative ease; it was about a two-hour drive away. Of course, as far as I was concerned, I would have traveled a thousand miles to perform for Tony Grant.

Tony Grant's Stars of Tomorrow was a showbiz staple for thirty-two years and gave thousands of eager young performers a chance to sing in front of live audiences. My mother saw an ad in the local Philly paper about *Stars of Tomorrow* holding auditions, and once I heard that, well, I was OBSESSED. Needless to say, the McArdle family took a day trip to New Jersey!

I can't say I was frightened singing on that stage. Yes, my heart was beating like a drum, but it was out of excitement, not because of nerves. That's not to say that I didn't get butterflies—I STILL get them before a performance—but not that day, not on the stage of the Steel Pier, my own magical dreamland! My only concern was that my hair was too curly. I wanted it pulled up and back—after all I had to look glamorous for my public! But my mother had other ideas. Little did I know "curly hair" was going to figure prominently in my future.

When they called my name, introduced me, and the band started up, I closed my eyes, opened my mouth, and had the thrill of singing take me over. I felt the connection of the audience, the Boardwalk, the music—everything. In that moment I understood the gift of performing, of connecting and sharing. It's safe to say I never looked back, and on that sunny afternoon, I was only looking forward. A little girl with big curls and even bigger dreams that suddenly felt like they were coming true.

That day also gave me a healthy dose of confidence— that's a gift that every young artist should have, knowing you are part of a community of singers, dancers, and actors. Knowing that there are other people just like you out there, supporting and inspiring you along the way, is an important part of the creative journey.

ANDREA McARDLE first captured the hearts of audiences in 1977 when she originated the title role in the megamusical *Annie*, becoming the youngest performer ever to be nominated for a Tony Award as Best Lead Actress in a Musical. She also received the Theatre World and Outer Critics Circle Awards. Andrea subsequently portrayed Annie in the West End, and played Judy Garland in the television movie *Rainbow*.

Andrea has starred in *Jerry's Girls*, the original Broadway cast of Andrew Lloyd Webber's *Starlight Express*, *Meet Me in St. Louis*, *They're Playing Our Song*, *Evita*, *Les Misérables*, the original Broadway cast of *State Fair*, *Oliver!*, *Joseph and the Amazing Technicolor Dreamcoat*, *Beauty and the Beast*, and as Sally Bowles in the national tour of Sam Mendes's *Cabaret*.

Andrea has also performed in major shows in Las Vegas and Atlantic City and other large concert halls throughout the country, including Carnegie Hall and the Metropolitan Opera House.

A MIDWINTER NIGHT'S DREAM

Jacqueline West

The day after Mara Crane disappeared, I chipped my front tooth on a coffee mug. A missing high school junior, a missing hunk of incisor—both of these things were tragedies, obviously. One of them just got more press coverage than the other.

At school that Monday morning, everyone was talking about Mara. Teary cheerleaders told each other how worried they were. Choir kids traded stories about where she'd last been seen. Even the teachers were whispering in doorways. I listened, slouching in my desk, while my tongue moved obsessively over the spot where a piece of me was suddenly gone.

When the lunch bell rang, I realized I hadn't said a single word all day.

I could have said something. Even if we hadn't exchanged more than a wave in the last three years of high school, Mara had once been my best friend. I could have joined the weepy drama kids and gushed about how worried I was, helped them concoct their stories about mysterious stalkers, alien abductions, the phenomenon of spontaneous combustion. But the truth is, when I heard Mara Crane was gone, my first thought was about who would take her place in the winter play.

Maybe I was better off with my mouth shut.

Tonguing the jagged tooth, I hurried past the cafeteria, ran the gauntlet of jocks outside the gym, skirted a group of mascara-streaked choir girls, and veered right, toward the auditorium.

The auditorium is in the old part of the school, built before the era of cinderblock and plate glass. Its seats are upholstered in worn purple velvet. There's a dusty balcony with brass rails, and plaster friezes of Greek gods on the walls. You can stand in the auditorium and forget that you're in a high school at all.

This is part of why I go there so often.

Liam was waiting for me on the edge of the stage. He had switched on a row of colored spots, and their beams fell across the apron, casting his shadow in triplicate rainbows.

Liam is the school's Light God. He has a permanent pass to the auditorium, because none of the teachers understand what he does. If a teacher ever questions why he needs to skip gym class—again— to work onstage, he says something like, "I'm prepping to adjust the lights on the first batten to hit the hot spot," and the teacher always just nods and goes quietly away again.

If I'm honest, I don't know anything about stage lighting, either. I'm the Light God's pretend assistant. I'm the Ineffectual Lighting Angel.

Liam glanced up as I slammed through the auditorium doors.

"I chipped my front tooth on a mug this morning," I announced, stomping down the aisle. My voice rang from the walls. "A huge piece fell off. A *giant* piece. And my mom can't afford to send me to the dentist until she gets her next paycheck, so I have to spend the next two weeks looking like a freak."

Liam shrugged. "One more reason not to smile."

I swung myself up onto the edge of the stage.

"What were you drinking?" Liam asked.

"Huh?"

"Out of the mug that chipped your tooth."

"Oh." I sat down facing Liam, cross-legged, and opened my bag lunch.

"That instant powdered hazelnut latte stuff."

"*That's* what makes you a freak."

"Shut up. We aren't all hardcore enough for black coffee."

Liam smiled, running one hand through his choppy black hair. I also have choppy black hair. Liam and I have similar builds, and we're both prone to dark plaid and Chuck Taylors. We often get mistaken for brother and sister, or boyfriend and girlfriend. Or identical twins. Which is especially awkward.

People used to mix up Mara and me, back when we were both tiny brown-haired grade-schoolers, always together, acting out our made-up plays. But that was a long time ago.

I took the green apple out of my lunch bag and tried to get my jagged front teeth through the skin in a way that didn't feel like rubbing an ice cube on a nerve.

"Did you hear about Mara Crane?" I asked, gnawing off a strip of apple peel.

"Yeah. I saw it on the morning news today."

"You watch the morning news?"

"While I'm drinking my black coffee." Liam swallowed a bite of sandwich. "They said she vanished from her own house. Her parents and her brother were all there, and she told them good night and went into her bedroom. And then on Sunday morning, she was just gone."

"It's crazy." I managed to nibble off another fragment of apple. "I mean—she's not the type to run away."

"Why would she?"

I shrugged. There was no reason. Mara Crane could do, or get, or *be* anything that she wanted.

First, she had grown up to be gorgeous. As we left elementary school for junior high, her hair turned redder and glossier, and her skin stayed as smooth and pimple-free as something that formed inside an oyster shell. Her parents could afford dance classes in Chicago, and Mara flitted through the school halls on legs that just got longer and more graceful while the rest of us lurched around like novice stilt-walkers. Then her parents started driving her to weekly voice lessons from some retired opera diva, and soon she was getting one choir solo after another.

I first saw the split between us when we were twelve. We signed up together for the Y's summer theater camp; it was cheap, so Mom said yes. At the end, we put on some generic fairy tale play. Mara was cast as the princess, and I was—I kid you not—a gargoyle. Afterward, the split grew wider and wider, with Mara and her lessons and her solos and her medals on one side, and me with my stringy home-dyed hair on the other. It's been years since I could say I *knew* her. But I knew her well enough to think she wouldn't run away.

"Her brother is in my math class," said Liam abruptly.

"I thought he was a senior."

"He is. He just sucks at math."

I laid down on the stage's black boards, smelling the mixture of paint and velvet and dust, letting it seep into my bloodstream. "I wonder what will happen with *Kismet*. We're supposed to start rehearsals next week."

"Well, if Mara doesn't come back—"

"—I'm sure she'll come back."

"But if she doesn't," said Liam, his mouth full, "then some other girl will finally get the good part." The rubber toe of his black All Star, covered with geometrical scribbles, nudged me in the shoulder.

"What?" I inched my shoulder away. "It won't be me. I didn't even make the chorus."

I flopped onto my back, staring up at the metal spiderweb of catwalks and light rods and electric cords that crisscrossed the ceiling high above. If I could sing, I might at least have gotten a small role. But that's one more thing that separates me from Mara, my life from her life. And I'd trade my whole real life for an imaginary one.

I'd spend it all onstage, changing costumes, walking through canvas rooms, getting to take on one existence after another. Never being just *myself* again.

I dug my fingernails into the apple peel. "Mr. Giatti asked me to do the costumes. I'll say yes."

"I know you will."

"It's better than nothing." I rolled onto my elbows, picturing the stage filled with plywood pillars and silk palm trees. I grinned at Liam. "It might even be fun. I'll put the choir boys in poufy harem pants and spangly—"

A crackling sound filled the auditorium. A moment later, a voice from the loudspeaker echoed through the room.

"Good afternoon, students," said Principal Barryman. I could hear pockets of dwindling sound from the hallways outside, the noise of other conversations rapidly fading.

"I'd like to take this chance to speak to you without interrupting class time," the principal went on. "All of us are upset today by the news about junior class member Mara Crane. I think I can rely on everyone in this school to do what they can for the Crane family, and for Mara herself, at this difficult time. The police are also depending on your cooperation, so if you know anything about Mara's whereabouts this weekend, please let someone know. And remember that our school counselors are always available if you need to talk.

"Finally, students . . . be cautious out there. Don't walk home alone. Stay in well-lighted, well-trafficked areas. Let someone know where you are and where you're going—a friend, a parent, a teacher. Let's all take care of each other."

There was a click, and the loudspeakers switched off.

Liam and I sat for a few more minutes in our patch of electric sunlight. Then I tossed my half-eaten apple back into its paper bag, Liam swallowed his sandwich crust, and we plodded together up the aisle, back into the real world.

. . . . .

I walked home alone.

I always do. Liam lives several miles away, my younger brother has football practice after junior high (and he would rather be dead than seen with me, anyway), and people don't tend to mess with the girl with black hair, black coat, and studded leather bracelets. Getting dressed every day can be like putting on a costume. I've been playing the role of brooding girl in black for years.

Besides, my mom knew where I was. Or I guess I should say my mom was *vaguely aware* of where I was. With her new job, and the house, and Kyle's football games, she's generally got too much on her mind to clear a spot for me.

The early December wind pushed little snowdrifts across the pavement, and I crunched through them, tonguing the broken spot in my mouth.

Alone inside the house, I grabbed a bag of stale tortilla chips from the half-empty cupboard and flopped down in front of the television. I had to chew with only my back teeth, which felt weird. I broke the chips into little pieces to fit them past the sore spot.

Every single local station was obsessing over Mara Crane's disappearance. Channel 6 had sent some poor, shivering reporter to stand in front of the Cranes' house, the huge white Colonial I remembered from when Mara and I were kids. The reporter was trying to look serious and sympathetic, but she was obviously more concerned about what the wind was doing to her hair. Every now and then, photos that had run in the local newspapers took the reporter's place on the screen. Mara in her Queen Guenevere costume. Mara with the rest of her dance troupe, her skin sparkling with little beads of postshow sweat. Mara after a concert, clutching a massive bouquet of white roses. Each picture was like an open safety pin. *Look how special she is,* they said, digging into my skin. *Look how pretty. How full of promise.*

On Channel 11, the Lincoln Grove police chief was speaking into a cluster of microphones. "... No signs of foul play, but we're not ruling anything out," he was saying, as another reporter shoved a microphone toward his bushy mustache. "We would like to ask all members of the community, and the young people especially, to be cautious."

Even on Channel 14, which broadcast from Chicago, a perky blonde anchor was interviewing some bald crime expert who looked like he'd been carved out of a bar of moisturizing soap.

"... area since 1987," said the expert, "when ten-year-old Lucy Porter disappeared during her walk home from a neighborhood park." A photo of a smiling, dark-skinned girl with long-lashed eyes flashed across the screen. "In the metro area, of course, there are many more cases of this type, but—"

"The circumstances would lead you to think that this was an abduction, then?" the anchor interrupted.

The gleam on the expert's scalp flashed back and forth as he tilted his head. "Well, they aren't consistent with most runaway cases. Additionally, just over a year ago, eighteen-year-old Peter Rostek disappeared under similar circumstances." A school photo of a boy with a chiseled jaw and wavy black hair floated in the TV's ray. "His family thought he was in bed for the night, but in the morning, his room was empty. Of course, that was in Carter, Illinois, a substantial distance from Lincoln Grove, but—"

I switched the TV off. Without it, the house was too quiet. I could almost hear the walls creaking as they leaned farther and farther away from me, and my own body felt strangely small. If I wasn't here—if I left right now, or if anything happened to me—no one would know. It would be hours before anyone even noticed I was gone.

I turned the television back on and flipped to the rock music channel, cranking up the volume. Then I headed to the kitchen for a cup of instant hazelnut latte, leaving the song to scream at an empty room.

. . . . .

That Wednesday afternoon, hundreds of students from Lincoln Grove High joined a volunteer brigade searching all of the nearby parks. No one found anything.

On Thursday evening, there was a candlelight vigil in the school parking lot. Liam and I went because anyone who didn't looked like a sociopath. We spent most of the time sitting side by side on a frosty cement divider, playing word games on his phone.

The next week, my mother got paid, and the dentist patched a big blob of enamel onto my front tooth.

The week after that, Mr. Giatti gave Mara's role in *Kismet* to a girl named Hailey, and three seniors got caught huffing glue in the shop.

In January, the school basketball team won at regionals, and Lincoln Grove lost its collective mind.

Mara's missing posters, which still hung on every bulletin board and telephone pole in town, grew worn and faded. Other, fresher fliers began to encroach on their edges, so that only Mara's face could be seen, smiling out at you from between the overlapping strips of weathered paper. And then, in February, the Camino Real Theatre Company went on tour.

. . . . .

You wouldn't expect a touring theater company to get a lot of attention at a crummy high school in a dying factory town like Lincoln Grove. But it did.

Maybe it was because Lincoln Grove was the kind of town where chances like this didn't come along very often. Maybe it was the posters, which popped up overnight like black and silver mushrooms along the high school halls, blaring things like: YOU HAVE NEVER SEEN A SHOW LIKE THIS, and TOKYO, MOSCOW, BERLIN, PARIS, LONDON, NEW YORK, *CHICAGO: ONE NIGHT ONLY*, and DAZZLING—MAGICAL—TERRI-FYING. Or maybe it was because the English department was offering extra credit and a free ride to Chicago to anyone who wanted to go.

I had exactly forty-nine dollars in my savings account. More than enough for the ticket. Enough not to have to ask Mom for it.

On the night of the show, Liam and I met up early in the school parking lot so we could grab a seat together in the back of the huge charter bus.

The ride to Chicago was flat and long, with snow-covered fields spread like dirty sheets on either side of the highway. By the time we reached the city, the sun had set, and the buildings were glittering hunks of electrified stone.

We were rumbling through the tight streets of downtown when Liam said, "It's weird to think I'll be living here soon."

I whirled toward him. "What?"

"I'm applying to DePaul."

I felt a prickle of ice deep in my chest. "Really?"

Liam nodded. "If I get a partial scholarship, my parents think they can cover the rest." He glanced at me. "You could apply. It's an amazing theater program."

I snorted. "Even if I was accepted . . ."

Liam waited for a second, watching me. "What? Is it the money?"

"You know it is."

Both of us went quiet. I slumped in my seat, scraping streaks of black polish off of my nails, until we pulled up in front of the theater.

The second the bus squealed to a stop, half the seniors bolted out the doors and ran into the streets, laughing. Three free hours in Chicago.

"More seats for us to choose from," Liam muttered into my ear.

Tuxedoed ushers hustled us through the marble lobby. We climbed curving stairs to the balcony doors. Liam picked our spot: in the center, near the front rail. I stared from the huge blue velvet curtain of the stage to the chandeliers hanging from the frescoed ceiling, and felt suddenly, pathetically small.

I slouched down next to Liam and studied the program.

A MIDSUMMER NIGHT'S DREAM BY WILLIAM SHAKESPEARE, said the

cover, in the same black and silver script as the posters. Inside, the program was almost empty. There were no cast lists, no actor bios. Just a scene-by-scene synopsis.

"Weird," I whispered, leaning over the armrest.

"Minimalist," Liam whispered back.

The remaining seats filled with city people in dark colors, suburban couples in heavy winter coats, old people with cough drops. At last the chandeliers began to dim, and I got that same feeling I always get just before a show begins: that prickling in the center of my chest that rushes out to the tips of my body, tingling in my fingers, flooding my toes. I've heard people talk about out-of-body experiences—the kind you have after life-threatening accidents or illnesses, when you float up out of yourself and look down at the world, and you suddenly see everything in a wider, clearer, luminous way. I've never come that close to dying. But I know what it's like to float out of my body. I feel it every time the houselights dim.

A hush spread through the theater. The curtain rustled open. Center stage, a huge fountain with three illuminated tiers seemed to spout actual water.

"Wow," I whispered.

"Light trick," Liam whispered back, but there was a tiny frown on his face. Glints of water reflected in the lenses of his glasses.

There was a rumble of music, and the actors entered.

It sounds stupid to say that they were good, even though they were. They were good in a way that made them disappear: they were part of the language, part of the set, part of the illusion. Maybe that was why no one noticed anything strange about them. Not at first.

Besides, we're all so used to seeing actors up close, on TV or in the movies, with cameras focused so tight on their faces that you can count every pore and nostril hair. In a theater, sometimes you can't see the actors' faces at all. And when you can't see someone's face, when you watch someone from far away, what you see isn't what they look like. You see how they move, how they hold themselves; you listen closely to their voices. The rest is an illusion. I know all this—I've watched enough shows from the light booth or the wings to know that you can brush past the actors backstage afterward, with all their insane greasy makeup and Aqua-Netted hair, and not recognize a single one of them. And still, through the makeup and the lights and the distance, I started to think there was something familiar about the actor playing Quince.

"Have you seen that guy in anything else?" I hissed at Liam. "Maybe on TV?"

Liam squinted at the stage for a minute. He shook his head.

I turned my eyes back to the stage too, searching the actors' painted faces. It wasn't just Quince. Several of them looked vaguely familiar. Maybe that was the secret of the Camino Real Theatre Company. Maybe they were all movie stars, carefully costumed and made up so that audiences couldn't quite be sure.

The first act ended. The curtain didn't close. This was where the crew should have darted out in their black clothes and headsets, moving the set pieces around, performing their invisible dance. Instead, a burst of fog billowed across the stage. Dry ice makes a thick, low-rolling swamp, great for creating atmosphere without smoking up the whole stage. But this didn't look like dry ice. This mist swirled up in tendrils of white, forming weird, twisted columns, spiraling and somersaulting, swathes of it soaring into the fly space like gigantic wings.

Quince's house vanished into the fog.

At the same moment, a forest of trees seemed to sprout up from the stage itself, their trunks swelling and branches unfurling, their limbs shimmering and solid in the pale stage lights. The buzz from the audience got louder.

"Whoa," I breathed. "How did they do that? Trapdoors?"

"All over the stage?" Liam shook his head. "It must be a projector or something." He craned over the back of his seat, looking for the light booth. I followed his eyes, but I didn't see what Liam was looking for. A few seconds later, he turned around, his frown growing deeper.

The fairies darted onto the stage. Their faces were sharp-featured but childlike, and their skin had been dusted or painted to look almost metallic, like moonlight on dark water. They were freakishly thin, without standard fairy wings, but with long, tapering fingers that made their hands look almost like twigs or roots—like something inhuman, but alive.

Liam leaned toward me. "What's with their hands?"

"Finger extensions," I whispered back. "Haven't you ever seen *The King and I*?"

We both turned back to the stage. Liam didn't say it, and I didn't say it either, but we'd both noticed that the fairies' fingers weren't stiff like the ones worn by the movie's Siamese dancers— they seemed to bend and move all the way to their pointed ends.

There was a flourish of orchestral music. The lights striking the boards grew dim. From the dark space above the stage, hundreds of tiny, silvery lights floated down and hung in space, like a sky full of stars, or the sparks of a firework refusing to die away.

There were audible gasps all around us.

"How the hell . . . ," muttered Liam.

And then Oberon and Titania, king and queen of the fairies, swept onto the stage with their retinues.

The buzzing audience fell silent.

Liam and I both sat up straighter in our seats.

The actors on the stage had the right number of limbs, the usual amounts of eyes and noses. The voices that came out of their mouths seemed natural, even if they were a little bit too loud and too pure for ordinary people. It was something about proportion. Or about the color of their skin. Or maybe it was their golden eyes, or the way their necks seemed so impossibly long and graceful, or the exaggerated, liquid slow motion of their too long, too slender limbs.

"They look like *puppets*," I breathed into Liam's ear. "But there aren't any strings."

"Those aren't puppets," he whispered back.

The twinkling lights changed from silver-white to red-gold. Masses of flowers seemed to sprout and bloom straight from the black floorboards. The buzzing around us resumed, growing louder. Liam actually wiped his glasses on his shirt, like a professor in some bad sci-fi film. He leaned on the seat in front of him, squinting at the stage, his eyes two dark pinpricks.

I leaned next to him. "How do you think they—"

But I couldn't even hear myself. Around us, the buzzing changed to murmuring, and then the murmuring changed to actual, out-loud, rude-guy-on-cell-phone-in-movie-theater talking. For a second, I thought about craning around and hissing at everybody to *shut up*.

"It's her. Look!" a girl two rows away was saying.

"No way . . ."

"Are you sure?"

In one of the upper rows to our right, someone stood up. He leaned toward the stage, his hands clenched around the back of the seat in front of him. In the dimness, I could see his silhouette, but not his face.

"Mara?" he shouted.

Everyone else fell silent: the audience in the house, the actors on the stage. The air around us seemed to have turned to glass, still and clear and breakable.

"Her brother," Liam whispered.

"Mara!" Jack Crane yelled again. I hadn't heard his voice in years. *"Mara!"*

Onstage, the cast remained perfectly still.

The fairies were crouched, not moving, beside Bottom and Titania in their patch of impossible flowers. They were all long-limbed and perfect-featured, posing with the grace of dancers.

And one of them had dark red hair.

Something about her face had changed. Her eyes looked larger, her jaw longer and narrower, her bones closer to the skin. But there was no question. It was *her*. Mara Crane.

Mara Freaking Crane.

The cast remained frozen.

Then someone downstairs shouted, "Lucy Porter?"

One of the smallest fairies gave a twitch.

She'd been ten years old in the picture on the news—the picture from 1987. She looked ten years old now. At the same time, there was something in her features, or in her eyes, that made her look much, much older.

The news: that was where I'd seen Quince too. Now that I thought about it, I was pretty sure I had seen several of the other actors' faces before, in black and white, without the tricks of light and makeup. If it *was* makeup. I'd seen them on posters, on TV, on those sad fliers that get stuck inside packets of junk mail. HAVE YOU SEEN ME?

Here they were, surrounded by faces that I didn't recognize, by Oberon and Titania and Puck, who looked even stranger, even older and thinner, even more inhuman than the rest.

The noise in the house was rising. Everyone was on their feet. Some of Mara's friends had scrambled into the aisles and were running toward the balcony rail like crazy fans at a rock concert.

And then, as the noise in the auditorium reached its peak, the illusion shattered. You could actual *feel* the moment it broke, its shards hanging there in the motionless air.

The actors stopped. Slowly, dropping their poses, their eyes flickering out into the darkness beyond the fourth wall, they became what they really were.

Something else.

Something not like us.

Something with limbs that were too long and voices that were too loud and teeth that were too sharp and eyes that were too wide and yellow and bright.

They gathered across the lip of the stage, forming one long, glittering, terrifying row. Together, they stared out into the darkened seats. Straight at us.

The audience froze: Downstairs, in the boxes, on the balcony. Every single one of us.

As though there had been some silent command, we all slunk back to our places and sat down.

The actors waited. When everyone was still, they glided back to their marks. There was a beat, like an indrawn breath, and then the show went on.

. . . . .

When the velvet curtain finally closed, the noise that filled the house wasn't quite applause. It wasn't theater applause, anyway, which is usually somewhere between a tennis match and a wedding where everyone knows the marriage won't last. It was a roar—a weird, rushing release of joy and fear and relief and awe.

The curtain stayed shut.

The crowd clapped, and shouted, and clapped, and waited, but no actors appeared to take their bows. A few ushers, who had been standing uncertainly in the downstairs aisles, disappeared into the darkness beside the stage. Another minute passed. Finally, the blue velvet curtains drifted apart.

The stage was empty.

The backdrops, the fountain, the strange growing trees, the impossible hanging lights. Everything was gone.

For a beat, the theater quieted. Then there was an even louder roar, as if half the audience thought that this was the last big trick of a magic show, and the other half thought that the trick was on them. While part of the crowd went on clapping and cheering, beaming up at the empty boards, the other part— the part that picked up Liam and me like two pieces of purple plaid driftwood—raced up the aisles, through the theater lobby, and out into the street. I caught a last glimpse of Mara's brother tearing down the snowy sidewalk, still shouting her name, before he disappeared into the flood of bodies headed toward the stage's loading doors.

Later, there were rumors of a huge black tour bus zooming out of the alley before anyone could get in its way. But I didn't see it. I'm pretty sure there was never one to see. There was nothing left onstage, or backstage, or coming out the doors. The Camino Real Theatre Company was gone.

Without speaking, Liam and I scuffed through the snow toward the waiting charter bus.

. . . . .

Back in the parking lot of Lincoln Grove High, the crowd scattered. The kids who had skipped the show hurried off to their cars. The ones who hadn't slumped softly, slowly away, holding on to each other. "It wasn't her," I heard someone saying, his arm draped around Jack Crane's shoulders. "It couldn't have been her."

Liam and I shuffled toward his ancient black Honda.

"Want a ride?" he asked, not looking at me.

"No, thanks," I said, not looking at him either. "I feel like walking."

I headed away from the school, along the deserted sidewalk. A few cars coasted slowly past me, their headlights slicing yellow strips out of the darkness. After I turned a corner, the streets grew quiet.

The air seemed to have gotten colder, or maybe I was noticing it—really noticing it—for the first time. The sky above me was clear as ice, with tiny stars prickling through it, small and very far away.

My house looked like something hibernating. The curtains were drawn, the front lights switched off. No one had remembered to leave them on for me. I tiptoed through the unlit living room, down the hall. The TV still buzzed behind Mom's door. A band of light slipped over Kyle's threshold; I could hear the click of computer keys.

I sat down on my own bed, in the dark, with all of my clothes still on, even my jacket and shoes. But I couldn't keep still.

I didn't want to be here. I didn't want to be in this room, this house, this little town. I didn't want to be in my own body.

I trudged out across the backyard, the puffs of my breath leaving smudges in the perfect air. The snow's crust snapped under my feet, dropping me through the surface with each step. I had never felt so heavy.

At the back of the yard, a ribbon of trees unwound through the darkness, leading away across the fields, toward the forested hills. The air was still. No wind. No sound. I stepped into the grove, into the black cobweb of bare branches, and tilted my face toward the sky.

For a second, I imagined that the stars above me were the same tiny, twinkling lights that had hung over the stage like the sparks of a frozen firework. I imagined that the bare black grove around me was unfurling with mist and magical leaves. I imagined myself in Mara's place, part of the illusion, not watching it from the darkness outside.

But the stars were high and small and cold, and the grove around me was perfectly still.

"Why?" I yelled. My voice shattered the frozen air. "Why did you take her? Why couldn't you choose *me*?" I reached out my arms. "Come on! Take me! I'm right here!"

The sound dwindled away into the dark and the snow.

I stood there, shivering, until my toes had gone from burning to numb, and the tears on my eyelashes had frozen in clumps. Then I turned back toward the house. I followed my own set of footprints, the hollow spots leading me back, taking me away from the dark, and the cold, and the trees and the stars, and everything else that might lie just beyond.

....

ANECDOTE: ANTHONY FEDOROV

....

I've been singing since I was barely two years old. It started back in the Ukraine, where I was born. It's always been in my family.

Both my dad and my brother played the guitar and accordion and my grandma was a singer. I think I got my vocal ability from her. What inspired me initially, though, was my dad; he had his own band back then. They played Russian pop music. We would sing old school Russian pop songs; at parties for friends, or at different festivals. It was just something we did as a family.

We moved to the United States when I was nine years old. When I was fourteen I started going to a restaurant called Golden Gates in our neighborhood in Northeast Philly. It was a Russian nightclub and restaurant that had live entertainment. One night I was out partying with my friends and I heard one of the singers, this guy called Gennaro (Tedesco). He had one of the most beautiful voices I'd ever heard. He sang a bunch of songs that night, some stuff in Russian, some in Spanish, and then he sang "Lady in Red." He sounded so incredible. I had a moment like, I want to sound like that, I want to do that, I want to work here. I remember just standing there and saying to myself, "I want to do that."

I knew the owner of Golden Gates and the musical director, so I asked to audition sometime soon after that night, and I did. I had a mini disc to sing along with, but I don't remember what I sang. They told me that I had a lot of potential but I just needed to work really hard.

So I took that advice and I started listening to Marc Anthony's music. And it was when I listened to his music that I knew I wanted to be a professional entertainer. Marc Anthony's music moved me—his voice moved me and I wanted to sound like him.

For the next two summers, I blasted my karaoke machine and tried to mimic everything that he was doing. At first, I sounded really bad; I didn't know how to sing properly. I remember our neighbors would knock on the ceiling and the walls because I was annoying as hell. I would come home from school, and instead of doing my homework first, I would start singing to Marc Anthony. In the span of two summers, I went from neighbors telling me to shut the hell up, to opening the window to see who was there, listening to me.

I was lucky enough to be exposed to music when I was a baby. So it grew from there. I would encourage parents and their kids to experience music and the arts together. Whether it's going to a musical or singing for friends and family for fun, anything. But the sooner you expose your child to the arts, the sooner they can discover that world, and I believe they become better people because of it.

ANTHONY FEDOROV, the *American Idol* season four finalist, has built an impressive list of credits in stage musicals, including Roger in the Off-Broadway revival of *Rent*, *Cinderella* with the Nashville Symphony, *The Sound of Music* at Paper Mill Playhouse, *The Fantasticks* Off-Broadway, and *Joseph and the Amazing Technicolor Dreamcoat* in several productions around the country. His sold-out New York City cabaret debut featured songs from his favorite stage roles, early pop influences, select songs from his debut EP, and a fun recap of songs from his *Idol* stint. Currently, Anthony is the lead singer for the Chicago-based rock band 7th Heaven. www.7thheavenband.com.

GRAVY AND MASHED

Tanya Lee Stone

Jess's stomach lurched. She grabbed for one of the bags she stashed in a secret spot in the wings. Strange to think of a brown bag as a comfort, but at the moment she needed it like a five-year-old needs a blankie to sleep through the night.

She relied on those bags to survive the every-Friday voice performance requirement at City Arts High.

Jess tossed the used bag into the backstage garbage and wiped her mouth. She stood next to the heavy folds of the thick, plum curtain. She took some comfort there, too—even with its close proximity to the danger zone that was the stage—the draping offering partial protection, like an overhang on a stormy day.

She waited for Mia to finish her song, every second further sealing Jess's fate—that inevitable walk to center stage approaching with every quarter note, each beat accelerating gripping fear, quivering legs seeking to root to the floor.

What if I screw up? Jess thought.

A battle ensued in her brain, her breathing, her body.

What if they think I'm no good?

She breathed slow and deep, intentional, in through the nose out through the mouth—good air in, bad air out—directing the breath to calm her shaking calves, thighs, belly, arms, hands, fingers. Drop shoulders, release neck.

Jess called on the trick her father had taught her, imagining a pretty blue light streaming into her with every deep breath, swirling, curling through her, filling her up. The exhale pushing out dark black air, like a dragon expunging plumes of smoke from its nostrils.

Blue light in, black light out. Blue light in, black light out. She steadied.

Onstage, Mia's crescendo rose then fell, settling into a satisfying low vibrato held to the half rest. She broke the spell with a small smile, a small bow, and strode offstage.

The audience, made up of their City Arts classmates from all the different disciplines—drama, dance, and music—stomped and cheered, whistled and woo-hoo'd, while the teachers smiled and took notes.

"Yeah, MIA!" one guy hollered. "Way to bring it!"

Jess didn't want to leave the shadows of the curtain folds to take her turn. But she did, one step headed toward the stage as Mia brushed past. With a faint tilt of her head, amber eyes narrowed, Mia gave a tug on her snug glittery top and gave Jess a condescending pat on the arm.

"I'm sure you'll do just fine."

. . . . .

Four years earlier, Mia and Jess had stood behind a different curtain, at a different school, waiting for their names to be called. City Arts was auditioning kids for their magnet performing arts high school. Jess's town could only afford to pay for the top three rankings. If you made top ten, you could still go, but tuition was high.

"How great would it be if we both got in?" Mia had said, her eyes opening even wider than usual. "Forget stupid chorus and school plays. We could actually train for the real thing!"

Jess's hand made small circles on her belly. "I don't feel so well, Mia," she said.

"You always say that, Jess. It's just nerves, we both know how awesome you are. Sing for them like you sing for me and you'll be fine."

It was easy for Mia to comfort Jess. They had bonded a long time ago, during a fifth-grade sleepover when they first discovered they both loved to sing. From that night on, whenever they were at one of their houses, they would belt out Broadway tunes from *Rent* and *Wicked* and *In the Heights*, singing and dancing and laughing.

Sometimes when Jess sang, it was so beautiful Mia cried. She once told Jess it was as if the world disappeared and Jess just *was* the song. Mia called her the Real Deal. But Jess only felt that way when no one was watching.

At school, Jess inevitably choked, her fear simply getting the best of her. That's why Mia always got leads and Jess was usually stuck in the ensemble. She had been an orphan to Mia's Annie, a guest at the tea party to Mia's Alice, a Lost Boy to Mia's Peter Pan.

. . . . .

Jess hesitated midstep, one foot off the ground. Mia's you'll-do-just-fine sneer snaked down inside her, touching the terror she had begun to conquer, taunting it to rise back up through her throat.

Jess put her foot down. Blue light in, black light out. She hurried to her mark, single white tape strip on the black floor, determined not to lose her nerve. She stood, looking into the audience, still Jess, raw, not yet embodying Lili from *Carnival*, as the accompanist played the opening notes of "Mira."

She sang on cue. Her voice sweet, a bit trembly, but nice. No wrong notes. Her peers sat patiently, waiting to be wowed.

Note by note, Jess began to fill Lili's shoes, a girl far from home, wrapping herself in memories of the place where everybody knows her name.

"*You're fine,*" Jess's thoughts poked through the song, occupying a parallel layer in her brain. "*You can do this. You can be Lili.*"

Jess anchored herself in images of Lili's touchstones, a familiar chair, house, street, just like she had done in her musical theater singing class earlier that week. Her voice lost its tremble, gaining in strength. From Row C center, Dylan smiled. Stella nodded her head in time with the music, unconscious acknowledgment. Jess was on the right track. She gave herself over to the sensation, fed by the growing connection with the audience. She could feel it now: they were seeing Lili/Jess, maybe even *just* Lili, not Jess *as* Lili.

The high note was coming. Jess could picture her sheet music, dark pencil marking where she had time to take a breath. She nailed it, solid, steady. The rest would be cake. She was in the clear.

Relief washed over her, and she smiled. But in that infinitesimal distraction Lili's presence peeled away like clothes falling to the floor. She was Jess again.

Naked.

Lost.

Midphrase.

The accompanist kept vamping, coming back around with musical room for her to jump in, but the words had vanished.

Jess's eyes darted around like a pinball in an arcade game, out to the back wall of the theater, down to Dylan gritting his teeth, behind him, to Stella, indecipherably feeding her the next phrase. How could she still not be able to kick this stage fright thing? It was even worse now that she was a senior. People probably had more sympathy for her when she was younger, but to have gotten this far and still freeze up onstage was ridiculous. She felt the eyes of her peers boring into her.

She turned her head toward the piano looking for a life preserver to be tossed her way as she drowned.

"I'm sorry. Line?"

"'Can you imagine . . . ,'" the accompanist said, giving her the prompt.

She finished the song, barreling through in a blur. She made no more mistakes, but the moment of connection was gone. She smiled weak, offered a quick obligatory bow, and half walked, half ran off.

Blinking rapid-fire, Jess tried to trick tears back, wiping the wet away.

She gathered herself in the wings, then went back to her seat in the audience next to Dylan, who pulled her in with a brotherly arm, whispering, "I'm just glad the dance department doesn't have to do this every week!"

Stella leaned forward, her auburn hair falling over her right eye. She squeezed Jess's shoulder. "You were great. Don't even worry about it."

They watched the rest of the performances in silence.

. . . . .

Later that day, Stella and Jess sat at the corner table in the lunchroom, and let the noisy chatter and rush of kids obscure them. Stella was a glass-half-full kind of girl with her own sense of style. She was always there with a look-on-the-bright-side and a practical solution. A musical theater major a year behind Jess, Stella was also a killer pianist and often played accompaniment for her friends. Stella pushed her cat-eye glasses up higher on the bridge of her nose.

"You really should eat, Jess."

"Ugh, I can't. So close . . . and yet so far. I was almost in the zone and then I choked. Humiliating."

"Everybody messes up lyrics, Jess. No big deal."

"Yeah, but just when I manage to stop shaking long enough to actually get into a song, I blank on the words?"

"So what? You nailed it up until then. It was great."

"I don't know, maybe it was a bad omen. That admissions rep from U Michigan will be here in two weeks. You know how I perform that day will decide whether they accept me into their musical theater program and it's one of my top choices," Jess said. "I'm never going to get my stage fright under control by then. Maybe I'm just not cut out for this."

"Honesty. Finally."

Mia.

Hip shoved out, smirk in tact, curly black hair irritatingly shiny, Mia. The heeled boots she wore every day made her two inches taller and it always took Jess by surprise. Jess still had the mental image of Mia as the petite, perky girl from middle school. She wondered if she still acted like that girl with her new friends, saving the snarky sass just for her.

"I was getting tired of your If-Only-I Didn't-Suffer-from-Crippling-Stage-Fright-You-Would-Understand-How-Fabulous-I-Am routine," Mia continued. "It's good that you're facing it. You really just don't have the chops, do ya Jess?"

Jess felt the familiar flip-flop of her stomach, bringing back her pre-performance jitters. Her gut grumbled, but she steeled herself.

"I'm not going to play your little mind games, Mia."

Mia pulled at one of her curls and released it. "You don't need *me* for mind games. We both know how well you play them all by yourself." She gave an irritated wave at Jess, dismissing her. "Just stay all tweaked like you are now and that admissions rep will zero in on ME. As it should be."

"You are so delusional, Mia," Stella said. "You seem to be forgetting there are other singers to compete with."

Mia laughed hard and sharp. "Yah. *Okaay*," she said. Then she spun around on the ball of her shoe and left.

Stella looked at Jess. "Let's assume she's not threatened by me because I'm a junior, shall we? Otherwise, I think she just insulted me." Stella laughed it off. "But seriously, what is her deal with you?"

"Long story," Jess said. "It's not important."

"Clearly, it is."

Dylan arrived at the table, balancing a tray with three heaping plates of mashed potatoes while still managing to wave hello to friends on the way.

"Sorry, no gravy," he said.

"What the . . . ," Stella started.

Jess shook her head and laughed.

"I once told him that when I was little, whenever I got depressed I would cheer myself up with a mountain of mashed potatoes and gravy."

"No big deal," Dylan said. "We got lucky. It was meatloaf day."

. . . . .

Jess and Stella unlocked a practice room down the hall from a dance studio where Dylan was stretching at the bar. It was late Saturday morning and City Arts was relatively quiet except for a few small-group ensemble rehearsals going on. Students were allowed limited access to the school on the weekends, ensuring what the faculty called "equal opportunity practicing."

"You need a different song," Stella said.

"You don't like 'Mira'?"

"It just doesn't do anything for you. It's like what Professor Langdon always asks us: How are YOU connected to the song? Why did you choose it?"

Jess shrugged. "Ugh, I don't know. I ran out of ideas?"

"Lame," Stella said.

"I know. So what should I sing about?"

"Why are you asking me?" Stella said. "You have to pick something you can emotionally connect to."

"Okay, now you sound exactly like Langdon!" Jess said. "I don't know. Maybe I should pick a song about being afraid or overcoming fear or something."

"Yes, that's perfect! How about 'I Have Confidence' from *The Sound of Music*?" Stella asked.

"Now who's lame?"

They laughed.

"'I Whistle a Happy Tune'?"

Jess picked up a pink eraser from the music stand and chucked it at her. "Hey!"

"What's going on in here?" Dylan poked his head in the door, little white towel slung around his neck. He wiped his damp forehead and tousled his hair, wet with sweat. He was wearing dark gray hip-hop pants and black plaid high-tops. The whole look screamed "I just finished a kick-ass dance routine."

"We're trying to pick a new song for when the admissions rep comes. Something about not being afraid or taking risks," Jess said.

Dylan jumped on a pretend broomstick. "'Defying Gravity'?"

"OVERDONE!" both girls yelled.

"Hmm, how about 'Make Them Hear You,' from *Ragtime*?" Stella said, twisting her hair up and weaving a pencil through it to keep it out of her way.

"Too civil rightsy, and it's a guy's song," Jess said.

"My mom used to calm me down at night with 'You'll Never Walk Alone,'" Dylan said.

"From *Carousel*? Aside from the dead husband factor, that could work," Stella said.

"Nah," Jess shook her head, "Feels too old."

"'Seize the Day'!" Dylan raised his fist high above his head in a move from *Newsies*.

"Yeah, cuz it makes perfect sense for Jess to sing a song performed by a bunch of dancing boys!"

They were quiet again, thinking.

"Would it be weird if I was sort of singing to myself, that 'Nothing's gonna harm you' song?" Jess asked. "I mean, I know Tobias sings it to Mrs. Lovett in the show, but I think I could make it work."

"Oh my god did you guys see Neil Patrick Harris do that scene?" Dylan said.

The girls just looked at each other.

"If you haven't, there's a clip on YouTube of him singing 'Not While I'm Around,' and he was so incredibly believable as Tobias, you have to watch it. I mean, I know he was playing someone much younger but he really nailed it and . . ."

"Dylan!" Stella interrupted him. "Focus."

"Oh, sorry, yes, sure, Jess, absolutely, that could definitely work."

Stella pulled out the *Sweeney Todd* songbook from the stack and played the song through while Jess sang, letting go in the safety of the tiny room. Singing in workshop class where everyone basically had to be vulnerable, or practicing with close friends wasn't so scary. It was being in the spotlight, all eyes only on her, that freaked her out. Her voice was haunting, sad, hopeful.

When it was over, Dylan let out a heavy sigh.

Stella took her hands off the keys and dabbed the corner of her eye. "Works for me."

. . . . .

Friday came around again, fast. As the City Arts student body shuffled into the theater, Jess checked on her stash of bags. Still there. The janitor must have figured out her little secret and taken pity on her. She reached for one and her stomach flopped, maybe just a knee-jerk response to the bag itself.

Blue light in, black light out.

She focused her breath. She slowly put the bag back, unused. At the signal, she walked onstage, took her mark, and began to sing. When she got to the line about demons prowling, Jess clutched her own arms, hugging herself.

She continued with the lyrics about sending them howling, her voice shaky, but a bit braver; more into the character with every passing note.

Jess was extremely aware of every sound coming from her, every move, and she wasn't sure what to do with her arms. She couldn't keep rubbing them, so she put them down by her sides. She sang well enough but never fully allowed herself to get lost in the music like she had in the practice room. She was overthinking it. She just had to get over this by next week. The weekly performances were one thing, but she only had one shot to prove to that admissions rep U Michigan should take a chance on her.

Fine described her performance. No mistakes. The song ended. The audience clapped. Dylan cupped his hands around his mouth yelling her name once or twice; she wasn't really sure in her haze of wanting to get through and get off the stage.

But Mia, she did notice, as she gave a few limp claps and half a satisfied smile from the front row.

. . . . .

Professor Langdon stood between the piano and the circle of chairs occupied by his musical theater singing students. Although they all wanted to impress him, his stance—in jeans and a faded blue Oxford shirt—was casual and calming.

"Who's next?"

Jess pushed her chair back, handed her sheet music to the accompanist, and walked to the front of the room. After the last line, "'Not while I'm around,'" the music stopped. There was some scattered clapping. Langdon waited.

"Okay, so how was your work? How did you feel?"

"Okay."

"Just okay?"

"Yes."

"Do you want to run it again?" he asked.

"Sure."

She sang, trying to forget about remembering the words, the breath breaks, everything she had practiced. Just letting go. Like a gypsy with a crystal ball, each time she felt herself drift back into uncertainty and lose the thread of her focus, Langdon was there, an improv partner injecting phrases related to the song, timed not to interrupt the flow:

"Trust me, I won't let anything hurt you," or "there are no demons here, kid," when she got to the prowling lyric.

She was used to his methods; she'd been in his class twice before. This was how he created a trusting environment—a space performers could experiment in and try different ways to connect to a song. It wasn't his fault his techniques hadn't fully worked on her yet.

The song ended.

Langdon put his hands in his jean pockets and offered a small smile. "How did it feel this time?"

"Better."

"Better than what?"

Jess raised her shoulders. "Better than last time?"

Langdon shook his head, just a little. "But I'm asking you how you *feel*."

Jess didn't say anything for a couple of seconds.

"I don't know," Jess said.

He smiled, slow, and nodded. It was a sympathetic smile. Her classmates quietly watched this process take place, all having stood before where she stood now. She wondered what they were really thinking as some smiled in encouragement and others kept an eye on Langdon, waiting to see what he would do next. Sometimes he would invite one of them to join the process as an acting partner, giving the singer someone to sing to; so they all knew to stay attentive and ready.

Langdon took his hands out of his pockets and used them to talk, as if their movements helped him find the right words. "Look, I get it, the nerves thing is hard. But you have to know *what* you're feeling, *where* you are, *who* you're singing to—or we're just not going to take the ride with you. And Jess?"

He took a few steps closer, put his hand gently on her shoulder, looked her straight in the eyes, lowered his voice, and said, "You gotta find a way to knock this thing, once and for all, if this is what you really want."

It didn't matter that he said it in front of the whole room. At one point or another he had said something to each of them that hit home. The other kids might not all suffer from stage fright but they were all working on something—every one of them had felt exposed in that room, been pushed out of their comfort zone, nudged, challenged to express something real, and not hide in the character. They all knew exactly how hard it was to be standing where she was standing.

If I can't do this here, I can't do it anywhere, she thought.

Jess's forehead wrinkled deep, she smashed her lips together, drew in a breath. Langdon smiled the kindest smile, like a father, or really, an uncle: all support; no judgment.

"So . . . how do you feel?" he repeated his initial question.

"I feel afraid," Jess blurted. *Do not cry, do not cry, do not cry,* her mind ran the mantra.

"Okay, fine, *use* that. Don't fight it, embrace it."

Jess's head bobbed up and down in the tiniest increments, as if the muscles in her neck were convincing her to leap.

"Okay, again please," he said to the accompanist.

Jess sang.

There were some rough spots, but by the end of the song, she felt better. And that *did* mean something to her.

. . . . .

On Wednesday, Jess stopped by Langdon's classroom.

He looked up from whatever he was reading and motioned her in to sit down.

"I think I want to change my song."

"Why?"

"I think I got what I needed from it, but this one will work better for me."

"It's only two days before the U Michigan guy comes. Are you sure?"

She handed him the sheet music. His mouth cracked in a tiny grin.

"Okay, if you think you can pull it off, go for it. I'm around after school for about an hour if you want feedback."

Jess worked through the song with Langdon after school, and then Stella met her in the practice rooms.

"How did it go?" Stella asked.

"You won't believe it. He actually said, 'I'm proud of you, kiddo. You really showed up.'"

"A compliment from Langdon, whoa. Okay, so let's hear it."

Jess handed Stella her Jason Robert Brown book, *Songs for a New World*, opened to the right page.

"Oh, this really is perfect," Stella said, and began to play for her. Jess flew through the first half, loving every second, feeling sure for the first time in forever.

As the next section began, Mia flung the practice room door open, looking like she was going to scream at them. But the noise of the door banging against the cinder block wall seemed to snap her out of her fury. Mia brushed off the sleeves of her sweater. She drew a sharp breath in through her nose and laughed a little.

"Sorry, don't know my own strength. You sound great, Jess," she said, spilling sarcasm. "I'm sure everything will be perfect now that you've chosen the perfect song."

Stella stood up too fast from the bench, and the fall board crashed and closed on the keys. "What is your problem?" she yelled at Mia.

"SHE is my problem." Mia jabbed a finger in Jess's direction. "Don't think you can fool these college admissions reps like you did the panel of locals that felt sorry for you when we were in middle school. We both know that's the only reason they ranked you higher than me and why my parents had to go into hock to send me here while you got a full ride. Least you could have done was prove them right. But *aww*, you can't, you're afraid. So quit already. You've always known deep down that I was the star. Maybe *that's* what always has you so spooked. A few extra sessions with Langdon isn't going to cut it."

Mia breathed in fast through her nose again and let out a shake-it-off sigh. "Have fun *practicing*." She closed the practice room door and left.

Stella and Jess waited for Mia to be truly gone. When they heard the outer hallway door close behind her, they looked at each other incredulously.

"You okay?" Stella half laughed.

"Yeah, but what was *that*?"

"Oh please, are you kidding? Obviously, she heard you singing and freaked out because you are amazing. She knows the only thing keeping you from outshining her is your stage fright. Talk about spooked!" Stella said.

Jess took a second to let this register.

"You really think so?" She hesitated again before asking, "Was it really that good?"

"Um, duh. Yes, Jess, it was. *You* are really that good."

"Thanks. Okay, let's just take it from the top."

"You got it," Stella said.

They ran through the song a few more times. Jess picked apart the lyrics, and the girls talked about the different things they could mean and how Jess might want to approach them. Satisfied, they quit for the night.

. . . . .

On Friday afternoon, the City Arts kids filed into their seats. The U Michigan rep was among them, clipboard in hand. Jess sat on the floor in the wings, knees curled up to her chest, arms wrapped tight around them, and head bent. Lost in thought.

Someone walked right up to her toes. She looked up.

Mia.

She was prattling on about something.

". . . don't worry, the rep won't pay much attention to you anyway . . . such a shame . . . stage fright always got the best of you . . . could have been so good . . ."

Jess never broke eye contact with Mia, but didn't say a word as she finished her rant. She got up off the floor, walked over to her stash of paper bags, pulled them out, looked back at Mia, and threw the entire stack in the garbage.

Jess strolled back to where Mia was still standing.

"You know Mia, once upon a time, we were friends. I'm sorry I got ranked higher, and I'm sorry you think I didn't deserve it. But are you really so small and mean that you have to put me down every chance you get?"

Jess's eyes widened as what Stella had said to her earlier really sunk in. "Or maybe, you're just scared that when I finally lose my nerve you'll have a real challenge on your hands. Well, guess what? My nerves? They're gone."

The hand Mia had on her own jutted-out hip dropped, as did her raised eyebrows.

And just like that, it was time.

Time to shed the stupidity of fear. What was she so afraid of, anyway? What's the worst that could happen? That she forgot some words? Missed a high note? Didn't get into U Michigan? What she had been doing all along was way, way worse. Wasting time. Wasting energy. The fear had turned into a bad habit; its small walls had become its own safety. She was sick of being afraid.

Jess walked on to the dark stage in a simple blue sheath dress, barefoot. Smooth wood on the soles of her feet a new comfort. She was grounded.

She looked out at the audience and felt welcomed by them. As if they were a group of children sitting at her feet, waiting for her to tell them a story. She sat on the black stool and took a moment to think about the answers to Langdon's questions: Where was she? What was she feeling?

She imagined herself in Mia's bedroom. She was eleven, holding a hairbrush as a mic, belting her brains out without a care in the world.

Unadulterated joy swept in, carrying with it the brightest, bluest light ever.

The spotlight came up and the piano played the opening notes of "I'm Not Afraid of Anything."

She was the girl in the song; the girl in the song was her, as she sang about things people are afraid of—the water, the darkness . . . love.

She got to the chorus and got up off the stool, bare feet firm on bare ground. The music swelled to the climax, her mouth open wide, arms outstretched, and she let loose, singing to the world that she was not a girl who would give up what she wants to a stupid thing like fear.

The audience believed her.

She believed her, too.

The song ended; the music stopped. Jess paused, smiled, and bowed.

The audience went nuts.

Whooping, hollering, feet stomping, and fist pumping, they cheered for her. Not sympathy cheering, or glad-you-got-through-it cheering, but true reaction, raw response.

She could see Dylan and Stella bursting with excitement. Jess put her hands over her mouth trying to conceal her utter glee, then gave up and started laughing. She couldn't fully feel the floor. It was as if she was floating.

Hers had been the last song of that Friday's lineup and no one waited for her to walk offstage. Within seconds, her classmates surrounded Jess, complimenting and congratulating her. Toward the back, she could swear she even saw Mia clapping for her just like she used to, back when they *were* eleven. The response from her peers made Jess float even higher, but it was the gravy on her very own mountain of mashed potatoes.

....

ANECDOTE: LISA HOWARD

....

When did I know I wanted to be a performer?

There were many stages of understanding what that actually meant, but I know that I fell in love with musical theater in elementary school. My parents took me to the theater from time to time, but I wasn't exposed to that much really. We lived in Akron, Ohio, so we could see local shows or touring companies that would come through town. I can distinctly remember seeing a touring production of *Annie* at E. J. Thomas Performing Arts Hall and thinking that was the most amazing thing I'd ever seen. I hoped and dreamed that one day I'd be up on that stage.

I went to an audition for a local community theater's production of *Annie*, but I didn't make the cut. Disappointed but not deterred, I tried out again the next year for *The Music Man* but didn't make it then either.

I did, however, have the record albums to several movie musicals, which were the next best thing. I used to sit in front of our record player in the dining room and listen to these albums over and over again. My favorites were *The Sound of Music*, *Grease*, and of course, *Annie*. I would pour over the album jackets, studying the pictures from the movies and pretending that I was a part of it all. I knew every word to every song, and I would sing them at the top of my lungs. My brothers used to yell, "Mom, tell her to shut up!" and my mom's reply was, "Let her sing. You never know, she might become a singer one day."

Thanks, Mom, you were right.

After I landed a solo in the fifth-grade holiday show, someone suggested to my parents that they get me voice lessons. They did. That year, when our teacher asked the class what we'd like to be when we grew up, I said, "I want to be on Broadway."

The road to Broadway wasn't always an easy one, and to a kid from Akron, Ohio, many times getting there seemed like an impossible dream. To my fifth-grade self, a Broadway stage felt like it was a million miles away, but with a lot of hard work, encouragement, and maybe a little bit of luck, my grown-up self is always happy and grateful to call Broadway home.

LISA HOWARD costarred in *The Twilight Saga: Breaking Dawn—Part 2*, portraying the role of Siobhan. Her Broadway credits include *Priscilla Queen of the Desert*, *9 to 5*, *South Pacific*, and the Tony Award–nominated *25th Annual Putnam County Spelling Bee*. She has also appeared in George Street Playhouse's production of *It Should Have Been You*, directed by David Hyde Pierce. Television credits include *Ugly Betty*. Lisa's voice can be heard on her debut album, *Songs of Innocence & Experience*. Please visit www.lisahowardNYC.com and follow her on Twitter @LisaHowardNYC.

A LOVE SONG

Antony John

"I'm Tamia," she says, and I'm about to say, "I know," when I stop myself. She's not really telling me her name; she's inviting me to share mine.

"Cooper."

Her skinny jeans disappear into black leather boots and a white camisole peeps out from under a gray cardigan. She's curvy, with shoulder-length chestnut hair and gently contoured features. Dark brown eyes narrowed, she watches me watching her. Her full lips are closed in an expression of quiet contentment. If she were a photo in a magazine, the caption would say she looks relaxed yet radiant. If I were looking at the photo, I'd have to agree.

"Cooper," she says, trying out the name for herself. She tucks a stray tendril of hair behind her ear and gives me one half of a nod. I guess she's embarrassed for never having noticed me before.

Which kind of makes sense. We go to single-sex Catholic high schools in St. Louis, but once a year there's a jointly staged musical. As the finest singer, Tamia has won a lead role for the past three years. As the finest pianist, I've performed in the orchestra for just as long. I've watched her onstage, bathed in light. But I'm not surprised that in the darkness of the orchestra pit, she hasn't seen me at all.

She opens the door to her school's best practice room. ("Best" being a relative term that means the piano is a Kawai baby grand, unlike the upright piano next door, which sounds like it has been stolen from a Western saloon.) The walls are coated in disintegrating acoustic tile. The carpet is threadbare.

"Really makes you feel like you've hit the big time, doesn't it?" Tamia asks.

"Yeah," I reply. "I mean, not exactly."

She opens a small leather portfolio and removes her music: *Der Lindenbaum* by Franz Schubert. She hands me the piano part and puts the vocal score on a music stand. I'm willing to bet she has already learned the song by heart. I certainly have.

"You ever done a classical music talent contest before?" she asks.

I lower the piano stool so that I can fit my knees under the keyboard. "No."

"Me neither. I think it's just an excuse to bring the two schools together. It's senior year, though, you know? I'd kind of like to go out on a high." I can feel her watching as I play a chromatic scale over four octaves of the keyboard. The mechanism is a little fast, the timbre aggressively bright, but the piano sings. "Dave says you're the best accompanist around."

It takes me a moment to realize she's talking about Mr. McCutcheon, head of music at her school. I've never even thought of Mr. Jeffries, my head of music, as having a first name.

"He says I'm lucky you're playing for me," she continues. She drums her fingers against the piano lid. "He also says you're a nerd. Which is a good thing, by the way. Nerdy is, you know . . . cool? So, uh, what have you heard about me?"

I've heard that she loves the sound of her own voice—which, as it happens, is a pretty incredible voice, especially when she sings—and that she wants to go to the Eastman School of Music. No one doubts she'll get in.

"I saw you in *West Side Story* last year," I say.

She raises an eyebrow. "And?"

"And . . . I wished you hadn't died at the end."

Tamia narrows her eyes as if she's searching for a hidden meaning in my comment. There's no hidden meaning, though—it's just as stupid as it sounds.

I flatten the music against the stand just for something to do. Then, so I won't have to say anything else, I begin to play.

The song opens with a piano introduction that sounds difficult but fits neatly under my fingers. Still, it's always a strange moment, the beginning of a collaboration. It's how I imagine a first date must be. Feeling each other out, trying to work out how much is too much, too fast, too soon.

"Faster," she says.

I stop playing. I'd only reached the third measure. "What?"

"You need to go faster."

I point to the music. "It says *mässig*. That's, like, *moderato*. A medium tempo, right?"

"We have a four-minute time limit. They'll cut us off if we go over."

"Oh. So why are you singing this piece at all?"

"My teacher, Bethany, chose it. I like Schubert *lieder*, and she thinks this one will stretch me. You know, a challenge." She produces air quotes for the last word.

It'll be a challenge to perform it in under four minutes. But I keep that to myself.

I start again. My fingers dance across the keys, almost trip in their haste to move along. So much for the music making me sound good. I haven't practiced playing this fast. Now I'm a kid on a bicycle with no brakes, flying downhill, blocking out any thought of where I'll land or how messy it'll be.

It's a relief when Tamia finally joins in.

She's quiet at first, the German poem delivered in hushed, almost secretive tones: about sleeping in the shadow of a linden tree. But as she moves through the second stanza, her voice becomes more focused. When she sings about carving words of love into the trunk, there's a purity to her tone that fills the room even though she's not singing very loudly. She sounds relaxed and in control.

In the middle, the poem turns darker. The music shifts to a minor key.

Finally, things become frantic. She sings about icy winds, and the already too-quick tempo becomes faster still. We're not together anymore. Tamia sounds like she just wants to get the song over with, or worse, as though she doesn't know what the words mean.

We end the song with a reprise of the opening—different words, but same music. But that's not all that has changed. Her heart doesn't seem to be in it anymore.

A piano solo closes the song, but I don't bother playing it. I spend every evening practicing alone in a cavernous room where each chord echoes, and composing music that exists only in my own head. It suits me well, being alone. But now I have an audience, and I don't want Tamia to think I'm wasting her time.

She slides a water bottle from her knit purse. "Okay, then. Thoughts?"

"It was pretty good."

She takes a swig. "And?"

"I'll need to work on keeping the tempo up. We don't want to get cut off."

"Agreed."

There's an awkward pause. "So what did *you* think?" I ask.

She wipes her sleeve across the piano. A cloud of dust rises up. "We weren't together in the middle. Or the beginning. Actually, the end wasn't much better either. You know?"

She looks disappointed. It was just one performance—not even a performance, a *rehearsal*—but Tamia acts like the problems are insurmountable. I don't know what to say to that.

"Okay, then," she says, filling the silence. "I think we're going to have to watch our balance when we get to the 'icy winds' bit." Another pause. "I can't compete if you play that loud," she says, spelling it out for me.

If she wants faster, I'll give her faster. If she wants quieter, I'll give her quieter. "Let's run it from the top," I say.

I don't wait for her to reply, just launch into the opening. She has thirty seconds before she has to sing. That should be plenty of time, even for a perfectionist like Tamia.

When she's about to come in, I look up and make eye contact. Tamia opens her mouth, and closes it again.

I stop after a couple measures. "I think you were supposed to come in there."

"I know." She won't look at me. "I'm sorry."

"For what?"

"The stuff I said just now. I do that a lot. Fill the silences, you know? Mom always says, 'If you never stop talking, you're bound to say the wrong thing sooner or later.'"

She hesitates and waits for a response. Only, I'm not used to shooting the breeze with girls like Tamia. Or any girls at all, come to think of it. I suspect her mom might be right.

Tamia leans against the piano. "You don't talk much, do you?"

I give a lopsided shrug. "You're the one with the vocal part."

For a moment, she looks confused. Then her face opens up in a grin, toothy and unselfconscious. "That's actually pretty witty," she says.

I didn't really mean to be witty, but I like the effect it has on her. She has a cute smile. "Thanks."

"Okay, then. Now that we know you're witty and insightful, how about you tell me what *I'm* doing wrong?"

"Nothing," I say.

"Nothing?" She narrows her eyes. "Seriously?"

I can't tell if she's disappointed that I have no criticisms to offer, or if she's disappointed that I'm unwilling to share them. Either way, saying nothing again will not impress her.

"Well," I begin. "Except for the stuff you already know."

"And what would that be?"

I swallow hard. "Your voice loses focus at the bottom of your range—it's why you want me to play quieter. In fact, the whole piece is too low for you. I'm guessing this has something to do with Bethany *challenging* you. Problem is, you're holding back. I can't even tell if you like the song—"

"I don't," she says quickly. "I mean, it's beautiful . . . for other people. Just not me." She lifts her water bottle but doesn't drink from it. "Bethany does this to me all the time—makes me sing stuff that doesn't sit well. She's really picky. Kind of intimidating too. She always says 'comfort breeds complacency.'"

"No way! Comfort is what lets you inside a song. Lets you *own* it."

Tamia sighs. I'm preaching to the choir here.

"What if I transpose it for you?" It would take me a couple hours, but it's easy work, and it's not like I've got a million other things going on besides schoolwork and piano practice. "Put it in a higher key, you know?"

"No. I appreciate it, but you're already doing so much."

I can tell she means it, but there's something else too. And I think I know what it is. "I get it. You don't want to sing this one in front of all your friends. And you *really* don't want to lose this contest. But you're afraid of annoying Bethany, and auditions for Eastman are coming up soon and you don't want her to give you a bad reference and—"

"Whoa." She's almost laughing, but not in a nasty way. "Anything positive you can share?"

"Well, your top range is . . . extraordinary."

The words come easily, teased out by her openness. But once I've said them, we're silent again. It's the right word, but I don't know how she'll react. *Resonant* is a musical term. Even *clear* and *warm* and *rich* are terms we can throw about meaningfully, but not *extraordinary*. It sounds reverential. I'm afraid I've just revealed as much about me as I have her voice.

"You need a song to showcase that range," I tell her, trying to salvage the situation.

"Right. One with lots of sustained high notes so I can really open up. And maybe a *pianissimo* top A, just to show off."

"Exactly. You want to win, right? You want people to be floored."

Belatedly, it occurs to me that maybe she wasn't being serious—doesn't believe such a song can possibly exist. She's wrong about that. Anything is possible in music.

Even though she's dubious, the corner of her mouth twists upward. I've found her weakness, this needs to be the best. "I don't know about winning," she says. "I just want to beat Kendra Nielson."

I've noticed Kendra onstage too—petite blonde with an incongruous powerful *mezzo* voice—but I don't mention that. "Your nemesis?"

"Moriarty to my Holmes." She steps around the piano and stands beside me. Runs a finger soundlessly across the highest keys. "So I suppose you know a piece like that, do you? A song so perfect that it might as well have been written for me? One that even my teacher doesn't know about?" There's a teasing challenge in her voice, like she wants to believe it. Wants to be impressed by me.

"Yeah, I do," I tell her. And even though it's a white lie, I know that with enough time, I'll make it true.

· · · · ·

I peer through the large glass panel in her front door and watch Tamia skip toward me. Literally *skip*. She kicks something to the side—it looks like a giant sausage—which gives me time to admire today's ensemble: denim skirt over black tights, a fluffy cream sweater topped off with a red scarf. Very festive. Very Christmas-y.

That's what happens when we get snow in November.

She opens the door and practically drags me inside. Closes it quickly and shoves the sausage-thing in place. "Keeps the draft out," she explains. "House is almost a hundred years old, you know?"

"It's a problem."

"Sure is."

I take off my jacket and gloves, and she drapes them over a radiator. "So," she says, "I got the music you sent. Now I can't decide whether to thank you or apologize."

"Why apologize?"

She shrugs. "I meant it when I said I like Schubert, but I never really believed there'd be a song that's so *perfect* for me. It must've taken you hours to find."

It did take hours actually, but I don't want to talk about that.

"That *pianissimo* top A near the end . . . just sublime."

My cheeks flush. I never imagined she'd be so impressed. "I'm glad you like it."

"I can't believe Bethany hasn't given it to me before."

I'm not used to gushy, and I don't think I can get any redder. "Schubert wrote about six hundred songs, right? It's a lot to get through."

"Well, thanks for finding the one-in-six-hundred song, then."

"It was my pleasure."

She opens her eyes comically wide. "Your *pleasure*, huh? Well, then, I match your pleasure with my undying gratitude." She gives what I think is a curtsy. "Living room's this way."

She leads me along a narrow hall that splits the one-story house in half. The kitchen is ahead—someone's cooking—and there are closed doors to either side. I wonder which of them is her bedroom.

"That one," she says, catching me looking.

A woman—her mother, I presume—appears in the kitchen doorway. She's shorter than Tamia, but the resemblance is uncanny. "You must be Cooper."

"Hi." I go to shake hands, but she's holding a spatula and bowl. "It's nice to meet you."

"Likewise. Tamia's been telling me all about you."

"She has?"

Tamia's mother looks amused. "Yes, Cooper," she says slowly. "She has."

Tamia grabs my sleeve and pulls me into the living room. Three boys are fighting over the controls for a video game, but she strides over and turns it off. "Rehearsal time," she tells them. "So sorry."

They take the disappointment well—at least until they're out of the room. Then the sound of fighting echoes along the corridor.

I give her a sympathetic look. "Must be pretty tough to have three brothers, huh?"

"Not really. Means I get my own room."

Tamia closes the door and shepherds me over to the piano. It's an old Baldwin, probably a family heirloom. The wooden legs are chipped where the boys have banged toys against them. The ivory keys are worn and discolored. I know without pressing a key that it'll be out of tune.

"My grandfather's," she says, watching me. "He used to accompany us."

"Us?"

"Mom and Dad and me. We used to sing hymns, chorales, folk songs, that sort of thing. I'd sing soprano, Mom on alto, Dad on bass. Grandpa would fill in the tenor and play the accompaniment." There's a hint of sadness in her voice.

"Not anymore, though, huh?"

"No. He died, and my brothers aren't big on music." She brightens again. "It's okay, really. Dad always sang flat, anyway."

I sit down and play an arpeggio, right hand only, just to get a feel for it.

It sounds amazing.

Tamia watches my reaction. "I got it freshly tuned for you—took most of my babysitting money. I know what you snobby pianists are like."

I try to hide a smile. "What are we like?"

"Oh, you know. Always moaning about having to play on other people's instruments."

"Unlike singers, who are always complaining that they've got a cold, or a sore throat, or stomach flu, or—"

"Cold hands. Which is why pianists can't play as well as they usually do. Can barely play a note until they've warmed their little fingers on a hot cup—"

"Of herbal tea that they use to restore the natural balance of their vocal cords."

Tamia snorts. "Exactly. Glad we straightened that out." She pulls off her scarf and tosses it on the sofa beside us.

"Bare neck. Living dangerously, I see."

"You have no idea." She opens up her score with a flourish and nods at the music stand on the piano. My score is already open there. "So, *Morgen* by Franz Schubert. Let's do this, Cooper."

With a deep breath, I begin to play. The piano accompaniment is far more difficult than the other song, but after practicing all afternoon, I've got it down cold. Cascading arpeggios fly beneath my fingers, a musical representation of the sun's rays in the poem. When Tamia enters a fraction late, I hope it's because she's pleasantly surprised.

"*Und morgen wird die Sonne wieder scheinen,*" she sings, her voice as high and pure as sunlight. Every word is clear; her German, impeccable. It's how I dreamed the song would sound. Even Schubert would have to be impressed.

Toward the end of the song, as the poem's lovers gaze into each other's eyes, she really opens up. She lets her voice soar, hangs on to notes that other sopranos would only grasp at. She sings with vibrato, but only a little. She's not reaching for these ethereal tones; she's landing on them. This is Tamia at her finest, and it's all I can do to keep playing.

The last line of the poem speaks of the happiness of silence. Tamia revels in it. Like a flickering flame being extinguished, she smothers the music until nothing remains but the husks of each word: softened consonants and muted vowels.

And then she is silent.

I keep playing for a few more measures, slower and quieter all the way to the final chord. It's so small and faint that I wonder if the judges at the contest will be able to hear it. I keep my fingers depressed for a few seconds and lift them at the same moment that I release the sustain pedal. There's not a sound in the house.

I look up at Tamia. She holds the score to her chest. "I love Schubert." Her voice is barely above a whisper. "Mom always wants me to sing Baroque music: Bach, Handel, that sort of thing. Dad likes Puccini."

"So you split the difference."

She mulls it over. "No. I just saw an opportunity to piss them both off."

"Language, Tamia!" Six quick footsteps and her mother pokes her head around the doorway. "I heard that."

Tamia does a convincing impression of someone who is embarrassed. Once her mother leaves, we try not to laugh out loud.

"So do *you* like Schubert?" she asks.

"Yeah."

"Course you do. You looked through six hundred songs, right?"

Not exactly, but I'm pleased that she thinks I did. "I like that whole early nineteenth-century period. Schubert, Schumann, Mendelssohn. I love the chromaticism, the seriousness of it, the way they wear their hearts on their sleeves, you know?"

"Yeah. I know."

She's staring at me again, and though she's smiling, I know she's smiling with me, not at me. It means so much, that look. It means that she understands, and we can share this. It means that for the first time in years, someone who isn't an adult truly *gets* me.

"So, comments? Criticisms?" I ask.

Tamia opens up her music again. She shakes her head. "I feel like we were meant to perform this song."

"Me too."

"So let's just keep going. It's Saturday, and I don't need to be anywhere. Besides, it's a love song—it'll get better every time."

I turn away so that she won't see me turn red. For the next hour, I play again, and she sings again, and our world is music. It's exactly where I want to be.

It's dark when we finish. Tamia walks me to the door and watches me pull on my jacket and gloves.

"So I have to ask," she says. "Why Rice?"

"What?"

"Rice University. That's where you want to go, right?"

I'm having trouble keeping up. "How do you know about that?"

"I asked around about you. Now stop changing the subject."

"Okay." I try to remember my list. There's actually a real list on the wall beside my desk. "Good music department. Good academics—"

"Hot and humid."

"I can stand the heat."

She cocks an eyebrow. "That was a very suave line, Cooper. Nicely done."

"Thanks. So why Eastman?"

She plays along, even though she knows that payback is coming. "*Excellent* performance program. *Great* faculty—"

"Cold and gray."

"I can be icy too. Haven't you noticed?"

She steps toward me, narrows her eyes, and arches one brow. She's wearing eyeliner too, which she wasn't last time we met. I need another suave reply—something confident and flirty. Only, dueling with words is harder now that she's so close. "Actually, no. I don't see that at all."

We stand at her door. She's looking right at me, and though I want to look back, something stops me.

"Where's your car?" she asks, wiping condensation off the glass.

"I walked."

"Walked?" She makes the word sound foreign. "It's snowing. I'll give you a ride."

She pulls on a bright red hat with tassels, and gloves to match. Everything I own is black, so we're a study in contrasts. "Be back soon, Mom," she shouts.

We walk side by side down her path, footfalls crunching on fresh snow, nothing but amber streetlights and the hush of winter. She unlocks the passenger door and I climb in. She hurries around and joins me. The wiper blades cast off the fresh coating of snow.

"Heater takes a long time to get warm," she warns me.

We pull out onto the empty street, and I give her directions. She sits way forward, almost hugs the steering wheel. "Seriously, though. Why

Rice? I figured you'd want somewhere with a better performing program."

"No. I like the piano, but I don't just want to play. I need to compose as well. Composing is like, I don't know, writing poetry without words, or something. One note can change a piece, and it's up to me to choose the note. To have that control, you know?"

When she nods slowly, I'm tempted to tell her more—the kind of things I've never told anyone. How I hear it all playing in my head, and there are times I can't get it onto the paper fast enough. How no one tries to decode my music the way they do poetry. No one draws conclusions about me and laughs at what they find. No one really thinks about my music at all, but that's okay. Being left alone isn't the worst thing in the world.

That's what I used to believe, anyway. But Tamia is still listening, and I like that she cares.

"I've been auditing this music theory class at St. Louis University," I continue, "and it's like I'm peeling back the layers of what music is. How it *works*."

She mulls this over. "I can tell you how music works, Cooper. You play the piano. Beside you, a girl swoons. It's really pretty simple."

I don't think we're flirting anymore. Tamia likes me, really *likes* me, and I don't know what to do. There's no musical score for this piece.

"Depends what I play though, right?" I say. "If I play Bach, your mom gets teary-eyed. If I play Puccini, your dad runs downstairs and gives me an awkward man-hug." Tamia chuckles, but it feels polite instead of genuine. "What I want to know is: What makes Bach, Bach? Or Puccini, Puccini? You get what I'm saying?"

"Yeah. I get it." But her tone tells me she doesn't really get it at all.

She asks for my address, but I continue to give her directions. She doesn't see through it, either. Doesn't decode the awkwardness until we're outside my house with the engine idling.

She peers wide-eyed between the wiper blades. "That's a big house," she says.

"Yeah."

"*Really* big." She tilts her head and peers at me from the corner of her eye. "Not that big is bad. It's just . . . big."

I need to say something, but I'm not sure what.

"You must have a whole bunch of siblings to fill that place."

When I look at it now, I see it through her eyes: austere and unwelcoming. "Actually, I'm an only child. My parents aren't even Catholic; they just like schools to be disciplined."

Her eyes flit between the house and me like she's seeing us both for the first time. "Well, like I say . . . big is just big. It's like, you know Kendra Nielson?"

"Yeah," I say a little too quickly.

She rolls her eyes. "Of course you do. Well, she has a great voice and small boobs. Whereas I have a great voice and big boobs. One isn't better than the other. They're just different. Do you see what I'm saying?"

"I . . ." I'm at a loss for words, to be honest. But that won't cut it. "I hadn't noticed."

"What? My boobs or hers?"

Reflexively, I check out her chest. She isn't lying, but I already knew that. "Um, either. I mean, neither."

"That's too bad." She bites her lip as if she's shy, but I'm not fooled—from the way her eyes sparkle, I know she's enjoying this.

She giggles, and I do too. It's about the least manly I've ever sounded. And when the giggling ends, everything is quiet. And it feels all right.

"I did it again," she says. "Filled the silence, I mean. I only do it because I'm nervous."

"About the talent contest."

She shakes her head once. "No, Cooper. Not about the talent contest."

"Oh." I make the word sound small and unimportant, when in reality it should've lasted several seconds. This is a *moment*, bigger even than a performance at a contest. Trouble is, I've got stage fright.

Seconds tick by and the heater hums. I need to say something, do something, but the air feels charged. Every moment, every action is vital, and it's a kind of pressure I'm not used to. By the time I remember to breathe again, she's not looking at me anymore.

"Well, I should let you get back," I say.

She stares out the windshield. "Yeah. I guess."

I pull on the door lever, but it doesn't open. Tamia leans across me and her hair brushes against my face. I smell her shampoo. She gives the lever a sharp pull, and the door pops open. Then she turns to me and kisses me on the cheek—just once, quickly, as if I might disappear.

I step out into a few inches of snow, but I don't feel the cold. I rest my arm on the doorframe and marvel at the beauty of the world. "Thanks for the ride."

"Sure. Hey, did you really walk to my house tonight, Cooper?"

I'm surprised by the question. "Yeah. Why?"

"It's almost three miles."

"I noticed."

She responds with a close-mouthed smile, as if the thought intrigues her. "I'm glad you did."

As I close the door, I think to myself: *so am I.*

. . . . .

Thirteen identical chairs are arranged in a circle. No one sits.

Half a dozen singers walk the perimeter of the small room, nervously adjusting their outfits, warming up their voices with lip trills and scales.

I'm not sure what to do. They can warm up their voices all they like, but the piano is next door and I'm fairly sure I won't be getting any more practice time on it this evening. I wiggle my fingers, but it feels pointless. Embarrassing too, especially when Tamia watches me, a laugh threatening to erupt at any moment.

I know that look because I've seen it a lot over the past three evenings as we've honed our performance—direct hits on every note and near misses on every kiss. I'm surprised it doesn't bother me more that we only kissed once. I'm surprised it doesn't annoy her that I'm too scared to make a move.

Kendra Nielson heads through the double doors that lead to the stage. She has just enough trouble with the door handles to disrupt everyone's flow. To make amends, she turns to us and smiles sweetly, offers an apology we haven't asked for and certainly don't need. And then she's gone, having ensured that we'll all be listening to her through the door.

"Come on," says Tamia. "We're up next."

In six minutes, we'll take the stage in my school's auditorium. In ten minutes, we'll accept the audience's applause. In twelve minutes, the judges will grade us. In less than an hour, we'll know if we've won. Then we'll say good-bye, and our collaboration will come to a sudden close. I'll continue to practice and compose every evening, but I don't believe it will feel the same. I don't want to be alone anymore. I want what we have to last.

"Here." Tamia adjusts the sleeves of her black dress, reaches into her purse, and pulls out an envelope. She hands it to me.

"Can I open it now?"

"Yeah . . . or later. I mean, it's up to you."

The stationery feels fancy. Expensive. I slide my finger under the flap and tear it open. Inside is a letter, folded perfectly in three. It has been handwritten in calligraphy—must've taken her ages. There's a voucher to a local music store too.

As Tamia wanders around the room warming up, her dress swirls around her ankles. I read the letter twice before she returns.

"Thank you," I say.

She waves me off. "You're welcome. I mean it. When you play, I feel . . ." Her eyes drift toward the floor. She looks embarrassed and demure all at once.

When she looks up again, she adjusts my bow tie. In heels, she's face to face with me, close enough that I can hear her swallow. "I guess what I'm saying is: We're in tune, you and me. And that's a beautiful thing."

"Yes," I agree. "It is."

The applause for Kendra is long and enthusiastic. Someone in the audience is very proud of his wolf whistle, which seems kind of weird. I hope it's her boyfriend.

When the noise dies down, there are a couple minutes of judging. Tamia warned me about this—it's kind of the point of a talent contest—but I don't like having my work graded five seconds after it's done. I'm a pretty good judge of when I flunk a test, and I really don't need the graders confirming it in front of my peers.

As if she can read my mind, Tamia gives my hand a reassuring squeeze. "It's okay," she says. "We'll kick ass."

A teacher nods at us, giving us permission to go into the auditorium. We open the doors together, stride through, and wait in the wings as Kendra saunters off the stage.

"Ah, geez." Tamia puffs out her cheeks and exhales slowly. "I didn't realize my singing teacher was one of the judges." She snorts. "Think Bethany will notice this isn't the song she gave me?"

I can't believe she's laughing it off. Not only will Bethany notice, but she'll have plenty of questions about the song we're performing too. I'm second-guessing everything now, but there's no time to talk about it.

The emcee introduces us and we walk onstage to enthusiastic applause. Pretty much everyone has seen Tamia in school musicals; I'm probably not the only one who thought she was amazing in them. The audience is a couple hundred strong, shadowy figures in orderly rows. The spotlight is fixed on us.

I adjust the piano stool down a couple inches and rest my fingers on the keyboard. It's a Steinway concert grand, a beast of an instrument. I've played on it before when I've accompanied the instrumentalists at my school, but there's still something intimidating about the immensity of it. Compared to my piano at home, it's like shifting from a Mini Cooper to a limo.

Tamia stands in the curve of the piano, watching me over her shoulder. When our eyes meet, I can tell she's not nervous at all. Impossibly, as the spotlight rains down on her, she seems to grow, not shrink from the glare. My fingers murmur above the pure white keys; my armpits are itchy with sweat.

Then I begin: a fluttering of arpeggios like dappled sunlight, chromatic harmony as subtle and complicated as love itself. I lose myself in it until Tamia joins in too. After that, it's a dialogue—a perfect conversation, perfectly in tune. And though I ought to be nervous, I'm not. Sharing the stage with Tamia frees me. Everything I do is on display here, but no one will be looking at me as long as Tamia is singing.

I'm in the music. I *am* the music. Silence and darkness surround us, but in our bubble, the world is as it's meant to be.

Tamia opens up on the higher notes, strikes them with laser-like intensity. Still she climbs, until at the climax of the song the lovers finally come together. Then she floats, as if we've left the real world and entered a dream. Or heaven itself.

Tamia's contribution over, I bring things back to earth, closing with a gentle *rallentando*. I haven't even let go of the keys before everyone cheers. I ought to be happy, but the applause feels rude and intrusive. Several seconds pass before Tamia takes a bow.

She signals for me to stand too. Reaches across the piano and takes my hand, eases me around the keyboard until we're side by side. It's standard practice, but when we bow, she continues to hold my hand, even slips her fingers between mine.

There's nothing standard about this anymore.

We bow again. On the third bow, we begin to laugh—partly because of nerves, and partly because it feels over the top. People are standing, cheering, whooping. I hadn't really thought about the reception we'd get, and it means a lot to see everyone appreciating Tamia's skill. I can stand losing, but I couldn't have stood anyone disrespecting her.

When the applause dies out, we stay exactly where we are. She still hasn't let go of my hand.

Mr. McCutcheon, her music teacher, leans across the table to speak into the microphone. "That was a beautiful performance, Tamia and Cooper. But, uh . . . it's not what we expected to hear."

Tamia gives a respectful nod. "There was a last-minute change of plan."

Bethany leans back in her chair, hands pressed together, watching us. Or rather, watching *me*. Her eyes drift down to our hands.

"It says *Der Lindenbaum* here," Mr. McCutcheon continues. A couple of people in the audience boo halfheartedly. "I'm just saying . . ."

Tamia squeezes my hand. "Different song, same composer. We wanted to show what we can do."

Mr. McCutcheon gives up the microphone and Bethany takes over. "Looking at the entry form you submitted, I see that the rules are stated quite clearly. You chose *Der Lindenbaum*, and we must judge accordingly."

Again, the audience expresses its displeasure, but Bethany doesn't even seem to notice. "I'm intrigued to know where you're getting your advice these days, Tamia." She pauses, as if she's giving her pupil a chance to respond, though it's clear there's nothing for Tamia to say. "But I'm even more intrigued to hear you explain how Schubert set to music a poem written half a century after his death."

Tamia's still smiling, but it's forced now. "I don't understand," she says.

Bethany looks straight at me, but addresses Tamia. "Of course you don't, dear. Because it's impossible. Schubert died in eighteen-twenty-eight. When Richard Strauss set that poem, *Morgen*, in eighteen-ninety-four, it was still quite new."

"So this piece is by Strauss?" Tamia's voice shakes.

"Not by a long shot. It is impressive, though. Truly a shame that a world premiere should count for so little—especially a love song." She addresses me now. "You have a remarkable ear, Cooper. But whom exactly were you trying to fool?"

Tamia loosens our fingers, and I feel the space where her hand used to be. She wants to face me, ask me if it's true, but the audience is whispering and snickering.

Besides, she already knows the answer.

I can't breathe. The distance between us is only inches but may as well be miles. In the frozen moment, I can't recall a single reason why I didn't just tell her the truth.

Tamia takes a deep breath and stands up straight. She refuses to cave to the humiliation. "Thank you for your consideration," she tells the judges.

She walks offstage, and I follow. When she turns the corner and the curtain hides her from everything that has happened, she runs. I try to keep up with her, but I'm barely into the warm-up room when Kendra Nielson stops me.

"You're such a jerk," she says. "If you did that to me, I'd—"

I brush past her and cross the room. Everyone is looking at me. They've already worked out that I wrote the song for her. They probably think I did it to impress her, but that wasn't the main reason. I did it so that she could be comfortable onstage, and so that for four precious minutes, everyone in the audience would understand what an astonishing instrument the human voice is. Now I'm faced with a mix of glares and sympathetic nods. No one is without an opinion.

I pull the door open, but she's not in the stairwell. She's not in the corridor at the bottom. I don't hear her footsteps anywhere.

Tamia has left the building. I can't kid myself that she wants me to find her.

. . . . .

I sit on my bed in the darkness, staring through the window at the streetlight outside. My parents haven't said a word to me. I don't know what they think—if they're shocked or confused or angry—and they don't know what I think either. It doesn't even bother me. Only one person's opinion matters anymore, and she's gone.

It's late, close to midnight, when a car pulls up. The driver doesn't get out, but I know it's her. She sits behind the wheel, as still as I am.

I tell myself she doesn't want to speak to me, but why is she here, then?

I tell myself that no apology will ever be enough for humiliating her, but does that mean I shouldn't try?

I go downstairs, slide on shoes, and head outside. It's her chance to drive away, but she doesn't. She climbs out of the car and closes the door almost silently behind her.

We stop a couple yards short of each other—a safe, respectful distance. Beneath her duffel coat, she's still wearing her dress.

"I'm sorry, Tamia." The words almost trip out of me. "I'm so sorry."

She doesn't react at all. It's like she doesn't even hear me. "I've just been to see Bethany. Said I should've talked to her, told her how I felt about things."

She runs a gloved hand across her nose. In the streetlight, her cheeks appear orange-red, the color of sunset.

"My parents were there," she says.

I close my eyes. "I'm sorry."

"Hmm. Well, don't be. Even though they like Handel and Puccini, they're actually pretty smart people. They asked me if I thought you did it to embarrass me—"

"Of course I didn't."

She holds her hand up to stop me. "I know that. And so do they. So then they asked me if I thought Bethany tried to embarrass me." She purses her lips. "And the answer is . . . yes. A grown woman, someone I've trusted for years, humiliated me tonight, just because she was annoyed with me. Just because she *could*."

Tamia has been stoic all evening, but now her eyes well up. I want to hold her, tell her I'm sorry again. Only, I don't think that's my place anymore. And so I just stand there, as helpless now as I was during the contest judging.

"I told her I'm going to find a new singing teacher, Cooper."

I can barely breathe. "But your auditions—"

"Will be fine." She blinks and the tears fall, but she laughs right through them. "Music is where I go to escape the world. Not to be reminded how ugly it can be." She sniffs, makes even that seem cute. "You wrote me a song. *Our* song. And I love it, and it's more perfect for me than anything I've ever sung. *That's* the world of music I want to live in."

I'm shivering like crazy now. I'm not wearing a coat, and when I rub my hands together it doesn't help at all. "I didn't know about the competition rules, Tamia. I promise I didn't. I only wrote Schubert's name on the music to see if you'd be able to tell. But then you said how perfect it was, and how it must've taken me hours to find, and I . . . I got scared you'd think it was weird. Or freaky, or something."

"Weird that you took the time to compose me my own song? That you know my voice better than anyone?" She takes off her gloves and stuffs them in her pockets. When she holds my hands, her fingers are warm. "I didn't get it when you said you wanted to know what makes Schubert, Schubert. I've never really thought about music like that. But after tonight, I understand. You gave me the gift of a song Schubert never got to write."

She pulls me closer and tries to wrap her duffel coat around us. It only reaches my arms, but we're touching now and her warmth radiates through me. Our breaths condense and mix in the cold night air until there's no space between us at all.

We're back where we were on Saturday night, just outside my house. This time, though, Tamia kisses me and I kiss her back. As snow begins to fall around us once more, we retreat to the happiness of silence, like a love song come to life.

....

ANECDOTE: LEA SALONGA

....

You'd think that the audition was the start of everything . . . the genesis, the "big bang" of an actor's career. With how the audition is one often-spoken-of step in the process of casting a show (and possibly launching someone into superstardom), it would seem as though it all starts here.

No, it does not.

There is no one actual first step (much like no two people have the same fingerprints or hair color). Everyone's story begins in very different ways. I can't speak for how others began their journeys, but I can speak about my own.

According to my mother, my journey began at the age of three. As a child, she said that I would stand on top of the coffee table and sing, using the plug of a nearby lamp as a pretend microphone. Whenever my cousin Betsy came over to babysit me, she'd whip out her guitar and teach me a few pop songs. It's strange, but I remember "We May Never Love Like This Again" performed by Maureen McGovern, and "Have You Never Been Mellow" recorded by Olivia Newton-John. My mother actually recorded those renditions on cassette, but unfortunately, we no longer have those early recordings. You'll just have to take my word for it.

Since it was quite easy to convince me to get up in front of other members of my very large family, another cousin took notice. Ria, who was at the time very active with a local theater group, Repertory Philippines, suggested to my mother that maybe, just maybe, I should be brought to audition for Rep's upcoming production of *The King and I*.

My memory of this actual audition is quite selective. I remember standing on the stage at the Insular Life Auditorium . . . reciting my Girl Scout Oath in lieu of a prepared monologue or a nursery rhyme . . . and feeling very, very comfortable.

The next memorable audition came for another of Rep's big musical productions, *Annie*. By then I was a veritable veteran with a few plays and musicals under my belt. I was told to prepare "Tomorrow" for the audition, and so with unrelenting commitment, I played the song over and over again to make sure I was absolutely ready. I made sure I memorized my song (I also prepared "Maybe" just in case another one was asked for) to avoid anything untoward on the day.

Oh, the day. I have no idea how it happened, but I had major allergies the day of my audition (I can't remember if I ate something or took medication that provoked an attack, but there it was). My eyelids were very swollen (I looked like bees had stung them), and I may have had some trouble breathing. But since this was the only audition day, I was not about to miss it. My mother wasn't going to let an opportunity like this slip by either.

My name was called . . . I got up onstage . . . and I opened my mouth to sing "Tomorrow." Those few minutes went by like a blur . . . the next thing I knew, the whole house was on its feet in front of me. I don't know why the audience gave me a standing ovation: for my actual singing ability, or for the fact that I didn't let an allergy attack stop me from making this moment come true.

Yes, there were more auditions that followed (including the one that would ultimately change my life and career, the audition for *Miss Saigon*), and while I remain active as an actor, there will be more. I'll win a few, I'll lose a few, but that's the name of the game. However, as I prepare for all of the ones coming up, I'll always remember those first few . . . and those early dreams and songs that got me there.

LEA SALONGA is a singer and actress who is best known for her Tony Award–winning role in *Miss Saigon*. She has also won the Olivier, Drama Desk, Outer Critics Circle, and Theatre World Awards. On Broadway, she has starred in *Flower Drum Song*, and was the first Asian to play Eponine in the musical *Les Misérables* on Broadway. She returned to the beloved show as Fantine in the 2006 revival.

Lea began her career in the Philippines, making her professional debut at the age of seven in the musical *The King and I*. She went on to star in productions of *Annie*, *Cat on a Hot Tin Roof*, *Fiddler on the Roof*, *The Rose Tattoo*, *The Sound of Music*, *The Goodbye Girl*, *Paper Moon*, and *The Fantasticks*. Lea was also the singing voice of Princess Jasmine from *Aladdin* and Fa Mulan for *Mulan* and *Mulan II*. In honor of her portrayal of the beloved princesses, Disneyland has bestowed the honor of "Disney Legend" to Lea.

To learn more about Lea, please visit her at www.leasalonga.com.

TUESDAY AT MIDNIGHT

Nina LaCour

To: Monica Livingston
From: Tori Fields
Date: 9/14/2013

Dear Monica,

Thirteen minutes after the seventh-period bell rang, I realized what the problem was. You say that I rush into things, tell you stories without giving you the context. You said it to me like it was something cute that I do, but I know (for a fact, actually) that it annoys you. I wonder how many of the other compliments you gave me weren't really compliments at all. It makes me sad to think about it. Okay. The context.

I finished the screenplay last month. You know how I'd been having trouble with the ending? Well, it finally came to me—the perfect solution, something that wouldn't seem too tidy but that would still satisfy. I hate that feeling, don't you? When the screen goes black and you're like, *what?* So it came to me: what would happen to Claire, where I would leave her. I wrote all through the end of world history and only felt a tiny bit guilty when Ms. Hendricks thanked me for taking such thorough notes when really I missed every word that she said.

There are still three main characters: Sophie and Eric and Claire, with Sophie at the center of the love triangle. Or, I don't know, at the top piece of it. At the pointiest point. The story is about love and friendship and the everyday agonies of high school. That sounds melodramatic but it isn't. I wanted to write a screenplay that felt real. I think I pulled it off.

We held auditions after school, so that brings us to the end of seventh period again. I didn't go straight into Mr. Samson's room where everyone was gathering. I thought that could be awkward since obviously I'm the one making the final casting decisions even though Mr. Samson makes the announcements, so instead I sat outside on the bench under the climbing vine that was specked with bright pink flowers and I made a list of what I wanted in a Sophie. I intended to write lists for Eric and Claire too, but I got hung up on Sophie and then ran out of time. The list included a lot of things. Black hair; dark eyes; slender wrists and ankles; delicate ears good for hair tucking; soft lips good for close-ups of kissing; a face capable of sarcasm, withering glances, and effortless cruelty. Also kindness and sincerity and openness. The kind of beauty that makes your bones ache.

Fifteen minutes passed while I was dreaming up the perfect Sophie. Matt (who gets to be cinematographer this year) was setting up his camera to film the auditions and the actors were assembling and rehearsing their lines and assessing one another. And then I put my notebook away and walked in to find all the usual people, sitting in a neat row: Kim and Samantha and Aubrey and Leah and Michelle and the rest of them. So many of the drama girls were auditioning for Sophie. And even though there were so many really great actors to choose from, I got this sinking feeling, this desperation. The problem became clear: none of them were you.

I know that you don't really want to hear from me, even though I never hurt you in any way. I hope that you are liking your new school and not missing it here too much. I'll stop texting and emailing you. I just wanted you to know.

Love,
Tori

Note written during 4th period, 9/18/13

Sean!!!

I thought about texting you but I didn't want your phone to get confiscated by Ms. Heung again. And plus, this news is too special for a text. You know all those times you said I was totally gonna get the part? Well, you were right.

I GOT THE PART!

I really need to trust you more and doubt myself less. Like, when I was rehearsing my monologue, and you said, "Babe, you're amazing," I shouldn't have said, "Do you really think so?" I should have said: "I know!" Because I could actually feel all the things my character was feeling in that moment: powerful and destructive and brave. For 2.5 minutes I was not Sam anymore. I was Sophie. And then, at the audition, I did it again. I knew that I was being a true artist up there, and that everyone else could feel it too. There's no other way to say it: it was magical.

How should we celebrate? I know. Take me out tonight! You can borrow your mom's car again, right?

I hope you aren't going to mind that I'm going to have to get it on with both Lily and Josh. It's totally nonromantic to fool around in front of a camera and the entire crew. I wonder how we're going to do the sex scenes. Eek, maybe I'll have to really be naked! Anyways, I'm so excited for tonight! Hint: I feel like Chinese!

I love you!

Your star,
Sam

To: Monica Livingston
From: Samantha Partridge
Date: 9/18/2013

Hey, Monica!

I hope Utah is awesome! As you might already know, I am to play the part of Sophie in *Tuesday at Midnight*. Since Sophie is based on you, I'm wondering if you'd help me out with something. When you hooked up with Tyler at Erica's party, what was going through your head? Did you not care that you were cheating on Tori? Did you feel like it was wrong but you couldn't help yourself? Or maybe you aren't comfortable being tied down? I'm trying to say this line right: "It's just me. It's the way I am." I've practiced a lot with different feelings behind it. I can say it tearfully or defensively or confidently, but I want to be authentic, because that's the word that Tori keeps using during rehearsals. She wants us to really feel what we're supposed to be feeling. "Aim for authenticity," she keeps saying. So I need to know the subtext, all the background stuff, you know. I know you won't mind me asking you this, because you understand the creative process too. The more detail you can go into the better because I really want to understand her/you. I want to give Sophie some humanity.

Thanks!

XOXO!
Sam

To: Bob and Martha Fields
From: Grady Samson
Date: 10/1/13

Dear Mr. and Mrs. Fields:

I hope this little note finds you both well. It's a pleasure to have Tori in my class again. She's just as creative as ever, and this year she is much more focused (due in part, I surmise, to Monica's family's move to Utah). As I'm sure you are well aware, her screenplay, *Tuesday at Midnight*, was chosen by her peers to be our class project this semester. If you have read it, you'll understand the delicacy of my situation. Underage drinking, teen sex, and profanity! The content isn't exactly PG rated.

I don't intend to bore you with the details, but it would be an understatement to say that it takes a battle to the death each year just to keep my film class alive amidst budget cuts and the increasing (and disturbing) privileging of the sciences over the arts. The administration doesn't understand the worth of art; they consider filmmaking frivolous. I ask them, where do you turn when you feel the world getting you down, when you need inspiration, when you need to feel alive again? To a Petri dish? No. You listen to a song that commiserates with you. You look at a painting that moves you. Or you go to a movie, feel that blast of air-conditioning, your skin on the plush seats, lean back, and look at the screen as it lights up with the promise of a story.

I need to tell you something. I wasn't planning on sharing this with you, but I feel for the first time in my twenty-seven-year career that I have found a protégé. In Tori I see an artist. A true filmmaker. Someone who can become what I didn't dare dream I could become when I was in my tender youth. But I digress.

To put it simply, it won't take long for the parents to discover some of the details of this film and go complain to the principal, and then I will be standing in her office getting my hand slapped. (So to speak.) And after the hand slapping, I will be the one having to break it to these adults that yes, their teenagers drink and have sex and curse and probably more things that we don't even know about, and that no, this movie isn't corrupting their poor young minds, etc., etc. *ad infinitum*. I am writing to assure you that I am behind Tori and her staggeringly beautiful *Tuesday at Midnight* 1000 percent. I have never encountered a screenplay that speaks so delicately and honestly about the complexities of youth, of first love and heartbreak. It isn't often that, in the midst of this mind-numbing beige suburbia, a cause worth fighting for arises, but it has arisen, and with it I too, am rising.

Yours,
Grady Samson

To: Tori Fields
From: Monica Livingston
Date: 10/3/13

Tori,

Are you aware that Samantha wrote me an email about how she knows that Sophie is based on me? She actually asked me personal questions so she could understand "her character." I shouldn't have to tell you this, but my life and my choices aren't just material for your movie. Please send me the screenplay. I need to make sure I'm comfortable with how I'm depicted.

I'm not going to get into the reasons I'm not writing you back and calling you and everything. I explained already that even though at first it seemed like the end of the world that my dad took a job in Utah, I then came to see Utah as a new beginning. And, to answer your question, no. I don't hate it when the screen goes black because I actually don't think, *what*. I think that life is not easily resolved. I appreciate that uncertainty reflected in art.

Monica

To: Grady Samson
From: Bob and Martha Livingston
Date: 10/3/13

Dear Mr. Samson,

Thank you so much for letting us know about the possible controversy surrounding Tori's film. We were, to be honest, less than thrilled with the number of expletives in her screenplay, but at the same time we agree that it's an accurate reflection of the experience of many of our children. Of course, we hope that other members of the Vista High School community will feel similarly, but we are ready to show support for Tori and your much beloved and valued film program in any way that we can.

Thank you, also, for your kind words about our daughter. We are tremendously proud of her.

All our best,
Martha and Bob (Fields)

To: Sean Lu
From: Samantha Partridge
Date: 10/17/13

Seany!

You will never believe what happened this morning! While you were in second period! It's still hard for me to believe that people at school were just in their classes sitting there staring into space or something while in the Admin hall things were going crazy!

Okay, so this is how it started. We walked into film class and Mr. Samson was pacing in front and he didn't say hello to us like he usually does so we all could feel that something was up. It was like there was this hush over us. But we were kind of whispering, too, because we were all wondering what was wrong. And then the bell rang and he just *kept pacing*. We were all like, Oh my God, what's wrong with Mr. Samson??? Then he said, "Tori, will you come talk to me for a moment?" And Tori got up and followed him into his office, and we all tried to hear what he was saying but we couldn't hear it. It was pretty silent for a little while, and then Mr. Samson and Tori BURST out of his office and into the classroom. Actually, it was more like Mr. Samson burst out and Tori walked out with him.

Basically, what happened was that some parent of a kid (who isn't even in the film class and who none of us have heard of, by the way) wrote to "express concern" about our film. I guess she's part of the parents' club and she said that since the parents' club funds the film class she would like to make sure the administration approves the movie. Whatever. So controlling.

So Mr. Samson was like a sports coach all of a sudden. "Are we going to let the parents' club dictate our art?" he kept yelling, and we yelled back, "No!" "What are we gonna do about it?!" he yelled, and we didn't really know what to do so we just kind of muttered some suggestions and shrugged and stuff until he said, "Are we going to go down to the office and tell them what we think about their 'expression of concern'?" And we were like, "Yeah!" And then, before I even knew what was happening, rolls of Duct tape were flying through the air and into our hands, and we were writing signs that said things like "Whatever happened to freedom of speech?" and "Art saves lives!" Mine said, "Get your parents off my movie!" Isn't that amazing? I don't even know how I came up with it.

We all covered our mouths with the Duct tape and then we marched to the Admin hall. Mr. Samson didn't tape his mouth right away, though, because he gave this speech as we marched. It was incredible. It happened so fast and he kept talking about all of this history stuff that I didn't really get but I could tell it was super awesome and relevant. When we got to the hall, he yelled, "Now make a star!" And we did it! We didn't even organize. *We just lay down in the shape of a star.* I thought about getting in the middle of it since I am *the* star, but then I figured I would stay with my cast.

Mr. Samson put the tape over his mouth, which was really powerful. And then we just waited for them to notice us. Finally the secretary came out and said, "What the?" and then rushed back in. Then Principal Monroe came out and shook her head. "What is this, Grady?" she asked, but Mr. Samson's mouth was taped so all he could do is point at us and our shirts. She walked in a circle around us reading our messages. She rubbed her face. It was clear that she really had a lot on her mind. Then she said, "Go ahead and make your movie. But you're not showing it at Open House, all right, Grady? Is that clear?"

Then she went back in the office. Honestly? I was a little bit confused. But then Mr. Samson peeled the tape off of his mouth. He gestured for us to do it, too. It really hurt! We were all watching him, rubbing our mouths, and wondering what we should do next. "Ladies and gentleman," he said—*to us*! "You have just been part of a successful preemptive strike. We have made Vista High School history today and preserved the integrity of *Tuesday at Midnight*." He actually had tears in his eyes. And you know what? I had some tears in mine too. I knew I was part of something really special. I really was.

See you at lunch!!!
Sam

To: Tori Fields
From: Monica Livingston
Date: 10/23/13

Tori,

I still haven't gotten a copy of your screenplay, and I'm feeling really uncomfortable about this, especially because Sam keeps writing to me—*even though I'm completely ignoring her*—with more questions and all of this rambling about how controversial your film is and whether I've heard about it on the news. *On the news?* Tori, all the things that happened to us were between us. I regret a lot of things but I'm trying to move on and I don't need my bad decisions haunting me. Just email it to me or something, okay?

Monica

To: Monica Livingston
From: Tori Fields
Date: 10/29/13

Monica,

Please. My movie wasn't ever on the news. Sam is being dramatic. There was a little bit of controversy, but Mr. Samson handled it (in a way that you would find really funny, by the way. It was extreme but, to his credit, effective).

When I said that you weren't in that room on audition day, I didn't mean that Sophie was you. I meant that I wrote the part with you in mind, like you were my muse, like when I wrote "Sophie laughs," I pictured you laughing. At first it was almost like a form of self-torture, because it was still so raw, what happened between us. But then it started to make me feel better to write it all out. Not the facts but the feeling of everything. It felt good to see all of the misery become something.

I'll tell Sam not to contact you anymore. I'll tell her that she misunderstood and that you aren't Sophie at all.
I hope you're doing well,

Tori

To: Tori Fields
From: Monica Livingston
Date: 11/8/2013

Tori,

You have got to be kidding me. Sam actually called me and left me this long voicemail asking why I made those lists about you that I made. I don't even know how you know about them. But the next time you choose to use personal details about my life please have the decency not to tell me that the character isn't based on me.

Monica

Text message sent from Tori Fields to Tyler Marsh, 11/8/2013

I need to talk to you.

To: Monica Livingston
From: Tyler Marsh
Date: 11/8/2013

Heeeeyyyyyy, Monica.

Okay, so I'm writing you this because Tori just yelled at me for five minutes because I told Sam about those lists you made. So here's the confession I promised her I'd give you.

Sam has been like stalking me for information about you. I finally just broke down and gave her something good so she'd leave me alone. And yeah, I told Tori about the lists, too, but I just thought it would be doing everyone a favor. Like I know you don't want to hear from either of us and that's no problem on my end because whatever happened between us is over and that's more than cool with me. But Tori's spent the last few months walking around like she's shell-shocked, so I thought telling her about the lists might snap her out of it.

So I told her.

And then I said, "What kind of person makes a list of the stuff that annoys her about the girl she's supposed to love? And then makes another one about the guy she's cheating on her with?" She was kind of crying, so she didn't answer me. Finally I answered for her. I said, "The kind of person we don't need in our lives." And she nodded. But I guess you weren't all worked out of her system yet.

As for me, you should be happy to know that I consider finding those lists on your carpet folded up into little squares to be one of the best things that ever happened to me. Also, it really isn't annoying that I point at my food with my fork when I think it tastes good. At least I don't talk with my mouth full. That would be rude.

Tyler

To: Tori Fields
From: Monica Livingston
Date: 11/10/13

Hey Tori,

I'm really sorry that I accused you of telling Sam about the lists, and I'm really sorry that I wrote them in the first place. I'm trying to let the old Monica go and become a better person. It doesn't help that I am constantly worrying about what's in your movie.

Monica

To: Bob and Martha Fields
From: Grady Samson
Date: 11/26/2013

Dear Martha and Bob,

Wow. That's all I can say right now. Wow.

Okay, I can say more. We just had our first morning of shooting. The production designer (a freshman!) and her crew did an incredible job of transforming my office into a bedroom. (I chuckle to myself every time I walk in there and see teen girl decorations. Ha!) We shot the scene where Claire falls in love. It's so subtle. No dialogue. But Tori's direction in concert with Lily's nuanced performance and Matt's cinematography was superb. Transcendent, even. I have never seen such a profound scene unfold in front of me, let alone by high school students. I feel invigorated and ready for tomorrow's shooting. The rest of this semester is going to be spectacular.

Yours,
Grady

To: Monica Livingston
From: Tori Fields
Date: 11/30/2013

Okay, Monica.

Maybe the movie is based on you and me. Maybe I am working through some of my inner conflict or heartbreak or anger. You, with all of your theories about art, should understand that. Here is where I disagree with you about endings, though:

In life, you're right, there is uncertainty. You might be completely in love with a girl who loves you completely back. You might wake up one morning, confident in that love, until you find your phone and learn that the girl who was supposed to love you made out with someone else at a party on a Tuesday night when you were sleeping. Probably dreaming about her. There may never be an explanation. You may never feel at peace with it. You may pace around your room and take down all your posters and decorations because everything you see reminds you of her, and then you might put most of them back up again because without them and the memory of her you don't know who you are anymore. You might feel tied up in her. You might have dreams that she comes back to you, and dreams that you're touching her face, and dreams that she's kinder than she ever was in real life. You might not be sure if the dreams will ever stop because even though you're only sixteen and your mother keeps telling you that life is long and vast and your father keeps saying that there are plenty of pretty girl fishes in the sea, you can't imagine kissing anyone else ever. That's what life is like.

But in movies and books and plays—in storytelling in general, I guess—we can offer an ending that feels like a gift. We can offer a world that makes sense, even if it's painful. I'm going to take myself seriously as an artist for a minute, and go even a step further. I consider it my duty to provide an ending that satisfies without simplifying. That makes people feel on their way to being healed.

I'm not sending you the screenplay. You can see the movie when it's finished. But I will give you something now: I'll tell you how it ends.

Remember Lily? She was a freshman last year in our aerobics class? She has long brown hair and big pretty brown eyes and freckles all over her face and she is beautiful in the movie. She is always so present. I cast her as Claire. After Claire finds out about Eric and Sophie, she avoids them for months. She trades her locker for one in a different building. She transfers sections of her Mandarin class. She does this because she can't help longing for Sophie every time she sees her, and she hates to feel that way about someone who betrayed her.

So I was stuck. I didn't know how to end it. Part of me wanted to make it happy, for them to get back together. I tried to write an apology for Sophie, but everything sounded hollow. And then, that afternoon in world history, it occurred to me that even though you are in Utah now, even though we don't go to the same school and we don't text or talk on the phone and you blocked me from your Facebook— despite all of these things, the chances are good that we will someday run into each other again in real life and will have to confront one another in some way. Maybe we'll smile and say hi as though it's no big deal. Maybe you'll want to talk to me and we'll go sit and have coffee and I will have to try hard not to yell at you or to cry. Maybe you'll avert your eyes and pretend not to see me. Or maybe I'll pretend not to see you. I don't know what will happen, but I do have this wish that keeps running through me, and so I took that wish and I turned it into a scene. Here it is.

It is winter. We've watched Claire agonize through the year, watched Eric apologize and be forgiven, watched Sophie struggle— maddeningly, but you should also know, endearingly, fumblingly—through her tempest of self-alienation. And now the weather has changed, and everything is gray-blue and frozen. Claire is rushing to her car against the cold, and there on the edge of campus, stepping off of the yellow curb, is Sophie. They haven't seen each other for weeks, haven't acknowledged one another for months. But this time, when Claire sees her, she doesn't turn away or feign blindness, and she doesn't feel like crying or yelling, and she doesn't especially feel like a conversation. She knows, by this point, that there are no questions between them worth answering anymore. Then Sophie catches sight of Claire and falters. She isn't sure what to do, and in her impossible-to-read face there may be a hint of hope or longing or regret. And then the camera pans away from her and back to Claire (whose story this is really, even if Sophie is the pointiest point), and we see Claire smile a small, kind smile. It says something like, I forgive you. Or, I loved you once. Or, I hope you're learning to be better to yourself. Or, maybe, just: hello.

She lifts her hand in a wave, and then she turns away.

The end.

Love,
Tori

....

ANECDOTE: BONNIE LANGFORD

....

I was three months old when I first appeared onstage. My mother carried me in her arms at the end of the annual show for the dance school that she ran. I'm told that I took to it like a duck to water, but I honestly don't remember it at all. It would be a little crazy if I could! But maybe that first of many appearances established the secure and comfortable feeling I have of being onstage.

I'm so glad I never had to make a decision to choose this peculiar profession; it was destiny and fate. I feel very lucky and blessed. I think it's so valuable to know where your focus belongs and your heart lies and, even though I was a shy, quiet child, I came alive when I was onstage portraying a role.

At the age of eight, I auditioned and was invited to play Baby June in the London production of the musical, *Gypsy*. It was the first time *Gypsy* had been produced in London, the first time Arthur Laurents (the book writer) had directed his show and was to star Angela Lansbury in her return to the West End stage. It was a theatrical event. The show was rapturously received, as was Ms. Lansbury. On the opening night curtain call, a member of the audience shouted "Welcome home, Angela!" I loved it so much and felt so fortunate to be on that stage to witness and share it all.

In England at that time, there were legal restrictions for children performing in theater, television, and on film. We could only work for a maximum of forty performances per year, which meant that I could only play Baby June for six consecutive weeks. At my final performance in London, I was devastated and cried buckets. However, after the performance, the producers, Barry Brown and Fritz Holt, asked my parents if they would consider allowing me to go to America to play Baby June on the production's forthcoming U.S. tour and subsequent Broadway season.

To cut an extremely long, detailed story short involving American Equity, AFTRA, and the British courts, a year later I was made a "ward of court" and my mother accompanied me across the pond to New York to begin rehearsals. It was such an adventure and such a learning experience in every possible sense. To be part of a brilliant, successful show, directed by a highly respected director, and to watch Angela Lansbury give such a heartfelt, truthful, and magical performance every single night, was a treasured gift. She taught me how to behave offstage too. She doesn't know it, but just being in her company makes you learn—especially at such an impressionable age.

The icing on the cake for me was the very final performance on Broadway at the Winter Garden Theatre. We had played to packed houses and were set to run and run, but Angela needed to rest and return to her home in Los Angeles, so the show closed at its peak. The final show was electric. The audience was with us through each moment, and they gave me the most wonderful experience that I will always cherish.

Gypsy incorporates every crowd-pleasing moment you can think of: I even had to twirl batons while tap dancing on pointe finishing in the splits! At the end of her vaudeville act, Baby June runs to the center of the stage to receive her applause before the play off. At this point I would look around the entire auditorium, from the balcony right to left, and the orchestra stalls left to right. Arthur Laurents had encouraged me to absorb every moment, every person, and "take my time." So much so, that I was directed to only say my next line when the conductor, Milton Rosenstock, put his glasses across his face and winked at me.

On that final performance, I stood center stage on Broadway with my arms out to the side and looked out at the entire audience standing and applauding. There leading the applause was Arthur Laurents himself cheering for me. Mr. Rosenstock was blowing kisses, and the orchestra members applauded too. I stood there for what seemed like hours, but was probably four or five minutes. It still makes me emotional when I remember those moments.

To do something you love and to know that you have touched people is such a privilege. It's not about plaudits and praise; it's just about feeling a universal emotion you can't buy, and sharing it with an audience. That's one of the reasons I love my job, through all its fickle ups and downs, sweat and tears—and sometimes blood! It sounds so sentimental, but it's not. It's just a unique profession, and I'm proud to be part of it.

BONNIE LANGFORD starred as Roz in the U.K. tour of *9 to 5*, and received a Drama Desk nomination for *Gypsy*. She has played Roxie Hart in *Chicago* on Broadway and both at the Adelphi Theatre and the Cambridge Theatre in London's West End. Other West End and U.K. tours include *Sweet Charity*, *Me and My Girl*, *Peter Pan*, *Cats*, *The Pirates of Penzance*, *Gypsy*, *42nd Street*, *Oklahoma!*, *Fosse*, *Gone with the Wind*, and Miss Adelaide in the Donmar Warehouse production of *Guys and Dolls*. Television/film credits include *Bugsy Malone*, *The Hot Shoe Show*, *This Is Your Life*, *Dancing on Ice*, and BBC's *Doctor Who*. Her solo albums *Bonnie Langford Now* and the top-selling *Jazz at the Theatre* are available on iTunes. www.Bonnielangford.co.uk.

STAGE KISS

Cynthia Hand

You've heard the term, "sweet sixteen, never been kissed"?

Yep, that was me.

Back then I was just your average high school junior, player-but-not-star player of the girls' soccer team, solid B student, blah blah blah—I was sixteen, is my point. I don't know how sweet I was, but up until that spring, the spring that changed everything, I had never been kissed by a boy.

Never.

Not once.

Not even in grade school when it would have been considered cute, or in middle school at one of those spin-the-bottle type parties. Not even on the cheek. I had never, as far as I could remember, *ever*, been kissed.

But I don't want you to get the wrong idea about me. I wasn't a social reject or anything. I had friends. I'd liked boys before, and they'd liked me. We'd just never made it to the kissing stage, is all. I was too busy. My parents were under the impression that the way to keep their kids out of trouble was to make sure they were monumentally busy. From the time I'd started school, it'd been pretty much one activity after another: piano lessons, track team, ski team, soccer, gymnastics.

Just call me Little Miss Extracurricular.

The problem with all the after-school fun, besides that it becomes, after a point, *exhausting*, is that you don't have time for anything else.

Like boys, for instance.

Hence my unkissed status at the end of my junior year.

Which, I had to admit to myself, was a little sad.

"So kiss a guy," my friend Becca told me after I fessed up on that fateful Wednesday morning in March. We were sitting on the floor of the commons in the break between second and third period, eating breakfast burritos. Becca had been telling me about how the current love-of-her-life, Peter, had taken her on a hike that weekend in the mountains near the Wyoming border. And how they had watched the sun go down together. And then he'd kissed her.

Cue the sweeping music.

"See, that's the way a first kiss should be." I'd sighed without thinking.

Then Becca said, "Oh, that wasn't my *first* kiss. My first kiss was when I was fourteen on the ski hill, you remember Stu, that guy on the ski team—Wait, what was *your* first kiss?" and she could tell by my lack of response and the beet-red color of my face that it was true: I was an official member of the VLC.

The Virgin Lip Club.

"Wow, really?" she said, wide-eyed. "Never?"

"Never."

"I thought you made out with that Justin guy in eighth grade."

"No. We just passed notes to each other in science class. No kissing."

"Hmm," she said thoughtfully and shrugged. "So kiss a guy." Like now, hop up, go get that taken care of. Pronto.

I scoffed. "Oh, right. I'll just walk up to a random guy and say, 'Hi there, do you mind if I kiss you?'"

"Sure. Why not? Seize the moment, Jo." She glanced around the commons at the dozens of unsuspecting males passing by on their way to the cafeteria. She grinned. "Pick a boy, any boy."

"I don't want it to be just any boy. I want it to be somebody—" *special*, I was too embarrassed to say out loud, because that was way too Hallmark card. *The right boy.*

Just then my gaze happened to fall on Ryan Daughtry.

Sigh, Ryan Daughtry. The hottest guy at Bonneville High School. Possibly the hottest guy in the entire state of Idaho. Possibly the world.

I'd had a thing for Ryan Daughtry ever since speech class in ninth grade when he gave a demonstration on how to bake chocolate chip cookies, and let me tell you, I wasn't the only girl in that class who thought he was delicious. There was just something about him—the combination of deep brown eyes and olive skin, the easiness of his smile, the close-cut dark hair that he styled to look purposefully messy. Adorable. That day in the commons he was going vintage—a white button-down shirt with a thin black tie, a black fedora perched jauntily on his head. It looked good on him.

Anything looked good on him.

Becca turned to see who I was staring at. "Oh," she said. "Well, that's setting the bar pretty high."

Yeah, he was out of my league. I was like a seven to Ryan's ten, and I knew it.

Becca shrugged again. "I bet he's gay."

I was startled enough by this out-of-the-blue remark to stop gazing wistfully at Ryan and frown at her. "What?"

"He's one of the drama people, right?"

Yes. He was almost always the male lead in the school play. But that made perfect sense. I mean, if you could see how beautiful he was. People would pay good money just to look at him.

"And he sings and dances, right?" Becca picked up the end of her long, chestnut-colored ponytail and examined it for split ends.

"Right . . ."

He *did* sing beautifully. Last year I saw him in the musical *Oklahoma!* (wearing cowboy boots and fringe chaps, and oh yes, it looked amazing on him), and he and Alicia Walker sang a duet, something about "people will say we're in love," that I had stuck in my head for days after. He kissed her, at the end of that show. Later that week I saw the two of them holding hands at a pep rally, and I could tell by their vibe that they were about an eyelash away from seriously getting it on.

"He's not gay," I said to Becca. "I think he's dating Alicia Walker."

"Alicia Walker? Blonde, skinny, Barbie-doll Alicia Walker?"

"That's the one."

"You could take her."

I laughed. "Good grief, Becca, this isn't wrestling."

Becca took a sip of milk, then nodded like the issue was settled. "So. Ryan Daughtry. Your first kiss. You should strategize on how to make this happen."

This was what I loved about Becca—she was nothing if not brutally direct. She set goals for herself and went after them with the persistence of a guided missile. It made her a beast on the soccer field. It was also the reason I generally avoided talking about my love life with her. I couldn't just moan about how I didn't have time for guys and have her pat me on the shoulder and say she understood. She was the type to try to make me do something about it.

Like now, for instance. "Did you miss the part where I said he had a girlfriend?" I reminded her.

She took a big bite of her burrito. "Are you sure he's dating Alicia? One hundred percent certain?"

"Um, no."

"I think you owe it to yourself to find out, at least," she said. "Why spend your life waiting for stuff to happen, Jo? You have to go after the things you want. Otherwise life is going to keep passing you by."

She had a point.

. . . . .

It was literally five minutes later, in English class, that the universe sent me a sign.

We were in the middle of a quiz on *Pride and Prejudice* when Alicia Walker breezed into the room. I looked up and saw her. I thought, ridiculously, that Becca was right. I *could* take Alicia Walker in a fight. She was so willowy and delicate. Even with a last name like Walker, Alicia never seemed to just *walk* anywhere. She floated, like her feet weren't connected to the ground. She was the picture of grace. Of beauty. Of exactly the type of girl that Ryan Daughtry would naturally go for. She was president of the drama club.

And she had kissed him. She'd felt his lips on hers.

Yeah, I hated her, just a bit.

She was also, as far as I could tell, a perfectly nice girl. Which made it impossible to out-and-out hate her. Which was annoying.

Alicia glided up to Ms. Yowell's desk. And then two important things happened:

1. She glanced over at me. Well, not at *me*, it took me about two seconds to figure out, but at the guy sitting next to me. Jonathan Renault, basketball player. At that moment he was tapping his pencil against his desk rhythmically, chewing on his bottom lip, agonizing over why he was expected to care about that darned Mr. Darcy, but then, almost like he could feel Alicia's eyes on him, he looked up. He saw Alicia, and the tapping stopped. The lip chewing stopped. He smiled. And she smiled back. It was one of those shared smiles like a current of electricity passing between the two of them.

And then?

2. Ms. Yowell said, "Yes, that would be fine," to answer the question I hadn't heard Alicia ask, and Alicia looked away from Jonathan quickly and handed Ms. Yowell the stack of bright blue papers she'd been clutching to her chest, stealing one more tiny peek at Jonathan as she slipped out of the room.

Interesting, I thought. Very interesting.

The blue papers turned out to be flyers, announcing the auditions for the school play.

MUCH ADO ABOUT NOTHING, it read in big loopy letters. SATURDAY, 9 A.M.–12 P.M., BHS LITTLE THEATER. There was a bunch of clip art arranged around the words: a rose, a sword, a crown, a heart, a cartoony illustration of two people kissing. ACTION AND SWORD FIGHTING! the flyer read farther down. ROMANCE! COMEDY AND DANCING! EVERYONE IS WELCOME! COME TRY OUT!

Most of the people in my class crumpled up that flyer and tossed it in the trash on their way out, or it ended in that layer of forgotten papers in the bottoms of their backpacks.

Not me, though. I folded the flyer carefully and stuck it in the front of my notebook, where later that night, after practice, in the privacy of my bedroom, I took it out again and stared at it every few minutes while I was doing my homework. I was thinking. About Alicia Walker making flirty eyes at Jonathan Renault. About what Becca had said about how life was going to keep passing me by. *Keep* passing me by, she'd said, as if life had already been speeding around me like a Winnebago in the slow lane.

Which was true, I had to admit. Because, for all my extracurriculars, there were times late at night when I stared up at my ceiling, my muscles aching, my alarm set for five in the morning for some practice, and I wished that I could just quit everything and be the type of girl who went to the mall with her friends on a Thursday afternoon. A person who had relationships. A boyfriend. A life.

I glanced at the flyer again. COME TRY OUT, it said. And another word caught my eye.

ROMANCE. Alongside the faces of a boy and girl. Kissing.

I sighed and fired up my laptop.

. . . . .

Much Ado About Nothing, the Internet informed me, was actually about a lot of somethings.

I tried reading a copy online, which was easy to find, but I didn't understand much, because here's the thing: *Much Ado About Nothing* is Shakespeare. It was written in the year 1600 or so. When I got to this point on the first page of the script: *"I pray you, how many hath he killed and eaten in these wars? But how many hath he killed? For, indeed, I promised to eat all of his killing,"* my eyes started to cross a little, but then I thought, life is passing you by—don't be a wuss, and kept on reading.

About fifteen minutes later I switched to Netflix and found a film version. I stayed up way too late that night watching it. The women in this film (Emma Thompson before she was Nanny McPhee and Kate Beckinsale before she was a vampire) run around all tan in floaty white dresses, eating fruit, and dancing and saying stuff like "Hey, nonny nonny!" Denzel Washington plays a prince, and Keanu Reeves plays his evil brother, which someone will still have to explain to me, but finally I started to get the gist of the story.

It's about how this woman, Beatrice, can't stand this guy, Benedick, and he can't stand her, either. Every time they're together, they bicker and mock each other and talk about how they never want to get married, because the opposite sex is dumb. But their friends play a trick on them and get them to think that they're actually in love with one another. Which they end up being, by the end.

And at the end, they kiss. It says so, right there in the script. I checked. *Benedick: Peace! I will stop your mouth. [Kisses her.]* it says.

That was good enough for me. Becca said I needed to strategize on this first kiss scenario, and strategize I did: I was going to get the female lead in the school play. Ryan was going to be the male lead, because that's what he always did. And then we would kiss. Ryan and me. Kissing.

Here's how it played out in my head: Ryan would be standing in the spotlight, which would cast a halo-like glow around him, all dressed up like a prince, and he'd give me this sexy half smile as he approached. "Peace," he'd murmur. "I will stop your mouth." And on the word *mouth* he'd look down at my lips, then up into my eyes, and his arms would come around me and he'd lean and kiss me. There'd be sweeping music. There'd be fireworks. He'd pull me closer, and the rest of the world would fade away, leaving just him and me alone there on that stage. And finally, at some point, he'd pull back, and he'd smile, and he wouldn't say anything but I'd be able to see in his eyes that the kiss had blown him away.

Okay, so it was a silly daydream, and trying out for the school play was a long shot. I'd never been in a play before, if you didn't count a disastrous stint in the church nativity play in third grade where I'd *dropped the baby Jesus doll* right on its head in front of everybody. I'd watched the drama crowd, which was a pretty tight clique at my school, and they always looked like they were having so much fun together. But I'd never for one second thought I could get up onstage with them. I wasn't like Alicia Walker. I was mousy-haired, my body was kind of straight up and down, and I was way more tomboy than girly girl. I wasn't the leading lady type.

But I wanted that first kiss. So I was going to try.

. . . . .

"Jolynn Dalley?" Ms. Golden called out.

The drama group, every single one of them, turned around in their seats to stare at me as I lurched to my feet at the back of the theater, where I'd been kind of hiding out since the auditions began. I made my way down the aisle and up onto the stage.

"It's Jo, actually," I warbled when I got there, blinking against the lights.

Ms. Golden shaded her eyes with her clipboard to get a better look at me. I had a sudden understanding of what an ant under a magnifying glass must feel during its final moments of life. I had a flashback to dropping the baby Jesus, like the whole world was watching me, alone there on the stage, waiting for me to mess up. I swallowed. My stomach heaved. I always got a bit queasy right before important stuff, like the PSATs or a big soccer game, but this was hands down the most excruciatingly nervous I'd ever been. This is a mistake, I thought. I shouldn't be here. I don't know what I was thinking. I have to go. Quick, before I puke.

I opened my mouth to say all of this, or maybe to just go ahead and puke, but then Ms. Golden said, "All right, Jo. Why don't you read from

Act Four, Scene One, around line two hundred and eighty-one, with . . . Ryan, why don't you read for Benedick?"

Someone handed me a script. I flipped to the right page, my heart like a drum solo, all runs and crashing symbols, as Ryan Daughtry in the flesh loped up onto the stage to stand next to me. His brown eyes were sparkling and curious, like he'd never seen me before. He probably *hadn't* really seen me before. Out of the two thousand students who went to our school, I'd been barely a blip on his radar.

"Hello," he said.

"Hi." I was staring at him. I needed to stop staring at him, but even now, on this bare, black-painted stage, wearing a simple gray tee and faded, holey jeans, he looked like a rock star. He was even better looking close up, all thick dark lashes and stellar cheekbones and full, perfect lips.

He glanced down at his script. "I think you have the first line."

I scanned down the page but couldn't seem to find it. I frowned at the script. "Uh . . ."

"Here." Ryan leaned over and pointed at the part of the page where my line began.

His breath smelled like cinnamon.

"Oh. Thanks." Heat rushed to my face. I cleared my throat, tried to focus on the words. "*Why then, God forgive me!*"

"*What offence, sweet Beatrice?*"

"*You have stayed me in a happy hour: I was about to protest I loved you.*"

"*And do it with all thy heart,*" Ryan said.

"*I love you with so much of my heart that none is left to protest,*" I murmured, suddenly wanting to look anywhere but right at him.

Hello, irony, I thought. I'd been standing next to Ryan Daughtry for all of thirty seconds and I was already blurting out that I loved him. It was too much.

"Okay," called Ms. Golden from the audience section before I could get out the next line. "Very nice, Jo. Can you try it without the British accent?"

Holy crap, was I speaking with a British accent? Suddenly I felt like an idiot for the hours I'd spent in front of my mirror for the past two nights, watching Emma Thompson on my laptop and trying to match her performance, her facial expressions, her gestures, and the way she said the words so crisply like she was tasting them as they came out of her mouth. I must be doing some kind of horrible impression of her.

"*Come, bid me do anything for thee,*" implored Ryan.

I gulped in a breath and glanced down at the script. "*Kill Claudio,*" I read. I tried to remember the story: Beatrice was mad because this guy Claudio just accused her cousin Hero of being a slut and left her at the altar. Heck, I'd be angry too.

"*Ha! Not for the wide world,*" Ryan said with a short, sharp laugh. He was really good. He was definitely going to get the part of Benedick.

"*You kill me to deny it. Farewell,*" I said.

"*Tarry, sweet Beatrice.*" He put his hand on my arm, pulling me closer to him. His face loomed inches from mine, cinnamon and brown eyes and too much.

I promptly lost my place on the page. Why were the words so freaking tiny? "Uh . . ."

Silence. The iambic pentameter swam in front of my eyes. "Uh . . . ," I said again.

Someone in the audience snickered. I could hear whispering, then another giggle. I glanced up at Ryan. He seemed to be trying to stifle a pitying smile. They were all laughing at me. Even my crush was laughing at me. For a minute I wanted to throw myself into the orchestra pit and crawl out again, oh, sometime around graduation.

But then a slow anger boiled up in me. I was trying, dangit. I had never done this sort of thing before, and it was Shakespeare for crying out loud, and all things considered, I was doing okay.

And then I decided this: I was going to finish the scene if it killed me. *There was no point in being nervous,* I thought. These people weren't my friends, so what did I care what they thought of me?

I jerked away from Ryan. I picked a line farther down the page and ran with it. "*O! That I were a man! What! Bear her in hand until they come to take hands, and then, with public accusation, uncovered slander, unmitigated rancor,—O God, that I were a man! I would eat his heart in the market-place!*"

Ryan tried to say something, but I kept going right over his line. "*O! That I were a man for his sake, or that I had any friend would be a man for my sake! But manhood is melted into curtsies, valour into compliment, and men are only turned into tongue, and trim ones, too. I cannot be a man with wishing, therefore I will die a woman with grieving.*"

Ryan looked startled. This time *he* was the one fumbling with the script. "*Tarry, good Beatrice. By this hand, I love thee,*" he stammered.

"*Use it for my love some other way than swearing by it,*" I said, and just for a minute there, I got it. Beatrice's frustration. Her fury. Her sadness. It all made perfect sense.

Take that, Benedick.

Silence again. I glanced down at the audience section and saw the drama crowd sitting there, staring up at me, stunned. Then Ms. Golden boomed out, "Very good, you two. You can sit down."

. . . . .

The cast list went up on Monday morning.

I sent Becca to go read it for me. I couldn't suffer the added humiliation of walking up to that piece of paper, taped to the door of the auditorium, past all those drama people who I knew would smirk and whisper as I went by. I couldn't let them see my pathetic, crestfallen face when I didn't find my name on that list.

It's for the best, I told myself as I watched Becca turn the corner toward the theater. It really was a stupid idea. How lame is it to get your first kiss from a play, anyway?

Becca came back looking solemn. Even though I was expecting bad news, my stomach dropped.

"So what, I didn't make it?"

"Sorry, Jo," she said. "I think you're going to have to miss some soccer practice. Coach is going to be furious."

She grinned.

"What?"

"You got Beatrice!" she crowed.

I stared at her, stunned. "You're punking me."

"Nope. It's right there at the top of the page. Beatrice, niece to Leonardo," she said. "Jo Dalley. You did it!" she called after me, because I was already sprinting toward the auditorium.

The drama people were all crowded around the door, all right, but the looks they gave me were friendly enough, even some congratulations thrown in there as I weaved my way to a spot where I could read the sheet.

My mouth dropped open.

For two reasons, really.

1: Becca wasn't yanking my chain. I was Beatrice. Somehow I had just landed the female lead in the school play. And Becca was right; my soccer coach was going to be ticked. I was going to have to quit, like everything, just so I could make it to rehearsals. My parents were going to wig.

But reason 2 was so much more interesting. Because one line down from my name it listed the role of Benedick.

Eric Bradshaw.

Ryan Daughtry, it turned out, had been cast in the role of Claudio.

I was going to have to kiss the wrong guy.

. . . . .

The first read-through was a joke. I was super frustrated by the ridiculousness of the whole thing: first, my crazy-stupid idea that I could get the guy I liked to kiss me by acting like I was an actress. Ha. Then, that I somehow actually managed to pull it off, and now I was going to be expected to act. Ha ha. And finally, that I wasn't going to even kiss Ryan. I was going to kiss Eric, a guy I didn't know. Ha ha ha.

I'm hilarious.

So we all sat around a big table in the drama classroom with high-lighters and pencils, and Ms. Golden went through the script cutting some of the longer bits out in order to get the show down to under two hours, because I guess Will Shakespeare was a little wordy, and we highlighted our lines. The mysterious Mr. Bradshaw sat at the other end of the table from me, and when he caught me looking at him he wiggled his eyebrows up and down playfully, and my stomach did a clenchy thing, and I thought, for the umpteenth time, this is all a huge mistake.

Ryan Daughtry sat by Alicia Walker. She was going to play Hero, my cousin. Which meant that she was going to kiss Claudio/Ryan. Again.

Sometimes the universe just isn't fair.

When we got to reading through the play, I stumbled over the lines. I didn't know what I was saying most of the time, and my mortifying British accent kept making the occasional appearance. There was nothing of the big brave moment I'd had at auditions. I sucked. By the end of the read-through, I was convinced that Ms. Golden must have realized that she'd made a huge mistake casting me. I started thinking about how I was going to grovel my way back onto the soccer team and go crawling back to my piano teacher.

After the read-through was over, I didn't stick around to chat with the cast. Call me chicken, but I fled.

"Jo, wait," someone called after me as I was making my lame getaway in the parking lot. "Wait!"

I stopped.

Alicia Walker floated up to me and smiled. She had very nice teeth, perfectly straight and even and white. Of course she did.

"Can I walk with you?" she asked.

"Um, sure."

We walked.

"So you were kind of nervous in there," she observed.

Um, duh. "I guess," I mumbled.

"Don't be," she said, like I had a choice whether or not to be nervous. "You're going to be an amazing Beatrice."

"Come on," I said miserably. "I was a disaster."

"Hey. You got the part for a reason. You were good at auditions. You *were*," she insisted when I laughed out loud. "Fine, you're a newbie, but you have a kind of strength about you, a kind of fire, you know, that's very Beatrice."

"You should have been Beatrice," I said.

She shrugged. "I wanted Beatrice, actually. I'm sick of playing the delicate flower all the time. Shakespeare always has a weak woman and a strong woman in his plays. So far I've played Juliet (weak), Bianca (so weak), and Desdemona (oh my God smother me now)." She sighed. "I actually faint in this play, did you catch that? My fiancé accuses me of sleeping around, and I collapse, and everybody thinks that I die from shame. Do you know how weak you have to be to *die* from *shame*? You, on the other hand, get to go around raving about how if you were a man, you'd tear Claudio's heart out of his chest and eat it, and I just sink to the floor. Oh, dear," she exclaimed softly, flailing her arms. "Whatever shall I do?"

"But you get to kiss Ryan Daughtry," I said. "That's a perk, right?"

Alicia rolled her eyes. "Just between you and me, Jo," she confessed. "Ryan's not a very good kisser."

Inconceivable. I stared at her.

"But you and Ryan were dating last year, weren't you?" I asked.

She grimaced like she found the idea totally embarrassing. "Oh that," she explained. "That was the verisimilitude."

"The what?"

"It's this thing in theater, where you kind of get lost in the part you're playing. So, if your character falls in love with someone, you kind of do too."

"Sort of like how Hollywood actors always hook up with their costars," I said.

"Exactly."

"So you and Ryan . . ."

"We had a little thing during *Oklahoma!* It wore off pretty quickly. Ryan's okay. He's pretty," she said, a bit wistfully. "But he's also a little . . . vapid."

Vapid. I was going to look that one up.

"Anyway," Alicia continued. "I'm glad you're in the play. I think you'll be great once you loosen up a bit. Shakespeare's challenging, but you'll get it. And you and me, we should hang out. We're supposed to be cousins, you know? Best friends."

"So there could be verisimilitude between us too?" I said. "Beatrice and Hero are friends, so we should be?"

She smiled that perfect smile again. "Yes," she said. "Something like that."

· · · · ·

Okay, here's what they don't show you on *Glee*: blocking.

That's the part in the beginning of the rehearsal process where the actors stand on the stage and go where the director tells them. I had to learn the geography of the stage: upstage and downstage, left, right, and center, and all the combinations: Enter down left. Walk to center right. Exit up left. It was initially confusing, but by the end of the first week of rehearsals, I had it down. I was a bundle of nerves, though, because the entire time I was thinking, how are we going to block the kissing? But when we got to the part in the script where Claudio is supposed to kiss Hero (So—Ryan kissing Alicia, as you'll recall—heavy sigh), they just kind of looked at each other and smiled knowingly and moved on to the next line.

I relaxed a little. Apparently we weren't going to be expected to kiss anybody yet.

Whew.

I wasn't supposed to be onstage for a bit, so I sat down in the wings backstage and started going over the lines for my next scene. After a while

I became aware that someone was standing in front of me. Someone wearing black Converse sneakers with ratty laces. I looked up.

Eric Bradshaw.

"My lady," he said, and gave a slight bow.

I stared at him, uncertain of how to respond. His shirt featured a guy with glasses and a mustache and the word PIZZA in large block letters, which I didn't understand. He smiled.

"Hi?" I said.

He stuck out his hand. "I'm Eric," he said, like I didn't know. "We were never formally introduced before, so . . ."

I took his hand. It was warm and slightly rough. "Jo."

"Jo, right," he repeated, squeezing my hand. "Are you a freshman?"

"Uh, no," I said with an embarrassed laugh. "Junior."

"Oh. Sorry. I'm a junior too, but I moved here last year, so I don't know everybody, and I've never seen you before. I mean, maybe I've seen you, but never in here." He finally let go of my hand and gestured to the auditorium around us.

"I've never really been in here before," I admitted. "Except for auditions."

"I loved your audition. You, quite simply, rocked."

I glanced away, hoping I wasn't blushing. "Right. When I wasn't speaking in a British accent, you mean."

His eyes, which were a deep blue, widened (dare I say) theatrically. "No, I thought the British accent was hot. I think we should all do this entire play in British accents. Shakespeare was British, after all. That's authenticity." He pressed his fist to his chest, his voice deepening into something that reminded me a bit of Charlton Heston. "That's truth, in theater."

I couldn't help but smile. "Thanks."

"Eric, you're up, dude," somebody said from onstage. Eric turned with an apologetic smile and tipped an invisible hat at me, then bounded out onto the stage.

I watched as he did the scene. I really let myself look at him, which I'd been too mortified by the situation to do before, and what struck me most about him was that he was an oversized little boy—tall, broad in the shoulders, a tad stocky, not overweight or anything, but solid. He smiled a lot. He had a large chin and deep blue eyes that twinkled under the lights. His hair was blond and all over the place, and his face was a bit scruffy, like he couldn't be bothered with shaving. Because he was too busy playing.

But he was attractive. Not in the way that Ryan was, but still.

He's cute, I admitted to myself.

And I was going to kiss him. The only question now was, when?

. . . . .

"We don't do the actual kissing until the week before dress rehearsal," Alicia informed me later that week when we were out getting Baskin-Robbins and becoming BFFs and all. Which was going pretty well, actually. "Are you nervous about kissing Eric?"

Yes.

"No," I said quickly, shrugging like it was no big deal. "I just don't know him very well."

"Eric's awesome," Alicia said fondly, like maybe she wouldn't mind kissing him herself. "But then, I have a weakness for the funny guys."

"Like Jonathan Renault?" I asked. I hadn't forgotten the way she looked at him in my English class.

"How did you know about that?" she gasped, and blushed prettily. Alicia did everything prettily.

"I'm observant," I answered, and it was quiet for a minute while she thought about Jonathan, and I thought about Eric.

Eric *was* funny. He always had everyone laughing, so much that he occasionally got into hot water with Ms. Golden for horsing around. For example, at rehearsal earlier, he'd produced a little flute-type instrument from his pocket and proceeded to play it with his nose. "He's cute," I admitted, out loud this time.

"I bet he's a good kisser," Alicia said, and I didn't know whether she was talking about Eric or Jonathan, but then we both kind of snapped out of it, went back to our ice cream, and went back to becoming friends.

· · · · ·

Here's some other stuff they never show on *Glee*: weeks and weeks of rehearsals.

Hours of time spent memorizing your lines. Costume fittings. Set building. Lights. Makeup. No, on *Glee* the actors simply arrive, belt out their amazing songs with their astounding special effects and their fantastic lighting and sets and dance moves, and then go on to win nationals. No effort required.

But they do get something right: the sense that comes through all those hours of seemingly endless preparation, that you are connected with the other people in your cast. You see them in the hall at school and you think, I know what that person sounds like when they're broken-hearted, I know how that girl's face looks like when she's feeling flirty, or I know the way that guy pronounces the word "bosom" when he's trying to get a laugh. And it's not exactly verisimilitude, at least not the way Alicia described it to me.

So we rehearsed for *Much Ado About Nothing* for a little under three months, six days a week, and in that time I started to feel that the other people in the play were a kind of family. My family. When I saw Alicia as Hero getting basically called a strumpet by the guy who's supposed to love and protect her, it wasn't too hard to conjure up some indignation. It definitely took some of the shine off Ryan, because I could see him too, in his acting, and Alicia was right.

He was vapid. Definition: *1. bereft of strength, sharpness, flavor. 2. boring or dull*. And he was vain. One time I caught him looking at himself in the mirrors in the backstage dressing room, just smiling at himself, as if he couldn't help it—he was just *that* good-looking. And if you wanted to talk about something besides movies or music, if you wanted to talk about the news or politics or the meaning of life, he always got this blank look.

I started to see him as maybe not the sharpest crayon in the box.

The less I liked Ryan, the more I liked Eric. Because Eric goofed off a lot, it's true, but he could also quote Plato when the situation called for it. He read books. He liked indie films and art. He knew how to deliver those difficult lines so that a normal person would understand Mr. Shakespeare's fine jokes. He was nice too. Whenever we'd go onto the stage together, he'd hold the curtain open for me. And when I saw him up there acting, showing a bit of his soul, I saw someone who was honest and genuine and intelligent.

He was special, I thought. Not to be too Hallmark card, but he was.

And I was falling for him a little, clearly. I couldn't tell if it was because of the verisimilitude thing or if it was real. But I liked it.

Like, when we did our scenes where Beatrice and Benedick mock each other, there was always a playfulness in the way Eric said his lines, as if Benedick was enjoying taking jabs at Beatrice, because, deep down, he admired her.

Admired me.

And I was enjoying taking my jabs right back, because I liked him too.

Me: "*I had rather hear my dog bark at a crow than a man swear he loves me.*"

Eric: "*God keep your ladyship still in that mind; so some gentleman or other shall 'scape a predestinate scratched face.*"

Me: "*Scratching could not make it worse, an 'twere such a face as yours were.*"

Eric: "Oh yeah, well yo mama is so ugly that I took her to a haunted house and she came out with a job application."

Me (laughing): "Oh yeah? Well, your mama is so ugly her pillow cries at night."

Eric (laughing too): "Come on, Jo. It's pronounced 'Yo mama.' And yo mama is so ugly she made an onion cry."

Me: "Yo mama is so ugly she made Obama lose hope."

Then we were laughing too hard to talk for a few minutes, and Ms. Golden just kind of shook her head, and finally Eric cleared his throat and said, as Benedick: "*Well, you are a rare parrot-teacher.*"

And I thought, not for the first time, I'm actually excited for this guy to be my first kiss.

· · · · ·

Which brings us to the week before dress rehearsal, when, after we'd all assembled on the stage, the girls in our petticoats and boys with their swords, and Ms. Golden said, "All right, everybody. Kissing time. For now I want everybody but Alicia and Ryan out while we block their kissing scene, and then we'll do the bit with Benedick and Beatrice at the end."

Here we go, I thought, my heart thumping wild. Showtime.

Alicia and Ryan stayed while the rest of us shuffled out into the hallway. I dared a look at Eric. He gazed at the floor like he suddenly found his shoes fascinating. It was the first time I'd ever seen him act nervous. He rubbed the back of his neck, then glanced up at me and smiled in a way that sent a flock of rabid killer butterflies to my stomach, then looked away.

We stayed that way, looking at each other and then not looking at each other, until Alicia came out to get us.

"You're up," Alicia said, and she slipped something into my hand.

It was a tiny can of Altoids.

I had to love Alicia Walker. Even if she was perfect.

Eric and I slunk into the auditorium and wandered up onto the stage. We took our places for the end of the play. My knees were knocking together, seriously. I tried to cover by making a big show of opening up the Altoids. I popped one into my mouth. It was so strong it burned my tongue. I coughed, then smiled.

"Want one?" I said to Eric.

"Heck, yes, please."

He took a couple. Then he pulled out a tube of lip balm and made his own big show of applying it. He held it out to me. It was Skittle flavored.

"Taste the rainbow," he said, his blue eyes dancing.

I laughed weakly and took it and dragged the tube lightly over my lips. I didn't want to put on too much and have us slide right past each other.

"Whenever you're ready," Ms. Golden said.

"Go easy on him, Jo," Ryan said, popping his head out from backstage. He smirked at us. "It's his first time."

"Ryan. Out," ordered Ms. Golden, and we could hear him laughing as he left the theater.

So yeah, Ryan was kind of a jerk. I turned back to Eric. "So . . . you're a lip virgin?"

Eric's face was very red by this point, clearly mortified, but the corner of his mouth lifted at my terminology. "Yeah. Lip virgin. Kind of pathetic, right?"

"Very pathetic," I agreed. I leaned close to him and whispered. "Don't tell anyone, but it's my first time too."

His eyes widened. "You've never been kissed?"

"Nope."

"Impossible. How could a girl as pretty as you have gotten this far without being kissed?"

I was blushing by this point. "Oh, Eric," I said. "Flattery will get you everywhere."

"All right, you two," Ms. Golden directed from the audience. "Time to face the music."

"Ms. Golden, I have a question, actually," said Eric. "Where do our noses go?"

I'd been wondering the same thing.

"Just kiss her, Eric," she retorted. "You'll figure it out."

I was so nervous I felt light-headed. Now, I thought, would not be a good time to puke.

"Okay. First kiss." Eric clapped his hands together like a football player breaking out of a huddle. He took a deep breath, closed his eyes momentarily, then opened them and said, "*A miracle! Here's our own hands against our hearts. Come, I will have thee; but, by this light, I take thee for pity.*"

I conjured up my best Beatrice smirk. "*I would not deny you; but, by this good day, I yield upon great persuasion, and partly to save your life, for I was told you were in a consumption.*"

Eric laughed. He took my hand and pulled me closer. "*Peace!*" he said. "*I will stop your mouth.*"

He kissed me.

His lips on mine were warm and smooth and tasted like mint and Skittles. Then we stepped back from each other.

"Excellent," Ms. Golden said. "Just like that."

Just like that. My first kiss. Check.

I tried not to let my disappointment show on my face. It wasn't that the kiss hadn't been good, exactly. It was nice. Quick, but nice. But it wasn't—how should I put this?—mind-blowing or anything. There were no fireworks, no sweeping music. It was just nice.

"Amazing," Eric said, his face flushed. "That was awesome, Jo. You rock at the kissing."

It was sweet of him, saying that. But I knew him well enough by then to recognize when he was acting.

My first kiss hadn't been such a big deal, after all. It was just a kiss.

· · · · ·

It was awkward between Eric and me for a few days after that, especially during the kissing scenes, which continued to be nice and all, but nothing to write home about. But then we hit tech rehearsal, and we were too busy to be awkward. We had stuff to get done. And then, like two seconds after that, it was dress rehearsal, and then it was opening night.

I'd dyed my hair red to match Beatrice's fiery disposition, and Alicia twisted it up into an elaborate mix of curls and braids that looked like something out of *Game of Thrones.* Then I put on my costume, a green velvet dress that hugged my body in a way a dress had never fit me before, because it'd been made just for me.

And finally I put on my makeup, starting with a thick layer of pancake foundation that felt heavy and gross and was definitely going to make me break out like crazy, too much blush on my cheeks, too much eye shadow, highlights and shadows painted on my nose and laugh lines and cheekbones so the stage lights wouldn't wash me out, plus thick, fake eyelashes glued to my eyelids, topped with two layers of eyeliner, and a layer of mascara. I was certain I'd look like a drag queen, but at the end of the whole process I gazed into the mirror and . . . mousy little Jo Dalley was gone.

I saw Beatrice.

And before it felt like I could even properly catch my breath, the curtain was going up, and I was saying my first line: "*I pray you is Signior Mountanto returned from the wars or no?*" and for a moment I was painfully aware of all the people staring at me, hundreds of people: Becca in the front row with my family and half of my old soccer team, my classmates, my teachers, and strangers—row upon row of strangers, all looking at me.

For about three panicky seconds I couldn't remember my next line, but then it was like some other part of me took over, and the words flowed out, not like I'd memorized them, but like I was actually saying them for the first time.

It was magic.

I was Beatrice. I teased Benedick, and I danced with the prince, and I laughed and raged and fell in love. Hard.

With the theater.

I loved everything about that night, the warmth of the lights, the little motes of dusts floating in the air, the smell of sawdust and fresh paint and hairspray, the whisper of my skirts as I moved, the charge of energy that swept over me as I took my first steps onto the stage, the way I could sense the audience listening, and the way my voice carried in the room. It was like being transported to another world, where I could be anything.

Anyone. And at the same time, myself.

All too soon, I was standing center stage with Eric, taking a bow. And all too soon, we'd done Thursday and Friday night, and it was Saturday night. Closing night. It occurred to me then that it was all going to be over. Sure, I'd see the people in the cast again, in the halls at school, in my classes, and around town. But it would never be the same.

I would never be the same. I'd never be Beatrice again.

I made it through acts one through four without crying over it, but around Act Five, Scene Three, I started to lose it backstage. Which was bad, because I was going to mess up my face.

"Oh, sweetie," Alicia whispered when she saw me. "It's like this every time for me too. That's the beauty of it. It's fleeting. But there will be other shows."

She floated away into the darkness of backstage, and I wiped carefully at my face with a tissue. When I looked up again, Eric was standing across from me.

"I have something I need to say," he whispered. "Before we go out there."

"Is it going to make me cry?" I asked in a whisper back to him. "Because I'm trying to pull myself together here."

"I like you," he whispered.

"I like you too."

"No. I *like* you. You're gorgeous, and smart, and you make me laugh, and . . ."

"Verisimilitude," I interrupted.

"What?"

"Maybe you like me because Benedick likes Beatrice."

He shook his head. "No way. I like you for you, Jo Dalley. I liked you the minute I saw you get up onstage all brave during auditions. I *loved* your British accent," he admitted, chuckling. Then he sobered. "What I'm saying here, or what I'm ineffectively trying to say is, I don't want this to end. You and me, I mean. So . . . will you go out with me, Jo?" he asked, his blue eyes all vulnerable and sweet and hopeful.

I believed him.

"Yes," I whispered, and he grinned, and I grinned, but we didn't have time to hug or anything, because then we had to be onstage. It didn't matter that we didn't seem to have that kissing chemistry in the play. This was real life, and I liked him, and he liked me. For me.

But let me tell you, when we got to the end, after Benedick and Beatrice admit in their silly way that they truly do love each other, Eric gazed at me in a way that had nothing to do with verisimilitude. I put my hand up to his cheek and felt the scratch of his stubble under my palm, and looked up into his twinkly eyes.

"*Peace*," he said softly. "*I will stop your mouth.*"

We kissed.

This time, the world spun around us, our friends watching, our family, the stage lights beating down on us, Eric's lips moving gently on mine and then not so gently, our breath mixing, our hands pulling each other closer, and when we came apart he whispered in my ear:

"Now *that* was a first kiss."

My knees wobbled, and he caught me by the waist and held me. The crowd got to its feet, and all around us there was thunderous applause.

....

ANECDOTE: ALICE RIPLEY

....

With all due respect to the Buckeye State, growing up in Ohio in the seventies supplied precious few chances to be directly influenced by creative artists and working actors.

Looking back, the odds were stacked against me that my life's passion to be onstage and the drive to be a successful working actor would spring from sitting in an audience in Ohio watching a pro work and thinking to myself, "I can do that!" There were very few productions at my disposal, and as one of eleven kids, money was tight in our household.

At the time, Cleveland's Ohio and State Theatres were about to be razed. A thriving theater district during the Golden Age of musicals, Playhouse Square was and is the second largest complex of theaters (New York City's Lincoln Center being the first). As the neglect and vandalism of the downtown Cleveland area in the late sixties collided with the onset of midseventies economic inflation, Playhouse Square was shut down.

It is a shame that when there are budget cuts to be made, the first slash is often to the arts, the heart and soul of a community. It is perplexing to me when people take art for granted or see the arts as disposable. Almost everyone in Cleveland could afford a television, so that is where many audiences were, including myself, seated in front of *I Dream of Jeannie* and *Bonanza*, instead of *A Chorus Line*. The plan was to swing the wrecking ball, destroy Playhouse Square, and build a parking lot. Yep.

I received a silver metallic wall hanging of *A Chorus Line* as a gift once, and I hung it on my wall. I stared at it for years wondering what the show was like, and even though I had never heard the score, let alone seen it— or any other musical—live, I pretended I understood when someone would notice the poster and say "I saw *A Chorus Line* in New York, and it was absolutely incredible. Did you see *Pippin?*"

On my fourteenth birthday, my stepfather, Bill Richard, took my mother and me to Playhouse Square to see a passionate production of *Jacques Brel Is Alive and Well and Living in Paris.* I had already decided I was going to be an actor and singer before that night. Being the middle child of a family shattered by divorce, I was struggling to attach meaning to my heartbreak. I had begun acting classes at Lakewood Little Theatre and had found an alternate family: an ever-changing brazen band of mix-and-match outcasts who rallied around each other for the sake of self-expression, also known as live theater.

Jacques Brel . . . was performed concert-style, in the lobby area, with the audience arranged around cabaret tables, close to the stage. What I witnessed stunned me, and a spark caught fire inside my trampled heart. As I watched the ensemble company perform one dynamic song after another, I found myself caught up in the theatricality of the score, the somewhat daring lyrics, and the awe-inspiring performances. I remember saying to myself, "I bet I can pull that off. I can do that."

Many years later after I won a Tony for my performance in the Pulitzer Prize–winning *Next to Normal,* I received a congratulatory letter from the director of this particular version of *Jacques Brel . . .* (the production of which was so fantastically successful it rescued Playhouse Square from demolition as it extended from a mere two week scheduled run into two years of packed crowds). The letter I received from director Joseph J. Garry Jr. read, "You most likely have never heard of my work, but I know you are from Cleveland . . ." and the letter continued, as he thanked me for my contribution to the lifeline that connects all of us to the grander stage of life and its players. Little did Mr. Garry know that by reading his words I was coming full circle with my own true savior: live theater and its imaginative, daring creators.

Alice Ripley received a Tony Award for Best Actress in a Musical for her performance as Diana Goodman in the Pulitzer Prize–winning *Next to Normal*. This performance also garnered her a Helen Hayes Award, a Drama Desk Award nomination, and an Outer Critics Circle nomination. Other Broadway credits include *Side Show* (Tony Award and Drama Desk Awards nominations), *The Rocky Horror Show*, James Joyce's *The Dead*, *King David*, *Sunset Boulevard*, *Les Misérables*, and the Who's *Tommy*. Her off-Broadway credits include *Wild Animals You Should Know*, *Five Flights*, *Vagina Monologues*, and *Li'l Abner* (Encores!). She has also received Helen Hayes Award nominations for her work in *Tell Me on a Sunday*, *Company* (both at the Kennedy Center), and *Shakespeare in Hollywood*. Alice has starred in the feature film *Isn't It Delicious* and the pilot *Modern Love*. She has written a hundred songs and records and performs regularly.

THE ARTFUL DODGER

Aimee Friedman

1. Food, Glorious Food

"Good mooorrrrnning, campers! Today is a very, very, *very* special day!"

The chipper voice bleated out of the loudspeaker, startling me awake in my bottom bunk. Through the fog of half sleep, I struggled to comprehend what I'd just heard. A very special day? Was it the Fourth of July? No. We were in early August. Blinking against the sunlight, I sat up and scanned a fuzzy mental calendar. Veteran's Day? Arbor Day? Was that even a thing?

"Today," continued our camp director, a frustrated actor who spoke extra-loud, in case Broadway was listening, "is Naaaational Cheese Day!"

Oh.

"Yes, that's right!" our fearless leader crowed. "Cheese for breakfast, lunch, and dinner! You'll need your strength for rehearsals, so don't miss out!" And . . . curtain.

I wanted to cry. I hated cheese. Pizza didn't count—everyone loves pizza. But I pictured the cafeteria taken over by oozing orange glop, and my stomach turned.

I could hear my psychotic roommate, Stephanie, moving around in the adjoining bathroom. Every morning, Stephanie roused herself from her top bunk before the loudspeaker wake-up, as if spurred on by some freakish internal alarm clock.

Reluctantly, I swung my legs off the side of the bed, my feet landing on the thin green carpet. Camp Backstage didn't truck with rustic cabins; we stayed, two to a room, in white-brick "dormitories" named after musical theater legends. I was eleven, so I was in the Liza Minnelli Dorm, which housed girls aged ten to twelve. As I padded over to the rickety chest of drawers, I imagined all the other campers getting ready in their tiny, airless rooms. I wondered if any of them felt the same dread I did.

I'd been at Backstage for four weeks; it was my first time at summer camp, and I wasn't adjusting too well. Mainly I missed the creature comforts of home. My soft bed, with no lunatic sleeping above me. The warm bath I took each night, as opposed to the freezing spittle that passed for a shower here. And most of all, I missed the food. My mother's roast chicken with crackly skin, the hunks of country bread we bought at Zabar's on Broadway, and the hot cocoa my dad prepared with a roof of foam on top.

With a sigh, I pulled on a black CAMP BACKSTAGE T-shirt and stepped into my denim shorts without having to undo the button or unzip the fly. I'd been a twig-thin kid to start with, but had gotten even skinnier since my arrival at Backstage. I twisted my dark curls up in a sloppy bun, and frowned into the mirror.

Yesterday, Theo—the gelled-hair, gleaming-braces prince of the boys' dorm across the lawn, who'd been cast as Conrad in *Bye Bye Birdie* (a rare feat for a twelve-year-old)—had smiled at me after lunch, and my empty belly had fluttered with hope. Theo had supposedly "made out" (I was fuzzy on the precise definition of that term) with Hannah, who lived next door, *and* with a fourteen-year-old girl who had the lead in *A Chorus Line*. Theo was something of a rarity at Backstage. It was increasingly clear that most of the other boys here were not remotely interested in girls.

"Ruthie!" my roommate shrieked. "Did you use my grease paint?"

Stephanie stormed out of the bathroom, wearing full-face clown makeup. This was a common sight at Backstage. Kids in all manner of sequins, wigs, prosthetics, and, as I'd seen yesterday, furry bodysuits (for the production of *Cats*) roamed the lush green grounds.

"No," I replied in the gentle voice one might use around a rabid Doberman. "I wouldn't need to—I'm not taking Stage Makeup, remember?"

Each camper had to take two "Theater Arts" classes for the summer. I had signed up for Dance and Stage Makeup, but Stage Makeup had been overcrowded, so I'd been moved to the least likely choice for a coward like me: Stunt Fighting. I'd been surviving that class by inventing headaches, backaches, and toothaches, sitting out while our instructor gleefully demonstrated fake karate chops.

The good news was that I got to avoid Stephanie entirely during the day; her other class was Voice, and her assigned musical was *Oklahoma!* Mine was *Oliver!* (Apparently exclamation points were as crucial to the theater arts as stunt fighting.)

"Whatever," Stephanie snarled as she charged past me toward our closet. "I'm not going to let you ruin things for me, Ruthie." Her menacing tone was somewhat undermined by the cheerful red circles on her cheeks.

The first night at camp, Stephanie had accused me of swiping her sleep mask and mocked me for not knowing what a "callback" was. After she'd commenced snoring, I'd sobbed into my pillow, feeling friendless and frightened.

Now, I still flinched at the sight of her, but I was beginning to understand that her fits of stress had little to do with me. This was Stephanie's second summer at Backstage. Many celebrities—movie and TV stars, winners of Tonys and Obies—had attended the camp, and she was determined to follow in their footsteps. She had an agent, had starred in a traveling production of *Annie*, and was on track, I supposed, to fame and fortune. This wasn't a fun getaway for her; this was a *job*. The fact that she had to room with me—an "amateur" (her word) who might have been from New York City but rarely went to Broadway shows—was clearly an insult from the theater gods.

Eager to escape Stephanie, I hurried into the pink-tiled bathroom. Hannah (of Theo-make-out-renown) and Tara were washing up at the sinks.

Hannah and Tara lived next door, and shared the bathroom with me and Stephanie. The two girls were kinder than Stephanie, though no less accomplished. Hannah was ridiculously beautiful, did modeling, and had the lead in *Oklahoma!*, which made Stephanie gnash her teeth. (Stephanie had been cast as the spinster-y Aunt Eller, and was wearing her clown makeup to rehearsals in some kind of twisted protest.) Tara was in my Dance class, and made my pirouettes and arabesques look like a clumsy toddler's first attempts at walking.

Tara and Hannah smiled at me as we exited Liza Minnelli together, the crisp, piney air of a Connecticut morning cool on our faces. But then the two of them linked arms and hurried ahead, no doubt whispering about their exciting professional futures.

What was I doing here? I wondered for the umpteenth time as I joined the masses streaming toward the cafeteria. I glanced around at the wooded campus that was dotted with other dorms, classroom buildings, and small theaters. No one had forced me to come. My parents were content with me spending the summer as I usually did—reading library books by the stack, scribbling stories in my bedroom, taking the crosstown bus to the Metropolitan Museum of Art.

I'd been the one to read an enticing article about Backstage in an issue of *Seventeen*. It had sounded glamorous: a performing arts camp built on the old grounds of a former resort hotel. I've always had a big imagination—a blessing and a curse—so I daydreamed about attending. I'd gazed longingly at the glossy photos of kids ranging in age from ten to fifteen, all laughing in the sunshine and wearing elaborate costumes onstage.

I was the opposite of outdoorsy, a city kid through and through. I couldn't swim or ride a bike, and nature seemed like an enemy to be conquered. So the idea of regular summer camp—hiking, building fires, encountering bugs—terrified me. But I was envious of all my friends being away for the summer, maybe kissing boys, coming back with stories and suntans.

Camp Backstage seemed like the perfect solution. I fancied myself pretty artsy—I loved to write, dance, look at paintings, and yes, even act and sing. I'd starred in my elementary school's production of *Pinocchio*, belting out the showstopper: our drama teacher's original composition, "A Real Boy (And Not Just a Toy)." By God, I'd played a male puppet with a fake nose, and I'd gotten a standing ovation! I was going to take Backstage by storm.

I snorted at this memory while getting in the breakfast line. The cafeteria always smelled like old socks and microwaved soup. Today, *eau de processed cheese* was added into the mix. Everyone here complained about the food, as was surely the case at every camp, ever. But I was a scared, picky eater who refused to try new things. I lived off toast, juice, and the candy bars Tara would get in her illicit care packages from home.

A stony-faced counselor stood behind the glass partition, slopping curdled white mush that I assumed was mac and cheese onto plates. As I passed him my tray, I squeaked, "Do you have anything else?"

"Sure," he replied dryly. He was British, like the counselor on my hall, Julianne. But Julianne was lovely and soft-spoken, and she called me "angel drawers," which made zero sense to me, but sounded very nice.

This counselor lifted the lid off a chafing dish to reveal undercooked pink strips of meat.

"For kids who're allergic to cheese," he groused.

"What is it?" I asked, worried.

The counselor smirked. "Electrocuted cow!" he snapped, then burst out laughing. Tormenting children was probably how he livened up his day.

I backed away, horrified. "I'll—I'll just get some juice," I stammered. My stomach growled as I pushed through the crowd, and his cackling echoed behind me.

There were two more weeks of camp to go. I wasn't sure I could make it.

2. I'd Do Anything

Post breakfast came rehearsal. The *Oliver!* group met in the Julie Andrews Theater, which was narrow, dimly lit, and perpetually dusty. I held back a sneeze as us cast members gathered onstage under the watchful eye of our director, Brad.

Brad was short, stocky, and stern. He seemed about my parents' age and had once acted in Shakespeare plays, which he mentioned regularly. He also liked to start off every day with a different warm-up ritual. Yesterday, we'd had to do jumping jacks and scream. Today, thankfully, it was just breathing exercises.

"In and out—*expand* your *diaphragm!*" Brad shouted, which made me want to laugh, since I knew the word also had a different meaning, but I didn't know what it was, exactly. Everyone around me was inhaling and exhaling with great seriousness.

The first day of camp, each camper had stood onstage in a different, bigger theater—the Judy Garland—and auditioned. Out in the blackness, the camp director, the voice teacher, and the dance teacher had sat at a table, judging us. I'd been nervous but uncharacteristically brave, singing "I Whistle a Happy Tune" from *The King and I* into the silent cavern. The next morning, cast lists had been posted in the cafeteria. We'd all been divided up into seven different musicals—*A Chorus Line, Cats, Pippin, Bye Bye Birdie, Oklahoma!, Oliver!,* and *The Fantasticks.* After much elbowing, I'd finally found my name on the *Oliver!* list. Under CHORUS.

Chorus! My spirits had plummeted. I was nothing special, one of the masses. What about my shining moment in *Pinocchio*? What about the fact that I adored watching movie musicals, and had memorized every line of *The Sound of Music, Fiddler on the Roof, Mary Poppins,* and *My Fair Lady*? I had even seen the movie version of *Oliver!* and knew the story well: a plucky orphan boy in a nineteenth-century London workhouse asks for more food and is cast out onto the streets, only to take up with a band of pickpockets.

Why hadn't I gotten a juicier role? I wasn't so arrogant as to assume I'd get Oliver himself. And the "grown-up" roles of saucy Nancy, scheming Fagin, and cruel Bill Sikes clearly went to older kids here. But couldn't I have been at least cast as Oliver's fun buddy, the pickpocket ringleader known as the Artful Dodger?

That role had gone to a pudgy, smug, redheaded boy named Josh, who had been in a *movie*! Or so the whispers went. On day one of rehearsals, I'd scowled at Josh as we sat in a circle and listened to Brad talk about the bleak Charles Dickens novel on which the musical was based. But later, when Josh performed "Consider Yourself," a cold understanding had washed over me. He was good, very good—he sang with a pure, clear voice that could tremble or thunder as needed. He strutted across the stage, all confidence and bravado. I wanted to be his pickpocketing friend, too (even though I hated him).

It was then that I realized that Stephanie had been right: I *was* an amateur. And this camp was meant for stars. Anyone else was relegated to the chorus.

"Chorus!" Brad bellowed, jerking me out of my thoughts. "Places, please, for the opening number."

I backed up and took my spot in the dusty far corner. Despite everything—my homesickness, my hunger—I felt a tingle of anticipation. It was still exciting, that beat before performing. Life onstage, however brief, was magical—the promise of people noticing your talent, applauding your efforts. There were no constraints of homework, school, or parental rules—just the pure opportunity to dazzle.

Both the best and worst thing about being in chorus was that you were onstage constantly. This was especially true in *Oliver!*, a show with lots of nameless kids—orphans, pickpockets—always singing in a group. But it was grueling work, hovering in the background. You had to be careful not to sing too loud or too low. The word *solo* had to be banished from your mind as you toiled under the hot stage lights.

Two days ago, I'd gotten carried away during "Be Back Soon," a number performed by Fagin and the pickpockets. I'd imagined myself in *Pinocchio*, and had let my voice soar and my arms open in a dramatic V.

Until Brad frowned at me and barked, "Keep your pitches even!" So I'd resolved to button my lip.

Today, though, on National Cheese Day, Brad threw us amateurs a bone.

"I've been thinking," he said, pacing back and forth, "about giving a brief speaking role to *someone* in the chorus." He peered intently at us.

We all caught our breaths. All except Hayden, the boy who played Oliver. He was only hidden in our midst for this number, and then he could shine all he wanted. For the rest of us, a speaking role meant a shot at glory. It meant that when the production of *Oliver!* went up on the final weekend of camp, with our parents and a few tantalizing "theater professionals" (as Brad put it) in the audience, we'd be *seen.*

I didn't care about some talent scout discovering me (although, if that happened, I wouldn't protest). I only wanted to experience the warm rush of pride I'd felt back in my *Pinocchio* days. I wanted confirmation of my specialness. That was all.

"First, though," Brad said, snapping his fingers and hopping off the stage. "Let me see your 'Food, Glorious Food.'"

Another audition of sorts, then. I exchanged glances with my chorus mates. A slouching girl named Meredith stood taller, and Andy, who was asthmatic, tried to cover up an anxious wheeze. It could be that this was just Brad's ploy to get us to up our games, but we weren't taking any chances.

I cleared my throat, preparing to sing. By now, I knew every song in the show by heart. They were all catchy earworms that stayed with me all day and during restless nights in my bunk. "Where is Love?," "Consider Yourself," "I'd Do Anything" . . . Unwittingly, I had made *Oliver!* the soundtrack to my life here at camp.

But "Food, Glorious Food" was my favorite song, and one I now related to with a kind of fierceness.

I opened my mouth and joined my fellow chorus-orphans. We sang, mostly in unison, about eating the same old awful gruel. I pictured the mac and cheese and the electrocuted cow, and it was easy to call up an expression of true misery.

In lockstep, we shuffle-marched across the stage, holding out invisible bowls. Some of the other camp musicals had already received their props and costumes, but we were still waiting on ours. Not that my costume would be one to write home about: a raggedy brown shirt and brown pants. I wondered if I'd been placed in *Oliver!* because I already had the waify, pale, big-eyed look down pat. No stage makeup required.

I tried to look as waiflike as possible as we sang about imagining "food, glorious food." Brad nodded in the first row, his expression unreadable. *Pick me pick me!* I wanted to shout, but I tried to keep my focus on the choreography. Step, step, turn, turn, pretend to set down invisible bowl.

I could feel dread building in my chest; we were coming up to my most hated part of this number. Of any number in the show. When we sang about peaches and cream being piled six feet high, four of us chorus members were to physically *lift* the three others onto our shoulders. This little maneuver was Brad's brainchild, and he couldn't have been prouder of it. I, of course, a master at shirking my duties, had complained of a shoulder injury the past few rehearsals so I'd get a breather from hoisting Meredith skyward. I'd simply stand there, singing, while three other weaklings struggled to bear the weights.

Today, though, I sensed there could be no shirking. I was going to do this, all the way. I gritted my teeth and let Meredith position her dirty sneaker on my shoulder. She stood, and I held on to her ankle, and my arm trembled like crazy and I remembered the camp director saying, "You'll need your strength for rehearsals!" over the loudspeaker. And I felt vaguely like this was torture, that if government regulators knew what was happening here, they'd send in cops to raid the place. But I bit my lip until I tasted blood and kept Meredith up until that particular lyric ended. I would never enjoy peaches again.

In the first row, I saw Brad shift in his seat, and make a notation on his copy of the script. *Pick me pick me!* I was sweating as we formed a line and shuffle-marched backward, singing the triumphant closing notes.

"Foood!"

"Thank you," Brad said tonelessly, rising from his seat. "Needs some work, but it'll look better once we get the bowls. My Hamlet didn't quite work until I got to actually hold Yorick's skull." I had no clue what he was talking about.

He got back onstage and walked a circle around us as we waited, tense and coiled. *Pick me pick me!*

"Okay," he said at last. "You."

My heart was racing. I couldn't look. I looked. Brad was pointing at me. *Me!*

"Me?" I whispered.

"Ruth Phillips, right?" Brad said, and I nodded, stunned. "You'll have a speaking line in the 'Boy for Sale' number," he told me, glancing down at his script. "You will say 'How much is that boy?' You can project your voice, obviously."

Was that a backhanded compliment? Who cared? My face was flushed, and I was grinning. It had all come together—my loudness, my longing for good food, and my determination to lift Meredith. Brad knew who I was. I had a solo!

Sort of. A semi-solo.

My chorus mates were scowling at me in much the same way I had scowled at Josh the Artful Dodger. I relished their scowls. I preened, even as I returned to my dusty corner for the next number. And when "Boy for Sale" rolled around, I strode to the center of the stage, as directed, and practically shouted, "How much is that boy?"

Brad asked me to do it again ("A little quieter this time"), but he didn't fire me. In fact, he told me more about the "role"—that I was a London housekeeper looking for a servant. I would even be getting a whole other costume for it!

National Cheese Day or no, things were looking up.

3. Where Is Love?

Dance class passed in a happy blur. We had moved on from ballet to jazz, and it turned out I was terrible at shaking my nonexistent hips to old show tunes. But I didn't mind. My imagination was off and running—I saw myself asking, "How much is that boy?" on opening night, and wowing the audience. I saw Brad handing me a bouquet and saying I should have never been in the chorus. By the time I entered the cafeteria for lunch, I was beaming.

That morning, I'd "eaten" my "breakfast" (a glass of juice) standing up by the drink dispenser. Now, I boldly accepted a half-melted American-cheese sandwich and sat with Tara and Hannah. Quickly, other girls from our hall (including a no-longer-clown-faced-Stephanie) gathered to sit around us; Tara and Hannah, like all the "star" kids at Backstage, were popular.

One of the first lessons of camp was that cliques and hierarchies formed more quickly than they did at school, due to the time crunch. Also, what counted toward popularity back home—athleticism, designer jeans, scoffing at hard work—did not apply here. You could even be unattractive (like Josh, my Artful Dodger nemesis), but as long as you had a big role and a bigger voice, you could be king.

I tended to hover in the background of the social stage. But today I nodded along while the girls nattered on about Capezio tights and Stephen Sondheim. I nibbled around the edges of the soggy Wonder bread, and asked Tara if she had any spare candy bars. She did, so we high-tailed it back to Liza Minnelli to nab some Twix from under her bed.

I headed to Stunt Fighting feeling almost hale and hearty. I wouldn't fake a headache today, I decided. I hadn't dodged out of lifting Meredith, and I'd been rewarded. I would bring the same can-do enthusiasm to this class.

Stunt Fighting met in the camp gym. I sat things out in the bleachers while our teacher, Kimberly, stood on the mats, schooling my classmates in the finer points of pretend slaps. There were only five other kids in the class—four boys (including cute Theo) who'd actually signed up for it, and another girl who, like me, had been transferred against her will. Her name was Jessica, and she had become my one real friend at Backstage.

Jessica occasionally sat out, but she was a more honest person than me, so she normally participated. "It's not that bad," she would tell me afterward in her sweet, earnest way.

Jessica was thirteen; she wasn't in my dorm, and mixed-age socializing never happened in the cafeteria. She was in the chorus of *Pippin*, and her other class was Voice. But Stunt Fighting, followed by the free hour before dinner, was our precious hangout time. We'd sprawl out on the patch of grass by Jessica's dorm, whispering about Theo or comparing our favorite books.

Today, when I entered the gym, I spotted her in the bleachers, reading a paperback. "Ruthie!" she said, jumping up. "I have to lend you this." She showed me the cover, and her dark eyes sparkled in her heart-shaped face. "You can start it during class if you want."

Jessica was like me: indoorsy, a big reader, and someone who'd had no clue how intense or "professional" Backstage was going to be before she'd arrived. But unlike me, she bore the whole experience with grace and good humor. She was grateful to be in the chorus, laughing to me about how off-key her singing was. The other class she'd wanted to take was Method Acting, but she was relieved she'd been moved out of it. "There'd probably be too much 'getting in touch with your emotions,'" she would say. I often wished Jessica's positive attitude would rub off on me, but it hadn't quite yet.

"Thanks, Jess," I said now, glancing out toward where Theo and the other boys were goofing around on the mats. Kimberly hadn't arrived yet. Theo looked in our direction and my cheeks got warm. "Listen." I turned back to my friend. "I'll participate today."

"What? Why?" Jessica asked, her expression alarmed. She put a hand to my forehead. "Are you okay??"

I laughed. "I'm great." I hurriedly filled her in on my good *Oliver!* news.

"Ruthie, that's amazing!" Jessica said. She gave me a hug. "We have to celebrate." She dropped her voice, flicking her long, shiny black braid over one shoulder. "Tonight, my friends and I were planning to sneak into the cafeteria after dinner to see if they have ice cream bars in the freezer. Our hall counselor swears they do. You should come!"

My heart soared. I was being invited to hang out with thirteen-year-olds? I'd been okay keeping separate from Jessica and her friends, though certainly envious when Jessica told me about their fun escapades and mature activities like leg-shaving. But now the tide could be turning. And getting ice cream would more than make up for National Cheese Day. My stomach rumbled and I smiled.

Just then, Kimberly entered the gym. Our teacher's blonde curls and angelic face were misleading; she worked as a stunt double on TV shows and could do roundhouse kicks like nobody's business. Fortunately, she only demonstrated those on the punching bag that hung from the gym ceiling.

"Ruth Phillips! Jessica Perez!" she called up to the bleachers. "Will either of you ladies be joining us today?"

"Both of us!" I answered, taking Jessica's arm and pulling her down the steps.

Kimberly looked as startled as Jessica had been. "Okay . . . great," she said, blinking. "Well, let's partner up."

Jessica and I looked at each other and grinned. Maybe this would even be fun.

Kimberly stood before our three groups of two, hands on her hips. On one side of me was Jessica, on the other side, Theo. His white T-shirt set off his tan skin and dark hair. He was chewing cinnamon gum, and it smelled so good. I wanted to tell him that I thought it was awesome that he had the lead in *Bye Bye Birdie*. And that I now had a speaking part in *Oliver!*, and maybe he'd come see the show on Performance Weekend.

But before I could work up the courage to whisper something, Kimberly spoke.

"Today, we're going to act out boxing," she said. "You'll often see punches being thrown in movies, on TV, or onstage, right? And they look really real, huh?" We all nodded, though I covered my eyes at any hint of onscreen violence. I knew Jessica did too. "Obviously, those stars aren't really slamming their fists into each others' jaws, because that would mess up their pretty mugs. And then they wouldn't be able to do all those fancy acting things *you* all spend the rest of your day doing here."

She smiled grimly and I realized then that teachers, weird as it seemed, could feel left out too. Kimberly must have been reminded constantly that her class was on the sidelines of Backstage. Nobody thought about stunt fighting when they imagined a career in the theater arts. So I'd been sitting on the sidelines of the sidelines.

"Why don't we face each other?" Kimberly was saying, clapping her hands. "Make a fist, draw your elbow back, and *wham*—" She mimed hitting the punching bag. "Try not to make direct contact. You can *lightly* graze your partner's cheek or jaw. At the same time, stomp your foot loudly to create a noise effect."

Jessica and I turned to each other and immediately started cracking up. Why hadn't I been participating in the class all along? This was hilarious. Jessica made a fist but then doubled over laughing before she could swing it in my direction.

"Girls," Kimberly said threateningly. All around us, the boys were dutifully stomping their feet and stopping short of knocking fists into chins.

"Sorry, Kimberly," Jessica said, trying to compose herself. "You go first, Ruthie."

I balled my hand into a fist, still laughing, feeling giddy and, for the first time in two weeks—maybe for the first time in my eleven years—immune to fear and uncertainty. Backstage wasn't so bad. I had a friend here, a true friend. I'd proven myself at rehearsal. *"How much is that boy?"* I heard myself saying. I imagined camera flashes from the audience. I'd started the day off miserably, but I was powerful now. I was—

I was letting my fist shoot forward with surprising speed and I wasn't stopping it and oh my God my fist was hitting something. It was hitting Jessica's nose. Hard.

I punched my only friend at camp square in the face.

"Owww!" Jessica screamed—a horrible sound. She doubled over, not laughing this time, her hands cupped over her nose.

I was trembling, staring in wonder at my fist. What had gone wrong? I was a weakling who could barely lift my weakling chorus mate. I hadn't eaten a proper meal in twenty-eight days. I wasn't capable of doing something like this.

"What happened?" Kimberly demanded, running over to us.

"I just—I think I—" I stammered, still glancing from my fist to Jessica, who was still bent over, wailing.

"She *punched* me!" Jessica cried, dropping her hands. I saw the blood trickling down to her upper lip and my stomach jolted.

"I thought you were going to move out of the way!" I cried, which I knew wasn't quite fair. In truth, I'd just been caught up in my own head.

"What? No!" Jessica screamed, wiping the blood with the back of her hand while Kimberly tried to calm her. The boys had gathered around us, buzzing with excitement and curiosity. "You were supposed to *not* make contact!" Jessica went on. "Didn't you listen? What's *wrong* with you?"

There were tears in her eyes, and I suddenly felt like crying too. Gone was my comforting, good-natured Jessica. An iciness filled my gut: I knew that, somehow, as crazy as this accident was, we wouldn't giggle about it later. Things wouldn't be the same between us.

"Jess, I'm so sorry," I said, meaning it with all my might. But it was too late—Kimberly was leading her away, saying they would get an ice pack from the infirmary.

Jessica threw a glance at me over her shoulder. "I knew I shouldn't have been friends with an eleven-year-old," she sputtered.

Kimberly looked back at me, too, as she and Jessica left the gym. "You stay right here and wait for me to get back, Ruthie," she said brusquely. "You're not slithering out of this one."

I groaned and sat down on a bleacher step, burying my face in my hands. If I had a punch like that in me, couldn't I have saved it for, say, my roommate?

And now I was in trouble too. Kimberly probably thought I was a black belt in karate who'd been hiding my talents all along.

I heard someone approach me, and I looked up. Theo was standing there, a grin stretched across his face.

"*Nice* going, Phillips!" he said, holding up his hand for a high five. "I have to say, that was pretty awesome."

I stared at him. Here he was, my sort-of crush, the cutest twelve-year-old at Backstage, talking to *me*. Acting like I was cool. Interesting. Worthy of his time. My first thought was that I had to tell Jessica, and then the harsh reality hit me.

"That was *not* awesome," I snapped, standing up and fighting the urge to bawl. Theo's mouth opened in shock. "Jessica's bleeding, in case you didn't notice. And you're a jerk if you think that's funny. Who cares if you have the lead in *Bye Bye Birdie*? Not me."

Then I really realized I was going to cry, so I lowered my head and sped past Theo, out the gym doors. I knew Kimberly would be furious that I cut out, but I couldn't stay there any longer, not after what I'd done to Jessica and what I'd said to Theo. Jessica was right; something was wrong with me.

I raced back to Liza Minnelli with tears streaming down my face. I passed by two fourteen-year-old girls who looked like they'd been let out of Stage Makeup early; they were made up like old women, with wrinkles painted like grooves into their cheeks.

"That girl must be coming from the Method Acting class," one whispered to the other, gesturing to me. "She's really good."

4. Consider Yourself

Later that night, long after Kimberly found me in my room and chewed me out for being careless (Jessica was going to be fine; as for me, I was excused from Stunt Fighting for the rest of camp), long after dinner (breaded cheese sticks that still tasted mostly frozen; I ate half of one, standing up by the juice dispenser), long after I tried to apologize to a swollen-looking Jessica on my way out of the cafeteria (she brushed me off and huddled with her friends), I decided to write a letter to my parents.

The rule at Backstage was: one phone call home per week, but no limit on letter writing. Over the past month, I'd sent my parents several short, breezy letters. My mom had been hesitant about sending me to camp in the first place. The night before they drove me up to Connecticut, I'd heard her whispering to my dad that maybe I wasn't ready. I'd been loath to prove her right.

Tonight, though, I didn't want to keep anything in any longer. What happened in Stunt Fighting had been replaying in my head all evening, eclipsing the usual *Oliver!* songs. I'd been so high on myself, so proud of my shot at semi-stardom. But now all of that seemed dimmed, almost insignificant. The punch I'd thrown at Jessica felt like it had landed on me too. Why had I been so obsessed with proving my talents onstage? So single-mindedly focused on getting my chance in the spotlight? Was that why I'd been unhappy here? Or was I just . . . not ready?

I sat on my bottom bunk in my pajamas, my box of stationery on my lap. Stephanie, to my relief, was next door, singing *Oklahoma!* songs with Hannah. My roommate must have forgiven the other girl for "stealing" the lead role. I heard them trilling together about it being a beautiful day.

I sighed.

Then I pulled out a fresh sheet of flowery paper, picked up my pen, and started writing.

Dear Mom and Dad,

Today was National Cheese Day here at Backstage. You can imagine how I felt about that. Here's the thing: I'm really hungry. All the time. Sometimes I feel dizzy in dance class, but I don't think it has to do with the pirouettes or turns. We rehearse all morning and don't even break for lunch, just go straight to our first class. Nobody else seems to mind, but I kind of miss reading under the air conditioner. I have a feeling most of the kids who come here all want to be actors when they grow up, and I'm not sure I really do.

I also have to lift a girl and hold her on my shoulder for I think ten seconds.

Something good happened today, and also something bad. The bad thing was that I punched my friend during Stunt Fighting class. I didn't tell you, but yeah, I'm taking Stunt Fighting. I'm not very good at it, but I guess I am stronger than I thought. The good thing was that I get to say a line in Oliver!*, but I don't even feel glad about that now.*

Also, remember how I told you I got cast as the Artful Dodger? Well, that was a lie. I'm sorry I lied. I'm only in the chorus. That's why getting to say a line was so exciting. I hope you won't be mad.

I also lied when I said my roommate was pretty nice. She's not. I think maybe she has mental problems. She keeps yelling at me that I'm stealing her stuff.

Also, I miss Mom's cooking. A lot.

Love,

Ruthie

Before I could change my mind, I stuffed the letter in an envelope, scrawled the familiar address, and ran to Julianne's room. She bunked with another counselor at the end of the hall, and collected the mail from us to send off in the mornings.

"Good night, angel drawers," Julianne said, adding my letter to the mail pile and giving me a kiss on the cheek.

I said good night and hurried back to my room. I crawled into my bottom bunk and pulled the covers up to my chin. I listened to Hannah and Stephanie singing until I fell into an uneasy sleep.

5. Be Back Soon

My parents showed up four days later to collect me.

"We're springing you," my mom whispered, giving me a hug as soon as I opened my door for them. "Good God, you're skin and bones."

"No, I'm not!" I said defensively. "What are you doing here?" It was before breakfast; our camp director had woken us up over the loudspeaker with the promise of pancakes (I was suspicious). Stephanie was washing up in the bathroom, and I'd just gotten dressed.

"Well, we got your letter," Mom said, closing the door behind her. She was wearing a long flowy skirt with a blouse and sandals. My dad was wearing his "driving" outfit: aviator sunglasses, a Polo shirt, shorts, sneakers, and, embarrassingly, socks pulled up to his calves. The realization of how much I'd missed them made my throat constrict.

"Oh yeah?" I said, trying to play it cool.

Mom studied me with her wide, green-blue eyes, so much like mine. "I know sometimes your imagination runs away with you, Ruthie, and you think things are worse than they are. But in this case, it really does sound like this isn't the right place for you. We understand that you want to come home."

"I don't know," I said. I needed them to leave before Stephanie witnessed this scene. This scene had *amateur* written all over it.

"Come on, sweetie," my dad said, sitting gingerly on my bottom bunk. "This place sounds awful. Constant rehearsing? Terrible food? Stunt fighting?" He paused, and said, "Okay, stunt fighting sounds sort of fun. But not for you, honey."

"I'm not in Stunt Fighting anymore." Since Kimberly kicked me out, the Stage Makeup teacher had grudgingly agreed to squeeze me in. This meant more quality time with Stephanie and grease paint, but at least I didn't have to encounter Jessica's hurt expression. "The food isn't always terrible," I went on, not sure who I was convincing. "Yesterday there were Sloppy Joes, and I'm pretty sure they were made with real beef."

My parents exchanged a look.

"And rehearsals aren't so bad," I continued, leaning against the dresser I shared with Stephanie, who would be showing up any minute. "I have a speaking role!" Over the last four days, my enthusiasm over my semi-solo had waned. But now, as I imagined leaving with my parents, I felt the tug of wanting to stay for that role. Who would Brad give it to in my absence? Slouching Meredith? Asthmatic Andy?

"All right, Ruthie." My mom held up her hands. "If you want to stay, you should. We were just worried about you. There's nothing wrong with leaving camp early. But it's up to you."

I studied my sneakers. I knew the right thing to do, the Afterschool Special thing to do, would be to stay. Stay on and fight. I'd be the star of the chorus and ace my one line. I'd rebuild my friendship with Jessica. I'd apologize to Theo for calling him a jerk and maybe even kiss him. I'd show up Tara in Dance class, and give Stephanie her comeuppance. I'd learn a lesson about perseverance, about not looking for easy ways out.

Stephanie walked into the room, her blonde hair stuffed under a cowboy hat. She eyed my parents with open hostility. She'd met them when they'd dropped me off and hadn't been any friendlier then.

"What's going on?" she demanded.

I stepped forward, and decided.

"I'm leaving," I said.

"What?" said Stephanie.

My parents exchanged another look.

"Yeah." I thought fast. "My parents won a prize—an all-expense paid family trip to Europe. We need to leave tomorrow or the prize goes to waste."

"Really?" Stephanie said at the same time as my dad. I saw my mom nudge him.

I nodded, surprised at how quickly I'd invented that lie. I had a thought then: I might not have been the best singer or dancer, but I was pretty good at fabricating things.

Stephanie frowned and bolted forward, flinging her arms around me. "I'm going to miss you so much!" she cried. "Promise you'll come back next year?"

I opened and closed my mouth but couldn't answer.

Finally, Mom put her hand on Stephanie's shoulder, and my roommate released me. "Yeah, maybe next year," my mom said.

I wished Stephanie good luck with *Oklahoma!* and watched as she raced out the door, clearly eager to spread the news of my early exit to Hannah, Tara, and beyond. So that was that, then. There was no undoing it now.

"You didn't need to make up a story," my mother said, shaking her head but looking amused. "Too bad there's no camp for fiction writers."

"I think you made the right choice, honey," Dad said, standing up and giving me a hug. "Let's get you packed."

An hour later, after I'd packed up my belongings and Mom and Dad had explained to the camp director about the Europe trip (they were now coming around to this story), I got in the car. I'd wanted to stop by the Julie Andrews to say good-bye to Brad, but the camp director told my parents it would be too disruptive. So I was left to buckle my seat belt and wonder if they were singing "Food, Glorious Food" now, and if anyone had noticed I was missing.

The car started and I felt immense relief mixed with melancholy. I had pulled off the ultimate dodge. I watched Backstage out the back window until it was a small green dot. Just like that, my experience with camp was over. I told myself I *would* try again next year, when I was older and wiser, more ready.

But I never returned to Backstage. I got busy with summer jobs and friends and most of all with writing. I put my too-big imagination to good use, and my scribbled stories became typed manuscripts. I ate well, and read books, and kissed a boy. I never saw Jessica again, but I was grateful for the friendship she lent me.

I may have been more ready for camp at fourteen or fifteen, but by then I'd made peace with being an amateur. Once I got to high school, I realized I could love theater, could appreciate the thrills of it, without needing to be a star.

I still dance and watch musicals, and I always sing along to the songs in *Oliver!* And singing along, enjoying from the sidelines, can be just as satisfying as having a solo. The performing arts are magical *because* they are inclusive: because everyone from the megastar to the bit player, from the stunt fighter to the scriptwriter, from the director to the audience member contributes to the dazzle. I'm not sure I would have fully understood that if not for all that had happened at Backstage when I was eleven.

Because of my abrupt departure, my time at Backstage often feels half-real. Unfinished. Sometimes I picture myself back there, on opening night of *Oliver!* I'm wide-eyed and skinny in my raggedy brown costume. The backdrop has been painted to evoke nineteenth-century London: all streetlamps and fog and cobblestones. There's the hushed anticipation of the audience, and the heat and glow coming from the footlights at the edge of the stage. I sing clearly and I move my feet in time to the music. I lift Meredith easily, and I stride forward and ask, "How much is that boy?" with the perfect British accent. When we take our bows, the applause makes my ears ring and my cheeks flush with pleasure.

Is that really how it would have unfolded, had I stayed on at camp that summer? I'll never know.

But I can always imagine.

....

ANECDOTE: LYNN COHEN

....

I guess I wanted to be an actress before I knew there was such a thing. Five years old? Could I have been five? All I knew was that it was more fun, more comfortable, to be someone else—Susie or Joan or John. Now, don't get me wrong, it wasn't like a split personality. I was just a shy girl child, an only child, pretending to be Bette Davis, with a martini glass (empty, of course) in one hand, a cigarette (unlit, of course) in the other, legs crossed, pretending. Acting?

I was sillier, happier, maybe even sexier (though I hardly knew what that was) as someone else.

Then came the idols who helped clarify this desire to pretend. There was Sarah Bernhardt (I knew about her because my mother at times called her oft-emoting child "Sarah"), then Eleanora Duse, Eva Le Gallienne, and of course, Olivier. That inspiration lasted a long time. I named my son Laurence after the great man. And even today I continue to find inspiration in people like Vanessa Redgrave and Cherry Jones, and the list goes on.

So, it's a "calling," right? We don't decide. We have no choice. Read such writers as Camus, or *A Mystic in the Theatre*, or Simon Callow writing about acting. They'll tell you about choice and the lack of it. It's a crazy thing we *must* do. So, there.

My first confrontation with the real profession of acting came at the ripe old age of fifteen. I somehow managed to get myself taken on as an apprentice with a summer stock company in Plymouth, Massachusetts. I arrived with a steamer trunk filled with tap shoes, formal dresses, and lots of scarves. I was ready for anything.

Mostly I washed dishes, cleaned bathrooms, painted sets, and ironed the stars' costumes. And it was heaven, because I was also allowed to go onstage. Small roles to be sure, but heaven.

In conclusion, there is no conclusion. Just the next role, the next challenge, the next mountain to climb, and the next stage to cross. Whatever and wherever that may be.

LYNN COHEN is best known as Magda in *Sex and the City* (and the two subsequent feature films based on the series) and for her critically acclaimed portrayal of Golda Meier in Steven Spielberg's *Munich*. Lynn has also been seen in such films as *The Hunger Games: Catching Fire*; *Synecdoche, New York*; *The Life Before Her Eyes* (with Uma Thurman); *Deception* (with Hugh Jackman and Ewan McGregor); *Invincible* (with Mark Wahlberg); Louis Malle's *Vanya on 42nd Street*; *Across the Universe*; and Woody Allen's *Manhattan Murder Mystery*. Her recurring roles on television include *Damages*, *Bored to Death*, and *Law and Order*. She has been seen onstage in *Macbeth* and *Ivanov*, and works at New York Theatre Workshop, New York Shakespeare Festival, Primary Stages, and Ensemble Studio Theatre. Lynn is a Fox Fellow, a recipient of a Bowden Award from New Dramatists, and a member of the Actors Studio, New York Theatre Workshop, Ensemble Studio Theatre, and Actors Center.

BECCA FIRST

Alex Flinn

It was my mother who started calling her Becca First, back in those early days of fourth-grade glee club. I would come home every Tuesday and Thursday, primed to recount the indignities suffered at the hands of Miss Hakes, our music teacher.

"Becca, first," I'd say. "It's always Becca, first—like the rest of us couldn't figure anything out without wonderful her."

I was referring to Miss Hakes's practice of having Becca sing whatever vocal line we were learning so we could hear it done "the right way" before the rest of the group—a ragtag mob, who'd mostly signed up for glee club because our parents wanted us to have something to do after school—came along and butchered it. Becca would stand in front of us, singing in her clear soprano, her dark ponytail bobbing to a rhythm which most of the group hoped—maybe—to pick up by ear sometime before the concert. Then the rest of us would get a try.

I sort of hated that because, hey, I knew my part just fine, thank you. But Miss Hakes never seemed to notice me. Only Becca.

One time, I came home and announced, "Guess who got a solo?" Then without giving Mom a chance to answer, I yelled, "Becca Marino!"

I was expecting big sympathy. Instead, Mom looked confused.

"Who?"

"Becca Marino," I huffed, "the one I talk about all the time."

Mom's eyes lit with understanding. "Oh, my goodness, Meghan. I thought her name was Becca First. That's what you always say about her."

I laughed. "That *should* be her name. Becca First. Becca First and Meghan Last."

"Not last with me." My mother ran her fingers through my curly, blond hair. "I'm sure you'll get the next solo. You were always a great singer. I even wrote it in your baby book: *Meghan loves to sing*." Then she took me and my best friend, Alli, out to Baskin-Robbins for Jamocha Almond Fudge sundaes.

But Becca First got the next solo and the one after that, and Baskin-Robbins became a regular part of our routine as the lineups for each winter and spring concert were announced.

"I don't get it," I said to Alli on one of those trips. "I have a good voice, don't I?"

"I think so. It's hard to get you to shut up."

I made a face at her, but it was true. "Then why can't I get a solo?"

"It wouldn't be so bad," Alli agreed, "if Becca wasn't such a snot."

I nodded sympathetically. Alli had learned the truth the hard way. Becca was friends with no one. She acted like it was some big thing if she looked at you in the hall. But Alli was one of those people who liked everyone, so she'd gotten it into her head to invite Becca First over to her house one day after school.

"Okay, I hate her too," Alli had reported the next day. "She said no, and when my mom asked her if there was another day that would be better for her, she said no, she just didn't want to come over."

"Well," I said, secretly sort of happy Becca wouldn't be playing over at Alli's anyway, "If she came over, she wouldn't be able to spend the whole afternoon, hanging around sucking up to Miss Hakes."

"Right? It's so weird that she stays after school," Alli said.

"Who needs her?" We went to my room to play our favorite game, where we dressed up in my mother's cast-off clothes and high heels and pretended to be pop stars. Usually Alli was Christina Aguilera because she was little and blonde, and I, taller and more serious, was Celine Dion. After I belted out her thrilling rendition of "My Heart Will Go On," I said, "Some-day, when we're famous, we'll come back and visit Cherry Hill Elementary in our limousine. Miss Hakes will be sorry she never let us sing a solo."

One time, we devised a plan: We'd both sing louder than everyone else in glee club. That way, we figured, Miss Hakes would have to notice our glorious voices.

"Meghan McGinley and Alli Hall!" Miss Hakes shouted over the din that day. "That is good enthusiastic singing, but a choir is supposed to *blend*. Would you please sing a bit more softly?" She gestured over to the usual side of the room. "Listen to how Becca does it."

And Becca First, with a satisfied smirk, showed us.

·　·　·　·　·

Middle school was a little better.

Mr. Oglesby, the chorus teacher, had a special "show choir," and while Becca First was the only sixth-grade girl to make it in seventh grade (boys being in short supply, any boy who breathed and sang kind of on pitch got in whenever), Alli and I got in too. Mr. Oglesby said I was really good. More than before, I started thinking of singing as my thing.

I dropped out of other activities like softball, where I'd never really excelled, and concentrated on singing. I practiced every day, not just karaoke with Alli, but real songs, even some classical stuff. My mom and Alli's got real involved in the choir activities, heading up car washes and candy sales and making headpieces to match our costumes. In eighth grade, I finally got a solo in one of our songs. It was a real high to hear the audi-ence applaud and know that they meant it, that my singing was that good.

That was the year we took an overnight trip to go to the state choir competition in Tampa. My solo was in one of our songs for state. My mother and Alli's fundraised their little hearts out and volunteered to be chaperones. Everyone was real excited about it. It was the first time our school had made it to state, and Mr. Oglesby kept saying it was because of "my three stars." But the day permission slips were due, Becca didn't have hers in.

"If you bring it first thing tomorrow morning, it will be okay," Mr. Oglesby said in choir that day. "I don't have to have them into the office until nine. I just said today to give us a little leeway."

"You can turn them in today," Becca said, looking him straight in the eye. "I won't have it tomorrow either."

"But why, Becca? You've worked so hard." Mr. Oglesby's bald brow furrowed. "We need you to lead the soprano section."

She looked at her shoes. "I have relatives coming from out of town that week. I can't go."

Frankly, I thought that was a pretty lame excuse. It was only one night, after all, and we'd be back the next day before noon. And much as I hated to admit it, I knew we sounded a lot better with Becca. There were still lots of kids who were in choir for an easy A. They didn't love singing, and everyone would be okay with them staying home. But not Becca.

All week, I glared daggers at her, not mentioning it. But the twentieth time Oglesby sighed and said how he'd miss Becca's voice, I got mad enough to say something.

"I think it's pretty sad," I said to her at the bus stop after school, "you not going to the state competition and letting everybody down. Way to support the group."

"What do you care?" She straightened her skinny shoulders.

"I do care. You're being a brat. I know the only reason you're not going is because I got a solo for once and you didn't." I hadn't thought of that before, but I bet it was true.

She laughed, a harsh bark that made some kids waiting around turn to look. "You think you're that important in my life? Is that what you think?" Her face looked pinched, like her ponytail was pulling too hard.

"It's what I know."

Becca kicked a rock. It flew up and almost hit me. "You only got that solo because your mother hangs around and helps all the time—like it's her life's work to assure that you get solos and special perks."

"My mother has . . . it's not like your parents ever help out."

"They don't have to. I can get my own solos."

"So you think you should just get everything? No one else gets a chance?"

She rolled her eyes. "Everyone gets a chance! Mr. Oglesby told me all about it the day he handed you what should have been my solo—sort of apologized, really. He said he had to give everyone a chance. 'If not,' he said, 'parents complain.'"

I recognized her implication but ignored it. My mom had in no way complained to Oglesby. "So you think you should just get everything? Well, that's fair."

"I think it's fair for the best person to get the solo." She pivoted on her heel. "My bus is here." She walked away, her dark ponytail bobbing as maddeningly as it had in fourth grade.

· · · · ·

Choir was first period, and the next morning, I went in early to talk to Mr. Oglesby about getting receipts for some raffle prizes my mom had gotten donated. I was standing in the hall when something stopped me.

The voice was high and light and would have carried out to the parking lot if the choir room hadn't been sort of soundproofed. It climbed the scales, reaching for the heavens, and when it fell down again, it was reluctant, yet inevitable. She didn't seem to need to breathe, like God himself was keeping her supplied with some invisible pump. She was hitting notes I couldn't think of, and it sounded *easy*. As I came closer, I heard her words:

> *Oh had I Jubal's lyre or Miriam's tuneful voice,*
> *To sounds like his, I would aspire.*
> *In songs like hers, rejoice!*

"Good job, Becca," Oglesby's voice said at the end of it.

Becca. Becca took private lessons with Mr. Oglesby before school, and it was really helping, helping in a way my own lessons weren't helping me. Each note, each run and trill, was an icicle through my stomach. I felt tears coming to my eyes, not tears of anger, or frustration, but tears at the sheer beauty of her voice. Becca was an angel, and in that moment, I knew she was right. I wasn't as good. I'd never be as good. She deserved all she got.

I left without asking about the raffle prizes. I came back fifteen minutes later, as class was starting.

That afternoon, I ran home from school and found my mother at the kitchen table. "Did you ask Mr. Oglesby to give me a solo?"

"No!" My mother was sewing a patch onto my sister's brownie sash. She didn't look up. "Of course not."

"You did," I said. "Oh, God."

"I didn't have to. Mr. Oglesby's a reasonable man. He knows he can't give every single solo to one girl even if . . ."

"Even if she deserves it."

"I wasn't going to say that."

"What were you going to say? She's a hundred times better than me, a thousand. I could never be that good."

"Of course you can be." My mother tried to smile. "You can do anything you set your mind to."

We got a rating of *Very Good* ("like a C," I told Mom) at state. The next week, I started private voice lessons with Mr. Oglesby.

. . . . .

In the next years, I worked my butt off. I went from voice lessons with Mr. Oglesby in eighth grade to lessons with a "real" teacher, a professor from the university in ninth. "It's worth the money," Mom told Dad, "for something that's so important to Meghan. Besides, maybe she'll get a college scholarship someday."

It seemed actually possible. I practiced hours each day and by senior year, was taking home *Superior* ratings at National Federation of Music Clubs competitions and Florida Music Educators Association. I didn't go out at night so I could rest my voice. I was adding notes to my range, high B-flat, C, even a C-sharp, and a squeaky D—each note a tiny victory, when I couldn't sing it one day. Then, I could. That year, my church did *The Messiah* at Christmastime. I had the soprano solo and, though I rolled my eyes at the slobbery compliments the old ladies there gave me, I loved it too.

Our choir director in high school was Mrs. Gower. Mom still made the headpieces, and Becca and I still alternated on most of the soprano solos, but it seemed more reasonable now. I never forgot about that morning in the hallway in eighth grade, but I liked to think that I—and my voice—had grown past it. I was really good. My voice teacher assured me that a career in music was possible for me. Alli and I were still best friends too.

As far as I knew, Becca had no friends.

About a week after my performance in *The Messiah*, I got a call from the director of the local civic chorale. "We're looking for two girls to do the solos in our performance of Andrew Lloyd Webber's *Requiem*," he said. "I saw you do *Messiah*. It was just gorgeous. Would you be interested? There'd be a small payment involved. Nothing much."

"Wow!" I could actually feel my heartbeat. "That'd be great."

Then, his next words: "Do you know anyone for the other solo?"

My first thought was Alli. But I knew Alli couldn't handle that difficult music. Maybe in the chorus. No way as a soloist. My second thought was . . .

"No, I'm sorry. I don't know anyone else. But I'd love to do it."

Actually, Alli was more involved in drama club and had quit choir in high school. At her insistence, I'd tried out for the drama club's Evening of One Acts sophomore year and got a small part, but it wasn't really what I was into. It took time away from singing. "If they did a musical, maybe I'd try again," I'd told Alli.

Then one day senior year, Mrs. Gower announced in choir, "The Palm-Aire High School drama and music departments have decided to try something very special this year. In cooperative effort, we will be doing a production of Rodgers and Hammerstein's wonderful musical, *Oklahoma!* I hope that many of you will come out to audition for roles in this production." As she said that, her eyes fell on Becca. "In addition to the major roles, there is a full chorus, so everyone who wants to should be able to participate." She looked at the rest of us.

Alli and I ran out and rented *Oklahoma!* that night. I knew that Alli—cute, funny Alli—would be perfect for the part of Ado Annie. And I could picture myself wearing a calico dress, my blond hair curled, as Laurey. I'd always wanted to be in a musical, ever since I was a little girl and my mother put me to bed with selections from *The Sound of Music* and *My Fair Lady*. Now was my chance.

I saw Becca several times in the days before auditions. I'd tried hard to keep her off my radar in high school, but that week, she was all that was on my mind. Mrs. Gower had practically issued her a written invitation to audition. But this should be my part. My chance. Finally, the day before auditions, I couldn't handle it anymore.

"Are you going to try out?" I asked.

We'd barely spoken since that day at the bus stop years earlier. She'd avoided me, and I hadn't objected. Now she turned and her green eyes swept up and down, taking me in. She smiled.

"Of course."

. . . . .

Mom had let me buy a new dress for tryouts, and a book of vocal selections from *Oklahoma!* I chose the song "Out of My Dreams" for the audition, figuring just about everyone else would sing "People Will Say We're In Love" or "Many a New Day" because they were easier. I had Mom finance an extra voice lesson that week, spending the whole hour working on "Out of My Dreams," getting just the right dreamy quality. Mrs. Gower might have looked at Becca when she made the announcement, but the drama teacher, Mrs. Sandler, was part of the decision-making process too. She'd remember me from the Evening of One Acts. Becca hadn't participated in anything. And Mrs. Sandler wouldn't have any preconceived ideas, like Mrs. Gower. If I was the best person at the auditions, I would get the lead.

I could barely sit still at the auditions, so it was a good thing there was a dance tryout first. I noticed with satisfaction that I picked up the steps much faster than Becca did. "Singing's next!" Mrs. Gower announced.

"Can't we do it privately?" someone asked.

"Sorry," Mrs. Gower said. "If you can't sing in front of people now, how will you do it in the play?"

Most of the auditioners were freshman and sophomores, hoping for, at best, a solo line among the chorus. They sang a few lines of a song from the radio and were gone. Alli nailed her rendition of "I Can't Say No," and I heard the drama club people whispering among themselves that she was a shoo-in for Ado Annie. Only drama club people would still use an expression like "shoo-in."

"Becca Marino is next!" Mrs. Gower called.

Becca stood and walked toward the piano.

Becca hadn't bought any special dress for the audition or done her hair any special way. She wasn't even a blonde which, to me, made her inappropriate for the role of Laurey. She stood in the curve of the piano, and I recognized the dreamy opening bars of "Out of My Dreams."

It had been years since I'd really listened to Becca sing. Oh, sure I heard her in class, but I tuned her out, and even when she had solos, she stood in front of the choir, her voice carrying forward. She didn't go to Federation competitions or take lessons with my voice teacher. She'd continued to take lessons with Mr. Oglesby at the middle school, so I was able to ignore her, to relegate her to a place of inevitability in my head. Becca was there, every day in chorus, in school, like humidity or homework, or rain.

But now, seeing her standing up there, singing *my* song in what should have been *my* place, I was back in that eighth-grade hallway again, and again, tears filled my eyes. But this time, they were hot, angry tears, tears I couldn't shed so they sat in my stomach and my throat, forming a hard lump like a wad of chewing gum. It wasn't fair! I knew how hard I'd worked, how hard I'd always worked. No way could Becca have done any more.

But part of me was transported to an Oklahoma cornfield, and I knew everyone else listening was too. She sounded like a real singer, a professional. The rest of us were just kids.

The audition list was in alphabetical order, so the next name called was mine. I stumbled through "People Will Say We're In Love," barely remembering the words. But I couldn't sing the song I'd prepared. Not after that.

The next day was callbacks to read for the principal roles, but I already knew it was decided. I did my best and hoped for a miracle.

I didn't get it. The next morning, the cast list was posted outside the drama room:

Curly . . . . Jared Davis

Laurey . . . . Becca Marino

Ado Annie . . . . . . Alyssa Hall

Jud . . . . David Hernandez

Will . . . . Nick Szpykowski

Aunt Eller . . . . . . Meghan McGinley

"Aunt Eller's a good part too," Alli said. "You have a big solo number."

"Yeah, about cows." But then I remembered myself and said, "Congratulations on Ado Annie. It will be fun, being in the play together. It will be, like, our last hurrah before college."

That day, at the first meeting to give out scripts, I could barely look at Becca. I was sure if I did, I'd see derision in her green eyes.

But Wednesday, when I got to rehearsal, Mrs. Sandler called me to the front of the room.

"Would you still be interested in playing Laurey?"

I drew a sharp breath. "I, uh . . . sure. But what about Becca?"

"Becca's had to drop out of the production."

I looked around, noticing for the first time that Becca wasn't there. I'd been trying not to look at her lately. "Why?"

"I have no idea. She called just this morning and said she couldn't do it. I'm afraid she's not a very reliable girl. She didn't even turn in her script sides and sheet music pages. You'll have to get them from her when you see her." Then she added, "I'm sure you'll do a wonderful job, Meghan. It was a hard decision to make. You were really equally good. I just thought you could be Eller because you're taller."

What a lie. But I guessed it was one she had to tell. She couldn't have Laurey doubting herself. I should have been elated, and I was in a way. But in another way, it was a letdown. I hadn't really gotten the part. And I dreaded running into Becca, knowing that I was second-best—as if I'd been caught rooting through her garbage, looking for leftovers.

She didn't show up for school on Thursday. And by Friday, I admitted to myself that I needed those script sides—the part of the script that had my lines on them. So that day, after school, I looked up her address in the phone book and walked to her house.

I stomped up the pitted driveway and knocked on a door with peeling once-white paint.

I barely recognized the Becca at the door. She pushed it open, just a crack, so all I could see were her red-rimmed eyes.

"What do you want?" she said.

"I . . . um . . . Mrs. Sandler asked me to come get your script."

"Oh." Without inviting me in, she walked away.

I pushed the door open a bit more and went in.

The house was small, so small that when I walked in the door, I was already in the living room and almost to the kitchen. And it was a mess. It was dimly lit, and it smelled like cat pee. Objects littered the floor and every available flat space. I moved my foot to avoid stepping on a used Q-Tip. On the sofa was a pile of what I first thought was laundry. Then I realized it was a woman.

Becca's mother.

I hadn't seen her in years, but I recognized her, sort of, from some assembly back in grade school. She'd changed so much since then. She was curled up sort of in the fetal position. Without thinking, I stepped toward her.

"Who said you could come in?"

The voice stopped me dead. I turned and looked into those piercing eyes again.

"I just thought . . ."

Becca thrust a wad of papers at me. "Here's your script. Now get out."

I didn't move. "Becca, I—"

I didn't even know what I was going to say. Whatever it was, I didn't get it out because Becca was on me, pushing me toward the door. "Get out!" she yelled. "Get out now!"

I went along. I thought she would have hit me if I hadn't. As it was, she was shoving so hard, saying, "You got my part. You get everything you want. Now, you can leave."

When we finally reached the front porch, I started again. "Becca . . ."

"Are you going to tell?" Even as she said this, her face wasn't apologetic or embarrassed, but defiant. "Are you going to run and tell everyone at school how I live, what I—"

"No." My voice was a whisper. "No, I won't. But Becca . . ." I struggled to put together the words. "Why'd you quit the play?"

"The play." She laughed. "Yeah, that's what really matters. The play." But in response to the question in my eyes, she looked away. "Howard. My stepfather. He said I couldn't do it. He didn't want me away from the house that much. I had too much stuff to do around here. He doesn't like me out evenings."

I thought back to eighth grade, to the overnight she'd missed. Since then, Becca had systematically missed every overnight trip, while attending everything else.

"He supports us, Mom and me," Becca continued. "We'd be on the street without him. So I have to do what he wants. He's in charge."

It floored me to think she'd had it so hard all this time, when I was worried about chorus solos. "How long has this . . . ?"

She shoved the script at me again. "Just leave. Please. You got what you came for. You got what you want. As usual."

Again, I found I couldn't look at her. I took my script, and left.

. . . . .

But at home, over the weekend, I couldn't stop thinking about Becca. I couldn't read the script without hearing her voice saying the words. I wanted the part, but not that way, not because the better person quit.

Becca came to school Monday, acting like nothing had happened between us, and I sleepwalked through rehearsal. Now that I had the part, I didn't want it. I was second-best, and Becca, who deserved it, didn't care.

The weeks passed, and I learned the part. I got the news that I'd earned a partial scholarship to study music performance at the University of Miami. My parents were thrilled. But at the dinner we had at a restaurant to celebrate, I told them I wasn't sure. "Maybe I should major in music education."

My father said, "Well, that seems like a sensible decision."

But Mom looked at me, stunned. "Why?"

I tried to put what I'd been thinking into words. "I just think if I can't be the best person in one little high school, I don't really have a chance of making it when I'm competing against the whole world. It would be a waste to major in performance."

"But we spent so much time . . . and money."

"I'm trying to keep you from spending more for nothing. I'm not good enough."

"You were always the best—one of the best. You got solos too. The university wants to give you a scholarship. You and that Becca are . . . equal."

I wondered if that was true, or if it was just my mother talking.

"They say success is ten percent talent and ninety percent determination," my mother said.

"But you still have to have talent."

"You *do* have talent. And you have determination too. You've tried so hard all this time, even when . . ." She stopped.

"Even when Becca always beat me," I finished for her.

"Not always," she said.

I shrugged. "I'll think about it, I guess."

. . . . .

Then, in March, the week of the performance came. Alli's mom and mine had gone shopping together to find the perfect calicos and had costumes made so we wouldn't have to suffer with whatever the drama department came up with. Mine was green. It was ready two days before, and as I stood in front of the mirror, my mother fussing over me, saying I made the perfect Laurey, all I could see was Becca's face. My whole body felt like the strings on a violin, and I couldn't stop thinking about it.

The next morning, I found her in the hallway before school.

"What are you going to do after school's over?" I asked.

She shrugged. "Get a job. Move out."

"But what about music? You're going to still do that, right?"

Her eyes filled with scorn. "Are you on drugs? No. I have three more months of putting up with this crap. Then I'm out of here."

"You could go away to college."

She shook her head. "You really are a piece of work—you know that? Away to college? I wish I could live one day in this fantasy world you live in, Meghan."

"I just figured . . . I mean, you're so good at singing and everything."

"Yeah, that's important." She looked through the books in her locker.

"You could get a scholarship."

"Maybe a partial scholarship for tuition. But no one's going to pay room and board. I'm not a football player." She seemed resigned, like she was talking about math homework. "I can't work full-time to earn it if I'm majoring in music. And my grades aren't good enough to major in anything else."

"But I figured . . . I mean, they must support you a little. The singing lessons and things."

"Oglesby taught me for free because he thought I had promise. I'm always sponging off someone else— that's what Howard says." She twisted around to see if anyone was listening. "I'll get a job after high school, move out. That's all I want, out. The singing was fun. It's something I was good at, one thing that was mine. But there are more important things in the world than singing. Lots more."

"But you're . . ." I stopped. Becca was something special. She had a voice the world should hear. I was ready to admit that now. "Maybe if you talked to Mrs. Gower, she'd be able to help, to see if there was somewhere you could go."

"Then what about my mom?" she continued. "I want to make money, now, soon, so I can help her too, so we won't be at Howard's mercy. What would you do in my place?" When I still didn't answer, she said, "Not that you've ever been in my place."

It was so unfair. It wasn't like she'd reached out to me. But I wondered, would I have done anything differently if she had? Or would I have been just as self-centered? It was nice to think I would have cared then, like I did now. But I didn't know. I'd always thought I was a reasonably good person. Now I was having my doubts. How could I not have realized that someone else had it so bad? How could I just have worried about getting a solo? It seemed so petty.

"It doesn't have anything to do with you, Meghan."

I nodded, though I didn't believe it. "Will you be at the performance this weekend?"

"I'll try to come. I really wanted . . ." She stopped, shaking her head.

"I know." I nodded. "Becca, I'm sorry I never . . . I mean, I'm sorry we weren't friends."

She slammed her locker door. "What makes you think I wanted to be friends with you?"

She walked away, the click of her heels on the terrazzo floor echoing in my ears.

. . . . .

That weekend, I looked for Becca at every performance, scanning the audience during my first solo, then again when the lights came up and I went out to accept the applause. We got a standing ovation, and an old lady came up to me, crying, saying I was "just like Shirley Jones." Becca never came. She was a ghost in school those next months and didn't show for graduation, even though the choir sang and Mrs. Gower asked her to do a solo. I ended up singing that too.

In fall, I started college, double majoring in music education. "I'm not giving up," I said to my mother, "just being practical. And besides, I like the idea of teaching. As a teacher, maybe I could really help a kid who didn't have parents as supportive as you guys." I thought of Becca.

But, in fact, I did pretty well in college, even getting a good part in the first Opera Workshop performance of the year, when few freshmen did. I wondered if, maybe, my competition with Becca had been a good thing. Maybe it had pushed me harder and harder, making me the best I could be.

I don't know what will happen in the future, but music will always be part of my life, somehow.

And I know I'll never see Becca again. I hope she's happy, wherever she is. And I hope she still sings.

ANECDOTE: MONTEGO GLOVER

We did not think we were misfits at all.

In fact, we weren't. We were twelve and thirteen years old—smart, arty (even if we didn't know it) students who had been afforded a grand opportunity: a school that provided us with exposure to theater as a very normal thing and a teacher who excelled not only at teaching, but at inspiring and caring about our growth as artists.

I found the bones, muscle, and breath of the theater in this class and have always known that without it, a central component of my training as an actress would be missing. I was first introduced to the arts through public television. I had always been so taken with the many, many ways to tell a story. So it was no surprise that theater class (up close and personal) was home.

We studied the classics, pulled them apart, reconfigured them to assist us in telling our stories (and our teacher in her teaching). This is how we did it: Read art. Practice art. Make art.

Read art. Students were to read all the time, especially the classics. Read. Read a play. Read a novel. Get accustomed to reading. Reading, interpreting, discussing. Reading alone. Reading aloud. To this day I'm not afraid or opposed to reading for work or pleasure.

Practice art. New and older students worked together on every aspect of making plays. But in class, new students observed acting coaching of older students. It's an amazing teacher observation. Also, new students had no speaking lines in any plays for the first two years. Amazing. The only tools you were permitted for the first two years were body, sounds (non-speech), and music if needed (not singing). It placed our attention on the process from the inside and gave us time to really work on that skill. No speaking lines gave our less verbal students a safe place to build confidence, and our more verbal students an added layer of training that only strengthened their words, once they were speaking, of course. Imagine the day you know you're permitted to have speaking lines! Speaking became a grand and glorious experience, words were savored. Words were respected. And less was more. A lesson I carry into my work (and my life) to this day.

Make art. Literally. We made costumes, and practiced and designed makeup on ourselves and each other—fun for some, dreadful for others, but learning all the time. We built sets and made props. Each student was encouraged to play to their strengths, but also encouraged to try other disciplines within the art form. To cross-train. In fact, it was a requirement, but one that every student understood because we were validated. And of course, once we discovered that our natural skills could contribute to the growth of other skills, the creative realm opened up even more. By the time we were ready to present our plays, we had poured ourselves (and every new thing we'd learned individually and as a unit) into every element of our production. And we were proud. We were proud whether our audiences got it or not. A lesson in and of itself.

In the end, it was in this class that I discovered my passion in life. I might've found it another way, but this experience, five years of learning this way, have turned out to be my bedrock.

MONTEGO GLOVER starred as Felicia Farrell in the Broadway hit musical, *Memphis*, for which she was nominated for a Tony Award. She also received both the Outer Critics Circle Award and the Drama Desk Award as well as a Drama League Award Nomination. Montego is thrilled to have been with *Memphis* since its conception, earning her third IRNE Award nomination as well as a San Francisco Bay Area Theatre Critics Circle Award nomination before moving the show to Broadway.

Born in Georgia and raised in Tennessee, Montego attended the Chattanooga School for the Arts and Sciences and continued on to receive her BFA with honors in music theater from Florida State University. She made her Broadway debut in *The Color Purple*. She has been privileged to travel around the country performing at the Geffen Playhouse, La Jolla Playhouse, Seattle's 5th Ave Theatre, The Huntington Theatre, and Pittsburgh CLO, among many others. Her favorite roles include Sarah in *Ragtime*, Lorrell in *Dreamgirls*, Hermia in *A Midsummer's Night's Dream*, Aida in *Aida* (IRNE Award for Best Actress in a Musical), and Ti Moune in *Once on This Island* (Helen Hayes Award nomination). Her TV credits include *Hostages, Smash, Golden Boy, The Good Wife, White Collar, The 2-2, Law and Order, Made in Jersey, Guiding Light,* and *Wonderful World of Disney.* www.montegoglover.com.

STRINGBEAN AND GOOSE

Laura Goode

1. Feet Filth in Five Days

After the relative popularity of "Feet Filth in Five Days," in which Goose didn't shower or change his socks for five days, and Stringbean filmed his feet in various stages of grossness, their YouTube channel, stringbeanandgoose, had 539 subscribers.

"This is disgusting," wrote one commenter, banjoqueen2904. "Freedom of speech gone WAY too far."

"Whaaat r this kidz smoking? ☺ ☺ ☺" added jaxrox42 thoughtfully.

"Uglytown, USA," wrote mizmichelle1985. "population: these kids and their weird feet. Why would anyone want to record ugly shit like this?"

"It's too bad you can't capture smell in video," noted minotaurXLZ, "because I bet the smell of this would knock over a steel duck."

Stringbean agreed, then wondered who in the hell had ever seen a steel duck.

2. The Thing About Ugly

The secret truth was that part of fifteen-year-old Stringbean loved these comments, was fascinated and titillated by them. In her own weird, contrary way, the more people vocally opposed what she posted on YouTube, the better Stringbean felt about how she was doing. Stringbean had read somewhere that all great performance artists started out being misunderstood and condemned. So, she concluded, if she was being misunderstood and condemned on YouTube, she was probably on her way to greatness.

The thing about being ugly was that the stakes were much lower than being beautiful. If you were beautiful, people only ever wanted you to be *more* beautiful, and lamented if you became less so. If you were ugly, nobody really cared about whether you got uglier or not.

Stringbean felt a kind of affinity with the ugly, the ignored, the dismissed, the damaged, the demented, the cast-off, the clearance rack and the five-dollar-box, the auto graveyard and the compost pile, the abandoned hotel and the broken machine. Stringbean just found ugly things more interesting than beautiful ones, she supposed whenever anyone asked, which was never.

Stringbean felt strongly that she was not pretty, not fine-boned, slender, and thick-haired the way Junie Mae and her mother were, the Italian side from Big DeeDee. Stringbean's own flat German face, inherited from her now-absent and lackluster father, was plain in an open, wholesome way: animated, vivacious, striking, but knock-kneed and gawky, too skinny everywhere but between her ribs and her collarbone. Stringbean had lived with this knowledge the way you might learn to live with a minor ache, a hangnail, or a chronic cramp. In two years, things would be vastly better, but Stringbean had no way of knowing that now.

3. James Bruce and Frances Rose

Nobody knew where Goose had come from except Stringbean, and for that matter, no one knew the origins of Stringbean but Goose. That is, everyone knew where the *people* Goose and Stringbean came from— Ladyslipper, Wisconsin, a town so small that your next-door neighbor probably knew your birthday more readily than Facebook did—but only the holders themselves knew the genesis story of the names. Still, no one, families included, called Goose and Stringbean anything but the same.

4. Good Worm Day

Goose and Stringbean were doing what they were usually doing on summer afternoons, which was shooting ugly things with Stringbean's old home video camera, which she got for free on Craigslist.

Goose took the trowel out of the garden shed, picked a remote corner of Stringbean's yard, dug the blade in with a stomp from his right filthy yellow Chuck Taylor high top, and flipped a clod of dirt. Stalking the scene as it unfolded, each time as though she'd never seen the action before, Stringbean paced back and forth a few times with the camera, then crouched down to the ground, wriggled onto her belly, and slithered up to the worms camera-first.

In a manner that Stringbean was still doing her best to ignore, her burgeoning boobs had started to get in the way of this pursuit. Goose's attempts to ignore them—Stringbean had started to notice despite her best efforts not to—were becoming less successful.

It had rained yesterday, and the worms were all at the epidermis of the soil, wriggling in exactly the glistening, disgusting tangle that never ceased to enrapture Stringbean.

"Cut," Stringbean said, upending herself onto her knees and setting down the camera. "Flip-flop ugly pop!"

This was Stringbean-and-Goosean for "that was a good shot."

"Yeah, that was flippin' awesome. They're juicy today," Goose remarked, wiping a film of sweat from his brow and replacing it with dirt. "Wicked good worms."

5. What Are You Supposed To: Age Fifteen

Stringbean had begun to wonder if they were too old for this. Not *this* as in making movies, which she was fairly sure she always wanted to do, always, but *this* as in getting so damn dirty all the time. This as in spending all her time with Goose. This as in doing what she always did, every day, all summer.

Stringbean was ready for things to be different, ready for things to *happen* already. Or at least some things. Maybe one of their 539 YouTube subscribers was someone who could get her out of here, Stringbean thought sometimes before she fell asleep. All the lucky ones were born somewhere more exciting, like Los Angeles: Carol Burnett went to Hollywood High School. She looked funny the way Stringbean looked funny, and she sang anyway.

Two facts:

Stringbean loved to sing.

Stringbean was afraid to sing.

Stringbean sang into the camera, late at night and sometimes even in that suspended place between sleep and waking. Stringbean sang with machines—an electric razor, a hand mixer, a vacuum—harmonizing with their hum, their whirr, their whine. Stringbean's singing was ugly, like all things she loved most, and she was afraid to sing for 539 people on the Internet. She was even afraid to sing for Goose.

What Stringbean didn't know: Goose had often stumbled upon footage of Stringbean's late-night machine duets when one or the other of them was digitizing tapes or editing. He hadn't ever said anything, but he had those videos at home, all cut and ready to go if she ever disclosed their existence. Goose knew how to wait for Stringbean's cue on things she didn't want to talk about.

6. Junie Mae and Goose, Sitting in a Tree

"Goose!" Junie Mae, Stringbean's seven-year-old baby sister, screamed, blasting out of the house. Junie Mae hurtled into Goose's arms.

"Hi, Goosie," Junie Mae cooed.

"Hey, kiddo," Goose said good-naturedly. Goose and Junie Mae had historically enjoyed a certain the-world-against-Stringbean camaraderie, one that Goose regarded as a joke and that Junie Mae regarded as indelible proof that they were forever meant to be together. Stringbean could hardly blame Junie Mae, much as she tried. It was hard to ignore, and equally hard to admit, that Goose's recent growth spurt, and resulting loss of baby fat, had made him sort of, well, tall and handsome. Right now, though, his face looked like he hadn't showered in a year.

"Oh my God, get your disgusting crush off of us," Stringbean teased, rolling her eyes. "Or at least put it to good use and get us some crackers and Easy Cheese."

"No. I came out to tell you that Mom says Big DeeDee needs you," Junie Mae said. "So why don't you and your big fat boobs go help her already." Junie Mae's eyes darted to Goose, who she knew she'd be alone with in a minute.

"Eat shit, Junie Mae," Stringbean said, crossing her arms as she stalked off toward the house.

7. Flip-Flop

This was Stringbean's least favorite part of the day: Big DeeDee, Stringbean's grandmother, had to be flipped. Big DeeDee had been a dancer once, but now she laid in bed all day. Stringbean stalked reluctantly into the house, where two DeeDees, Big and Little, were waiting. Little DeeDee had wheeled Big DeeDee's hospital bed parallel to the couch.

"Ma, we've been over this and over this," Little DeeDee, Stringbean's mother, said. "If we don't move you and change the sheets, you'll get bed-sores."

"The mother of unhappiness is a desire to control," Big DeeDee said calmly and cryptically, which is to say characteristically.

"Yeah, well, the mother of me is you," Little DeeDee retorted. "Stringbean, get on the other side."

"Hi, BeeDee," Stringbean said to her grandmother, kissing her on the forehead as she crossed to the far side of the bed. "How you feeling?"

"I love you far more than I love polite questions," Big DeeDee responded, patting Stringbean's hand. "Up and away, I suppose."

In a practiced, choreographed motion, Stringbean and Little DeeDee hoisted the sheet underneath Big DeeDee and gurneyed her over to the couch. Little DeeDee swept away the hospital bed's sheets, then Stringbean and Little DeeDee gently rolled Big DeeDee over to pull out the sheet underneath her. Little DeeDee threw the new sheets, faded pink plaid, over the bed, and tucked one under Big DeeDee to regurney her back off the couch.

"One. Two. Three," Little DeeDee said, and she and Stringbean lifted Big DeeDee back to the bed.

"Four!" Big DeeDee said, pumping a fist midair, just to be contrary. Big DeeDee had cancer in her guts but she didn't act like it, except for being in bed all the time. Sometimes, morbidly, Stringbean wished she could *see* Big DeeDee's ugly guts, to understand the whole thing better. The doctors just kept saying *it won't be long now*.

Little DeeDee breathed a sigh of relief. "Well. That's done. I'm going to get Junie Mae fed. Stringbean, you can make yourself a sandwich and get BeeDee something, right? I've got to get in the shower and get to work." Little DeeDee was a waitress at a fried chicken restaurant called Chicken Fair.

"Sure," Stringbean said, internally rolling her eyes. Between taking care of Junie Mae and taking care of Big DeeDee, Little DeeDee didn't have much time left over to take care of Stringbean, whom she knew could pretty much take care of herself. Stringbean knew her mother was busy and stretched too thin, but she couldn't ever fully rid herself of the thought, *Don't I get a little mothering too?*

"You want ice cream?" Stringbean asked Big DeeDee, rising to go into the kitchen. Big DeeDee nodded. Since her grandmother was now in hospice care, she got to eat whatever she wanted, which usually meant she opted to indulge her notorious sweet tooth as much as possible. Stringbean came back with half a ham and cheese sandwich in her mouth and a bowl of coffee ice cream in her hands. Chewing, she sat down and spooned up some ice cream.

"Here you go," Stringbean said, leaning over to feed Big DeeDee a bite.

8. Interlude: So Sweet and So Cold

Little Stringbean had always loved Big DeeDee's refrigerator, back in Big DeeDee's big old house. There was always ice cream and pop and maraschino cherries. Stringbean liked to pour herself a glass of Sprite and tip cherry juice from the bottle into it for a homemade Shirley Temple, and then watch an actual Shirley Temple movie with Big DeeDee. Big DeeDee had lots of good old VHS tapes. Their favorite was a tape of highlights from *The Carol Burnett Show*.

Stringbean liked Carol Burnett because Carol Burnett seemed to like ugly things, and because she had grown up with her grandmother, too. She had a maid outfit that made her look like a Raggedy Ann doll.

Stringbean liked that: Carol Burnett didn't care too much about being pretty all the time. She just wanted to sing, her way. Carol Burnett had a drunk dad too. Stringbean wondered how she had it in her to be funny all the time, or if being funny was just what Carol Burnett had in her. Was Carol Burnett ever afraid to sing?

9. Nipple Stickers

Big DeeDee peered down Stringbean's shirt collar as Stringbean leaned over.

"Bean," BeeDee whispered, coffee ice cream pooling in the corner of her mouth, "do you have duct tape on your nipples?"

Stringbean sat down quickly and took an evasive bite of her sandwich, looking at her shoelaces. She felt herself blush an alarming shade of purple. The truth was that Stringbean had tested a variety of materials in her ongoing attempts to tame her seemingly untamable breasts. When they were smaller, an A-line men's undershirt under her T-shirt mostly did the trick. Then two months and another whole cup size later, she added a layer of sports bra. Then she went up another cup size and bought a sports bra a cup size smaller.

Finally, to contain the C-and-a-half-cup spillage, Stringbean's daily boob-constriction routine went like this: too-small sports bra, tight mummy-like layer of ACE bandages over the sports bra, then undershirt, secured by a quick lap of duct tape, T-shirt, and if it was cooler than eighty degrees, sweatshirt. It was ninety-five today, and Stringbean had been forced by massive pit stains to abandon the sweatshirt.

"It's—it's nothing," Stringbean muttered lamely.

"Doesn't it hurt?" Big DeeDee opened her mouth slightly, like you do before the priest puts the crispy Communion wafer on your tongue: *more ice cream*. Stringbean obliged.

Stringbean sighed. This was the problem with her boobs: they insisted upon themselves. They were always protruding into things.

"I'm sort of used to it," Stringbean said.

"Don't you know rich ladies pay good money for ta-tas like that?"

"BeeDee. Don't say *ta-tas*."

"Why not?" Stringbean fed Big DeeDee another bite in an unsuccessful attempt to shut her up. "I've got them, don't I? Even if they look like pissed-out pig bladders now."

"Christ on a bike, BeeDee."

"Now who's got the mouth?" Big DeeDee chided Stringbean uncon-vincingly. "I'm done with the ice cream. Stomach's starting up again."

"Drink some water," Stringbean said, handing her the pink plastic cup with the pink plastic straw.

The truth was her boobs had gotten Stringbean to thinking. They seemed like an omen, an indication of things to come: Stringbean was out-growing the body that had gotten her this far, and she was wondering where the new one could take her. Out of Ladyslipper. Out of her fear.

10. Ignore

The home phone rang in the kitchen; Stringbean got up to check the caller ID.

"Who is it?" Little DeeDee called from the shower.

"Eight hundred number," Stringbean called back, knowing what that meant: bill collector.

"Press IGNORE," yelled her mother.

About a year ago, Big DeeDee's treatment, and then hospice care, had forced them to sell Big DeeDee's big house, which Stringbean and Junie Mae had been born and raised in, and to move into the smaller, rented two-bedroom house where the four of them now crowded. Stringbean's mother, to the best of Stringbean's understanding, had to ignore money most of the time because she had to pay so much attention to everything else.

Another fact about Stringbean: Stringbean didn't really have a dad, at least not anymore. Junie Mae didn't either, but a different one. The family had pressed IGNORE on the subject of Dad.

Stringbean heard a cough behind her and turned. Goose gave an uncertain wave from the front door with one hand, the camera hiked by the other on his shoulder. Junie Mae bounded in from behind him, feeling no such uncertainty.

"Honk, honk!" Big DeeDee called happily at the sight of him.

Goose's face brightened at the welcome. He'd sensed for a moment that this was a bad time, though the amount of time he spent at Stringbean's had at this point pretty much transcended the boundaries of good and bad times. He crossed the threshold and came over to give Big DeeDee a kiss.

"How's the weather today, BeeDee?" Goose asked, sitting down on the couch.

"Hot as hell and getting worse." Big DeeDee sighed. "But cooler for the sight of you, dear. Long time." Sometimes Big DeeDee didn't remember that Goose had been here yesterday. Or every day this week.

"BeeDee, have you ever been out to the old hotel on the island?" Goose asked.

Stringbean saw Goose's hand start to reach toward the camera. Stringbean shook her head firmly. *She isn't ugly,* Stringbean meant, *so don't film her.* Goose nodded subtly and reached instead for a butterscotch candy on the end table.

"Sure, before it burned down," Big DeeDee said. "Big dances. Cotillions. Rich kids' summer weddings. The owner liked to call it 'The Coney Island of the West.' God knows why."

Predictably, Junie Mae bounded onto the couch beside Goose.

"Goose, can I be in your movie today? You said I could be in one soon. It's soon now. Pleeeeease?"

Stringbean rolled her eyes. "We have enough footage for today."

"Why don't you two sing our song for me?" Big DeeDee asked. When Stringbean was little, Big DeeDee had taught her the harmony line to "Amazing Grace," and they'd sing it together. Later, she had taught Junie Mae the melody, and she liked to hear the two girls sing it together.

Stringbean blushed, bashful at the idea of singing in front of Goose. If Goose thought she was bad, then singing would pretty much be over, and Stringbean didn't want singing to be over.

"Maybe another day, BeeDee."

"Not so many days to sing, String," Big DeeDee said cryptically. "Not as many as you think."

11. The Grand Hotel Sault St. Marie

Stringbean and Goose had decided to go out to the island.

Ladyslipper had a big lake on the east side of town, dotted with cabins and trailers, docks and boats, Friday night fish frys and fireworks after dark. Stringbean's mother hated the lake life because it made tips at Chicken Fair, off the lake at the intersection of Highways M and 40, pretty dismal on summer weekends. But Goose's family had a little summer place, and it was where Stringbean had learned to swim.

In the middle of the lake was an oblong island, like a banana-split dish thick with trees. It had taken Stringbean and Goose awhile to screw up the courage to make the trek out to the island, seeing as local law enforcement strictly prohibited it, but they figured if they did it close to dark on a Friday night, when the whole cop shop was at the bar anyway, probably no one would care enough to stop them. On the island, local folklore recalled, there had once been an upscale lake resort, a real white-tails-and-fresh-towels joint. Some said Al Capone had hid there for hot stretches in the twenties.

12. Celebrity Ghost Stories

It was 7 p.m., the first fingers of sunset over the dock, as Goose and Stringbean loaded up the paddleboat for their expedition: camera, extra tapes and batteries, trigger spotlights that were the kind you used to catch deer in a hunting field, flashlights, a hammer, trail mix, and Cokes.

Stringbean paused a moment, hoisting the camera on her shoulder. An August sunset over the lake was an affordable luxury, a mundane extravagance, and it wasn't the least bit ugly, but she wanted a shot of it anyway. Stringbean faced the lake with the camera. Tiger lilies and cantaloupe smiles and the end-of-the-movie glow of E.T.'s translucent throbbing heart spread across the sky, silhouetted underneath by the banana-split-dish shape of the island; a fishing boat hummed across the water, heading home for dinner. Because of the long northern days of the summer, they had maybe two hours of fading light left to explore the island.

"Give me an intro," Stringbean said, turning to face Goose in the boat. Goose was an aquatic machine with boats; he was thinking about joining the Coast Guard like his uncle, and that way he could go to college for free. Stringbean thought she'd prefer to skip the Coast Guard part and go straight to college, but she wasn't sure how that was going to happen, so she tried not to think about it. Stringbean had seen on one of her many visits to Carol Burnett's Wikipedia page that she had gotten a scholarship to UCLA. Stringbean wondered how you got one of those.

Goose snapped to attention. "Ready?"

"Hit it."

"The date is August fourteen. The setting is dark with history. We are at Amy Bell Lake, the oldest part of the mostly insignificant town of Ladyslipper, in the great state of Wisconsin. Our destination: The haunted, burned-down, long-forgotten Grand Hotel Sault St. Marie. Opened to serve illegal liquor in 1922 and torched under suspicious circumstances in 1978, the hotel supported much of the growth of Ladyslipper, providing jobs, parties, and a place on the map for this sleepy little factory town. When the hotel was gone, a piece of Ladyslipper's history went with it.

"Tonight, for the first time, my fearless partner Stringbean and I will actually witness the island's wreckage for ourselves, avoiding the watchful eye of the law and providing, as always, the top-notch flip-flop ugly pops this side of the mighty Mississippi for our viewers. We're live from Ladyslipper, and"—Goose pointed an Uncle-Sam-Wants-YOU finger at the camera—"you *know* that's a Goose." "That's a Goose" was a catchphrase Goose had been trying to attach to their dispatches. It made

Stringbean giggle.

"Pop, pop," Stringbean said, loading the camera in the paddleboat and hopping in behind it. "Let's go."

Goose untied the paddleboat, and they pedaled their way toward the island. Once she got comfortable, Stringbean brought the camera back.

"So, Goose," she said, "how are you feeling about your first rummage through the ruins?"

"Like I'm finally going to have something to talk about for my *Celebrity Ghost Stories* cameo in five years," Goose said. "Now give me that. You talk." He peered into the lens, probably giving the fans a graphic shot of the inside of his nostril. "Now, a rare few words from our camera-shy director. Stringbean, how are *you* feeling about your first rummage through the ruins?"

"I always wanted to be a reenactment actor on *Unsolved Mysteries*," Stringbean said, stiffening up at the sight of the camera. "Like, look normal, then look concerned, then look really paranoid and scared, then either die or spend the rest of the episode convincing the police officers you really did see a dead person."

"I bet a lot of really famous people got their start looking concerned on *Unsolved Mysteries*." Goose nodded. "It's either that or *Law & Order*, right?"

"I don't really want to be an actor, though," Stringbean continued, a little to Goose's surprise. "I don't want to play other people. I only want to play myself or people that I make up myself. Like Carol Burnett did on her show."

"That's cool," Goose said. "Your self is the best." Goose smiled in a way that made Stringbean feel like the boat was rocking, but the water was glass-calm. Stringbean swallowed, crossing her arms, pedaling harder.

"Why do you like to film ugly things?" Goose asked, slowing his feet. Goose had never asked her this before. The necessity of filming ugly things had always been tacit, agreed-upon, unquestioned.

"I don't know," Stringbean stammered, stumped. "I mean, why not?

Nobody else does."

"But why do *you* like it?"

"Because I'm ugly," Stringbean said simply, surprising Goose even more. "I feel connected to ugly things. I see myself in them."

"Stringbean," said Goose, looking at her over the camera, but not turning it off. "You're the farthest thing from ugly."

"Shut up," Stringbean snapped. This was starting to leave her comfort zone in a major way. "You call me ugly like every day."

"No, I don't," Goose said with unexpected solemnity. "I've never said that."

As soon as Goose said that out loud, Stringbean realized it was true. Goose had never called Stringbean ugly. Only Stringbean had.

"Besides," Goose went on, "who gets to decide? I mean, who says what's ugly and what's beautiful?"

"Exactly," Stringbean said. "I want to decide."

"But if you can decide, if you accept that you have the power to decide," Goose said, steering the paddleboat toward the sunken-down dock on the island. "Why did you decide that you're ugly?"

"Oh, I didn't decide that," Stringbean said simply. "That's a fact."

"But you just said—"

"Pretty's on account of what you're around all the time. I'm the ugly one in the family. My mom is pretty, and everyone knows Junie Mae'll be the pretty one like her."

"You know, I thought you had a good theory going there for a minute," Goose said, inconspicuously shutting off the camera, so as not to remind Stringbean it had been on, and throwing their rope line onto the dock, "but now that you kept talking, you sound pretty full of shit."

Stringbean threw a peanut at him, and they maneuvered the boat up to the dock.

13. Flip-Flop II

The air beyond the shoreline was damper, chiller, grown-over with unfamiliar smells: must, rot, growth, neglect. Stringbean tracked old roads under decades' worth of leaves and vines, kicking herself for wearing flip-flops instead of sneakers, which clearly would have been the sensible choice for woods exploration.

"I wish we could record the smells out here," Stringbean mused. "It smells like—I don't know, old fire. And decay."

"That's good," Goose said. "It does."

Stringbean barked suddenly, feeling something slimy underfoot. She reached down to pull a slug off her big toe, swearing under her breath.

"You okay?" Goose asked, shifting the weight of their supply pack on his shoulders.

"Yeah. Just a slug."

"Wow," Goose mugged shock at her, chuckling. "You don't like ugly slugs?"

"Slugs are the only ugly thing I hate."

"Interesting. I guess there are still things to learn about people you've known forever."

Stringbean paused, contemplating this. There was so much longing Goose didn't know.

They pushed deeper into the woods. The outline of the hotel's main building was visible through the thick tapestry of trees: fir, pine, oak, birch, all deep in their summer bloom. The two waded through the carpet of leaves and needles, vines and roots.

"We are approaching the remains of the Grand Hotel Sault St. Marie from the south side," Goose said into the camera. "It smells like fire and decay."

14. Interlude: Back at The House

Junie Mae watched as the big machine next to Big DeeDee blinked and beeped. Big DeeDee shifted slightly in her sleep, narrow in the hospice bed since she'd lost so much weight, her arm sliding off its edge. Junie Mae crawled into the space at Big DeeDee's side, burrowing into her nook.

"BeeDee," Junie Mae whispered. "It's me, Junie Mae."

"I know that, pumpkin," Big DeeDee whispered back, wiping a trace of drool out of the corner of her mouth. "What you got?"

"Do you remember how you told me that we should be grateful that Princess Diana wasn't in pain anymore? Because she had been sad, and because she was in a car crash and it probably hurt a lot?"

Big DeeDee gave a dry laugh. "You woke me up to ask me about Princess Diana?"

"No, I wanted to ask you if we're supposed to want you not to be in pain anymore. Because I think that might be hard for me, but I don't want you to hurt a lot, either."

Big DeeDee looked deeply at Junie Mae. "Well, that's a tough one, pumpkin pie. I suppose I'll make a deal with you. How about for now you don't think too much about me hurting, but after I'm gone, you can be grateful that I'm not anymore?"

Junie Mae looked deeply at Big DeeDee.

"Deal."

And they both went to sleep.

15. Broken Machine

Goose was trying very hard not to pee his pants in excitement: for one, this old, burned, rotting hotel was *so flipping cool*, and on the other hand, he'd been plotting getting here, particularly getting here alone with Stringbean, all summer.

There had been, in a way that felt undeniable to Goose, a tectonic shift this summer, a quickening, and even though Stringbean didn't want to talk about it, he was beginning to think they needed to. It felt enormous, and he just couldn't go on playing her weird machine songs in the dark and feeling all funny inside when he watched his sister's old *Dawson's Creek* DVDs instead of acknowledging it anymore. It was all getting too embarrassing.

It was impossible to overstate how much time Goose now spent thinking about Stringbean's boobs. He didn't *want* to spend this much time thinking about them. But they were always *there*, under the camera, under her layers of bondage, under her crossed arms. And in his dreams, in the cinema of his mind every time he closed his eyes. Stringbean seemed to have absolutely no idea that she was rapidly transforming into a high-octane *babe*. But this fact, the transformation of his oldest friend, his partner in crime, into a newly strange and beautiful creature, was as profoundly disrupting to Goose as anything ever had been. The only hidden part of Stringbean that mesmerized Goose as much as her boobs was her voice.

"We are in the main lobby of the hotel," Goose said excitedly as Stringbean swiveled to capture the rotted Persian carpet, the sunken velvet chairs, a moss-covered reception desk, and vine-ravaged grand piano. "Stringbean, see if you can play the piano."

"You play," Stringbean said from behind the camera.

"I'm afraid of the bench," Goose said, standing at the keyboard. He played a few bars of "Nearer My God to Thee." The piano sounded wet, diseased, and demented. A key fell off.

Stringbean watched, mesmerized: this was great. She hoped the fading light and the flashlights would be enough to get it all onscreen.

Softly, as Goose picked at the ancient, soggy piano, Stringbean hummed the damaged notes along with his playing. This piano was a broken machine. Stringbean was in love with it, with its broken song.

Goose looked sharply at Stringbean. "I know you sing, String," he said. Stringbean's humming ceased with a gulp. "What?"

"Come on. You're not that careful about switching out the tapes. Why don't you just sing? I like the way you sing."

Stringbean crossed her arms and grimaced. "No."

"But no one's here." A tinge of panic rose in Goose's throat: had he pushed her too soon? "It's just me. Here, I won't look."

He closed his eyes and kept playing. Softly, faintly, almost imperceptibly, after a moment, came Stringbean's voice, her wordless tones, small but open-mouthed. Goose's heart thrilled at the sound of her: her voice rangy and sonorous, the loveliest snarl. *You're beautiful, String,* he said to her, inside his head.

16. Room 15: Goose

Covered in dust and elated, Goose and Stringbean pushed farther into the hotel. Goose's heart thundered as he pushed open the least-burnt of the rooms, 15. The bedspread was still laid perfectly on the imploding queen-sized bed, lace and soot and spongy green growth. The last rays of sunlight withered from the broken window.

"See what happens if you put weight on the bed," Stringbean said excitedly, zooming in on Goose.

Goose sat gingerly on the edge and the bed creaked impossibly, more a groan of exhaustion than a squeak of springs. Stringbean sang more earnestly now, trying to match the sickening tone of the bed. Goose now stared openly at her: from the piano, he'd tried to keep her from noticing that he noticed her singing, but the fact of it seemed to be acknowledged now, unleashing the secret of Stringbean's voice.

Goose shifted around on the bed, not wanting Stringbean to stop singing. He laid back, sinking into its center: more groaning, a kind of hiss. He flipped over on all fours and gave a cautious bounce: a cough, a crack as a board burst below. Stringbean harmonized with the bed's destruction. Goose watched her and her open mouth with the camera, transfixed.

More recklessly now, he stood up on the bed, transferring his weight from foot to foot: deflating, cracking, groaning, crunching. Stringbean sang her lunatic melody louder.

Goose was bewitched by her excitement—he had never seen Stringbean look quite so uninhibited, quite so unselfconscious, quite so alive. Stringbean was a *part* of this video in a way that she hadn't been before—a voice on the tape, a performer and not just an eye. Her face emitted a light.

Goose began to jump up and down on the rotten, rickety bed. Stringbean's spontaneous song reached a crescendo, screeching wildly, the sound of her bizarre and primal and pure. Goose jumped higher as she sang louder, trying to push through the ceiling for her. He didn't want her to stop, never wanted her to stop, could hear a thousand little imaginary ceilings shattering inside her, wanted to see what kind of Stringbean emerged from that wreckage.

It was just then, at the soaring climax of Stringbean, Goose, and the bed's strange trio, that the bed gave way under Goose and collapsed entirely, pitching Goose dangerously over its edge and shoulder-first onto the floor, knocking down a sign from the wall that read CONEY ISLAND OF THE WEST: THE IDEAL RESORT OF THE NORTHWEST. It took everything Stringbean had not to drop the camera as she ran to him.

"Oh shit, that was so stupid of us! Are you okay? Can you breathe?" Stringbean asked frantically, rolling him over to examine him.

"Oooowwwwww," Goose groaned in a tone not unlike the bed's. "That one's gonna bruise." He rubbed the floored shoulder.

"Do you think it's broken? Is it dislocated?"

"Naw. I can move it okay." Goose winced as he rotated the arm. "It just hurts where I hit the ground. Did you get it all on tape?"

Stringbean burst into laughter. "Yeah. I think so. No, I definitely did."

"We're using that clip. No arguments." Goose stared hard at Stringbean. The gut-tingle she gave him was starting up again. "I like it when you sing. You sound kind of like Carol Burnett."

17. Room 15: Stringbean

"Okay," Stringbean said quietly.

The room reverberated, stunned after all the raucous action into sudden silence, and Stringbean felt a tectonic shift somewhere, one plate slipping under another, a new intersection. She was still out of breath and flushed, overheated from the plunge into the other side of her inhibition, unburdened and bare.

Goose sat up, still looking at her, not far from her face. The look made Stringbean feel something like indigestion.

"It's, um—kind of nice to be alone."

"What do you mean?" Stringbean said uneasily. "We're alone all the time."

"I know, but there's always your family or mine, and Junie Mae running around—it's quiet out here. It's nice," Goose said.

Stringbean immediately thought about running, but where? It was an island, and it'd get dark, and she'd get lost in a haunted old hotel. Then she thought, *why am I thinking about running? It's just Goose.*

"I guess so," Stringbean said. She smirked. "You're lucky you didn't hurt yourself any worse. You were just about to be another cautionary tale about kids and trampolines."

"Stringbean, can I tell you something?" Goose blurted out, like he was in pain.

Stringbean was taken aback. "You can tell me anything. You know that."

"IthinkI'minlovewithyou." Goose's words all swirled together like melted ice cream.

"What? No, you're not." Stringbean exclaimed, shocked. "Did you bang your head?"

"No, I'm fucking serious," Goose said fervently. "You can't tell me that things haven't been sort of—different, in the last few months. That something's changed between us."

"I mean, we're not ten anymore, sure," Stringbean said, oddly warm and squirming.

"But don't you feel the difference? Because it seems like you feel it too, but you don't want to talk about it."

The thing about Goose was that he was always willing to admit things: Goose was an open channel, a present force, an untainted reflection of things. With Goose, what you saw was what you got, and it was what made him such a good story-hunter, such a good partner in crime, such an easy addition to the yard and the kitchen and the living room and Junie Mae and the boat and the island and the business of dreaming.

Stringbean knew she loved Goose, but *in love* wasn't something she'd let herself think much about. Because she thought that's what other girls did, and scoffed accordingly. Because, deep down, she knew that ugly girls who thought about *in love*, who let themselves get attached to it, were probably heading for an emotional plane crash.

"I guess—I guess maybe there's been an, I don't know, a tension that hadn't been there before," Stringbean admitted.

"Yeah. I mean, um, I think in general there's some stuff that wasn't here before," Goose said, coughing.

Stringbean glared at him, her message stern and silent: *Don't you know that we are never to talk about my boobs, ever?*

"Don't be disgusting," Stringbean said.

"Don't be mean," Goose shot back. "Look, I've been trying to work up the guts to tell you all this for a while, so you could at least be nice about it."

"I'm sorry," Stringbean said, softening. "Look, you know I love you, Goose. You're like, my everything. You're the only person in this godforsaken town who I actually *want* to spend time with. Everyone else I'm just stuck with."

"Well," Goose said, "maybe I want you to be stuck with me too. Maybe I'm a little stuck to—on—you."

Stringbean fought to avoid rolling her eyes.

"Come on, dude, think about this. Don't you think it's kind of weird? I mean, we've literally known each other since we were toddlers."

"I don't think it's that weird," Goose said, looking more crestfallen than Stringbean would have preferred. "I mean, how do people get together with people they don't know first?"

"What exactly do you mean by *get together*?" Stringbean asked suspiciously. "I'm just saying, don't you think there's a point at which you know someone too—"

Stringbean was cut off, abruptly, by Goose's mouth on hers. She was appalled. In any of the few imaginings of this moment that she'd ever permitted herself, she'd never dreamed that her first kiss would happen as she was literally midsentence.

A moment went by, Goose's lips still pressed to hers. Cautiously, Stringbean pressed back. Goose happily pressed a little more. Stringbean moved her lips some.

No one was more surprised than Stringbean herself to discover that she liked it.

18. Interlude: How Stringbean Met Goose

It was back when Stringbean still had a dad, way back. There was a meeting he went to every Thursday night in the basement of the church where Reverend Gerald H. Nelson preached. And because Little DeeDee had a shift on Thursday nights, Stringbean came with her father and played with the ladies in the church playroom upstairs while he went to his meeting. Goose's mom was there, and so was Goose. Goose introduced Stringbean to the kaleidoscope, Stringbean figured out how to break into it and mess it up, and that was it. They were inseparable. When Stringbean's dad left about a year later, Goose's mom just picked up Stringbean every Thursday night, out of habit or kindheartedness or both, and they kept playing with the kaleidoscope.

One night, Goose's mother had run out to the grocery store, and the pair went exploring in the church—before the days of the video camera, but a portending of them. After successfully jimmying a lock into the office belonging to Reverend Nelson's associate Reverend Andresson, the two discovered a cavern of wonders. Reverend Andresson was an avid hunter, and his office was crowded with mallards and pheasants, stag heads and foxes, a gaze of raccoons and a brood of chicks. In the center of the room, above the desk, was a majestic Canada goose, wings spread and neck darted as if in eternal flight, clearly the prize of the collection.

Young Goose was so transfixed, he reached up to pet the goose, to feel the avian feathers of its giant wingspan—and promptly snapped off the bird's wing. It took a frantic thirty minutes of Krazy Glue, dental floss, stick pins, and other effluvium to repair the wing before Goose's mom returned, during which Stringbean laughed so hard that the nickname affixed.

The fact of Stringbean's becoming Stringbean was much simpler. According to Goose, it was just how she looked.

19. Roam Free

Stringbean and Goose were as tangled as the roots and vines poking through the hotel's ancient, mottled parquet floor, rolling around together on the ground as they were. Stringbean had rationed herself so little anticipation of this moment that it had never occurred to her that she might enjoy it, but suddenly the possibilities of her body seemed to extend beyond dragging herself through the dirt (though, in a sense, that was also what they were currently doing) and bringing Big DeeDee ice cream, beyond her daily boob-bindings and other mummifications.

And it was Goose, Goose whose smell she knew, Goose who had spent his life down in the dirt with her, Goose who had previously accepted the boundaries of what she would and would not discuss, Goose who could not possibly be fooled into thinking Stringbean was anything but what she was: a strange, rangy, curious girl who rarely remembered to brush her hair, an apprentice eccentric, the girl who loved ugliness because it sang to her. Goose, for whom she sang, even through the veil of the camera; Goose, for whom she could be brave enough to sing.

For all these reasons, Stringbean had decided to keep kissing Goose. He had wrapped his arms all the way around her as things progressed into tongue-touching territory, his chest pressed to her layers of breast-suppression. Rubbing her back under her shirt, Goose brushed the ring of duct tape.

"Sweet Jesus, Stringbean," Goose breathed, "what the hell have you got going on there? Is that duct tape?"

Stringbean hid her hands with her face, but for the first time, her impulse to dodge was intercepted by her own laughter.

"Yes." She giggled. "It's so embarrassing. There's, like, nothing I can do to contain them."

"Why would you want to?" Goose said, gape-mouthed.

"Because they just get in the way of *everything*."

"But how do you know, if you've never let them, um, roam free?" Goose laughed with her.

Stringbean cocked her head. "Huh. I never thought about it like that. I think I was just hoping that if I could just sort of get a hold of them, they'd stop growing."

Goose snorted. "I mean, I'm no expert, but I don't think that's how it works."

They giggled for another moment, then silence fell again in the gathering darkness.

"Take your T-shirt off," Goose said quietly.

Stringbean looked at him in horror.

"Relax. Haven't you got like an undershirt and a billion other layers underneath that? You look like you're wearing a bulletproof vest most of the time," Goose reassured her. It was totally flabbergasting how relieved Stringbean felt by just having this discussion. Leave it to Goose to be the one to dig it out of her.

Slowly, Stringbean shucked off the used-to-be-white T-shirt, tossing it aside.

"Can I?" Goose asked gently.

Taking a deep breath, Stringbean nodded. With poignant care, Goose picked the end of the tape ring free and began peeling off the tape, going two full revolutions around Stringbean's torso. Stringbean took another deep breath, delighting in the unhindered expansion of her diaphragm.

"Does it feel better? Didn't it hurt, the way you had it before?" Goose asked.

"I'd gotten used to the way it hurt," Stringbean said. "But I gotta admit—it does feel better now."

It felt so much better that she leaned in and kissed Goose again, and there they tangled for another immeasurable while, Stringbean's bare arms still warm in the full darkness.

20. Interruption: Phone Call

Neither of them had any idea what time it was when Stringbean's cell phone rang.

"String," Little DeeDee said on the other end of the line, her voice troublesick. "I think you'd better come on home."

21. Soon

When Stringbean got home, Junie Mae was asleep on the floor and Little DeeDee was crying at the table. She looked up and saw Stringbean, filthy and wild-haired, and rolled her eyes in an expression that reminded Stringbean of herself.

"I'm not even going to ask where you were," Little DeeDee said, running a tired hand over her eyes and through her hair. "The nurse just left.

They think—with BeeDee—they think it's going to be soon."

Stringbean looked bug-eyed at her mother. "They think *what's* going to be soon?"

Little DeeDee gave her a hollow look, a *don't make me spell it out for you* look, and lit a cigarette. "I think you should go in and spend some time with your grandmother."

22. The End of Ugliness

Big DeeDee's breathing didn't sound right when Stringbean walked into the living room. Her breathing in sounded like a lot of work, and her breathing out came with a terrible rattle, a rattle that sounded like the insides of a broken machine.

Stringbean could transpose that ugly music of Big DeeDee's. She had to. Big DeeDee had said it herself: not so many days to sing. Today, on the island, Stringbean had sung until the room was wreckage. Now, even though she was afraid of wreckage, she could feel her harmony was needed here.

When Stringbean sang for Big DeeDee, she left the camera out of it. Big DeeDee was at the end of ugliness, and it was Stringbean who was in the thick of it, anyway. She sang, through the tears, all of Big DeeDee's favorites: "Amazing Grace" and "You Made Me Love You" and the song Carol Burnett sang at the end of her shows that went, "I'm so glad we had this time together."

Afterward, Stringbean snuggled into Big DeeDee's crook. Big DeeDee moved slightly, her head resting on Stringbean's.

"BeeDee," Stringbean whispered, "can you hear me?"

Big DeeDee made a humming sound: *yes.*

"I came to tell you that—" Stringbean said, her throat catching, "it's okay to die, BeeDee. You can let go."

23. Letting Go

In the morning, she was gone. Stringbean watched the medics take away BeeDee and the bed and the big beeping machine. In Big DeeDee's honor, that afternoon, Stringbean went to Wal-Mart and bought her first nonsports bra.

24. The Wreckage of Stringbean and Goose

Stringbean and Goose called the Grand Hotel Sault St. Marie video "We Killed Room 15." It got 13,274 unique hits and 5,024 new subscribers the week they posted it.

"That's the weirdest thing I've seen today, but I can't say I didn't like it," commented johnmonroe54.

"That girl sounds kind of like Janis Joplin," wrote chcltbnnyxoxo.

"DUDE WHEN THAT KID FELL OFF THE BED I ROFLD MY ASSS OFFFF!!!!!" wrote mrsquashhocker1979, echoing the sentiments of many others in the thread.

Stringbean and Goose refreshed the page endlessly, screaming with laughter as they watched the bizarre, anonymous commentary unfold. They were working on a new concept for a series of webisodes, "The Wreckage of Stringbean and Goose," in which Stringbean sang along with the sounds of Goose destroying various abandoned things.

Junie Mae had excitedly reported back about an old hunting shack in the woods that looked ripe for this afternoon's destruction, and tomorrow, they were going out to the auto graveyard on Route 40 to see about a car. The kissing continued in manic, stolen fits and spurts, still unpredictable, still undefined. Sooner or later Goose would probably make Stringbean talk about it, but for now, they had to find a tractor or four-wheeler to borrow. Stringbean hummed with happiness, imagining the crunches and crackles of the hunting shack as they razed it to the ground. Its broken song.

....

ANECDOTE: TELLY LEUNG

....

My love of musicals came about in a very unexpected way.

When I was eight years old, my parents made it clear that they wanted me to focus on my studies. They forbade me from watching "junk cartoons" after school. Instead, I was expected to do my homework, practice the piano, and I was only allowed to watch PBS—because the programming was educational. My TV diet consisted of *Sesame Street*, *Square One*, *3-2-1 Contact*, *Nova*, and lots of nature shows.

One day, I'm watching PBS and a life-changing event occurred. *Great Performances* came on, and they were showing the live telecast of the original Broadway cast of *Into the Woods*. I had found a new religion (Broadway), and I found a new god to worship (Stephen Sondheim). To this day, when my parents try to convince me to quit acting, I tell them it's their fault! They were the ones that forced me to watch PBS!

I grew up in New York City, the son of Chinese immigrant parents. They escaped the Communists (very *Joy Luck Club*) and came to this country with two hundred dollars and a pair of suitcases, crashing on friends' couches in Chinatown when they first arrived. They saved every penny they made, working blue-collar jobs in the garment industry and the restaurant business. They could only afford to have one kid (me), and they placed all of their hopes and dreams on this one child-to-be. Like so many immigrants, my parents came to this country to achieve the American Dream. To them, the Dream was a monetary one. I'm sure that when my parents first held me in their arms in the hospital that cold, January day I entered the world, they saw in me an Ivy League degree that would then result in a six-figure-a-year job as a doctor or a lawyer or an engineer. The last thing they wanted me to be was a starving artist. "Actor" and "artist" might as well be four-letter words in my family.

I was eight years old when we went on a family vacation to Boston. It was a guided bus tour, but my dad decided to ditch the tour guide and take me to Cambridge. We stood outside the ivy-laced gates of Harvard University. He held my little eight-year-old hand and said to me, in his soft-spoken, heavily accented voice: "Son, do not do restaurant business like your father. You study hard. Go to Harvard. Become Doctor. Lawyer. Engineer. Make a lot of money. Then, you buy a nice Rolex for Daddy."

So—I did just that. I studied hard and got stellar grades. My parents were so proud to have their son on the honor roll (scoring not just As, but A pluses on every test). It made me happy to see my parents so happy at my scholastic success. All that hard work hitting the books paid off when I was accepted into one of the specialized high schools in New York City, Stuyvesant High School. I was on my way to Yale or Princeton—maybe even Harvard. My parent's American Dream was about to come true. I was on my way to that six-figure job in a steady, respectable profession.

Getting into that dream college also meant working hard on the SATs, and I went to every Princeton Review and Kaplan test-prep class I could. It was a grueling schedule, and I couldn't wait for the whole daunting college application process to be over. I took my SATs on a Wednesday morning, and when it was all done, I wanted to give myself a treat—a reward for busting my butt in school. I decide to buy a ticket to a Broadway show. I'd saved up my allowance money, and so I walk over to the TKTS booth in Times Square, where they sell discounted tickets to Broadway shows.

There, I see 50-percent-off tickets for the revival of *Hello, Dolly!* starring the legendary Carol Channing! I am about to witness a living theater legend, performing her star turn for, what would likely be, the last time she'd do it in her career. (Although, Carol is *still* going strong these days, and still performing all over the country. It wouldn't surprise me if she put that red dress on again and descended those Harmonium Garden stairs in yet another revival.)

Suddenly, the storm clouds roll in and the biggest torrential downpour I've ever experienced completely drenches me from head to toe. But, it doesn't matter. I have a front mezzanine seat to see Carol Channing, and "a little fall of rain" isn't going to stop me now. (Can you tell I like musicals?)

I take my seat at the Lunt-Fontanne Theater, and by the end of the overture, my teeth begin to chatter. Being soaking wet in the intense air-conditioning in the Broadway theater was not a good combination. But Carol was electrifying. The whole production was a masterful recreation of the original Gower Champion production, and I felt like I had jumped into Marty McFly's DeLorean and gone back in time. I didn't feel cold or wet at all.

Carol begins her big closing number at the end of Act One. She is center stage, and it's at this moment that I understand why she's an enduring, timeless talent. She doesn't have the most technically proficient, trained, polished voice in the world. What she *does* have is the ability to make everyone in that Broadway theater feel like she's singing right to *them*. It's a personal, intimate experience. She is a brilliant communicator, and there is something about her performance (especially as Dolly Levi) that breaks your heart because you feel like she is reaching deep into the core of your heart.

When she began to sing "Before the Parade Passes By," I knew right then and there. I wasn't going to Harvard. I wasn't going to become a doctor, a lawyer, or an engineer. I was going to do what I wanted to do. I was going to pursue a career in acting. I was going to have a career on Broadway, and make a life of it, just like Carol had all of these years.

Carol Channing ended up giving me one of the *worst* colds I'd ever had. But she also gave me a new perspective—and a personal show biz anthem. A new perspective. She gave me the courage to follow my heart and live my life—before the parade of life passes by.

TELLY LEUNG's Broadway credits include *Godspell*, *RENT* (final Broadway cast), *Pacific Overtures*, and *Flower Drum Song*. TV credits include *Glee* (Wes, Dalton Warblers), *Broadway or Bust* (PBS documentary), and *Law & Order: Criminal Intent*. Other favorite roles include Sammy in the world-premiere of Broadway-bound *Allegiance* at the Old Globe, Angel in *RENT* at the Hollywood Bowl (directed by Neil Patrick Harris), and Song in *M. Butterfly* at the Philadelphia Theatre Company. His debut solo album, *I'll Cover You*, is available on the Yellow Sound Label. Website: www.tellyonline.net. Twitter: @tellyleung.

A DATE WITH DESTINY

Josh Pultz

INT.—IAA OFFICES, CONFERENCE ROOM—AFTERNOON

The view is spectacular.

This is one of my favorite parts of the day. Not algebra, not biology, not even lunch (which is usually spent outdoors, sitting in the courtyard reading some celebrity gossip blog or tweeting about some big Hollywood scandal on my iPhone). *This* part. The part of the day after the final bell rings, when I get to walk down Avenue of the Stars from Los Angeles PS 3 to my father's office, go through the revolving door, and be ushered up to the very top floor of the building.

I sit in the conference room at the end of a long hallway. I'm surrounded by glass. As far as my eyes can see, all that exists are tall, shiny buildings and palm trees. Right now, I am at the head of the polished rectangular table. I close my eyes and pretend that I'm the world's biggest pop star or an important actress here to talk about my next project. I pretend that I'm famous.

"Good afternoon, Imagine Artists Agency."

I open my eyes and sigh. I hear Trish, my father's secretary, on the phone just outside the conference room. "How may I help you?" she asks in a crystalline voice.

While I sit, barely (not at all) concentrating on my homework, the office bustles with ringing phones, shouting voices, and the click of computer keyboards.

Dad has been a talent agent at IAA for as long as I can remember. Whenever Dad and I are watching television together or spend a lazy Saturday afternoon at the movies, he's always pointing out all of the famous people he's met or talked to on the phone. Once in a while Dad'll take me along to a movie set or to a premiere. Those are the days I remember the best: all the lights and the cameras, getting to shake hands, and talk with Dad's famous clients.

FYI: I'm obsessed with celebrities. With fame. And truth be told, even though it may sound a little shallow, I want to stop *pretending* that I'm famous. I want to *be* famous.

"Hi, sweetie," Dad says, leaning against the doorframe. He's wearing his usual work uniform—a crisp suit. Today's is blue with light gray pinstripes, and the black tie with tiny zebras on it that I gave him last Christmas. On his ear hangs a wireless telephone headset. Sometimes he looks like a crazy person, wandering around the office seemingly talking to himself.

"How was school?" he asks.

"Hi, Daddy," I say, looking up from the *People* magazine hidden inside my social studies textbook. "School was great. Did you hear about the big breakup?"

His forehead crinkles. "G-Puppy and what's her name again?"

"First of all it's C Doggy and second of all, no!" I say, annoyed that he doesn't take this as seriously as I do. After all, Dad works in show business. He should know what's going on. I decide to let it go; I have bigger fish to fry with him today.

Dad walks over and kisses me on the forehead. Stealthily he reaches down and grabs the magazine from inside my textbook.

"A-ha!" he shouts, like a magician who has just pulled a rabbit out of his hat. "Is there going to be a quiz tomorrow on the summer's twenty hottest beach bodies?" He sits down across from me and tosses my magazine into the trash can. He leans back in the cushy brown leather chair and frowns. "If so, you're sure to get an A plus. Should I quiz you?"

"Just so you know I took that from the coffee table in your lobby." I grin. "So, Daddy, I was just reading about the new Danny Roberts movie and that they're looking for a pretty, young, actress to play his love interest." I pout my lips and twirl my hair, just for effect. "Can I ask you a question?"

Dad nods.

"Danny is your client, isn't he?"

"Yes. It's a very exciting project."

I bat my eyelashes. "And who is the prettiest, most talented girl you've ever known in your whole life?"

"Let me see," Dad says, tapping his finger to his chin, considering the question. "I mean, I've got so many talented people on my list. . . ."

"I was talking about me!" I interrupt.

"But you're not an actress, are you, Monica?" He pauses, letting his words sink in. "I mean, you won't even join the drama club at school. How can you expect to star in a movie with Danny Roberts?"

It's true. I haven't joined the Nuclear ReACTors, but that's because, in all honesty, it's a giant waste of time. No one in the drama club even borders on popular. I mean, most of them can barely dress themselves in matching outfits in the morning. Last week I got partnered with Molly Farkus in biology lab. Molly is the leader of the ReACTors and an A-class drama geek. I tried hard to give her a pop-culture makeover during our forty-seven minutes together, but it was hopeless. She couldn't have cared less about last week's best dressed list, and she thought Ryan Seacrest was a coastal town in Maine. I couldn't bear it.

"What good is having a high-powered agent for a father if he's not going to help me be a star?" He helps all of his clients realize their dreams . . . so why won't he help me?

"Monica Sarabeth Perlstein. I love you, but I've told you a thousand times: when you get serious about being in this business, then I'll get serious about you *being* in this business. Do you think Danny Roberts just woke up one morning with a movie deal? No, he went to school, and college, and studied music and acting."

"This isn't fair." I swing my chair away from my father. I stare out the conference room windows, silent.

"There's more to life than being famous, Monica," Dad says after a few seconds. "The sooner you learn that lesson, the happier you'll be."

I don't say anything.

"Okay, well, I have to get back to work. I'll see you at home later for dinner. Be sure to finish your homework before you pick up a magazine again, please. I'm asking nicely."

"So what?" I turn around as my father is walking out the door. "I asked *nicely* for an audition and it got me nowhere."

"It's about to get you grounded for a week." Then he disappears from sight.

I feel deflated. Dad knows how important being a star is to me. I spend all of my free time reading magazines and tweeting and imagining what it would be like to be read about and tweeted about. I want to know what it feels like to walk down the red carpet. To have people look up to me, take my picture . . . for everybody in the world to know my name.

The walls in Dad's office are lined with movie posters and headshots of all the famous people IAA represents. As I sit in that conference room in the middle of Hollywood, so close to all of the celebrities I have grown to admire, I feel farther away from stardom than I ever have before.

"I'm sorry, he's not available at the moment, may I take a message," I hear Trish say from her desk outside the conference room door.

I eye the *People* magazine poking out from the trash, but I decide to pick up my pencil and go back to social studies. Ugh.

"Right now?" Trish's voice sounds alarmed. "Well, we weren't expecting her this afternoon. Mr. Perlstein has a very busy schedule today. Perhaps we could find another time—"

I get up and poke my head out the conference room door to get a better listen.

"You're *where?*" Trish begins rapidly snapping her fingers, trying to get my father's attention through his open office door.

Dad reappears with a perplexed look on his face.

Trish hangs up the phone. "Destiny Jean Sparrow, downstairs!"

Dad's eyes widen. "Downstairs where? Here?"

Trish nods. "I'll get the Diet Coke and the organic almonds; you meet her at the elevator," she says, already in motion running down the hallway toward the kitchen.

"Monica." Dad looks to me, fixing his tie. "A very important client is on her way up. Come sit in my office; we'll have to put her in the conference room."

"Her? You mean Destiny Sparrow?"

"Yes." Dad pops a few breath mints into his mouth.

I can't help myself. "'I'll go to the moon and back for just one of your sweet alien kisses,'" I say, quoting a line from Destiny's latest movie.

"Monica, not now." Dad shakes his head. "Besides," he whispers, "that's a terrible movie."

"Speak for yourself." I go back into the conference room to grab my book bag off the floor and algebra textbook from the table. "I thought *Smooches from Saturn* was brilliant. Two thumbs up!" I actually give him two thumbs up.

Dad immediately gives me the you-know-better look.

"Can you introduce me?" I ask. "You know how much I love her. I mean, we even *look* alike, it's creepy."

More than once I've gotten stopped at the mall or while walking down Santa Monica Boulevard, and have been asked for my autograph. After awhile I stopped trying to explain that I wasn't really Destiny Sparrow and just started signing her name.

We're both fifteen and born just a month apart from each other. Last year, while having my birthday dinner with Dad, our waiter mistook me for Destiny and brought a big cake to our table, candles and all, and proceeded to have the whole waitstaff sing happy birthday . . . to "Destiny." Dad wanted to correct their mistake and send the cake back. It was chocolate with buttercream icing, my favorite, so I told Dad to zip it and we didn't say a word.

"You're more beautiful, but don't tell Destiny I said that. See you later, back at home!" Dad says, ignoring my question, buttoning his suit jacket, and heading down the hall toward the elevators.

INT.—IAA OFFICES, WOMEN'S BATHROOM—AFTERNOON

I wish the part of the story where we met happened in a more glamorous setting.

I'm standing at the sink, briefly admiring how the hand soap in the bathrooms at Dad's office always smells really good. I'm singing the song of the summer, a little ditty by Marci Fresno.

"'Oh boy you look so fine, I wish I would make you mine,'" I sing to myself in the mirror. Not to sound too pretentious, but I sound pretty darn good. (I've been a professional shower-singer since I was old enough to shower.) "'Walk with me, talk with me, be my teenage fantasy—'"

"Ahem," a voice says from the bathroom door.

I turn, startled.

In an instant I am in awe.

Standing in front of me is one of the biggest stars in the world: Destiny Sparrow.

It's just me and her. Alone.

She locks the bathroom door behind her. A second later, there's a knock at the door; it's aggressive, someone wants in.

"Just leave me alone! Can't a girl get a little privacy once in a while?" she says.

Destiny is wearing a white baseball cap, ripped denim jeans, and a baggy T-shirt that's hanging off one of her shoulders. She's dressed so simply, and on anyone else it might look messy and tragic, but on Destiny it looks chic.

We stare at each other.

I've seen Destiny on TV and in the movies, but seeing her in person is weird. We really *do* look alike. Her features are fair, with deep brown eyes and dirty-blond hair. Her eyebrows are perfectly arched and manicured. Her lips are covered in soft pink gloss. Same shade as mine.

I try to act casual, like I don't care that I'm five feet away from a girl I was just reading about in *Us Weekly*. I glance back into the bathroom mirror and return to washing my hands. I can feel her eyes on me—her red, teary eyes. She's been crying.

"I was hoping that no one would be in here," she says. "So much for that!"

I turn to look at her just as she rolls her eyes.

"Sorry for living," I say instinctively.

I hear a chuckle. I look up into the mirror. She walks to me and wipes underneath her eyes.

"Hey, I'm Destiny," she says in a softer voice than before, extending her hand to me.

She wants to shake my hand? No way!

"Hi." I am practically quivering with nerves. "I'm Monica." Our fingers touch. *I'm never washing that hand again.*

"And you're sassy!" Destiny flashes me a bright white, perfectly straight smile. I can't help but smile back. "It's just been one of those days. Sorry for getting all crazy."

"I'm sorry too," I say, even though I'm not. "I've just never had anyone try to kick me out of a bathroom before. You caught me off-guard."

"I guess we're *both* having one of those days." Destiny lifts herself up onto the edge of the countertop, letting her feet dangle above the floor. For a second I forget that she's famous, that she has everything I've ever wanted.

"Tell me about it." I try to find some familiar ground for a conversation. "All I want is to be in a movie and make out with Danny Roberts, but it doesn't look like that's going to happen, so whatever. What's wrong with your day?"

This is, of course, a rhetorical question. Destiny Sparrow is one of the biggest celebrities on the planet. She has a famous, gorgeous boyfriend and the number one song on the radio, is starring in a big new movie, and has people waiting on her hand and foot. Obviously, she's having a good day.

"Do you want a list?" she says, much to my surprise.

"A list? Of what?"

"Of all the things wrong with my day." She wipes another tear from her eye while simultaneously blowing a bubble with her gum. It's a strange move, but one that I immediately want to copy.

"Sure," I say almost too enthusiastically. It's exciting enough to be stuck in a bathroom with a celebrity, but to be stuck with a celebrity going through a crisis is almost too much for me to handle.

"Well, for starters, did you read *People* this morning?" Destiny punctuates her question with a question mark *and* a pouty face.

"Are you kidding?" I am almost insulted. "I read it *twice* cover to cover this morning and once again this afternoon."

"So you already know that he's cheating on me," Destiny sobs. "Can you believe it?" She pulls a paper towel from the dispenser to wipe her nose. I have to admit I'm sort of shocked; I always thought Destiny would be a little more . . . glamorous. "With that evil witch Marci Fresno. I mean, she's not even that pretty."

I was so blinded by Destiny's Hollywood aura that I temporarily forgot she's dating Tyler Potter. I almost feel bad about Destiny walking in on my singing a Marci Fresno song earlier. Whatever, though. I sounded fierce.

"There are pictures of them everywhere—smiling, holding hands, feeding each other sushi. It's disgusting," Destiny scoffs. "Come to think of it, he's not really that cute up close."

She takes off her cap and runs her fingers through her hair. "They make a good couple, I guess. Dumb and ugly. Dugly!"

"Sounds like you're better off without him," I say, trying to comfort her. "Besides, don't you have a million other things going on? How do you even have time for hand-holding or sushi?"

"The million other things I have going on . . . You mean all those other problems?"

"But isn't that your, um, job? And don't you love it? Making movies and wearing expensive clothes and getting your picture taken?"

Destiny is looking down at the ground, gently shaking her head.

"World hunger is a problem," I continue. "Global warming is a problem. AP Social Studies? *Major* problem. I wouldn't have ever thought being famous is a problem." I lower my voice just slightly. "For real, it's all I've ever wanted!"

"It's not all it's cracked up to be," Destiny says with a heavy sigh. "I mean, this movie I'm about to do—"

"*Tidal Wave?* The summer movie that everyone is talking about?"

"That's the one." Destiny cringes. "Are you an actress?"

I shake my head. "I wish! I just want to audition for a movie, or be on a TV show. I mean, it doesn't look hard. But my dad says I have to study acting and join the drama club. Who has time for that?"

"You do have a great voice," Destiny says with a hint of a smile. "Even though you were singing that dugly girl's song earlier."

We both laugh. "Yeah, sorry about that," I say, happy for the compliment.

"Can you act?"

"Totally," I reply with confidence, even though I've never really thought about it. I've just assumed everyone will love me and, like I said, it doesn't look that hard. I've never really "acted" before, but . . . why couldn't I?

And then, it happens.

"Well," Destiny asks, "do you want to give it a try?"

"What do you mean?" I am stunned at the prospect of being a real actress. "Do you think I could be an extra in *Tidal Wave?*"

Destiny's lips curl into a smirk. "I'm not talking about you being an extra."

Slowly, she reaches up and takes off her hat, placing it on my head. It fits perfectly. She tilts her head, examining me for a second. Then she strolls over to one of the bathroom stalls and opens the door. "In here." She motions toward the stall.

Truth be told, this is getting a little weird—but I think that Destiny is about to cast me as an extra in her movie. So I oblige.

She closes the stall door behind me. I hear her walk into the stall next to mine. The next thing I know she throws a T-shirt over the divider. It's the shirt she was wearing.

"Here, put this on," Destiny says, "and throw over your jeans!"

"Huh?" I mutter, unsure exactly what is going on.

"Do you want to be a star or not?" Destiny doesn't even give me time to answer—not that she needs to. "Then throw over your jeans!"

Minutes later, Destiny Sparrow and I emerge from our respective stalls, dressed just as the other was minutes ago. She gives me a good look up and down, and pulls down one shoulder of my T-shirt.

"Always do something a little different, a little quirky. That's sure to get you in the fashion blogs," Destiny says, not realizing, of course, that I will never be featured on a fashion blog. "I think this is going to work for sure. They'll never know. You really look just like me. It's uncanny."

"What? *Who?*" I am not able to form a complete sentence.

Destiny takes a tube of lip gloss from the small purse she's carrying. "Here, put some of this on."

We stand in front of the bathroom mirror, staring at the girls before us. We look like twin sisters. Identical.

Only I look differently than I normally do in these new clothes. A little quirky. A little hip. Like I could show up in a photograph on a fashion blog. Like Destiny Sparrow. Like a star.

EXT.—GLOBALPIC STUDIOS—AFTERNOON

"Destiny, look this way!" someone shouts as soon as the car door opens.

"Over here, please, Ms. Sparrow!"

A line of photographers waits outside the studio. A hand reaches through the door of the black sedan and into the backseat where I'm sitting. It's Jacques, my—I mean *Destiny's*—driver. He's been driving Destiny around Hollywood for a while now, since her big break as an actor in some awful television movie about being different and special or something, but he doesn't seem to suspect that his cargo isn't the real thing.

I grab his hand, step onto the sidewalk and, in an instant, I'm the only thing anyone is looking at.

The photographers keep shouting. I let go of Jacques's hand, which I instantly place on my hip—it makes you look nice and thin, and I've seen it a million times in magazines—and smile the most dazzling smile I can muster. I switch hands and make a pouty face, turning my attention to the photographers on the other side of the car.

"What's going on with you and Tyler?" someone shouts. "Is it over?"

I didn't know I'd be taking questions! I have to think fast.

"No comment," shouts a voice from down the sidewalk.

High-heeled boots, ponytail, bright blue nail polish, clipboard—it's Stacy, Destiny's assistant.

Stacy whisks me past the photographers, avoiding the questions and the flashes. She moves fast. I have no time to think; she seems to be doing the thinking for me.

INT.—GLOBALPIC STUDIOS, DRESSING ROOM—AFTERNOON

When we finally slow down, we're inside the studio and coming to the end of a long hallway. At the end of it is a door. MS. SPARROW it says in bold block letters in the center of a gold star.

My dressing room.

Stacy opens the door, and turns to bolt back down the hallway. "I'll be back for you in a little while, Destiny. The new scene and your music are on your vanity."

"Huh?" I ask. Back in the bathroom, Destiny had mentioned that we could trade places for the afternoon. I was going to work instead of her, and she was going to take some "well needed time off."

I only *sort of* realized that going to work for Destiny meant filming a movie. I may have fooled Destiny's driver and her assistant, but would I fool the director? And all of her costars? What if I got caught . . . what would happen to me? Would they send me to jail?

Or even worse: Call my father?

I look around. Destiny's dressing room is beautiful; a large white, cushy, sofa is pushed against a crisp pink wall. Above it hangs a large headshot of Destiny. On the other side of the room, the wall is lined with mirrors surrounded by bright white lights.

I walk over to it. Makeup of every sort is laid out on the counter beneath the mirrors, along with hairbrushes, curling irons, and a blow-dryer. Tucked underneath the makeup counter is a wood-framed chair with a fabric back—on the chair is MS. SPARROW. In one corner of the counter sits a tray of fruit and a big bowl M&M's, only they're all green. *That is what is means to be a real star.*

I'm here. I'm finally here. Everything I've ever wanted is at my fingertips.

I reach into the bowl to grab a handful of M&M's. Something jabs me in the side, gently.

I let out a little yelp, and my hand sends the bowl crashing to the floor. I feel tiny chocolate pieces hit my toes.

"What the . . . ?" I turn to see who is speaking.

On the outside I simply smile what I'm sure is the goofiest smile ever. My inner monologue, though, goes something like this:

OMG OMG OMG OMG OMG (breathe) *OMG OMG OMG OMG OMG*

It's Tad Preston.

Tad is Destiny's costar in *Tidal Wave*, and another in a long list of hunky guys I may or may not have photos of on my bedroom wall. He's tall, almost six feet, with crystal blue eyes, shaggy dirty-blond hair that falls just below his shoulders, and the most perfectly clear, tanned skin I've ever seen. The kind of flawless complexion that no cream or chemical could ever help a normal human to achieve. He's wearing a white T-shirt that shows exactly why he has one of those "best beach bodies" that Dad threatened to quiz me on earlier. He's standing so close I can smell his freshly brushed, minty breath.

"Whoa, Sparrow, chill out. I didn't realize you were so skittish!" He bends down and scoops up a handful of runaway M&M's.

"Sorry." I try to regain my composure. "I didn't realize the door was open." I take a quick peek at myself in the mirror while Tad is picking candy off the floor. *Not bad. But will he notice that I'm not really Destiny?*

"I caught your segment on *Inside Hollywood* last night," Tad says, dropping handfuls of now dirty candy back into the bowl. "Thanks for saying such nice things about me."

Tad smiles, big. I didn't watch *Inside Hollywood* last night. Is he being sarcastic? Had Destiny said some terrible things about Tad? Or is Tad being serious and they actually like each other?

I quickly run down the facts of the situation in my head: big smile, gentle tickle/poke, so handsome, dreamy really. . . .

"Of course!" I decide to go with the they-actually-do-like-each-other option. "You're the best!" I give Tad a light punch in his *very* firm chest.

Awkward.

"Ow," Tad pretends that my little smack hurt him. He runs a hand through his hair, sweeping it off his forehead. "Do you want me to help you run lyrics for a bit?"

"How was your night?" I'm much more interested in the *celebrity* part of my life as Destiny than I am the *work* part. "Did you hit the town? Go to any hot clubs?"

As soon as the words are out of my mouth, I wince. *Hit the town?* Does anyone even say that anymore? I am going to give myself away if I don't watch my language and sound more like Destiny.

"Nope," Tad replies simply. "I knew we had a big day today, so I was just going over lines and stuff. Nothing crazy."

This was almost too much for me to comprehend. Tad is famous, gorgeous, and rich. He can get into any restaurant or party he wants. Surely he has a long list of girls knocking on his door. I imagine him not being able to keep all of his dates straight! He's too amazing to be stuck at home on a perfectly good night for having fun.

"Plus," he continues, "I had a bunch of homework I needed to get done by today, or Mrs. Traywick would have given me a hard time for sure. You know how she is."

Mrs. Traywick? Mrs. Traywick? My mind races trying to figure out who this Mrs. Traywick is. *Don't blow this, dummy. Act fast.*

"I see you're playing the part of brownnoser today," Tad says before I open my mouth. He picks up a stack of papers from the counter and holds them up for me to see. It's a math exam with Destiny's name written on it. On one corner, in red pen, is a giant *A*. There's a little note stuck to the other corner. Printed on top of it, in bold letters, is: FROM THE DESK OF MRS. DAPHNE TRAYWICK, EDUCATIONAL TUTOR. Of course! *School.*

"I know, she's *so* annoying." I try my best to make an A in math look cool.

"Well, I mean, she's just doing her job, Destiny. Cut her some slack; what she does is important. You should appreciate it, not give her a hard time."

What just happened? Tad Preston just gave me a lecture on gratitude and how much I should love learning. What would Destiny do? I decide to return his serve with some Sparrow sass.

"Okay, Einstein. Sorry," I say, though it doesn't sound like much of an apology. "You're always so busy getting your photograph taken with some bimbo; I guess I just didn't realize that you had time for school."

"You know I'm not into all that superficial stuff, Destiny. We've talked about this. It's one of the reasons we get along."

He looks at me strangely. "The photo-ops, the parties, the paparazzi . . . it's all part of the job, but it's not me. I'm here to work, not to have fun." Tad puts Destiny's test back on the counter. "Being famous is just a sometimes nice and sometimes nasty side effect. I'm just a kid with chores and home-work and parents like every other kid. Only I get to be in movies too. I thought you felt the same way that I did, but I guess you don't."

"But Tad, I really—"

He holds up his hand. "The sooner you learn that, the better off you'll be."

Tad turns to walk out the dressing room door. I need to save this. This day is supposed to be fun, exciting—my dream come true. I can't spend the whole day with Tad mad at me.

"Listen." I rush up to Tad and place a hand on his shoulder. He stops at the doorframe. "You're right." I put my head down to the ground and make a sniffling sound with my nose. "I guess I was just a little nervous about shooting today, and I took it out on you." I look up with my eyes, keeping my head pointed toward the ground. "Forgive me?"

He nods. "It's okay. We all have bad days, right?"

"Yeah, you're right," I say in the most pathetic voice I can muster. "Thanks for understanding."

Tad holds out his arms. *Oh my God, he's going to hug me.* I freeze. Tad wraps his tan, toned arms around me and squeezes. I feel like a gooey batch of cookies that have just been taken out of the oven.

"Now," Tad says with a slight whisper in my ear. Shivers run down my whole body. "Are you ready for your big song today?"

Did I just hallucinate? I need Tad to repeat that. "What do you mean?" I chuckle, trying to act as nonchalant as possible.

Tad releases his bear hug and points to the script sitting on the makeup counter. Next to it, I see pages of musical notes and a bold, black title at the top that reads, YOUR LOVE IS LIKE A TIDAL WAVE.

Tad's eyes widen. "Everyone on set is *really* looking forward to shooting this scene today. I mean, it's your singing debut! Aren't you excited? I'd be freaking out."

I press my hand to my forehead. Freaking out doesn't begin to describe how I'm feeling.

"Oh?" I say. "Is that today? I thought we were shooting this scene tomorrow. . . . I must have my dates mixed up."

Tad gives me a quizzical look. "But we've been talking about this song for a week already. I know you're nervous but—"

"It's probably Stacy's fault." I try to think of how I'm going to get out of this one. "I'm sure they can record the actual track some other time, and we can shoot a different scene today."

"Oh, I get it." Tad flashes his pearly white smile. "You're messing with me. Good one. As if you didn't know that we're doing the song live."

Live?

Tad checks his watch. "I think the band is warming up right now, actually. Wanna go have a listen?"

I pull the fabric-backed chair with Destiny's name on it out from under the makeup counter and sit. I begin flipping through the music to "Your Love Is Like a Tidal Wave."

I wave Tad off with my hand. "Um, no, thanks. I need some time here alone." I stare at all the music notes and lyrics and feel myself start to go dizzy. "Please shut the door on your way out."

"You'll be great," Tad says.

I hear the door close.

Something has gone horribly wrong. Why would Destiny pretend to do me a favor by letting us trade places for a day and *not* tell me I was standing in on such an important day in her career? A big movie with her first singing role—surely that was a huge deal, something she'd be super excited about.

Unless . . .

She can't actually sing.

I think back to a few hours earlier, when we met in the bathroom. She heard me singing and even told me how much she liked my voice. I've been duped! Destiny only wanted to trade places with me so she could get out of singing live and embarrassing herself on set today.

My first instinct is to give up. Go home.

For a second, I think about calling my dad and explaining the situation. Begging for him to pick me up.

No. A few hours ago I was sitting in Dad's conference room wishing I was some big movie star. Well, I got my wish. Maybe it was time to see firsthand what I had been wishing for all along. If I can't handle it now, then I probably can't handle it at all. No one knows it's me, Monica

Perlstein, ordinary girl from PS 3. I have to do well for Destiny. I have to do well for myself.

I pick up the packet of music, and something stuck between the pages falls to the floor. It's a CD. There's a stereo that's sitting silently on an end table next to the sofa. I pop the CD into the machine, and with the touch of a button the stereo begins playing. It's the demo recording of the song Destiny is meant to sing today, so she can practice, I guess.

I flip through the music, following along. I start to hum. Then I sing in a soft whisper just to get some of the notes and melody down. The words are easy enough, and decently catchy.

Can I pull this off? Can I really be Destiny Sparrow for a day?

There is only one way to find out.

INT.—GLOBALPIC STUDIOS, STUDIO 1A—AFTERNOON

The soundstage is huge and full of sand.

Within this giant room they have replicated a beach, complete with water, umbrellas, lounge chairs, and multicolored beach balls. Thirty or so extras—tan, pretty people in bikinis and board shorts—mill around eating cookies from the craft services table and drinking Diet Coke.

This is it, I think to myself. *A real movie set.*

I stand, surrounded by the team assigned to Destiny for the day: Stacy, a bodyguard, a production assistant whose sole job is to bring me anything I ask for when I ask for it, another PA just to hold my bottle of water, and a wardrobe stylist with a lint brush permanently attached to her hand.

I'm furiously going over song lyrics, moving my mouth and bopping my head to the beat pulsating through my brain. I probably look like a crazy person.

I can feel the sweat gathering on my forehead. Jackie, the stylist who has spent the last hour painting my face and blow-drying my hair, blots my forehead with a tissue in a desperate attempt to save her work. I have always wanted to be pampered like this, but I can't even enjoy it—I'm too nervous about messing up the song. But at least no one has accused me of being a fake Destiny.

Yet.

"Destiny, daaaaahling, you look fabulous!" says a man with a British accent who I've never seen before in my life. He's tall and skinny with a thick goatee on his chin, wearing a black T-shirt, black skinny jeans, black boots, and sunglasses—very Los Angeles.

I steal a quick glance at the studio ID hanging from the lanyard around his neck. *Quincy Dash, Director.* He leans in to give me a quick peck on the right cheek and then the left—very British.

"Are you ready to make love to our ears, my little starlet?" Quincy puts his sunglasses on top of his head either because he wants to get a better look at me or because, well, we're indoors.

"We are ready for you," he continues. "Now take off that robe, get some sand between your toes, find your light, and sing your heart out!" He throws his hands in the air dramatically. "Ready on the set!" Quincy yells, making his way back to a row of cameras.

"Break a leg," Stacy says, coming behind me and removing my robe. As if having to sing a brand-new song in a huge movie surrounded by a bunch of strangers wasn't bad enough, *I* have to do it wearing a bathing suit. This couldn't get much more strange and surreal.

"Places, please!" Quincy barks.

I have no idea where I'm going. Then I spot Tad's familiar face.

He's standing on the set, in the center of the action, flashing his perfect smile at me. He motions me over with his hand. He's wearing a pair of bright red swimming trunks and a red T-shirt with the sleeves cut off. LIFE-GUARD is printed on the front.

He can give me CPR anytime. Then I think, *Concentrate!*

"You okay?" Tad says. "You look a little pale."

"I'm fine. Some bad tuna for lunch, I think." I give my stomach a little pat with my hand. "I totes forgot where we're standing for this scene."

"Destinyyyyyyyy," Quincy says. "I heard that." He points above my head. I look up to see a microphone hanging above me. *Caught.*

"We're good!" Tad shouts. I look at him. "Just follow my lead," he says softly, giving me a wink. "Don't worry about the cameras or what anyone else on set thinks. I know you can do this."

Even though he is encouraging Destiny, not me, his words give me the bit of confidence that I need. I know what I have to do. There's no more pretending I'm famous. This isn't about being famous at all—this is about doing my job. *Destiny's* job. None of the people in this giant room really care that I'm famous; they only care that I finish my work so we can all go home for the night.

I close my eyes and really concentrate. Is there more to being a star than parties and pictures and having fun? Was Dad right? Is becoming an overnight sensation just a fairy tale? Is this going to take some work? I think about what it means to be an actor. I think about what it means to be a singer. I know the words. I know the music. I've got Tad to make sure I know where I'm going. I'm going to be all right.

I think.

"Marvelous!" Quincy shouts. "Quiet on the set! Roll playback!"

The familiar melody of the song I've been practicing all afternoon blares in the background. Out of the corner of my eye, I see extras start to dance and move to the music.

Tad grabs my hand and pulls me toward a row of beach chairs. He stands behind me and wraps his arms around my waist.

"Smile," he whispers. So I do, staring at the wall ahead, imagining it's some beautiful ocean view—the kind meant solely for postcards and the covers of magazines.

"And . . . action!"

INT.—LA TRANSIT BUS—EVENING

I manage to slip out of the studio unrecognized wearing an old sweatshirt and a brown, floppy hat I found in Destiny's dressing room. My face is wiped clean of all the makeup that had been applied that afternoon. Not a trace of celebrity on me anywhere. No more limousine, no more paparazzi to greet me at the front door.

I'm Monica Perlstein again.

I catch the express bus from nearby the studio to Beverly Hills. I sit staring vacantly out the window. It's hard to take it all in. It's the sort of day that people only have in the movies.

I couldn't have asked for my time at the studio to have gone any better. Sure, we had to start over a few times because I forgot the words. And sure I was nervous and freaking out the whole afternoon, but in the end, it all turned out okay. I think back to being surrounded by a wave of well-wishers after we finally finished filming the musical number. People I had never met or seen before in my whole life congratulating me on a great job.

"Who knew you could sing like that?" Quincy asked me. "I mean, darling, I wasn't even sure we were going to make it through today. I guess we can stop looking for a vocal double for you now."

If I were actually Destiny, that comment would've really offended me, but as it turns out, I *was* the vocal double, more or less, and I'd performed beautifully. I let the comment pass with a smile and a hug. No harm done.

I hop off the bus at my street corner. I see Dad's car in the driveway and the lights on in the living room. Luckily I texted him earlier saying that I would be studying at a friend's house all afternoon.

Destiny and I promised each other never to tell anyone about the switch we had made. I won't have to tell Dad about the incredible yet exhausting afternoon and evening I've had. I don't think that he would believe it anyway.

INT.—PERLSTEIN HOME—EVENING

"Hi, sweetie!" Dad says the moment I open the front door. "In the kitchen."

I take off my shoes and throw them into the closet just inside the door. Then I drop my book bag on the floor and head into the kitchen. Dad is sitting at the table, alternating between reading a script and watching the evening news. The smell of Chinese food fills the house; a dirty plate and an empty plastic container sit on the kitchen table.

"There's dinner for you in the fridge," Dad says, looking up from his script. "How was the rest of your afternoon? You look exhausted."

"Big math exam tomorrow. We were cramming for hours."

He squints. "Is that what you were wearing earlier?"

I stare down at my clothes. I'd forgotten that Destiny and I switched clothes earlier today. I wonder if I'll ever get the skinny jeans and new top back from her. Surely this old sweatshirt and baseball cap weren't a fair trade.

"It was dumb, really. I spilled a whole glass of diet soda on myself at Stephanie's house—a freak studying accident!" I laugh. "So she let me borrow this."

"Klutz." Dad chuckles and shakes his head. "I left you an egg roll in the microwave." He motions to the kitchen counter.

"Dad, listen, I've been thinking." I spoon some General Tso's chicken onto a plate. "What would you think about my signing up for drama club at school and maybe taking acting lessons? Is there someone you could recommend for me to go study with?"

Dad puts the script down on the table, picks up the remote control, and mutes the television. "Seriously?" He takes the reading glasses from his nose and slips them into his shirt pocket. "Earlier you were only interested in a quick ascension to stardom. Now you're willing to put some work into it?"

I think of my conversation with Tad, how he said that he was a normal kid—that acting was a privilege. Then I think of what it felt like to be on set, to be performing in front of a camera. To have Quincy tell me that I did a great job.

I can feel a smile begin to creep across my face. "I know, I know." I sit down across from him. "Sometimes I *do* listen when you talk to me, you know?"

"So, that's it? That's all it took?" he asks, with a slightly vexed look.

"I think I've been concentrating too much on magazines and blogs lately, and not enough time thinking about what I really want to do with my life. It's not just about getting your picture taken and going to fancy parties. Acting and singing is hard work. It takes discipline."

"You realize, of course, that's what I've been saying to you all along, right?" Dad grins from ear to ear.

"Of course." I take a bite of chicken. "Sometimes it just takes a little time out in the real world to make you come to your senses."

Dad leans back into his chair. "Well, if this is what happens after you spend an afternoon at Stephanie's, you should see her more often!"

"It's not Stephanie. I think it's more like fate. Or . . . destiny."

Yeah. Destiny.

. . . . .

I never saw Destiny again after that day.

Well, that's not exactly true—I did see her, in the movies.

I went to *Tidal Wave* by myself one afternoon after school. I sat in that dark theater, waiting to see myself onscreen. Would I look any different in my scene than Destiny did in all the others? My stomach tied in knots waiting for that moment. Fortunately or unfortunately, that moment never came. My scene got cut.

I would read later, in an interview that Destiny and Tad gave, that it was cut for time so the movie wouldn't be so long. Quincy also told some big magazine that the musical number was the absolute best part of the movie and that everyone was sad when they decided it had to go. I cut out that article and pinned it to the bulletin board above my desk.

I never saw myself onscreen, and none of those photos taken outside the studio that afternoon made their way into a magazine. I wasn't *really* a star. That was okay with me, though. My favorite memories of that day aren't of being famous. They're of being happy.

And maybe I *will* be a big, famous actress one day. But if not, I'll be happy just being me.

CONTRIBUTOR BIOS

Clay Aiken has evolved into a versatile and beloved popular entertainer since coming to national attention on the second season of *American Idol*. In October 2003, he launched his first solo album, *Measure of a Man*. The record sold three million copies and debuted at number one on the *Billboard* 200. It was the highest-selling first album for a solo artist in ten years, going double-platinum and netting Aiken an American Music Award. He has released five well-received albums total, selling over six million copies worldwide.

In 2004, Aiken penned a best-selling memoir, *Learning to Sing: Hearing the Music in Your Life*. It was an instant *New York Times* bestseller, holding the prestigious spot for seven weeks.

In addition to taking the stage on nine separate tours, in 2008 Clay began his critically lauded stint as the inept yet endearing Sir Robin in the Broadway musical *Monty Python's Spamalot*.

Clay has been an ambassador for UNICEF since 2004. The same year, he started the National Inclusion Project with cofounder Diane Bubel. NIP supports the integration of children with disabilities into the same environments as their nondisabled peers. In 2012, Aiken was runner-up to Arsenio Hall on the fifth season of NBC's *Celebrity Apprentice* to raise funds and awareness for the National Inclusion Project.

Marc Acito wrote *How I Paid for College: A Novel of Sex, Theft, Friendship and Musical Theater*, which won the Ken Kesey Award for Fiction, was Editors' Choice by the *New York Times* and a Top Teen Pick by the American Library Association. Translated into five languages, it inspired a sequel, *Attack of the Theater People*. He is also a book writer of musicals, including *A Room with a View* and *Allegiance*, which broke the box-office record at the Old Globe Theater. His comedy *Birds of a Feather* won the Helen Hayes Award for Best New Play. A product of the musical theater program at Carnegie Mellon, Marc has written about theater for *Playbill*, the *New York Times, American Theatre*, and National Public Radio's "All Things Considered." A book doctor to writers of all mediums, he teaches story structure at New York University. Visit him online at www.MarcAcito.com.

Josh Berk is the author of *The Dark Days of Hamburger Halpin*, which was awarded a Parents' Choice silver medal and named a best book for teens by *Kirkus Reviews* and Amazon.com. His second comedy/mystery teen novel was *Guy Langman: Crime Scene Proscrastinator*, and his series for younger readers begins with *Strike Three, You're Dead*. He is the executive director of the Memorial Library of Nazareth and Vicinity and lives in Bethlehem, Pennsylvania. Josh was the star of the 1986 Hanover Elementary School fifth-grade musical *Hanover Goes Around the World*. He still knows all the words to "Waltzing Matilda."

Alex Flinn was nine when she took semiprivate violin lessons with a far-more-talented girl whom her mother dubbed, "Nancy First." Though violin (and—ahem—clarinet) didn't work out, Alex found her stride with vocal music, studying musical theater in high school and opera in college. She drew on these experiences for "Becca First," and for her novel, *Diva*, about a performing arts high school. Alex is the author of such novels as *Beastly*, a #1 *New York Times* bestseller; *Bewitching*, a companion to *Beastly*; *A Kiss in Time*; and *Cloaked*. Her books have been translated into over twenty languages. She is a nonpracticing attorney who lives with her husband, daughters, and way too many pets in Miami, Florida. She is also the author of *Towering*, a modern retelling of *Rapunzel*.

Garret Freymann-Weyr's seven novels have been published both as young adult and literary fiction, and have been translated into several languages, including Japanese. Her stories have been published in the *Greensboro Review* and the now sadly missed *Christopher Street*. She is a Printz Honor Award winner for *My Heartbeat*, and her novels have appeared on several "best of" lists, including the ALA, *Publishers Weekly*, and New York Public Library "Best Books of the Year;" and the *Booklist* "Editors' Choice Top of the List." Her short story, "The Ugly Ducking," was shortlisted for the Manchester Fiction Prize, and her first picture book was *French Ducks in Venice*. She is a native of New York City and now makes her home both in Davidson, North Carolina, and Chevy Chase, Maryland.

Aimee Friedman is a *New York Times*–bestselling author of many young adult novels, including *South Beach*, *French Kiss*, *Hollywood Hills*, *The Year My Sister Got Lucky*, and *Sea Change*. She also writes for younger readers under the pen name Ruth Ames. Aimee is an Executive Editor at Scholastic, where she has worked for over a decade. A native of New York City, Aimee graduated from the

Bronx High School of Science and received her BA in English from Vassar College. She attended a performing arts camp as a child, but had her parents take her home early. Aimee now lives in Manhattan and regularly partakes in New York's rich performing arts scene, but only as a spectator. Visit her online at www.aimeefriedmanbooks.com.

Laura Goode is a novelist, essayist, poet, and screenwriter living in San Francisco. Her first novel for young adults, *Sister Mischief*, was called a "Best Book You Haven't Read of 2011" by *Vanity Fair* online, as well as "a provocative, authentic coming-of-age story . . . full of big ideas, big heart, and big poetry" by *Booklist* in its starred review, and a 2012 Best of the Bay pick by the *San Francisco Bay Guardian*. Laura is the cowriter and producer of the feature film *Farah Goes Bang*, and her work has appeared in *New York* magazine, the *Los Angeles Review of Books*, *BOMB*, the *Rumpus*, the *Faster Times*, *Boston Review*, *Racialicious*, *Feministing*, the *New Inquiry*, *IndieWire*, *Denver Quarterly*, *Dossier*, *Slope*, *Fawlt*, and other publications. She received her BA and MFA from Columbia University. Visit her online at www.lauragoode.com and via Twitter @lauragoode.

Claudia Gray is the author of the Spellcaster trilogy, a young adult witchcraft series, and the upcoming Firebird young adult science-fiction trilogy. She has also written the historical werewolf novel *Fateful* and the *New York Times*–bestselling Evernight series. Before becoming a full-time writer, she was a radio announcer, a lawyer, and a very poor waitress.

Cynthia Hand is the *New York Times*–bestselling author of the Unearthly series. During high school and college, she acted, teched, and directed in more than twenty-five plays and musicals, in which she got to kiss a variety of interesting guys. She currently lives with her husband and two small children in Southern California, where she teaches creative writing at Pepperdine University. Find out more at www.cynthiahandbooks.com.

Antony John is an award-winning author and musician. As a teen in England, he spent every free moment singing in choirs, and playing flute in orchestras, double bass in jazz bands, and piano for anyone that would listen. He would regularly blow off his friends to compose late into the night. He graduated from Oxford University with a degree in music, and received his PhD in composition from Duke University. After teaching at Duke and the University of South Carolina, he became a stay-at-home dad, and turned to writing books instead of music. His novels include *Five Flavors of Dumb*, *Thou Shalt Not Road Trip*, and *Elemental*. He lives with his family in St. Louis, Missouri. Check out his website, www.antonyjohn.net.

Nina LaCour was born and raised in the San Francisco Bay Area. She has tutored and taught in various places, including Alameda County's juvenile hall, Berkeley City College, Maybeck High School, and Mills College, where she received an MFA in creative writing. Nina's first novel, *Hold Still*, is a William C. Morris Honor book, a Junior Library Guild selection, an ALA Best Book for Young Adults, and a Chicago Public Library's Best of the Best Books of 2009. Nina won the 2009 Northern California Book Award for Children's Literature and was featured in *Publishers Weekly* as a Flying Starts Author. Her second novel, *The Disenchantments*, received five starred reviews.

Josh Pultz knew show business was his calling after co-starring in his sixth-grade production of *Alice in Wonderland*. His portrayal of the Caterpillar earned him rave reviews from both the school newspaper and his parents. While he no longer appears onstage, he is a frequent theatergoer, avid writer, and enjoys singing in the shower.

Tanya Lee Stone is an award-winning author of books for kids and teens. Her young adult novel, *A Bad Boy Can Be Good for a Girl*, received multiple starred reviews and was on several state lists, as well as an IRA Young Adult Choice, ALA Quick Pick, *SLJ* Book of the Month, and New York Public Library Book for the Teen Age. When she was a teen, Tanya attended a performing arts high school in New Haven, Connecticut, and went on to study voice at Oberlin Conservatory. Like her main character in "Gravy and Mashed," she has battled those stage fright demons and is still singing today.

Jacqueline West is the author of the award-winning middle-grade series the Books of Elsewhere. *Volume One: The Shadows* garnered starred reviews, several state award nominations, and a spot on the *New York Times* bestsellers list. In addition to the US, the series is published in such countries as Italy, Spain, Greece, Turkey, Indonesia, Sweden, Norway, France, Germany, and Catalan. Jacqueline's short fiction has been widely published, and her poetry has received many honors, including two Pushcart nominations, a Rhysling Award nomination, and a Dorothy Sargent Rosenberg prize. Jacqueline lives in Red Wing, Minnesota, surrounded by large piles of books and small piles of dog hair. Visit her at www.jacquelinewest.com.

Kiersten White is the *New York Times*–bestselling author of the Paranormalcy trilogy, the Mind Games series, and several other upcoming novels. Being able to sight-read alto parts is a skill she sincerely wishes she had never developed, as it leads to awkward requests for duets when really her voice is best left on paper. Visit her at www.kierstenwhite.com.

Maryrose Wood made her professional acting debut in the original 1981 cast of the now legendary flop Broadway musical *Merrily We Roll Along*. The show's magnificent score by Stephen Sondheim lives on in the original cast album and many subsequent revivals. She spent years as a playwright, lyricist, and librettist before working up the nerve to write fiction. These two worlds collided in her novel, *My Life: The Musical*, which captures the crazy fandom of two theater-obsessed teens. Maryrose has published a dozen books for young readers. She is the author of the Incorrigible Children of Ashton Place, a critically acclaimed middle-grade series set in Victorian England about a young governess and her three unusual pupils, who were actually raised by wolves. Visit her online at www.mary-rosewood.com.

Eve Yohalem grew up in New Jersey, where she got kicked out of piano lessons in fourth grade. She survived high school thanks largely to her theater kid friends, including fellow *Starry-Eyed* contributor, Marc Acito. After a brief, unremarkable stint as an opera singer, Eve became a writer of children's books. She's the author of the novel *Escape Under the Forever Sky* and the series for young readers Grandpa Hates the Bird.

EDITOR BIOS

Ted Michael is a graduate of Columbia University and the Juilliard School and a Presidential Scholar in the Arts. He is the author of *So You Wanna Be a Superstar?: The Ultimate Audition Guide* (a YALSA Popular Paperback and a YALSA Quick Pick for Reluctant Readers nominee), *The Diamonds*, and *Crash Test Love* (a Books-A-Million and a Seventeen.com Book Club pick). He is thrilled to be collaborating with Josh on editing this exciting collection. Favorite high school musical roles include Anthony in *Sweeney Todd*, Freddy Eynsford-Hill in *My Fair Lady*, and Billy in *Anything Goes*.

Visit him online at www.tedmichaelbooks.com and via Twitter @tedmichaelbooks.

Josh Pultz is the senior agent at DGRW Talent, and his clients include stars of television, screen, and stage. He attended Pace University and Baruch College, worked for five years on-air at two New York radio stations and once owned a Halloween haunted house. He regularly appears as a guest and speaker for such venues as the American Musical and Dramatic Academy, the School for Film and Television, Actors Connection, and One on One Studios. Follow him on Twitter @joshpultz.

ACKNOWLEDGMENTS

Special thanks to all of the fantastic writers, performers, and agents who made this anthology possible with their thoughtful and touching contributions. This collection wouldn't be possible without your hard work, enthusiasm, and extraordinary talent.

As well, thanks to everyone at Running Press Kids for making this dream come true, especially the incomparable Lisa Cheng, who believed in *Starry-Eyed* from the beginning and made it possible for you to hold this anthology in your hands.

From Ted:

Thanks to all of the teachers who believed in me as a young artist, especially Nina Pfeffer, Scott Stickley, and John McNeur at Herricks High School, and Lorraine Nubar, Jorge Parodi, Andrew Thomas, and Marlena Malas at Juilliard. Much appreciation goes out to the National Foundation for Advancement in the Arts (NFAA YoungArts) for helping to encourage and support so many teens—including myself—in their artistic pursuits. Heartfelt thanks go to Elizabeth, Steven, and Abby Malawer; Eileen, Alan, Laurie, and Leigh Honigman, and in loving memory of Arnold and Mark Honigman. And, of course, thanks to Josh for being an incredible partner on this journey.

From Josh:

To anyone with whom I shared a stage, taught me a box step, coached me on a song, or who came to watch me perform in a cafetorium, thank you.

To my parents, who supported my every move, saw all my shows, and helped me survive in the greatest and most expensive city in the world, thank you.

To my incredible friends and NYC-family, without whom I would be lost, for your support, encouragement, laughter, and advice, thank you.

To my mentor Jim and the incredible team at DGRW for being the best work family a guy could ever hope for, thank you.

To my astonishingly talented clients who I am honored to work for each day, you make my job exciting, challenging, and fun, thank you.

To the ridiculously gifted writers and artists who have shared their stories with us, you are all stars, thank you.

Finally, to Ted, without whom this remarkable project would not exist. Words can never begin to express my thanks. LTP.